"LOOK, I'VE SAID I'LL STAY UNTIL YOU SLEEP."

"He'll come back again," Sonnie said.

It was there again, the unfocused stare. "Sonnie, tomorrow you must go to the police and explain what's been happening here."

"Tell them about a gift of lilies and a card about a baby's death?"

Chris shook his head, bemused.

"Tell them he told me to leave because he'd kill me if I stay in Key West?"

"Yes." Rubbing her arms, he leaned over her. "Yes, you must tell them that." He would not ask her who she was talking about. To do so would be to ask to be dragged in deeper, and he didn't want to go there.

She scooted away from him and closed her eyes tight. "Thank you," she said. "You were very kind to come. I apologize for the terrible intrusion into your life."

"It isn't a terrible intrusion. You've been through too much. You're still recovering from a catastrophic accident. Most people wouldn't be doing anywhere near as well as you are. But I think you're trying too hard and it's taking a toll on you."

"You think I'm mad, too."

BOOK YOUR PLACE ON OUR WEBSITE AND MAKE THE READING CONNECTION!

We've created a customized website just for our very special readers, where you can get the inside scoop on everything that's going on with Zebra, Pinnacle and Kensington books.

When you come online, you'll have the exciting opportunity to:

- View covers of upcoming books
- Read sample chapters
- Learn about our future publishing schedule (listed by publication month *and author*)
- Find out when your favorite authors will be visiting a city near you
- Search for and order backlist books from our online catalog
- Check out author bios and background information
- Send e-mail to your favorite authors
- Meet the Kensington staff online
- Join us in weekly chats with authors, readers and other guests
- Get writing guidelines
- AND MUCH MORE!

**Visit our website at
http://www.zebrabooks.com**

KEY WEST

STELLA CAMERON

Zebra Books
Kensington Publishing Corp.

http://www.zebrabooks.com

For Kate Duffy

ACKNOWLEDGMENTS

Jerry Cameron—Thank you for marching the streets of Key West with me and for being patient when I made that march again, and again.

Key West Police Department—You were generous and wise.

Island City Flight Service—You coped so well with the weird questions—even if you did laugh! And you stopped me from making a fool of myself. Thank you.

Mike and Mae Nunn—I'm grateful you're hooked on fabulous cars. You gave me so many ideas.

Applause for the folks who bring us Key West Sunset, even when it doesn't ...

And Key West. What an island, what a history, what a wild and wonderful present. You are irresistible.

One

"Hush little baby, don't you cry. . . ."

Tropical wind in the night reminded her of times when she'd made the mistake of pretending to be happy, safe, although she'd known she was fooling herself.

That kind of wind slapped banana leaves against the jalousies and sent warm, frangipani-scented air across the skin. Lulled you—even in hurricane season. Mostly the big storms never really hit, but eventually one did. Even if it was a long time coming, you could take one thing to the bank: another hurricane *would* hit Key West. And the less prepared you were, the more devastating the onslaught.

Sonnie Keith Giacano's personal storm had arrived eight months ago, on just such a wild night. It had changed her forever. She hadn't expected what happened, and she'd almost snapped under the horror of it. But driven by her need to discover the truth she was convinced had been hidden from her, she'd started the long trail back from despondency. That trail had led her here again, to Key West and the place where everything she'd like to forget had taken place.

It's over, Sonnie. You can't go back. You can never go back.

Maybe she should have sold the Key West house. There was nothing here for her anymore. Never had been, other than during the few weeks of euphoria before she'd told Frank about the baby. His career had been slipping for some time. With each tournament he was convinced he would win again, only to go down to one more early round elimination. Sonnie timed her announcement for his return to Florida after the latest Wimbledon defeat—another step downward toward public oblivion for Frank Giacano, former wonder boy who lived for the flash of the camera, the adoring crush of the fans. That visit—and rapid departure—had happened only weeks before Frank had sent an unexpected message telling her to be ready for him to come home again because they had to talk.

On the first occasion, she had waited for him, hopeful that her news about the baby would transform him, make him want to spend time with her, give him a reason to see there was more to life than tennis—and the people who were his friends because of tennis, rather than despite the game. He'd been rich before he'd won his first title, and he'd at least quadrupled his fortune in the twelve years he'd been at the top. But all that had changed, had begun to change even before Sonnie met him. The more defeats he suffered, the faster he lived and the more he spent—or lost at the tables to dealers who saw him more often than his wife did. Get out now, was what Sonnie had asked him to do. Get out and help her make a family, a real family. And give the two of them a chance to be what they'd never been: a husband and wife who knew and liked each other, and not just in bed.

Frank had listened to her, so silent she'd talked faster and faster, babbled, broken into bursts of laughter, until she stopped, breathless, and as silent as he.

Later that same day he'd left again. "Take care of yourself," he'd said. "I'll be in touch. Sorry I can't be better at this sort of thing, *cara,* but I am not the domesticated man. And, well"— he made one of the eloquent hand gestures that had once so captivated her—"what can I say? I do not find pregnant women sexy. You would not want me here, looking at you, and knowing I was wishing you were . . . otherwise."

Sonnie had been unable to answer him.

"I'll contact you. And I'll be here at the right time for the doting-papa pictures. The press will help me make them so touching. And the fans, they will love that.''

He had gone, had not so much as called for two months. Then he'd surprised her with his announcement that he was returning, that she should make herself available to help him with some business matters. He had not even asked how she was, or how the baby was.

Sonnie remembered his voice as it had sounded on the phone that last time, and narrowed her eyes. So cold. ''Be at the airport.'' He meant he'd be coming in on his private plane. ''I won't have much time.''

She'd tried to forget the anger she'd felt in his words.

Had that really been the last time she'd spoken to Frank?

Another gust of wind tossed leaves against windowpanes. ''I just wanted you to love me—and the baby,'' Sonnie said into the fragrant darkness. Two weeks ago she'd arrived back in Key West and made the parlor her safe place. Just once, on the day she first walked into the house, she had forced herself to go into every room. And she'd closed each door as she left. The doors were still closed.

If she were not so convinced of the need to surround herself with what had once been familiar, she would have left immediately. But she was convinced. If she was to grasp for pieces of a night she had blocked from her mind, she must be exactly where she had been when it began.

''Hush little baby, don't you cry. . . .''

If she was to go on, to start living again, peace must be welcome in her head and in her heart—and in the places filled with an ache she had clasped so tightly she still couldn't let go.

''She'll come out of it. She's young and that's on her side. The young forget—even when they don't think they will.''

Her father's voice. Her mother's. And big half-sister Billy's—Billy, who still thought of Sonnie as a kid, even though she was twenty-eight and had the kind of ugly miles on her shoes that were guaranteed to make her real old inside.

Frank's voice.

Soft?

Shouting?

Pleading?

Why couldn't she remember the words, or when she'd last heard him speak to her? On the phone before he was to arrive, everyone insisted, yet she couldn't be sure. Had there been another call? Why did she hear voices saying things they shouldn't say, making threats, goading, promising the unspeakable?

Noises, always noises. Noises tore apart the words until they weren't words anymore. She pressed her hands over her ears and said, "I can't do this. I can't."

They were right—the doctors who spoke in whispers. She was losing her mind. Coming back to the place where everything she cared for had blown apart had seemed the one way to pull it all together again, but she couldn't think long enough without the noises, and the voices, breaking in.

Sheer white draperies drifted over the windows, lifted by wind through the jalousies. Moonlight fingered a fuzzy blue glow between shadowy stripes from the shutters. Shifting, shifting.

Sonnie Keith Giacano. Wife. Daughter. Sister. Almost a mother.

The tears had turned to burning dryness months ago.

"These things happen. You'll have more babies. You were only five months along. You'll get over it. One day you'll know I was right."

They didn't know how she felt. They didn't know what she would or wouldn't get over, or if there would be another child. And if there should ever be another child, the tiny girl who had slipped away that night wouldn't cease to be Sonnie's daughter. No one else knew, but she had named her Jacqueline, and inside a locket Sonnie wore around her neck were inscribed the name and the date of . . . just one date.

What really happened that night?

"High-speed crash. Distraught. The news was too much for her. Her brother-in-law had told her about Frank and she snapped. Pregnant woman, you know. Hormones. Poor kid. She'll need a lot of TLC. '

And so they had talked on and on over her hospital bed, talked as if she weren't there. She had withdrawn to a place where she heard snatches of conversation, but where she could be alone with the horror of all she'd lost, alone to think and to try to grasp what she couldn't remember. Later the doctors had told her about the brain's ability to wipe out events too painful to relive. She shouldn't even try to recall the actual accident when her car had smashed, at high speed, into a concrete wall about a mile from the airport in Key West. The news her brother-in-law, Romano Giacano, brought and delivered when she'd expected to see Frank get off his plane had destroyed her delicate balance, and she'd fled.

So why couldn't she accept what she'd been told in the hospital and start to move on?

That was why she was here: to convince herself that the story was true, that there was nothing else to know.

She might be a widow, or a wife. Frank had been kidnapped. That was what Romano came to tell her that night. Frank had been kidnapped and they must wait for a ransom demand. That was what they said had made her snap.

But . . .

Holding her wrist to the moonlight, Sonnie saw that it was almost ten. She had an appointment. An appointment with a man she didn't know, had never really met. And the man didn't want to see her.

Maybe she didn't want to see Chris Talon, either. From what she'd heard he'd been a hotshot detective once. He wasn't so hot anymore. But his brother, who had given Sonnie a job she didn't need except to force her out of this house, insisted Sonnie and Chris would be good for each other. Roy Talon said his brother was brilliant and would help her if there was help to be had. "And," Roy Talon had said obliquely, "Chris needs a kick in the pants. Get his mind off himself for a change."

So tonight—couldn't be earlier than ten-thirty because the gentleman had "things" to do until then—tonight they would meet and see just how good they might be for each other.

The phone rang. Sonnie hesitated a moment before picking up the receiver. "Yes."

"Sonnie, darlin', it's Roy. Just checkin' in to remind you you've got a date."

"I have an appointment," she told him. "And I'll be there. Then I'll help close up."

Roy laughed his hoarse laugh. "I been closing this run-down, beat-up bar for enough years to do it in my sleep, babe. You just get your pretty ass over here and get my brother out of . . . make my brother listen to you. He's good. If anyone can convince you there aren't any ghosts to chase, it's Christian J. Talon. See ya."

The line went dead and Sonnie let the receiver drop into its cradle.

She was as ready to go as she'd ever be.

Frank had disappeared, kidnapped by people it was hinted might be Italian terrorists. But there had been no ransom demand. Eight months had passed since the night when she'd set out to meet him at the airport, and not a word had come to Sonnie, or to any member of the Giacano family. She knew that was so because Romano made certain he was never very far away from her. The thought that he didn't know where she was now didn't make her happy.

He was a good friend and he would be furious. But she had to do this alone.

The heels of her sandals clapped on the polished slate tiles that covered the whole ground floor. She went into the airy entrance hall where a staircase rose from the center to the second story. Above Sonnie's head more moon shadows sifted through the faceted panes of a lofty, domed skylight.

A dream home for a star-kissed couple.

A hell for a woman left alone with her disappointment.

The rented Camry sat to the right of the front door. Sonnie ignored the car and set off to walk to the Rusty Nail on Duval Street. Ten minutes in the fresh air would help her think more clearly—maybe.

If this Chris Talon, private investigator and ex-detective, decided she wasn't too boring to talk to, he might help her at least decide how and where to begin looking for leads—if there were any leads to find.

All he had to do was ask the right questions in the right places. If there were any right places, and Sonnie was certain there were. She was sure she'd managed to stuff truth out of sight and that if it could be pulled back into the light, she might face more terror than she could have imagined, even after what had already happened. But in the middle of that terror was truth, and without that truth she would never be free.

"Hush little baby, don't you cry. . . ,"

Eight months since she'd hit that wall hard enough to be thrown many feet from her vehicle.

Eight months since she'd killed her baby.

Two

"Quit feedin' the g—damn cats, will ya?"

Chris Talon tossed another oyster to a rangy orange tabby that sat between his dusty brown loafers. "You're cute when you're angry, Roy," he told his brother. "But I bet Bo tells you that all the time." Bo Quick was Roy's partner in the Rusty Nail, a Key West drink-and-cheap-food institution. They were also partners in life.

"Quit feedin' the g—damn cats," was all Roy said from behind the bar.

In the mood to goad his older sibling, Chris scuffed at the worn boards beneath his feet. "This place could use a face-lift, bro." He poked at sagging coconut matting on the wall beside him. "You ought t'have to pay people for coming in here. Health hazard, that's what it is."

"Yeah, yeah. Lot of folk like it just the way it is. Have for years. You just sit there and keep your mouth shut for once."

"The boys are fighting again," Bo Quick said, swiping a wet rag along the bar. He grinned engagingly at the row of regulars who had probably been warming the green plastic on their stools for hours. "Added attraction around here these days. The Talon brothers' daily mix-up."

It was too late, and too many beers had wetted the throats

of the glazed-eyed patrons. Not a flicker of interest showed. Or maybe they were engrossed in the tinny reggae that squawked from ancient speakers.

"Save it, Bo," Roy said. "My no-good brother loves to stir it up. Disappoint him."

Chris yawned and reached from his stool to stroke the sinuous marmalade tom. "Reckon I'll get on out back. Time for my beauty sleep."

"Hold it," Roy said. "Just you g-damn hold it there, bro. You're not going anywhere."

"If you want to cuss, why not cuss? Why tippytoe around like a goddamn fairy?"

Roy aimed a cocktail cherry at Chris.

Scrawny Bo sent up a cackle, and when he could control himself said, "He is a goddamn fairy, that's why."

"On that note," Chris said, "I'll bid you a fond nighty-night."

"Get back on that stool or you don't have anywhere to *go* nighty-night, smart mouth. In case you forgot, you've got a date."

"I *had* an appointment," Chris said. Not that he should have agreed to meet the pale, forgettable, wispy creature Roy had hired when he and Bo didn't need the extra help. "The lady didn't show, so sayonara."

"She will show," Roy bellowed.

"Wassamatter?" A man dozing over his beer came to life and swung around so hard he fell off his stool. "What's the f—ing matter?"

Chris groaned. "How'd you do that, Roy? Don't get me wrong. I'm impressed. Yessir. You've got 'em all cussing like they were in Sunday school."

"Keep it down," Roy said, coming from behind the bar, although Chris had yet to raise his voice and rarely did so anyway. "Play something, will ya?"

"Huh?"

"*Play* something," Roy repeated. "G—damn storm's been coming up for hours. Got everyone uptight. We're not over the last one yet. So play. You always could charm a room into forgetting why they don't have somewhere else to be.''

''I'm going to bed.''

''You leave this bar and you'll be looking for a new bed.''

''What is it with the woman?''

Roy stared. Nearly ten years older than Chris, a fit forty-five with red hair and light blue eyes he'd inherited from their mother, Roy Talon had taken a lot of knocks in a cruel world and bobbed up stronger for every one of them. Despite Chris's marked physical resemblance to their abusive father, Roy regarded him as the relative he loved most in the world, and as currently needy. Much as Chris didn't like the attention, he wasn't about to hurt the best man he'd ever known.

Roy's sudden smile brought the boy back into the man. ''Humor me, huh? All I know about Sonnie is she's got trouble. She won't say a lot, but she did agree to talk to you.''

''Agree? You mean you browbeat her into talking to me? If you've got some fool notion about the two of us hitting it off, forget it.''

''Hitting it off?'' Roy rolled his eyes. ''She's a nice, gentle woman. Why would she hit it off with a beat-up hard-ass like you? Play something, Chris. For me, huh?''

Chris looked at the war-torn upright. It was set to one side of glassless windows open to Duval Street, and a tasteful Hawaiian-print runner flapped on top of the instrument. ''Wind gets much worse, you'd better batten down the hatches.''

''Leave the shutters to me. I worry about you, Chris.''

''Yeah.'' Enough of that. He threw the last oyster on his plate to the tom, took up his glass of bourbon, and went to the piano. On the way he felt the first drops of hot rain fly out of the night and into the Rusty Nail.

''You shave today?''

''Huh?'' You never knew what Roy would ask next. ''Hell, no. Not yesterday, either. So what? You expecting a talent scout for the movies?''

Roy shrugged a muscular shoulder. ''Just wondered.''

''She's not coming,'' Chris said, smiling with one side of his mouth. He set his glass on the piano and sat down. ''You goofed, bro. You should have tried for the casual approach. Waited till she was working, then called me to help put out a fire in here. Something like that."

He sat at the yellowed keys, made a tentative pass, and shook his head. "How d'you do it? This monstrosity ought to be on a junk heap, but it's always tuned." And Roy never let anyone but Chris play it, so it sat idle, sometimes for years at a stretch.

"Turn off the music," Roy hollered to Bo. "Chris is gonna serenade us."

But for the muted murmur of patrons, silence fell. "Pressure could be too much," Chris said. "Critical audience like this—"

"Zip it up, and play for me."

Chris looked into his brother's eyes, saw so many shared moments from the past hovering there, and played.

" 'Smoke Gets in Your Eyes,' " he said, grinning because it felt like the thing to do. "Dad's favorite."

"Bum," Roy said succinctly. "D'you know how much you look like him?"

"What can I say? He was a mean son of a bitch, but you've got to admit he was a handsome devil. And I got his good looks."

Roy sniffed the liquor in Chris's glass and set it down again. "It's going to be a wild night. This place is a hellhole this time of year."

"Yep. Even the bugs are too smart to come out of the shade."

"I'm glad you decided to come to me."

The message was implicit. Roy was glad Chris had come to Florida when the floor dropped out of his life. "I came to Key West," Chris said. "Bottom of the world as I know it. End of the world. No place farther to run. You just happen to live here." Only partially true. He'd needed to be with Roy.

"Thanks. You're still one helluva piano man. Know that?"

Chris glanced past his brother and winced. The world's least likely bartender had arrived, a waif of a woman with a limp he tried not to watch. "Your other charity case is here," he said.

"What?" Roy looked over his shoulder and grinned. "Sonnie. Good. I told you she'd come. And she's no charity case."

"You took her on in your slowest season because of her vast experience in the business?"

"Just talk to her, damn it. And keep your thoughts to yourself. She's special—not that you would understand the finer things of life—and Sonnie's one of the finer things. So hold yourself back. One of your wiseass snarls and she'll bolt."

"Snarls? You malign me. Anyway, it's past my bedtime. Give the lady my apologies. Explain I've got a headache." He kept on playing because he wanted to. He fought against letting music trap him, but it always won in the end. Damn thing was that it quieted the gnawing in his gut, and he didn't want it to quiet; he wanted to feel it, needed to feel it.

"Hey, Sonnie," Roy called. "Come on over and meet my brother."

"Shit," Chris muttered.

"Cut it out," Roy said under his breath. "If you want incentive, I took her on because I've got a feeling about her, okay? She wasn't looking for a job; she was drinking tea next door and minding her own business. She was there every day for a week, and what I saw in her face scared me."

"What—"

"She's barely hanging on. That's what I saw." Roy unfurled a wide grin. "Storm's rolling in, Sonnie. Did you get wet?"

Chris stopped playing and crossed his arms.

The woman needed a good meal. A lot of good meals. "Not really," she said. He couldn't place her accent, or almost lack of one.

"Feels like a doozy coming," Roy said, rubbing his hands together in a manner Chris knew was a sign of nervousness. "Meet Christian J. Talon. Chris, this is Sonnie Giacano."

He hadn't known her last name before. Sounded familiar but didn't ring any bells yet. He rose to his feet and stuck his hand over the piano. "Hi, Sonnie." He'd seen her several times, but never up close. "Time we met formally."

She shook, her grip surprisingly firm. "Hi." Her grip was the only thing about her that didn't seem shaky right now. She was fair, not exactly blond, just fair. Fair hair and skin. Thin face. All cheekbone. And a way of bowing her head and looking up at you with big eyes that were dark. Dark what, he wasn't sure. The fact that she was smiling didn't immediately occur to him; when it did, it was too late to smile back.

Roy cleared his throat. "Well, I'll leave you two to get to know each other better."

When Chris opened his mouth to compliment his brother on his smoothness, he got a glare that induced him to change his mind. Roy walked away.

Chris stood on his side of the piano.

Sonnie Giacano stood on hers.

He took up the bourbon and sipped, narrowing his eyes against cigarette smoke that held its own even against the wind.

"Roy suggested—"

"We should meet. Yeah, I know. Roy's full of great ideas."

That earned him a very direct stare. Maybe her eyes were very dark blue. They made him uncomfortable—not easy to do.

"You'd prefer that we don't talk?" She ran the fingers of her left hand through hair cut to go back from her face. "Of course you would."

Now he was supposed to argue with her. Tough. "Roy gets some strange ideas. Comes from living down here too long."

He got another stare and wasn't sure how he felt about his reaction. Mildly interested, maybe?

"You aren't like your brother, are you?"

He digested her words. "Gay, you mean?"

Her face flushed. "You know I don't mean that. I was thinking that he's a genuinely nice guy who wants to make the world happy."

"Oh. Thanks."

She bowed her head again, looked up at him again.

His stomach did something it hadn't done in a long time: flipped. *Definitely interesting.*

"I didn't mean to be rude," she said. "This was a bad idea. You must be embarrassed. I'm sorry."

"I don't get embarrassed."

"I'm still sorry."

"Don't be." He was being a jerk. "I'm the one who's sorry. My social skills are a bit rusty. Will you join me for a drink?"

She shook her head and said, "No, thank you." Then she glanced toward the bar, toward Roy and Bo, who were both watching. "Um, well, I am thirsty. Lemonade would be nice, but I won't keep you long."

"Lemonade?" She'd sit and drink with him to please his brother. *Great.* "Lemonade for the lady, and a refill for me," he called to Roy and wiggled his empty glass in the air. "A view seat windward? Or something more intimate?"

"View, please. I like the wind."

And she didn't like even a suggestion of being somewhere intimate with him.

He led the way to a ringside table onto the street. They sat down facing each other, but not looking at each other. Chris peered across the street, at the bars and shops they faced, and sensed Sonnie doing the same. Somewhere a door or window slammed. Palm crowns chattered together, and their trunks were swaying black wands against an even blacker sky.

"Lemonade." Roy was beside them, setting a tall glass in front of Sonnie. "Bourbon." Chris's drink was exchanged. "Enjoy."

Sonnie made lines on the side of her sweating glass. Droplets fell into fine grains of coral sand that had blown onto the table. She said, "You play well."

"I used to." He used to do a lot of things well.

"Sounded good to me."

"How long have you been in Key West?" He was still a good boor.

"Not long. Couple of weeks."

"Why did you come?"

"Unfinished business."

He hadn't expected an answer like that. "Sounds serious."

"It is. It is to me."

Maybe he didn't want to know more. Or maybe he did want to know because he was naturally curious. He sure as hell didn't want to get involved.

"I lived here before. For three years. I . . . I left last winter."

"Why?"

She looked startled. "Because we . . . I had some problems."

"Uh-huh." He nodded, kept on nodding. Where was he supposed to go from here? He'd like to slip out of the back door and down to the two-room guest house he now called home.

"Roy said he thought you could help me," she said in a rush. "He said you're a detective and—"

"Whoa." Chris held up one hand, and used the other to take his glass to his lips. He sucked a mouthful of bourbon, more to buy thinking time than because he was thirsty. Not that thirsty had much to do with drinking bourbon.

Sonnie whatever-her-name-was had gotten enthusiastic enough to lean across the table. Her lips remained parted. When she flushed a little she was pretty in a doleful way.

A scar in front of her left ear continued past her jaw to her neck. There was a fairly new pinkness to it. It wasn't pretty.

"I used to be a detective," he told her, and sent his oh-so-busy brother a glare. "I retired."

"Retired?" Her fair brows fashioned a frown. "You're not old enough to retire."

"Thirty-six is way past old enough to retire from—" He whistled tunelessly. He'd almost said he was old enough to retire from hell, but she didn't need to know anything personal about him.

"I'm sorry." Her voice was small now. "I guess I misunderstood Roy. Not his fault. I tend to misunderstand a lot of things." She gave a laugh that was nothing but a puff of air.

"Blame Roy. I do whenever I can. He likes it. Gives him something to feel indignant about."

She wasn't finding him funny.

"Hey, don't look so beaten," Chris said. "You should be glad. Who wants to hang out with detectives? Slime of the earth."

"I need some help," she said very quietly.

Chris was grateful she didn't follow the statement up with

one of her deep looks. "Don't we all?" he said, and felt like the heel he was.

Sonnie nodded slowly. A heart-shaped gold locket, very small and fine and hanging from a thin chain, settled in the hollow of her neck. She was all shadows and air and ... softness.

She was soft, and gentle, and whipped enough to keep on talking to a tough, unapproachable man who had already caused more than enough pain in other people's lives. "Look, I'm sorry, okay? Forgive me for being rude—or rough, or whatever I am."

"I don't care how rough and rude you are. Roy told me you're a detective. A private detective. You take on cases for people. Investigate things. He said you're very good at what you do when you want to be." Her eyes did that thing again, damn it. "When he got me to agree to talk to you, I didn't want to. I was embarrassed. Now I see you aren't interested in more cases. 'Retired,' is your way of saying it. Because I already bore you. That's because you can pick and choose, isn't it?"

"Well—"

"Yes, well, *I'm* a good case. And I want you to take me on because it's not going to be easy. D'you understand?"

"No." No, he surely didn't understand.

"Something awful happened to me. I don't know how, but I do know when. And I think there's a why, too. And I don't just mean it happened because things happen. It could have been ... I just don't know if I should accept the story I was told about it all. There could be something else."

Chris pushed aside his bourbon. "That, ma'am, is as clear as mud. I'm sorry for your trouble. I wish you luck finding some peace. But I'm not your knight on a charger."

"Are you a private investigator?"

Hell and damnation, he'd get Roy for this.

"You are. That's what you do here in Key West. You find things out. You tracked down that man who said his boy had been kidnapped. It turned out the father had locked his own son up at home all the time, and—"

"I don't talk about old cases."

"You aren't retired, are you?"

He made himself smile and knew the result wasn't inviting. "Why would you want to hire someone who doesn't want to be hired?"

When the lady's stubborn streak surfaced, she looked different, alive. "I want to know why you've decided—without even finding out what I need—that I'm too boring to waste your valuable time on."

Rather than start to relax, he felt the tension tighten. "You aren't boring. You're just . . . You're inconvenient." Wow, he was refining his insult skills to new heights.

"Okay." She was giving up. Her fine-boned hands curled on the scarred top of the many-times-lacquered table. "You've got enough work already. I understand."

He hadn't taken a case in a month. "Yeah. Sorry."

"Don't worry about it. I'm the one who's sorry. I shouldn't have pushed myself on you like that."

Shit. "You didn't push. You're worried is all. I understand."

"It's not fair to expect strangers to care about your problems. I can handle it. I don't know what came over me."

His *brother* was what came over her. She wasn't wearing a wedding ring.

Why would he care?

He didn't. Just the old observation habit. "Don't beat yourself up if you don't have to, Sonnie. Life will do it to you without any help. Feel that wind?"

"Uh-huh." Her hair flipped across her face and she pushed it back. "Funny how storms here make you excited, even while you're scared."

He looked at her again. *Refined.* That was the word. She looked refined and fit in around here about as well as any lady would. But she wasn't cool, this one. Nope, her words, the little things she said, gave her away. There was some fire behind the delicate exterior. Not that he cared about those things anymore.

"Don't let me keep you," she said.

"You aren't."

She wore the collar of her white shirt turned up. When she turned her head, a point brushed her sharp chin. There wasn't a whole lot of her in that shirt, but what there was might be very nice. He hadn't had a chance to study the rest of her before they sat down. The limp was something he'd like to know about.

"Why did you say you were retired? Really, I mean?"

"I am. I did. I thought you were talking about something else. When I was on the force. I used to be. Up north. I didn't retire; I quit." End of topic, and that was more than he'd said to anyone in the months since he'd arrived on Roy's doorstep.

Sonnie Giacano was staring at him. Not a comfortable experience.

He tried a real smile. "Felt like a change of pace."

She looked at his mouth.

Chris watched her face. "Sometimes you need to accept that it's time to move on." That wouldn't earn him a place among the great philosophers.

"You're hurting, aren't you?"

"What?" *Hurting?* How did you tell a woman who was obviously feeling something she didn't like, that you'd quit feeling anything at all? "No, I'm not hurting."

"Right."

"I'm not hurting, Sonnie."

"This is a strange conversation, isn't it? Between strangers, I mean."

He considered. "Not so strange, given the reason we're here."

"If you love someone, you'll do anything. You'll lie to yourself. You'll lie to other people—just to give yourself an excuse to keep on believing in the other person."

A lot of thoughts came to him. Not one would make it past his tongue.

"When you run out of excuses, the darkness opens up at your feet. You walk on the edge of a hole. Then maybe you have to get away. Maybe you have someone else you've got to put first."

"Is this code for your being in some sort of man trouble?"

She shook her head once and looked up at him. "There

aren't any men in my life. Not anymore. This conversation feels too personal."

"Trouble is always personal." She was an enigma. If he didn't know how dangerous caring about someone could be, he'd care about Sonnie's problems. It was way too dangerous.

"You don't have too many cases, do you?"

He didn't answer.

"It's me. You're one of those people who can only work with things that interest them. I respect that."

"You're interesting."

They both studied the buildings across the street again. "Duval Street," she said quietly, "where the bars hardly ever close—except for the Rusty Nail."

Roy and Bo believed in as close to a regular schedule as they could grab. "That's right," Chris said.

"Why did you quit? Really?"

"I was a lousy detective."

Her incredulous laugh annoyed him.

"That's not what I hear," she said. "Why are you so hard on yourself?"

If he'd needed a therapist he'd have found one a long time ago. "I'm not hard on myself. I'm a realist. I hope you find someone who can really help you, because you're nice. Very nice. And you deserve better than me. I'm washed-up. Used up. I'm working at getting my own shit together." Offending ladies wasn't a favorite pastime, but she'd hit too many nerves he wanted permanently dead. "I'm no good anymore. To anyone." Least of all himself. He considered finishing his drink. He didn't want it.

"Can I do something to help you?" she asked, her voice so low he only just caught the words.

Pity. "Save the help for yourself," he said, and stood up. "I hope you find someone to take on your case. To tell the truth, I've kind of priced myself out of the general marketplace. You might even say I've become too dangerous to afford."

Three

The night whined.

Wet grit whipped against Sonnie's bare ankles and stung. Despite the rain Duval was crowded, and it was late enough for drunks to rule.

Chris Talon had offered to bring her home. Offered while he looked at a space somewhere above her right shoulder—probably longing for her to leave. Leave the Rusty Nail, and leave him alone.

He'd get his wish. She'd leave him alone. But she would continue to work for Bo and Roy because the job got her out and gave her an opportunity to gather information on what was going on around the island, and because she'd accomplish nothing if she stayed at the house and stewed.

Somewhere on the island there was someone who knew something; there had to be. It could be some small detail that didn't seem to mean anything to them, but to Sonnie it might be the key to the door she'd been unable to as much as crack.

Chris Talon thought she couldn't afford him.

She could have argued that point but hadn't felt like it. Lack of enthusiasm oozed from his every pore. She didn't need help from a man whose disinterest was that obvious.

He didn't even know what her problem was.

She wasn't sure what her problem was. But she knew she had one, and if she couldn't get it resolved, she'd never be able to put the pieces of her life back together. She wasn't sure she could anyway—too much had happened that couldn't be reversed—but she had to try.

"Too dangerous to afford."

Why? He hadn't been referring to money at all, had he? He'd been a detective somewhere up north, he said. And he'd retired—quit—at thirty-four or thirty-five. Old enough, he'd said. But there'd been something else, something he wasn't talking about.

Chris Talon was hiding out. Of course he was; that was why he gave an impression that he needed a solid barrier between himself and any intruder—even a harmless one, like one crippled and not very impressive woman. *Used up. Worn-out.* Or whatever he'd said to discourage her. It all amounted to his having something to hide—just like she did.

Maybe she didn't want help from someone with baggage. But maybe that was just what she did want—a man who, no matter how hard he protested, had his own reasons for needing to find new focus.

Sonnie checked her uneven stride and looked back. Shadows punctuated garish light. She'd known Roy and Bo only a short time, but she trusted them. Roy wouldn't suggest his brother could help her if he'd thought it was a bad idea.

This was what being absolutely alone felt like. And the feeling should be an old friend by now.

She continued on to Truman Avenue. The street was a hodgepodge of nineteenth-century wedding-cake mansions—most of them converted into boardinghouses—and tiny, three-room clapboard houses that had once belonged to cigar makers.

The house Sonnie's father bought for her when she'd convinced him she intended to marry Frank Giacano had two stories. In front, a balcony ran the length of the second story. On the ground floor a veranda wrapped around the entire house. A pretty place with old-island charm. Bob Keith hadn't understood his daughter's choice in husbands, or Frank's complete lack of interest in the house, other than wanting his name on the title. But Sonnie's dad had gone along anyway and presented her with the deed. Frank's name had not been on that deed.

Sonnie's sister Billy had brought home Frank and his brother Romano. Billy had shown great promise as a tennis player in the junior leagues. And she might have gone far as an adult if she'd been able to control some of her habits. As it was she'd hung on for several years, occasionally qualifying, but always going down to an early round defeat. She met the Giacanos on the circuit. The family liked Frank's brother, Romano, who had originally dated Sonnie. They did not like Frank.

Sonnie slipped rapidly past the low white stucco wall in front of the grounds and turned in at the driveway. She kept the iron gates open. When she'd flown down from Denver, home of Keith Beers, she'd rented the Camry, but she rarely drove anywhere.

Everything was dark. This was the season of the year—the low season for tourists because the heat kept them home—when the locals ventured forth again, but they'd gone to ground to wait out the storm. Between July and November, tropical storms were a way of life, and *hurricane* was a word on everyone's mind. This storm was predicted to blow itself out by morning.

Despite the heat in the wind and rain, Sonnie shivered. She rubbed her arms and glanced at the house. It seemed unbelievable that she and Frank had lived there as man and wife . . . when he wasn't on tour. He'd spent most of their married life on tour, and he hadn't liked her to travel with him. He said she was a distraction.

The key to the front door was in the pocket of her cotton wraparound skirt.

The fronds of a fan palm swayed sideways to the ground before her, and the branches of a giant poinciana tree rustled. In the morning, petals from the red poinciana blossoms would carpet the ground.

Sonnie stood still beside the fan palm.

Her skin prickled.

She narrowed her eyes to look upward, toward the small,

rightmost second-story window. She'd caught sight of a light there—inside what was now a storeroom. Hadn't she?

The rain grew heavier by the moment. She was soaked.

No light showed now. It had probably been moonlight on the glass. . . . There wasn't a moon anymore. A streetlight a few yards past the property gleamed on the downstairs windows. That was what she'd seen.

She studied the upper windows again. If what she'd seen had been a reflection from the streetlight, it would still be there.

One thing she'd never been was easily frightened. Just as well. If she had been, she couldn't have dealt with these last months. She hadn't really seen a light—an impression of one could be caused by many things.

A hot shower; then she'd lock herself into the room where her suitcases stood open on the floor and her hanging clothes were draped over several chairs.

She must force herself to open the house properly. She'd start on that in the morning, take her things to one of the bedrooms and put them away, make the place feel alive again.

If she could become convinced that the story she'd been told in the hospital was true, she'd find peace. That was the best she could ask for now—peace. And when and if she found that peace, what then? Where did you go when the one plus in your life was a chance to start over? How long did it take to forget the past and grab the chance?

Billy hadn't wanted her to come here. Older by five years, Billy worried about Sonnie. But the time had long since passed when Sonnie could allow her sister to lead the way.

This was ridiculous. Rain drizzled down her face from hair plastered to her head. Her shirt and skirt clung to her, and her feet squelched in her sandals. Accompanied by a popping sound at every step, she went to the front steps, climbed, and crossed the veranda. Once she'd found pleasure in filling pots with the tropical flowers that thrived here, then clustering the pots about the veranda posts. Why not try to get interested in those things again?

The screen needed oiling. It didn't just squeak when she opened it; it screamed. Sonnie gritted her teeth at the noise and slid the key into the lock. Once inside the broad entry she noted that the smell of disuse hadn't gone away yet. Tomorrow she'd open all the doors and windows and let the sweet air in.

"You'll stay where you are, Sonnie. You understand me, girlie?"

She stood still again. Her father's voice wasn't one that came to her often. There were others that set up a discordant cacophony in her brain, but Daddy's usually remained silent. He'd been afraid she might decide to leave Denver again. He hadn't known where she might go, just that she was restless and distant. Daddy loved her, but he didn't understand her, and the only way he knew to reach out was through orders and demands.

"Just let yourself go, Sonnie. Go on, let go. Go to your baby now. You know you want to. She's waiting, Sonnie. Your baby's waiting."

She threw her hands up before her face. "Stop it."

An androgynous voice. A sexless whisper. She'd heard it twice before, or was it three times? But not since she'd left the hospital.

Sonnie backed to the wall beside the front door and fought for breath. When she'd been close to death, someone had told her to let go and die. Yet when she'd fully regained consciousness and there was increasing hope of her recovery, everyone around her had insisted she would get better, and had shown her in so many ways that they wanted her to. And, despite her injuries, her physical rehabilitation had been dramatically rapid because she was fit, and because she had things she wanted to do.

She had dreamed the voice.

And now she was remembering the dream again.

Sweat had joined the rainwater. She was burning up. And sick to her stomach. And afraid.

Drawing herself up, edging away from the wall, she pushed the door shut, put the key on top of a wicker chest, and walked toward the parlor. Sleep was what she needed.

A single, mighty slam came from somewhere high up in the house.

The wind had blown a door shut.

The doors were already all shut. And the windows.

Sonnie reached the foot of the stairs and stood, gripping a newel post with both hands while she listened. The storm moaned outside, yet there was stillness inside. Her heart beat hard, almost painfully. Her back, still healing from torn muscle and ligament, ached from holding herself stiff. So did the areas where her ribs had been crushed on impact—and her left leg, her right foot.

Why tonight? Why would she be jumpy tonight when she'd been fine, or more or less fine, since she'd returned?

Somewhere in this house other ears strained to catch sounds, the sounds of her movements.

She shook her head, her throbbing head. Billy was right; she shouldn't have come here alone. But why not? If everything she'd been told she should believe was true, she had nothing to fear.

She wasn't alone.

A presence filled what should have been a void. No one would understand if she tried to explain, but she was right. Someone was in the house, biding time, waiting to . . . Waiting to what? Kill her?

Sonnie backed from the staircase until she connected with a wall. Then she turned, wrenched open the front door, and fled back the way she'd come.

Still it rained.

And still the wind blew.

There was nowhere to go—except a motel, maybe—until it was light. She didn't have a purse with her. No credit cards.

Ahead, several figures, their arms linked, swayed and roared out the incoherent lyrics to a song she didn't recognize. Sonnie ducked behind a wall and waited for the drunks to pass. This wasn't a good idea, not in any way. She was putting herself in fresh, unnecessary danger, and dragging back the phobic state she'd taken months to overcome.

There was someone in her house.

She ran, and felt every recovering injury protest. She dragged in air that burned her throat, and dashed as fast as she could.

Not fast enough to quell the panic. Her body wasn't ready for this, but she couldn't stop.

At Duval—she'd known she would go to Duval Street because the only people she could ask for help were there— at Duval she hovered at the curb, panting and shaking.

Roy and Bo had been good to her, more than good, and they owed her nothing. There wasn't a soul here who owed her anything.

But she could pay for what she needed—someone to help her sift through the past, a particular part of her past, and find out the exact details of a night filled with fire—and blood.

Christian Talon's opinion of her had been as clear as if he'd told her aloud. He thought her colorless, uninteresting, and not worth his time. She might be colorless and uninteresting as a woman, in his eyes, but she could turn out to be a whole lot less than boring, and she could certainly be well worth his time.

Also, Mr. Talon had given himself away. While he'd been so busy convincing her that he wasn't what she wanted or needed, he'd shown a piece of his own vulnerable underbelly. She hadn't been married to Frank Giacano for three years and learned nothing from him. Frank had believed that the way to bind an ally to you was through discovering their weakest point. Chris Talon had a weak point that had made him, carelessly, refer to himself as dangerous. If necessary, she'd find out what he really meant.

He'd made a mistake. She might be colorless in some ways, but she had a big will that had brought her from death when there'd supposedly been no hope of her living.

She had never, ever, forced herself on anyone. But she had never, ever, been as out of options as she was tonight.

The weather had all but closed the street down. The shutters were up at the Rusty Nail, and several lights showed in the apartments above, where Bo and Roy lived. Sonnie knew that if she went to them, the two men would do their best to comfort her, but comfort wasn't what she needed anymore, not the kind of comfort that patted the head, but did nothing for the endless motion inside the brain.

A skinny alleyway opened between a T-shirt shop and an establishment where a psychic held court when she wasn't too tripped out to do business. The alley led behind the row of buildings, on the same side of the road as the Rusty Nail. Roy's brother was living in some sort of guest house behind the bar. Sonnie had heard it spoken of a number of times.

Most of the Duval Street establishments had storage buildings or garages in the back. Despite the lack of light making every step dangerous, Sonnie kept going. Rainwater ran underfoot, turning dirt to mud that splashed her legs.

An abrupt rush of desperation filled her eyes with tears.

No time for tears.

No time for the clogged sensation in her throat.

"Hush little baby, don't you cry. . . ."

"Not now. Please, not now." What she knew, what she'd known from the instant this trip had become inevitable, was that she was trying to convince herself that somehow Jacqueline's death hadn't been her fault, at least not her fault alone.

She'd never been out here. Roy and Bo's "guesthouse" was a small building, evidently with painted metal sides and a tin roof.

She shouldn't wake the man.

Unless he slept with a light on, he wasn't asleep.

Sonnie approached a door that faced the back of the Rusty Nail. She would convince him of two things. The first, she hoped without clueing him in to how little there was to go on, would be the worthiness and the strangeness of what she needed to find out. The second point, and the one most likely to bring him onto her team of two, was her ability to pay just about anything for his services.

Metal slat shades covered two windows, one on either side of the door. Music—violin?—sounded as if it would be loud inside. Sonnie looked down at herself. Regardless of her mood, she always took care with her appearance. Tonight—or this morning now—she could pass for a member of the homeless.

It didn't matter. There was no one to impress. She knocked, and crossed her arms to wait. He was probably the type who wouldn't answer unless he was in the mood.

The door swung open almost at once.

If the man who blocked light from inside were not Roy's brother, Sonnie would flee.

"Holy . . . What are you doing, you little idiot?"

"Coming to see you." She felt horrified, horrified by the disbelief on his face, and horrified that she was there and looking wild.

"I told you there's nothing I can do for you."

"I think there is. You just don't want to."

"You've been walking around in this, haven't you? Walking around in a storm, in the dark? Alone?"

"I haven't been walking around. I went home, then changed my mind, is all."

"You should have stayed at home."

Crying wouldn't accomplish one thing with this man—much as she felt like doing just that. "May I come in, please?"

"You don't know when to quit. You just don't know." He stood aside to let her pass. "If there were anything that mattered around here, I'd tell you not to drip on it. You're going to be sick."

"You don't get sick from being wet."

"You do get sick from doing what you're doing to yourself. There isn't one damn thing in this life that's worth that much pain, Mrs. Giacano."

He'd have to be from another planet not to see her desperation, but she didn't like it that he could look at her and see exposed emotion. "Don't mistake sartorial disaster for anything else, please."

"Whatever you say. Get in here before you collapse."

The violin music sounded like something intended for snake charming. "Nice of you to care," she said, entering a crowded room.

"I don't. A body on the doorstep could ruin a man's day."

She smiled and it almost felt good. "I'm not close to death. Just wet and muddy." She looked around, gauging where she could safely stand without making something dirty.

"Ah, hell."

Sonnie looked at Talon sharply. With his hands on his hips,

he bent forward so she couldn't see his face. She'd swear he'd spoken aloud without knowing he'd done so. He wore only jeans. His feet were bare.

Nice chest.

She glanced around again. A door led to what was probably the bathroom. Everything else was right here, including a Murphy bed pulled down from the wall and neatly made, a tiny sink and stove with minuscule cupboards above, a prehistoric refrigerator that clanked, an open laptop computer on a table built into a corner—and a very large, black Harley-Davidson parked crosswise, and filling almost every inch of spare space.

"I'm not your man," Talon said.

Adrenaline ebbed, and exhaustion crowded in its wake. "I'm not looking for a *man,*" Sonnie said. "I'm looking for an investigator. Roy told me you're an investigator."

She'd seen him on a number of occasions and noticed he was a big man, a big, muscular man with dark curly hair on the wrong side of too long. She also noticed he might be good-looking without a few days' growth of beard and a tendency to appear too bored, or too cynical to wear any particular expression.

He wore an expression now. The man was angry.

"Did you hear what I said?" She was angry, too. So she'd interrupted his cozy evening with his bike. He was mooching off of Roy, and refusing to do anything for himself. That was what this was all about. He was probably every bit as good at his job as Roy suggested, but he was lazy.

"We already had this discussion," he said. "And I already told you I can't help you."

"Won't help me." Her stomach contracted. "Because you're too lazy to help me. That's it, isn't it? You're one of those men in some sort of second childhood. Riding around on the bike you couldn't have when you were the right age to have one."

His dark brows shot up.

He had light brown eyes, or hazel, maybe. And she'd definitely gotten his attention. Sonnie shifted in her soggy sandals. Her clothes weren't just wet; they were also growing cold.

"Why would a supposedly normal woman decide to come to the home of a man she doesn't know in the middle of the night and insult him? Push him?" Talon's South Carolina roots became more pronounced as his temper deteriorated. He stepped closer, so close she could see the faint sheen on his chest, beneath smooth black hair. "Are you fearless? Or stupid?"

"I'm . . ." Oh, no, she wasn't going to admit to being desperate. "I've got to find something out and I'm not getting anywhere on my own because I don't know how. There. Absolute honesty. And I trust Roy. He said I could trust you, too, so I do." Brave words. A pity they didn't make her feel more confident.

"If you were absolutely honest, ma'am, you'd have finished what you started to say. You're desperate. Isn't that what you mean?"

A mind reader. She thought for a moment before saying, "Close. You seem like a smart man. You've got to know I wouldn't come to you like this if I had anywhere else to turn."

"Thank you," he said, with that smile that touched only one side of his mouth—and only slightly. "Flattery like that could go to a man's head."

She didn't want this—this banter. Maybe she just wanted to close her eyes and be silent, feel nothing, think nothing.

The sensation of a large hand closing on her upper arm jolted her, and she realized she had actually closed her eyes. She stared at him.

"Are you okay?" He was too close. "Sonnie? You'd better sit down."

Drawing herself up straight took effort. "I'm just fine, thanks."

"I doubt it." He kept his grip on her arm. "You're exhausted, and you're wet. When did you eat?"

"Eat?" She wanted to hire him as a detective, and he'd decided to become a stand-in mother? "I eat regularly. Are you going to take my case?"

"Sit down."

"I don't—"

"Sit *down*. You're about to collapse, and I don't feel like picking you up."

He led her to a sagging chair draped with a brown-and-orange afghan, and plunked her on the seat.

"I'm sorry." She had no right to come here like this. But she would do what she had to do. "I've probably shocked you, turning up like this."

"It takes a lot to shock me. This isn't the way you are, is it? Not really."

She coughed into a fist. "Annoying, you mean? It doesn't matter how I really am. I have to find some things out. I came back to Key West thinking . . . I probably wasn't thinking. That's the trouble now: I didn't think anything through. Because I suddenly knew what I wanted to find out; I just came without figuring out how I'd do that."

"So you told Roy all about yourself and he elected me your right-hand man."

"No."

"No?" He retrieved a denim shirt from a hook on the wall and pulled it on, but not before Sonnie caught a glimpse of a tattoo on one shoulder. "No, you didn't tell Roy, or no, he didn't elect me?"

"Either. Neither. I mean I didn't tell Roy much except that I'm in trouble. Maybe in danger. I could be. I don't know."

He stopped in the act of buttoning the shirt and let it hang. He approached until he stood at a bottom corner of the bed. So large a man who could move so silently disconcerted Sonnie. He sat down and leaned toward her. Their knees almost touched.

"What kind of danger?"

She jumped, then laughed, felt foolish.

"I'm not for hire. Let's be straight about that. But I am interested in what makes a woman like you act out of character. You're scared out of your wits."

Sonnie shook her head, spraying drops of water from her hair. "I'm not the kind who gets scared."

Talon rested his hands on his knees. Spots of moisture had hit his shirt and begun to spread. "So you often change your mind about going home. You bang on strangers' doors instead—in the early hours of the morning?"

"Of course I don't."

"Okay." He drummed his fingers. His hands were huge. Not meaty. Lean, but with wide palms and long fingers—and prominent tendons extending to powerful forearms.

Strong hands.

A strong, strange man who kept a Harley-Davidson in the middle of his living room and played eerie violin music . . .

"If you aren't afraid of something, and you're here by mistake, we don't have anything else to talk about, Sonnie."

She didn't have a right to be here. He owed her nothing. If he wasn't interested, he wasn't interested.

"Hmm?" He leaned closer. "Do we?"

"I have a house here on Key West," she said, avoiding his eyes. "That's where I'm living."

He crossed his arms.

"After we spoke this evening, I went back there. I went inside and felt as if there was someone there." Sonnie did look at his face then.

The expression in his eyes changed subtly. "Felt?"

"How do people ever explain these things without feeling foolish?"

"If they do, I'm less likely to take them seriously."

"So you do take me seriously?"

"I didn't say that. It was just a feeling?"

He would never give her the smallest break. "A door slammed upstairs."

"You're living there alone?"

"Yes."

"Probably a draft." His stillness didn't help her discomfort. "Either from an open window or when you opened the front door."

Mentioning a light she might or might not have seen was out of the question. "Probably."

"But because of other things you know, you're afraid it might not have been."

The beating of her heart pounded at her eardrums. "I'm just going to tell you what I need to find out. Okay?"

He bent a very long leg and rested a bare ankle on the opposite knee. He did not encourage her to continue.

"I want to know if I'm a wife or a widow."

"If the people who abducted your husband don't make further contact, that's something you may never know. Not for sure."

"How . . ." Sonnie hesitated, made to get up. "I didn't tell Roy "

"No, you didn't." He shrugged and indicated the computer. "I did a little checking."

"And found out my history? On the computer?"

"Not hard if you know where to look—and have some connections. Don't worry. Most people don't know. But the question's the same. What I said about your husband's abduction."

Face-to-face with voicing at least a facsimile of what she believed, Sonnie felt as if her diaphragm had been cut out. She would not say that what she needed most was her memory.

"Isn't it true?"

"It may be. If he was really abducted."

Another subtle shift in expression. His eyes narrowed then, and his nostrils flared.

"I don't think the crash I had near the airport—Smathers Beach—was an accident. I think I need to find out if someone tried to kill me, and I can't risk asking anyone I know for help."

"So you're trying to dump a guilt trip on me. I'm supposed to take you on because I'm too honorable to let you go it alone."

Sonnie stood up. "I hadn't thought about it quite like that. But, since you mention it, won't it make you feel bad if you send me away now and you read about my murder in the morning?"

Four

"Hello, hello, hellooo." A white-haired woman wearing a yellow muumuu that reached her ankles slid sideways through a gap in the fence between Sonnie's house and the pink stucco immediately to the west.

"Old friend?" Roy said.

"No." Sonnie watched the woman advance. "Although . . . I think I do remember her. She used to wave from a distance—pretty much like she's waving now."

"Mrs. Giacano? Yes, it is you; of course it is."

Sonnie, with Roy beside her, stopped reluctantly at the foot of the steps to the veranda and said, "Good morning." It was a good morning, the sun so bright it made her squint. Except for leaving scattered red poinciana petals like a telltale fingerprint, the storm of the night before might never have happened.

The woman arrived before them. Up close she was younger than she had appeared at first.

"You probably don't remember me. No, I see you don't. It's just Ena. From next door. We only met a few times in passing. But then, you and that handsome husband of yours were always so busy. I didn't like to push myself. And I never saw you when he was away." She tutted and shook her head. She held a long florist's box. "I'm certainly sorry about those dreadful people. The ones who kidnapped him. Imagine that—kidnapped. How long has it been now? Eight months? How are we supposed to feel safe in our own homes when a man like that is snatched away and there isn't a word more heard?'' She paused for breath. ''I wanted to come sooner—once I saw you here again—but I don't intrude. There hasn't been any news, has there? About your husband?''

Sonnie took an instant to recover from the onslaught and say, ''No, no word.''

''Fancy that. And such a talented man. I just know he was about to make a comeback. And he will. You just wait and see. I was telling Edward—he's my lodger Edward Miller''—she pointed toward her own house, at a man playing with a small dog near the front door—''I told Edward how Frank Giacano will show up one of these days and he'll take his rightful place. He'll be number one, and you'll be proud to be beside him. The cameras are so kind to him. Not that they have to be kind. He's so handsome.'' She rolled her eyes. ''Those Italian good looks. No wonder all those women run after him. Charisma, that's what it is. And when they let him go, he'll be even more mysterious.''

Sonnie felt her fingernails digging into her palms but couldn't relax enough to uncurl her hands. All she could think to say was, ''Yes, yes.'' This woman was one more of Frank's fans. She probably bragged about living next door to him.

Ena closed in on Sonnie and stared hard at her face. ''Oh, you poor dear,'' she said, shaking her head and sighing. ''What a mess you've made of yourself.''

''If you'll excuse us, ma'am,'' Roy said, gripping Sonnie's elbow, ''we wouldn't want to take up a woman's time.''

''Not at all,'' Ena said, batting a soft hand from a loose wrist. ''Being neighborly is close to being godly in my book. I suppose you have to wait a while before having plastic surgery. Didn't I hear that?''

Sonnie's scars, the ones not hidden by her clothes, felt as if they swelled and throbbed. ''That's right,'' she said. ''Thank you for coming over.''

''Oh, it's nothing. You poor girl. All you have to do is shout and I'll be here." This time Ena studied Sonnie's legs. "I'll be more than glad to run errands, too. Save that leg—and your foot."

Sonnie's heart pounded. She said, "Thanks."

Ena peered at Roy. "Don't I know you? Where have I seen you?" Her unlined face bore the sheen of some lotion or cream. The white hair was a platinum bleach job taken too far.

Roy, who religiously avoided the sun, wore a straw Stetson. He also wore Western boots with tooled-silver toe caps. "Well, ma'am—"

"I'm Ena Fishbine, but it's just Ena."

"Well, Ena, I reckon you may have seen me. I'm Roy Talon. I own the Rusty Nail on Duval."

Ena shuddered and averted her face. "A *bar*. No, I wouldn't know someone from a bar. I don't believe in imbibing." She returned her full attention to Sonnie, who noted a flush on the woman's face. "I want you to let me do what I can to help you. There isn't any task I won't tackle. I noticed you haven't gone through and taken off the dustcovers yet. Probably hard to do with all the worry about your husband. Let me help you."

"I hadn't planned—"

"You look awful, dear," said Ena. "My, oh, my. What's happened to your hair, your clothes . . . your sandals?"

Sonnie couldn't think how to respond.

"Got caught in the storm last night," Roy said, and Sonnie noted that his drawl was more pronounced than his brother's.

"Well," said Ena, ignoring Roy. "I'm sure you don't need me making you feel even worse, Mrs. Giacano. Some secrets are meant to be kept." She gave Roy a rapid, sideways glance. Then she pressed the florist's box into Sonnie's arms. "I promised I'd make sure you got these. I'll check back on you later, help you get settled in."

"Oh, you don't have—"

"That's what neighbors are for," said Ena, already making for the gap in the fence. "You need a friend. A good friend. Then you won't want to spend nights in bars. I'll be back. I'm coming, Edward."

Roy gave a low chuckle and said, "Yup, you've got to give

up all that drinkin', Sonnie. Shouldn't be a problem with Just Ena's help.''

She grimaced and led the way to the house. "She's a victim of her tongue. I do seem to recall her now. One of those people with a heart of gold—according to people around here. Not that I ever got to talk to many of them.''

Roy leaned around her to open the door, and she forced herself to walk in without hesitation. "Thank you for bringing me home,'' she said. "And thank you for allowing me to spend the night.''

Roy chuckled some more. "We were glad to have you. But that brother of mine made it pretty clear you'd be staying. Chris in his forceful mode isn't someone you buck. Good to see him that way again.''

When she frowned at him, Roy smiled. "Good to see my brother worked up about something. It's not easy to get him riled up these days, but you sure managed. Only gets ruffled over things that interest him. Like the Harley. Had to put a wider door in that shack he calls home, just so he could sleep with that bike where he can see it. Yep. In fact I don't recall the last time I saw him like he was when he brought you over. I'd say you got him interested enough to be ruffled, all right.''

There hadn't been any discussion since Chris Talon had all but marched her to the back door of the Rusty Nail in the small hours of the morning and hammered with a fist until Bo appeared, with Roy close behind him. Talon had thrust Sonnie at the two men and told them she needed a bed, and that she needed "to be saved from herself—and me if she tries to make me responsible for her again.''

She grew hot all over at the thought. Roy couldn't be farther from the truth about Talon's feelings about her. He considered her a nuisance. She said, "Thank you for putting up with me. I've been such a burden to you.''

"Nope.'' Roy shook his head. He'd removed the hat, and his red hair was still damp from the shower. "Not a burden at all. There's plenty of room, and we like company. Sonnie, why don't you stay on with us until you're on your feet again? Chris was right to bring you to us last night—this morning. We didn't talk much, but you were so scared.''

"I was embarrassed at disturbing everyone. Thanks, Roy, but I need to make myself settle in here.''

"I don't push people. And my brother never used to. You must have hit a nerve. But you can change your mind and come to us anytime. Pick up the phone and I'll come get you. Understand, now?''

"Thanks, Roy, but I—''

"Don't say what you won't be doing. Just leave it that you can. Okay?'' He looked at the box in her hands. "You going to open that? I'll be takin' a look around the house before I go.''

She started to protest but he was already starting up the stairs. "Your brother must have said something to you about me being scared,'' she called after him, annoyed that Talon would wait until she was shut away in Bo and Roy's guestroom, then spill everything she'd told him in confidence. "It's not true.''

"All Chris said was that you might be a bit too uptight to be alone here yet. That's all. And how you'd gotten jumpy here last night and gone to him.''

Increasingly irritated, she followed up the stairs. "In other words, he did say I was frightened.''

"You were, weren't you?'' He'd reached the landing that circled the second floor.

"No.'' *Why pretend?* "Yes, I was. But I . . . Well, when I met him last night I hoped he would help me, and when he wasn't interested, I think I was confused. I went back to see if I could convince him I wasn't a flake. Hah! Great job I did. Look, Roy, this isn't your problem. You've already done too much for me.''

"Good ol' Chris is going to help you. You've got to be patient with a fella like him. Give him time to convince himself it was his idea to work with you all along. You two will be just dandy together. You heard a door slam up here?''

Good ol' Talon had spilled *all* the beans. She bit back what she'd like to say about confidentiality and told Roy, "I'm sure the wind blew it shut."

"I didn't notice if there's a floor above this." He studied the domed skylight with a chandelier suspended from its center, and the high walls that rose on all sides of the second story.

"Just the attic. I'd considered raising the roof to build more rooms—" She stopped. She'd wanted it converted to more rooms for the children she'd hoped to have. "Don't worry about me, Roy. The daylight makes everything look very normal." White on white paint glistened. Plaster medallions at the centers of beaded panels bore yellow roses.

"Night always follows day, kid. That's one of those absolutes. It'll come around again. Just let me put my mind to rest. I'll take the tour—if you don't mind."

"I don't mind. I think you're just about the nicest man I ever met."

"You don't know Chris well enough yet."

She wouldn't tell him she thought his arrogant, rather nasty brother was emotionally crippled and she didn't much care why. She also wouldn't discuss her problems with Roy again. The idea of Chris Talon being coerced into helping her made her ill.

"Chris hasn't had an easy time of it. But he wouldn't appreciate my mouthing off about his personal stuff."

"He didn't mind mouthing off about mine to you." Her tongue could be too quick, and too undisciplined.

"All he said was that you're stretched too thin. And he doesn't think you're well enough to cope—physically well enough. These doors are all shut, Sonnie. Were they shut when you left the house last night?"

Talon thought she wasn't physically fit? She wasn't, but how would he know? A limp, sometimes with both legs, and a few visible scars didn't mean you were an invalid.

"Were they shut, Sonnie?"

She held a banister to steady herself. "They were shut when I was last up here." She took a breath and admitted, "I've been sleeping on a pullout sofa in the parlor. I do need to get properly moved in."

Their eyes met, but Roy was too diplomatic to comment. "So the doors couldn't . . . Well, they probably couldn't have slammed shut, could they?"

"No."

She and Roy looked at each other again and didn't have to say that they both wondered how a door could slam if it hadn't been opened by someone.

"You felt someone in the house?"

Talon again. "Stupid, I know. Just that weird sensation. I'm too touchy."

"You've been through a lot. The accident. The recovery had to be hard. Then finding out your husband had been grabbed like that."

She took a moment too long to say "Yes," and knew by the quizzical expression in Roy's eyes that he had noted the hesitation. "What else did your brother say? About my stupid visit? And about what he found out on his wonderful computer?"

"He didn't say your visit was stupid. He only said you needed a place to stay for the night."

"But he told you about my accident, and—"

"This isn't such a big place. I didn't need Chris to tell me your history. Your husband is a celebrity. That makes you a celebrity. The whole island talked about your accident and how you were airlifted to Miami. Then there was the story about what had happened to Frank Giacano. A lot of stuff gets talked about in a bar. Liquor does that."

"I guess it does." Sonnie regarded him somberly. "I didn't . . . I didn't think people would remember anything about me. I suppose there are lots of theories about Frank."

"Open the flowers."

In other words, there were a lot of theories about the Giacanos. Sonnie untied a green ribbon from the shiny white box and slid off the lid. The heavy scent of white calla lilies swelled forth. Sonnie hadn't eaten and the aroma sickened her.

"Hmm," was Roy's reaction.

She picked up the enclosed envelope and opened it. Typed on the card inside was: *Lilies, as velvet white as a baby's skin—*

as white as the satin in her only bed. Take care, Sonnie. She bowed over the box and struggled to catch her breath.

"Your favorite flowers?" said Roy.

She shook her head. "I hate them." *White satin in her only bed.* Jacqueline's tiny casket. Who would do this? Who hated Sonnie enough to torture her—and why?

"You'd better let your admirer know you don't like them," Roy said, and laughed self-consciously. They both knew he wondered who had sent the bouquet.

"The card isn't signed."

He settled his thumbs into the waist of his jeans and frowned. "Florist must have left the name off. Call and ask 'em to check."

"I will," Sonnie said. "Later." She crammed the lid back onto the box and quelled an impulse to throw the whole thing in the garbage. The horribly obvious message terrified her.

Roy proceeded to open the nearest door and walk into a bedroom draped with sheets. Sonnie looked past him at blue-flowered paper above white wainscoting, and sheer white draperies closed over French doors with a clear fanlight above. She had fallen in love with this house the day she'd found it. In disrepair then, it had swiftly become as beautiful as it was meant to be.

"Leave the doors open," she told Roy. "Please."

"You've got it." Following Sonnie, he went from room to room.

The only times Sonnie hesitated were when Roy went into the nursery next to the master bedroom, and into the storeroom where she thought she'd caught sight of a light the night before. She stayed out of the nursery. Nothing looked out of place in the storeroom.

Back on the ground floor, they went into the kitchen. "Can I make you some coffee?" Sonnie asked.

Roy shook his head. "I do need to get back. But I'll check on you later. You'll be at work tonight?"

"Oh, yes," Sonnie said. The idea of spending an entire evening there overwhelmed her. But she had to ask, "If you knew all about me, why did you offer me a job?"

"I didn't know who you were when we met, Sonnie. You were a pretty woman drinkin' tea alone each afternoon. You looked sad, and I've always been real good at makin' it my business to cheer people up. I thought you could use company."

She rubbed his arm and smiled up at him. "You were right—about everything. You are one nice guy, Roy Talon. And so's that Bo. Are you sure I don't put off customers, though?"

He frowned at her. "Put off customers? How would you do that?"

"I don't remember jokes and I'm not . . . Roy, I'm not a real asset to the Nail."

"You're a great asset. Some of those assholes—shit, I mean . . . Don't listen too close, please. Some of our fine clientele are even starting to ask when you'll be in. I've even heard it said that you bring class to the joint. Can't imagine anyone thinkin' it didn't already have enough class, can you?"

"No, Roy," Sonnie said. He was absolutely one of the best.

The phone rang and they looked at each other. When Sonnie made no move to answer, Roy picked it up. "Hello? Uh-huh, you're in luck, bro."

Sonnie slid the flowers onto the counter and backed away. Roy signaled for her to stay in the kitchen.

"A-OK," he said. "Nope. Looks fine. Nothing unusual unless you count bouquets from anonymous admirers."

Sonnie's stomach made a leap. The only people who knew where she was were Billy, their Dad, and Sonnie's Mom. They weren't likely to send flowers with notes that weren't signed, and they knew she'd detested calla lilies since her grandmother's funeral when she was a young teenager.

"That fancy florist on Whitehead Street. Moss Corner? Okay, I'm on my way now." Roy covered the mouthpiece and said, "You sure you're okay, Sonnie? On your own, I mean?"

"I'm fine." She would be fine.

The instant Roy left, and without giving herself time to think, she started pulling drapes from the downstairs furniture. Dust flew and swirled in sunlight through the windows she opened.

Already the day was heating up.

By noon every grimy sheet was piled in the laundry room or already taking its turn in the washer or dryer. The familiar domestic sounds made Sonnie feel almost carefree.

Twice she'd caught sight of Just Ena, or her lodger, on the opposite side of the shrubbery fence, and waved. Then she'd turned purposefully away. These people meant well, but Sonnie wasn't in the mood to make small talk. And she didn't like knowing she was being watched.

The crunch of wheels on the gravel driveway stopped her. Her body tensed and her scalp felt too small.

People—normal people—had visitors for a variety of completely harmless reasons.

A car door slammed.

Roy was back to check on her. She quelled a giggle.

Before she could reach the front door, a key turned in the lock and Romano Giacano walked in.

Five

"Chris? Do I know a Chris? No, I don't know him anymore, but would that be ace schmuck and deserter Christian J. Talon, formerly of NYPD?"

"Save it, Flynn," Chris said into his cell phone. "I need a favor. And fast."

"A favor? Fast? I'm about to hang up this friggin' phone."

"Thanks for all the understanding you've always given—"

"You quit the force and left town. You didn't give me a chance to be understanding. I haven't heard a friggin' word from you in two years. I don't even know where you are."

"Yeah," Chris said, keeping his eyes on Sonnie Giacano's pretty and very expensive house. "Sorry about that. I always intended to make contact. I thought I'd do it when I finally got my shit together. When I do, I will. I'm looking at a New York plate. I need to know who owns the car. Will you fix that for me, Flynn?"

"I'm a cop—you're not. Cops don't run makes for civilians. Against the law. Gimme the plate. And a number where I can reach you. Someone in Traffic owes me a big one. Shouldn't take more than a few minutes."

Chris grinned and recited his cell phone number, and the particulars from the back license plate on a white Jag XK8 parked in Sonnie's driveway. He doubted it was hers because he'd seen her driving the rented tan Camry parked to the left of the house and covered with poinciana petals. The Jag's windows were tinted his least favorite color—as close to black as they came. There was no reason Sonnie shouldn't have a visitor with New York plates, but everything she'd told him had made him think she didn't have a whole lot of friends.

And he had a feeling, the kind of feeling he'd forgotten about, but which he recognized the instant it hit. When he and Aiden Flynn had been partners, Flynn would know Chris was "visiting dark places" just from his still silence.

Sonnie was frightened. Her supposedly funny comment about showing up dead in the morning hadn't been all joke. She'd already said she thought someone might have tried to kill her.

In the past half hour Chris had ridden his Harley slowly past Sonnie's house—twice—trying to convince himself he was doing so to please Roy. Roy was worried about his latest good cause, and Chris ought to want to help his brother.

The Jag had shown up in the last few minutes—while Chris was too far away to witness the arrival.

What help would it be to Roy to have Chris cruising back and forth on Truman Avenue and looking at Sonnie's house?

He didn't like the Jag.

He didn't like the feeling he was having. Someone sent Sonnie calla lilies with an unsigned card inside the box. And she not only disliked them, but, according to Roy, she had turned pale and looked as if she might collapse.

Calla lilies were funeral, weren't they?

His phone rang and he clicked it on. "Yeah?"

"You there, schmuck?"

Chris ignored the bait. "What you got?"

"Leased to Giacano Enterprises. They buy surplus goods and ship 'em overseas. Mostly Russia."

"Damn, you're still quick, Flynn." He frowned. There had been nothing in the research he'd done that mentioned Giacano Enterprises, at least not in relation to either Sonnie or Frank

Giacano. But he'd obviously lost his touch for significant feelings. Sonnie had a family visitor, nothing more.

"You still there, schmuck?"

"Yeah. It's good to hear your voice."

There was a pause before Flynn said, "Likewise. What're you doing in Key West?"

Chris laughed. "What makes you think I'm in Key West?"

"Just a hunch."

"Good hunch. We'll talk about the meaning of my life one of these days," he said, "when you need something to put you to sleep."

"It's still the woman, isn't—"

"One of these days we'll talk about it," Chris repeated, but the muscles across his shoulders had already clenched.

"Sure you will," Flynn said. "I'll expect to hear from you in a year or so—or when you need information I'm not supposed to give you. You remember the 'sixty-seven pink pony I bought?"

Chris looked at Sonnie's house again. This wasn't a good time for a buddy chat. "The Barbiemobile, you mean?" he said. "Who could forget? A rusty pink heap of Mustang junk with a missing seat. Let me guess—you've finally accepted that it's tasteless, too tasteless even to live in your warehouse with the rest of those useless junk Mustangs. Congratulations."

"It's mint now, perfect," Flynn said. "And it was only the third exception to all the other Dusk Rose vehicles. Guess why?"

Chris figured he was paying for the information Flynn had given him. "I don't have a clue," he said. "Why?"

Flynn chuckled like the proud father of a brilliant child. "They all had black seats, unless they were custom. I know of two others with parchment seats. This baby's got a history."

"Congratulations. You'll hear from me." Chris hung up. He meant what he said. But just not too soon.

He lifted his helmet from his lap. It could be that Frank Giacano had chosen today to reemerge from the void.

Sonnie was an odd little bird. An odd, wounded little bird. He doubted she'd ever been real substantial, but she must have had more body than she did now. He almost laughed. Maybe he ought to rephrase that thought.

Feeling negative at the prospect of Frank Giacano's return was way out of line.

Chris eased on his helmet. Sometimes he missed the days when he'd worn a regulation brain bucket and ridden with the wind raking his then-shoulder-length hair. On more than one occasion his chief had accused him of enjoying his job too much. Chris had never protested because, dirty as Narcotics might be, it was a duty that really counted. Sometimes really counted, unless the perp mattered enough to the money men. In that case, he or she would be back on the streets before the ink dried on the warrant. After Narcotics, he'd moved to Homicide—the beginning of his end.

He looked over his shoulder and prepared to start his engine.

Sonnie's front door opened.

Chris rolled his booted foot from toe to heel, eased the bike backward and onto the sidewalk until a vine-draped telephone pole gave him some cover.

Sonnie herself stood in the doorway, her arms crossed. She faced straight out, but from her stance, Chris doubted she was looking at anything in particular.

A man came to stand behind her. Sonnie stepped onto the veranda that ran around the house, and she turned aside as if she refused to look at her visitor.

Chris looked at him. The distance between them was too great to allow more than a general impression. Average height, dark curly hair, tanned. Chris thought the guy looked fit.

The man touched Sonnie's arm. She hunched her shoulders and walked away, to the corner at the right side of the house. Her visitor followed and Sonnie broke into an uneven run out of sight toward the back of the house.

The man was chasing her.

Tearing off his helmet, Chris hauled the Harley back onto its stand. He took off across the street and sprinted along a crushed coral path that skirted the veranda. He didn't slow down until he'd almost reached a trellis loaded with shocking purple bougainvillea. Built between a veranda pole and a high hedge at the east edge of the property, the trellis divided the front garden from the back.

Chris had put a foot on the veranda decking and made to swing a leg over the rail when the man's voice, raised but not angry, reached him. Caution finally kicked in and Chris finished climbing—very quietly—over the railing.

"Listen to me, please," the man said with a heavy Italian accent. He sounded shaken. "Listen, Sonnie. You and I are friends. We were friends before you met Frank. I wanted—"

"Stop. Please stop." Sonnie was harder to hear. "You've been a good friend to me, the best."

"And I always will be. I will watch over you as long as I live. This is a promise I have made to myself, a promise my brother would expect me to make."

"Romano, I'm grateful for your kindness, but I can't allow you to tell me what I must or must not do. And I don't expect you to be angry because I choose to live my own life. You are a busy man. Don't worry about me, please."

Chris stood close to the house and waited.

"You have been through a great deal," Giacano said. "Too much. You need someone to care for you at all times. You are an attractive woman, and—"

"I'm an insignificant, *married* woman," Sonnie said, her voice sharper. "No, don't argue with me. I'm used to the truth. I've lived with it for months. I'm grateful for the recovery I've made, but I know what I look like."

Chris breathed in slowly. She had a lousy opinion of herself and she was dead wrong. She limped and had scars. Big deal. She was interesting, damn it. She interested him. . . .

"What is inside you shines out, my dear," said Sonnie's subtle brother-in-law. "That is what matters. But an opportunist who discovers what a wealthy woman you are could flatter you, take advantage of you. There already is someone, isn't there? That's why you came here alone. Who is he? Give me a name and I'll find out about him."

"How did you know I was here?" Sonnie asked.

After a short silence Giacano said, "You don't need to know that. I'm here; that's what matters. There will be nothing for you to worry about anymore. Let me take you back to your family. I'll stay tonight and we can leave in the morning.''

"No. What are you saying? No.''

The man's sigh was loud and frustrated. "These are not the decisions for you to make. In Frank's absence, I must decide what is best for you.''

"You aren't Frank,'' Sonnie said, and Chris thought he heard the start of angry tears. "You aren't my husband. I don't even know if I've *got* a husband anymore.''

He ought to feel uncomfortable, Chris thought, only the lady had come to him with a story about her life being in jeopardy. It was his duty to take her request for his services seriously— even if he hadn't agreed to work for her.

"I know I am not your husband.'' Romano had taken a long time to respond. "But I am the head of the family. That means it is my responsibility to look after you. Sonnie . . . Sonnie, have you heard something about Frank? Did they contact you?'' The man's voice rose.

"No, nothing.''

"Please, my dear, don't hold back anything about my dear brother. I cannot tell you how I have suffered thinking of what could be happening to him.''

"I haven't heard anything about Frank. Billy told you I was here, didn't she?''

"Billy loves you.''

"She's my half-sister and I ought to be able to trust her. She promised she wouldn't tell anyone where I'd gone.''

"Come back into the house, Sonnie. I need to be sure you're all right. You are as much a part of my life as . . . You are very important to me.''

Chris narrowed his eyes. Mr. Giacano was too smooth, and he wasn't Sonnie's type. And there was something about him that raised Chris's antennae.

"I will be staying in Key West,'' Sonnie said, and Chris smiled with one side of his mouth.

"Your family wants you to come home.''

"Frank did his best to keep me as far from my family as

possible. He didn't want me to have them near me, and he didn't want me to have friends."

Shrugging away from the wall, Chris went on alert. He hadn't only imagined that Sonnie was covering up more than she had actually shared with him. A husband who cut her off from other people. Classic behavior for an abusive spouse. Not that he had any proof that Frank Giacano had been abusive— yet.

"Let me hold you, Sonnie. I look at you and I just want to take you into my arms. You have suffered so much for one so gentle. Come, my dear."

Chris bowed his head and listened even harder. He studied his fingernails. Surely she was too smart to be taken in by lines like that.

"You are confused," Romano said. "You don't even accept an offer of comfort from the one you trust the most."

Maybe Romano was trying as much to convince himself as Sonnie. Chris didn't blame him for wanting to hold her, but he didn't quite believe she trusted him the most, as Romano said; in fact, he'd put money on her wanting to get rid of him.

There was a pause in conversation from the other side of the bougainvillea. Chris rubbed a hand over his mouth. Had she accepted Romano's offer of "comfort"? "Well, baby," he murmured softly, "if you buy that one, I've got a real nice bridge for sale."

He didn't want to think of her in Giacano's arms—or any man's arms.

Now there was a confusing admission. Ah, he'd flipped into protective mode; that was all. For a tough man, he'd always been weak when it came to letting women open doors for themselves, or carry their own bags. Too bad. He guessed he must be one of those Renaissance men people spoke about. There were definitely some who referred to him as a "throwback," not that he thought they were complimenting him.

"Very well," Romano said. "Perhaps it will take time for you to remember the trust we have shared."

She hadn't let him get his clammy paws on her.

"I will stay here with you. If you are searching for some

clue to Frank—not that I can understand why you would choose this place—but if you are, I will help you.''

Sonnie didn't answer.

"You were never sure of yourself. It will be good for you to know there is a man in the house.''

Chris held absolutely still.

"I'm quite sure of myself,'' Sonnie said. "I've had to learn to be.''

In any other circumstance, Chris would have cheered.

"I am glad you feel so,'' Romano said. "I will help you become even more sure—while we try to help each other. But this decision of yours to come here is not, er, easy to understand. If, as you insist, you came here to be alone, and you are not involved with someone else, then we must examine what has happened in your mind.''

Those words brought Chris to attention.

"I have enough of my things to manage for some days. Then, if I can't persuade you to leave with me, I must send for more. I will take the bedroom nearest to yours and Frank's, just in case you need me in the night.''

Damn the slimy little bastard, Chris thought, setting his teeth. In case she needed him in the night for what?

"That wouldn't be a good idea.'' Sonnie was barely audible. "I have neighbors. People talk.''

"But, my dear —''

"No,'' Sonnie said, with more force. "You can't stay here. I suggest you go back to New York. We'll stay in touch, and the moment I find out anything useful, I'll call you.''

"I will do as I have said and remain here.''

"You will not stay in this house, Romano. It's not that I wouldn't love to have your company, but I can't. If you insist on being in Key West for a while, you'll have to find another place to stay.''

"How can you say that?'' Anger edged those sexy, reasonable Italian nuances. "You wound me, my dear. It is exactly as I feared. You are not yourself. Very well, I will stay at the club. At least until you stop being afraid of gossip. But I insist that we bring in a doctor to examine you.''

"Examine me?"

"You know you are not ready to be without medical supervision."

"Are you talking about bringing in a psychiatrist?"

The man laughed. "Leave these matters to me. I will call the Sunset shortly and arrange for a room. A good thing we kept up our membership."

In other words, he did intend to try to make Sonnie submit to some psychiatric examination.

"There will be no doctors brought here," Sonnie said. "I'd like to be alone now."

"Alone is the last thing you should be. It's obvious I must care for you. I will call your father and he will agree with me."

Making sure he made plenty of noise with his boots, Chris walked to the next corner of the house and stepped out. Sonnie sat halfway down a flight of steps from the veranda to a paved terrace with a pool beyond. Romano Giacano stood on the top step looking down at her, or he had been looking at her until he heard, then saw, Chris arrive.

"Hey," Chris said, his best grin in place. "Hey, Sonnie. Sorry I'm late. Don't tell Roy or he'll have plenty to say about it."

Romano stared at him blankly.

Sonnie smiled with such pathetic gratitude that he wanted to laugh. He felt a whole lot more pleasure than he should feel over something so small.

Romano moved to cut Chris off from Sonnie's line of sight. "Who are you?" he asked. "What are you doing here?"

"Chris Talon, at your service," Chris said, leaning forward and extending a hand. "Friend of Sonnie's."

Chris's hand was ignored. "A friend? How could you possibly be a friend of our Sonnie's?"

"*Friend*," Chris said slowly and distinctly. "You know. As in someone you like, and rely on sometimes."

The other man looked back at Sonnie. "Do you know this . . . man?"

"Yes," she said, and her delighted grin gave Chris a charge. "We know each other very well."

Chris almost shouted with laughter. The odd little bird wasn't above her own brand of opportunistic torture.

Romano's hair waved tightly back from a broad forehead. His eyes were unexpectedly blue. Chris guessed that meant he was a northern Italian but wasn't about to ask. As he'd suspected, the man appeared very fit. Chris guessed some women might find him attractive—if they were into males whose testosterone level had to be something they prized more than their IQ.

"How could you possibly meet such a person?" Romano asked, not looking at Sonnie, but at Chris's faded T-shirt inscribed, *If All Assholes Could Fly, This Town Would Be An Airport,* and jeans that were soft and faded, and thin enough to show skin in places. The boots were expensive, but Romano didn't bother to get that far. "Sonnie? This is exactly what I've been afraid of. Frank would not approve, and neither do I."

She started to get up but had evidently sat too long in an awkward position. Chris walked past Romano without a glance and held out his hands to Sonnie. She looked straight into his eyes and let him pull her to her feet.

"You okay?" he asked quietly. "After Roy called, I decided to take a turn down here and make sure everything was okay with you."

"Thank you." She held his hands so hard he was sure she was unaware of not having released him. "Roy's a dear."

"He wanted me to check on you and see if you wanted a ride tonight."

"My God, what has happened to you, Sonnie?" Romano caught at Sonnie's wrist and made to pull her hand away. "Let her go at once. She is a fragile woman in need of constant supervision."

Immediately, Chris released her hands. "Really," he said. "I think you're wrong about that, buddy."

There was no doubt that Romano weighed Chris and decided they were too unevenly matched to make any physical move on his part a good idea.

"You can leave now," Romano said. "Sonnie needs to be quiet. We have to call her family."

"And call in a shrink, too, maybe?"

Romano sneered, but looked taken aback at the same time. "You make a habit of listening to the conversations of others? Despicable. But what else would one expect?"

"Expect from whom?" Chris asked. "And the lady doesn't need a shrink, by the way. She's doing very nicely all on her own. My brother considers her the best employee he's ever had."

He saw Sonnie bite her lower lip, but that wicked little smile was still there. She was actually enjoying parts of this.

"Employee," Romano said, managing to look more confused than Chris would have thought possible. "My sister-in-law doesn't work. She doesn't have to work."

"Careful now," Chris said. "You wouldn't want me to dream up any ideas about getting cozy with a wealthy, unattached woman."

Romano's face reddened. "You listened a long time. My sister-in-law is not unattached."

"Is that right? Well, since we're being honest, she's right in not wanting you moving into her house, then, isn't she?"

"Get out," Romano said.

"When Sonnie tells me to go, I will," Chris said. "She's very good with the customers, y'know. They look out for her. Say she raises the tone of the place."

Romano turned to Sonnie and said, "You have never worked, my dear. There has never been any need. Giacano women look after their husbands and homes."

"My husband seems to be missing," Sonnie said. "I would very much like to see him come back. We've got things to work out. But he isn't here now and I choose to fend for myself. I work for Roy Talon and Bo Quick at the Rusty Nail."

Romano shook his head. "This is insupportable. Do you answer phones? Type letters? What? You have no training."

"That's an error I intend to make good," Sonnie said. "I've got time to go back to school. Meanwhile, I'm a barmaid at the Rusty Nail on Duval Street."

Six

The phone was ringing as Sonnie let herself into the house. She dropped her keys on the wicker chest inside the front door and went into the parlor. Without turning on the light, she picked up the receiver and said, "Hello."

"At last you answer," Romano said. "Where have you been?"

Sonnie sat on the edge of the couch, then pushed to the back. She was so tired. "I told you earlier today. I've got a job. I work."

"Sonnie," Romano said, dropping his voice, "I am beside myself. Let me come to you."

"This makes no sense. You have nothing to worry about—not about me. I'm fine."

"Your car was at the house all evening."

Now he was watching her. "You have been the one I relied on," she told him. "I relied on you because you were on my side. Or I thought you were. You supported me when I insisted I would get well faster if everyone stopped fussing over me and telling me what to do."

"I still support you. I am your champion. But you are not being yourself. I asked you about your car. How could you have gone to that place tonight without your car? Did that biker person take you?''

Biker person. Sonnie grinned at the description, but she guessed that was fairly apt. Chris Talon was a biker person. ''Chris didn't take me. I walked.''

Romano's following silence made her edgy.

''I cannot believe it,'' he said at last. ''Surely ... It is a long way even in daylight. You don't mean that you walked home in the darkness.''

''It isn't far, and yes, I walked home.''

''Sonnie, please listen to me. I do not want to stay here at the club. I do not want to be in Key West at all. But I cannot leave you alone at such a time.''

''Such a time?''

''While you are not yourself, dear one.''

She felt shivery. ''Why do you keep talking about me not being myself, about bringing in doctors to examine me? You aren't responsible for me. I don't want you to be. I want you to go back to being the friend I can call on when I need him. I can't understand why you're so upset. We've spoken regularly and everything's been okay. As okay as it can be until we know—until Frank comes back.'' If Frank came back she would have to pray for the strength to do what must be done.

''Frank will come back,'' Romano said, but without conviction. ''You have done so well since the accident. I thought you would continue to improve—as long as you didn't do something foolish and possibly dangerous, as you have now.''

Sonnie propped an elbow and buried her face in one hand. He was a good, kind man who had always done his best for her. When she'd been in the hospital, he'd rarely left her side. Her family loved him. In fact, they loved him as they had never seemed able to love Frank.

''Are you still there?'' he asked.

Perhaps she should stop trying to fight alone, and with so little idea of what she hoped to find, to do. ''I'm here,'' she said. If she asked his help, he would give it. He might well tell her she was imagining things, but she was the one who heard the voices and saw, if only briefly, those vague impressions of faces and movements, of fire in the wind, of reaching hands.

"Sonnie?"

"Be patient with me, Romano. I came because I felt I must. I felt there were things here that I should know about. Or perhaps things that would lead to information I should know about. You know how important you are to me. I don't want us to become enemies."

"Oh, my dear, we could never be enemies. No, no." He expelled a long, uneven breath. "Tell me what you think you may find. Or what you want to find. Let me help you, please."

She smiled. He hadn't changed. "You are the man you always were," she told him. "Thank you for that. I don't know what I hope to discover here. I only know that I . . . I just wanted to come here and think. There are decisions I need to make about my future." This wasn't the time to reveal exactly what had brought her back here, not when he was talking about getting her reevaluated by a psychiatrist.

"What decisions?" He sounded tense and worried.

"I don't work tomorrow evening. Come for dinner. Around seven?"

"Let me come over now. Then we'll spend the day together tomorrow and I'll bring you to the club for dinner."

"Always the persistent one," she said. "No, thank you. I need to be alone. That's one of the reasons I decided to return to Key West—to be alone. You should play golf tomorrow. Or get on the courts—you will anyway." Romano had been his brother's coach and was a first-class tennis player in his own right.

"Sonnie—"

"Good night, Romano. I'll see you tomorrow evening."

He was talking again when she hung up.

Business at the Nail had been brisk all evening. She'd wanted to stay longer and help, but Bo insisted she go home. Roy wanted to drive her, but she talked him out of it with a small lie: her car was parked a block away, she'd said. She was used to the walk back and forth now and knew it was strengthening her leg.

But she was exhausted. The day had been an emotional one, and the prospect of sleeping in what had been her bed with Frank made her jumpy. All of her clothes were hung in the closets. She'd changed the sheets and put a bowl of jasmine in the room. The rest of the house was far from back to normal, but she'd get it there within days.

She left the light in the parlor off and made sure the windows were closed and locked. Then she toured the ground floor, checking all doors and windows before climbing the stairs.

Milky blue light penetrated the sky dome over the two-story hallway. Clouds, shifted by the wind, dappled patterns on the shadowy pale walls inside. She didn't fear darkness. When all was dark, the odds of seeing and being seen were even.

It felt good to look around and see into rooms where the furniture was no longer draped. Part of the reason for her being here was to brush aside specters. Living in one room surrounded by closed doors wouldn't help her reach her goal.

A quick shower, and then she slipped into a favorite pair of soft, satin pajamas. The sprigs of jasmine she'd used to fill a bowl scented the whole room. She left the window to the balcony open and slid between cool, white sheets.

The last time she'd slept in this bed, she'd been pregnant.

Would there ever come a time when she could think of that tiny girl and not have her eyes fill with tears? She placed both flattened hands on her stomach and lay very still. How she'd loved to feel the baby move. The first time it had happened she'd felt almost faint with shock and excitement. She had sat on the couch in the parlor and stared down at herself, trying to actually see a tiny elbow or knee or bottom poking around to make more room.

"I loved you so," she whispered into the night. "I wanted you so. You will always be with me, little Jacqueline. Forgive me, baby mine." Tears slipped from the corners of her eyes and ran in hot lines down her temples.

This was something she'd promised to keep at bay, this falling back into the desperately sad place where her baby waited for her mother to comfort her.

The night was hot—too hot.

The sheer drapes billowed inward.

Sonnie turned on her side, then rolled to her other side. She felt sick and her scalp grew damp. She threw back the covers and took long, slow breaths. In her tote bag were the bottles of pills she kept for pain, or nervousness—or for when she couldn't sleep. Slipping from the bed, she put on a small light beside a chair and found the sleeping pills. She hated to take them, but sometimes, when she knew the gulf of sweaty blackness might be opening up before her, she gave in.

In the bathroom, she swallowed two pills with water and returned to bed. As she stretched out she began to feel herself relax just at the thought of drifting away. She'd been going to stop by the florist, Moss Corner, and ask about the lilies, but she'd forgotten. They were a deliberate effort to frighten her. Romano had seen them and hadn't even asked where they came from. In fact no one seemed concerned, so maybe she shouldn't be concerned either.

. . . *Her only bed. White as the satin in her only bed.* Sonnie tossed some more. The suggestion was horrible, and it had been intended to horrify her.

She gave in to a veil of unconsciousness that drew itself slowly over her warm body. The veil grew thicker and softer and closed out everything—even her hearing.

But she never quite slept. Each time she felt the last shreds of wakefulness grow thinner, she was drawn back up through shades of mist and darkness to an ever-increasing heat.

A crackling—distant, but clear—nibbled at the edges of her brain. There was a shooting blanket of fire. The flames within the blanket spun like elegant orange tongues, molten gold at their margins. Swirling, swirling, until they merged.

She couldn't breathe. "Help me," she whispered. "Stop. Please go away. I'm sorry."

Her body was awash in sweat, her pajamas sodden and twisted around her.

"No." Her own voice was pathetically small. *Breathe, Sonnie, breathe. Lie still and breathe, and shut everything else out.* He was trying to drive her away. She wasn't supposed to try to find out what had really happened to her.

The crackling rose, rose to a roar, ripped at her ears, heated her skin until it was parched. Her mouth was parched, her lips dry and cracked. Her hair streamed and stuck to her face and neck.

"Go away from here. Do as you're told. Get out, before I make you get out."

Her eyes wouldn't open. They were fused shut, and when the poking fingers attacked and she tried to fend them off, she couldn't catch them. She was helpless before a shrieking audience with sharp fingers. They screamed and prodded her, prodded her stomach and howled, *"Baby, baby, baby, all gone."*

"Stop it!" She wanted to be silent. She wanted to be dead here and now. "I didn't mean it. Let me go."

No, no, she was giving in. That's what he wanted. He wanted her to be frightened to death. Then he'd have his wish. She'd fought through this over and over again. He'd gone away, she thought. But now he was back again, and he had her alone this time. But she knew she could beat him only if they were face-to-face, alone.

The fingers poked her stomach again, and the voices chanted, *"Baby, baby, all gone away."*

She screamed, then crammed her hands over her mouth, trying to force the sound down. No one must hear. They'd say she was mad—and they'd put her away. She'd heard them talk about that when she was in the hospital, how they didn't know if she'd ever be able to be alone again. Perhaps she'd need to be "cared for somewhere," they'd said when they thought she still couldn't hear.

The scream bubbled up. She opened her mouth and filled it with sheet, forced it inside until she gagged and rolled to let her head hang over the side of the bed.

"Sonnie. Cara mia? *Look at me."*

Please, no. "Go away!"

"Do as I tell you. Look at me. You will do as I tell you. You will not do anything unless I tell you that you may. Do you understand? I will never let you go. Not alive. The only way you'll be free of me is in death."

"Don't hit me. Oh, don't hit me." All the air left her space and only heat and pulsing remained.

A crack smacked her head back against the pillows. She started to pull herself up. A blow to the back of her head threw her forward, and she drew up her knees to meet her face and muffle the next scream.

"Look at me."

She opened her eyes and stared. The window wall was a sheet of flame. She would die here.

"That's right."

Sonnie slid from the bed to the floor and curled up as small as she could. Frank's face. Trembling, too weak to hold her head up, she raised her eyes once more and, through the flames, she saw a face. Frank. His lips drawn back from his teeth, his eyes glowing sockets.

She closed her eyes and waited, and the heat lost its intensity. Her body, bathed with sweat, turned cold. Her teeth chattered. When she opened her eyes, there was no flame, no leering face, no host of stabbing fingers.

But they had been there, hadn't they?

They could come back.

Whatever she did, she must stay awake. She must never close her eyes and try to sleep again. She needed help or she would die here, alone, with only demon hallucinations to greet her.

Scooting on her bottom, she backed up until she sat against the bedside table. She kept her eyes on the window and managed to grapple the phone down into her lap. Romano would come at once. She should have listened to him when he warned her she was in trouble and needed help.

After several attempts, she managed to punch in numbers. What numbers? She usually forgot them. Did she know the number of the country club? She'd never liked the place. It had been for Frank, and for Romano when he was in Key West.

"Yeah?"

A cry worked from her lips and it took both of her hands to hold the receiver.

"Who is this?" The voice on the other end of the line sharpened. "Answer me. Who is this?"

"S-sorry," she said. "Wrong n-number." Chris had made her repeat his number before he'd left that afternoon, only minutes after Romano. She'd written the figures on a board by the kitchen phone, then put them in the little book beside her bed. But she'd dialed it automatically.

"Sonnie? It is you, isn't it?"

Romano hadn't wanted to leave her with him, but she'd insisted, and finally her brother-in-law had gone, but not before she saw how badly she'd hurt him. Chris had seemed anxious to leave soon after. He'd done his duty to Roy and checked on her, nothing more.

She hung up the phone. Her breathing was easier, but her head ached. What was the matter with her? She'd had another nightmare—one of many—nothing more. Just because her nightmares were so real, she'd managed to persuade herself there was something she had to find out, that they brought messages intended to send her on a mission for the truth.

Always in those desperate moments when the flames came, and the face, or sometimes faces, she expected to die, then wanted to die.

There was no fire.

There were no faces.

Heaving, she hauled herself onto the bed and lay facedown, praying for coolness, for peace, for dreamless sleep.

"Hush little baby, don't you cry."

She covered her ears. She would talk to Romano in the morning, apologize to him, tell him what she feared, and ask him to help her. He would do that.

Time stretched while she lay there in her damp pajamas, among damp sheets. As one area grew warm, she moved to another, then another. She needed to shower and change the bed, but she hadn't the strength.

From below came the sound of knocking at the door.

Sonnie sat up and hugged her shins.

The knocking sounded again, and again.

"Go away," she said softly. "Leave me alone."

More knocking, insistent, steady.

On legs that threatened to collapse beneath her, Sonnie got off the bed and went into the upper hallway. She held the banisters with both hands and began to climb down the stairs, placing first one, then the other foot on the same step before taking another. Her injured hip trembled. The pain that never quite left her foot became sharp. She moved so slowly, and the knocking went on and on.

Another step. And one more.

The knocking stopped.

Sonnie sat down at once and covered her face. If she didn't get some help, she wouldn't survive, and she wanted to survive.

A scraping sound reached her, and she raised her head to look downward. Only an instant passed before the front door swung inward and a large figure stepped quickly inside. The door closed again.

She opened her mouth but no sound would come past her aching throat.

A flashlight beam shot across the foyer, swung from side to side, then upward, upward to hit her face. Sonnie crossed her forearms to ward off the glare, and she did scream then.

Seven

Chris ran to the stairs and took them two at a time. "Sonnie, sit still. Don't move or you'll fall." She looked as if she were about to slide downward. "Gotcha. Hell, what's happened to you? Hey, relax, I've got you."

He gripped her beneath her arms and started to lift. She struggled against him, tried to fight him with thin hands, and arms encased in damp satin. Suddenly jerking up to stand, she almost sent them both down the stairs. He was no stranger to the kind of strength adrenaline produced. She pummeled him, kicked at him, even though he knew she must be hurting herself.

"Sonnie? Hey, hey." Holding his flashlight and the banister with one hand, he wrapped his other arm around her and held on while she struggled. "Sonnie, it's me, Chris. It's *Chris*. You're okay."

She was crying, sobbing. He knew she was trying to say something but couldn't understand a word.

"Okay, that's it. *Enough*. Do you hear me?"

"I won't die for you," she said, her eyes huge and glassy. "Kill me again, but I won't just die."

He cataloged every word. She could be sleepwalking, but he didn't think so.

Her bare feet raked his shins repeatedly. Beneath satin pajamas her too-thin body was slick, and he released the banister long enough to hike her over his shoulder before she slithered away from him altogether.

Taking her upstairs seemed the only thing to do. She must have been in bed. And to have made the call he was now sure she had made, she must have been very frightened. The question was, by what? Or who?

The house was in total darkness. Had she dialed his number without putting on a light?

Moonlight shone through a domed skylight. When Chris reached the top of the stairs, he swung Sonnie down from his shoulder and carried her in his arms. She slumped there, limp, her head lolling to one side. That didn't mean he got careless. With the hand he'd passed under her shoulders, he kept a grip on her arm. Now that the fight seemed to have gone out of her, she might not pack much of a punch, but he didn't want to find out.

One door stood open, wide open, to a room on his left. He carried her in that direction, then inside and directly to a large bed. Nothing more than moonlight was needed to show sheets tangled into ropes and trailing to the floor.

French windows were pushed wide onto the balcony outside, and pale curtains filled softly with the breeze. He smelled the unmistakable scent of jasmine.

She moved slightly in his arms, but only to curve toward him and press her face against his chest. Did she know who he was? Did it matter who he was? Her breathing was quieter, but she still hiccuped.

"Sonnie," he said quietly. "Sonnie, can you hear me? It's Chris Talon. You called me, so I came. Can you hear me, Sonnie?"

"Yes," she whispered.

"I think you're ill. I'll call—"

"No." She didn't, as he expected, resume writhing. Instead she grasped the collar of his shirt and tugged. "I'm sorry I woke you up. I dialed the wrong number. I'm not sick at all. I'm just fine. Please put me down and go home. It was a nightmare, that's all. Just a silly nightmare. You can go—"

"Hush," he said. "Hush, Sonnie. It's okay. I'm not going to call anyone if you don't want me to. Now I'm going to set you down on the bed. Is that all right?"

Again she began to pant.

"On a chair? Do you want to sit on a chair?" He felt her nod and took her to a chair near the windows, put her down, and fumbled to switch on a floor lamp.

Light burst across the chair. The woman who sat there was bent so far over at the waist that her face rested on her knees. Her pale hair was damp and clung to her head and neck, her too-fragile neck.

She shook. Chris raised a hand and let it hover over her back. One wrong move and she'd fly at him, and maybe hurt herself—if she hadn't already hurt herself. He looked rapidly around the room. Apart from the wildly disordered bed, there was no sign of struggle.

He dropped to his knees and leaned close to her to ask, "Was there someone here? Did someone do something to you?"

Her response was to resume crying, but softly this time. She cried and trembled, and he saw the line of her spine through moist white satin. A web of shiny, discolored scarring extending from beneath her short left sleeve. Where her collar gaped, the raised welt he'd already noted continued and widened.

"Help me."

Chris held his breath. "Tell me what you need."

"Not like this."

He frowned. "I don't understand you."

She kept her face down, but pushed her hair back. "Wait for me. Say you won't go away."

"But"—he glanced around again—"where are you going?"

"Shower," she murmured.

"Shower?" He puffed up his cheeks. He was the man who wasn't ever getting close enough to another woman to be considered involved. He was also the man who had vowed to avoid anything that felt sticky enough to drag him in, to make him care. He was finished with being responsible—for anyone but himself.

She turned her head enough to peer at him with a swollen, reddened eye, and she put a hand on his shoulder while she pushed to her feet. "Please don't leave."

A wise man would contact that schmuck Romano, as Flynn would call him, and put Sonnie into the hands of someone who was at least some sort of relative. "I'm not going anywhere," he said, maneuvering himself into the chair she vacated. "Maybe you should just go to bed. You're . . . you're not real steady on your feet."

Her laugh scaled upward. A vaguely hysterical laugh. "I haven't been steady on my feet for a long time." She laughed again, before the sound choked off. "But I'm on my feet, aren't I? They didn't . . . I'm a miracle." Raising her arms, she used them like wings and crossed the room with her awkward gait. "I can't just walk, I can almost fly. One day I'm going to fly. I'm going to fly away where no one will ever be able to catch me again."

Chris set his flashlight on a table beside the chair and rubbed a fist over his mouth. The sensation in his gut wasn't completely new, just all but forgotten. Desperation. Wanting to help, but not knowing how.

She opened a drawer and pulled something out. Then she went to the door of what must be the bathroom and, just before she went inside, wagged a finger at him and said, "Now, you won't go away, will you, Chris? You don't want to be here, but you won't leave me alone?"

"I'll be here. Are you sure you're up to the shower?"

"Oh, yes." Her smile wobbled and failed. "Oh, yes."

A second later the sound of water burst forth. Soon steam issued into the bedroom. He smelled lavender—her soap, he guessed.

"Hush, little baby, don't you cry. Hush, little baby, don't you cry. Hush, little baby, don't . . ." High and clear, and so sweet it tightened his throat, she sang the same words again and again; then her voice faded.

A short time longer and the sound of gushing water ceased. A shower door slid open. He moved farther toward the front of the chair, straining for the sounds of her falling.

Water poured again, probably into the sink.

Then she appeared, her hair slicked straight back, and wearing a fresh pair of white pajamas—silk, not satin—and with a spray of yellow roses embroidered from her right shoulder and diagonally across her breasts to the left hem of the top. The pajamas were too big.

He got up and waved her toward him. At first she stopped and frowned, but then she came, although she stopped again just out of his reach.

"Sit here," he said, mustering a do-you-think-it's-going-to-rain voice.

Without waiting for her to agree, he went to the bed, touched the sheets, and found them as damp as he'd expected. Quickly he removed them and tossed them aside.

"I can do that," Sonnie said, and he heard her coming up behind him.

"You can, but you're not going to. I did as you asked and stayed put. Now you do as I ask and sit in that chair. Where are the clean sheets?"

"I don't want—"

"Humor me, please. Where?"

"Second door to the left outside this one. Linen cupboard. Queen size. Top two shelves."

He went, whipped out the first set he came to, and returned to make the bed in record time. When she came to put the pillows into their cases he allowed her that much. He was a hardheaded son of a gun, and he knew another one like him when they met.

"What a mess," she said when they'd finished. "I'm so embarrassed. What did I say?"

Chris regarded her speculatively. "You think you said something to me but you don't remember?"

Tears welled in her eyes and she gasped as if shocked by them. She put her fists on the mattress and breathed through her mouth. Her eyes closed.

He was around the bed in two strides. She didn't shrink from the hand he slipped about her waist. "You're . . . Sonnie, I don't know what you are, but it isn't good. Help me out here.

Tell me what's happened. And what's going on. Should I call your brother-in-law?''

"No. Oh, no. Romano's a good man. He's my friend. But there are reasons I have to watch them all."

"Do you want to elaborate on that?''

"I can't." She leaned against him. "I need to lie down."

"You've got it, kid," he said, and pulled back the covers. Without waiting for permission he swung her up and settled her gently on the bed. Beads of sweat stood on her forehead again, so he didn't cover her.

"This was all stupid tonight," she said, rolling to her side and putting her hands beneath her cheek. "Just a bad dream. It's been stressful getting settled. There's been a lot of stuff. That must be what made it happen again."

"Happen again? What exactly is it that happens?''

Once again she said, "No." But she shot out a hand, fingers reaching, until he held them. "Sit beside me, please. Don't go away."

She kept asking him that. "You can't tell me what's wrong, but you don't want me to go away because you're frightened. You can't have it all ways. Not that I intend to get involved here, Sonnie. I've already told you that."

To his horror, tears slid from her eyes and ended in her hair and against the pillow. This was one troubled woman—exactly the kind he would never, ever get tied up with again.

She was pretty. In an unconventional way, but definitely pretty. All her features were pointed and their smallness drew attention to the size of her very blue eyes, and the fact that her mouth was what some would consider too wide, and too full. Chris liked the entire package.

Out of line.

And stepping into deep water.

I must be horny. Scrawny women had never appealed to him. Besides, he had made it a career rule not to have sexual thoughts about women who came his way in the line of duty.

Christian J. Talon didn't have duty anymore, except to himself and his principles. Right now he wasn't sure about his principles.

Time to duck out. After all, he'd had plenty of experience doing just that. Not that he wouldn't keep an eye out for her. Half an eye. But she was probably a wacko in need of that psychiatric attention Giacano had implied he intended to seek for her.

Chris didn't like Romano Giacano. He was just a little too smooth, a little too quick with the right words at the right time. And he wanted something from Sonnie. Not just her shoulder to lean on while they waited for a final word on her husband, but something else. If Chris were on the case, he'd go all out and discover Romano's hidden agenda, but he wasn't on the case.

"You did come," Sonnie said, her voice husky.

He spotted a box of tissues on the bedside table and pulled out several. These he pressed to her eyes and cheeks. Where his fingers touched her skin, was incredibly soft.

"You wouldn't be here if you hadn't decided to help me."

Ah, yes, the trap could so easily close. "I'm a hard man, Sonnie. Hard and battle worn. I've already told you about me. I'm washed-up, worn-out. A loser. A bum living by his brother's good-heartedness."

"I don't believe you."

"Believe me, kid. I'm here because this is the end of the world, as far as the States goes. South and the sea. And I'd go there before I'd willingly head north again. I've lost too much up there, mostly because I let myself care too much. Caring too much cost me too much. But that's my story, not yours. I can't be good for you. I can't be what you need."

"But you came." She was pleading.

He hated it when a woman pleaded. Turning her down was harder then. "You called and I could hear you were crying. I didn't know what the score was, so I came. Anyone would have done the same thing."

"Most people would have called the police. Even knowing that it would be the wrong thing, they'd have done it anyway."

Would he ever learn to be as tough as he wanted to be? "Go to sleep. I won't leave until it starts getting light, and I'll make sure everything's locked up."

She sat up. "There's a garage. You could keep your bike there."

He wasn't sure what she meant. "It's under the fan palm. It'll be all right for now."

"Your place at Roy's is small." She grasped his hands again, and the wild look was back in her face. "You could have rooms here, big rooms. And your bike would be safe. You could come and go whenever you want to. And then if . . . Will you stay here, please?"

Good God. He pulled a hand free and stroked back her drying hair. And he smiled at her—not hard to do. "Sleep. You don't mean what you're saying, and if I were to agree, you'd be embarrassed and have to tell me later that you didn't mean it."

"No, I—"

He put his fingers on her mouth and pulled his belly tight. Touching her only made him want to touch her some more.

"I'm cynical, selfish. Not what you think I am at all. I don't know why you'd think otherwise, unless you've made the mistake of believing my brother. He's a relative. You never believe what a man's relative says, especially when he just about brought me up."

"But you came by this afternoon. Why did you do that if you aren't interested in taking my case?"

This could turn into a tightening noose around his neck. "Roy's been worried about you. I decided to cruise by and see if everything looked okay. That's all. Nothing deeper than that." A little lie, maybe, but for the best.

"Yeah," she said, and the fight was gone again. "Yeah, I understand. I need to go to a florist. You know a florist called Moss Corner?"

Chris took her by the shoulders and eased her firmly down against the bed. "I already went there. Roy told me about the lilies you received."

She turned her face into the pillow. "I hate them."

"So Roy said." What the hell was he going to do there? Nebulous as the whole mess was, there was no doubt that Mrs. Giacano had problems. "The flowers were probably bought at

Moss Corner. They were busy at the time, so the woman who bought them didn't make much impression. She was in a hurry; they did remember that. She paid in cash and took a blank gift enclosure. They were preparing a big order for a funeral. The woman was relieved because they had plenty of lilies.''

He knew his mistake as soon as she covered her mouth.

"Look, I've said I'll stay until you sleep."

"He'll come back."

It was there again, the unfocused stare. "Sonnie, tomorrow you must go to the police and explain what's been happening here."

"Tell them about a gift of lilies and a card about a baby's death?"

He shook his head, bemused.

"Tell them he told me to leave because he'd kill me if I stay in Key West?"

"Yes." Rubbing her arms, he leaned over her. "Yes, you must tell them that." He would not ask her who she was talking about. To do so would be to ask to be dragged in deeper, and he didn't want to go there.

She scooted away from him and closed her eyes tight. "Thank you," she said. "You were very kind to come. I apologize for the terrible intrusion into your life."

"It isn't a terrible intrusion. You've been through too much. You're still recovering from a catastrophic accident. Most people wouldn't be doing anywhere near as well as you are. But I think you're trying too hard and it's taking a toll on you."

"You think I'm mad, too."

He looked at her white face, at the perspiration in the dip above her top lip and in her fair brows. "I think you're in trouble. I don't have much idea what kind of trouble. You ask me to help you; then you won't tell me what's supposed to be wrong."

"There were voices," she said, and her own voice became fainter. "In the darkness. Voices. Threats. They said I was supposed to be dead and that I would be dead. They said I was in the way."

"When you were in the hospital?"

"Yes. Then afterward. When I went home to my parents in Denver. At night when I thought I'd gone to sleep, they came again. And the fire."

"The fire?"

"I'm crazy. I've said enough. Go away and forget about me."

Oh, sure, that was going to be real easy. "Is that what happened tonight? You thought someone came to you while you were asleep?"

"I don't know." She rolled onto her face. "I heard the flames and then his face was there, on the other side looking through at me. He threatened me."

"Who is he?" he asked very carefully.

She shook her head. "No. I'm mad. But I won't hurt anyone but myself."

"You're not mad," he heard himself say with something near dismay. "You're in trouble, Sonnie. Please go to sleep. You won't solve anything while you're like this. You're overwrought and weak."

"You'll wait till I'm asleep and leave me."

He should do just that.

"No. One of the things a cop learns is to sleep standing up. Sitting down's a breeze."

"He said I should go to my baby." She was slipping into sleep. "He said she was waiting for me. The fingers poked me. They felt like she did when she was inside me. It's not real but that scares me more. It feels real."

He looked beyond her at the flowered wallpaper. God, why was there so much tragedy and misery in the world? "Go to sleep. When you wake up it'll be morning, and I'll be sitting in that chair looking like a bum."

"I like the way you look when you look like a bum."

Chris digested that, not that she really knew what she was saying. "Good enough. I won't desert you, Sonnie. Don't expect too much of me, because I don't have it to give anymore. But I'll try to be a friend."

She remained on her stomach, but she raised her elbows

and crossed her hands under her forehead. "If you'll be my friend, I'll live," she said, and he heard her slipping into sleep.

The lady might or might not need a shrink. What he'd just agreed to meant he definitely needed one.

He stood up and looked down on her. Her back rose and fell gently with each sleeping breath.

The top of her pajamas had hiked up, and the elastic in her pajama bottoms was so loose they had worked down low on her hips.

Chris experienced a twisting in the region of his heart. Her narrow rib cage and tiny waist were almost childlike. The sweet flare of her small hips was not childlike. Her rounded bottom made him want to do things guaranteed to relegate him to the ranks of those who took advantage of perceived weakness. He had seen her nipples through satin and then silk, and her small breasts.

This was not his type of woman. Maybe she was intellectually his type, only he'd never know that for sure. Physically she couldn't be less like any female who had ever messed with his hormones.

Running parallel to her spine, on the left side, was what looked like a surgical scar. The suture marks were still raised. Other scars, jagged as if the flesh had torn, had also been sutured, but he assumed there would be further work done to reduce them.

There were burn marks on the top of her right buttock, disappearing into the indent between.

Without intending to do any such thing, he stroked the backs of his fingers down her spine and spread his hand over the shiny web of burned skin. Nerves twitched, but she didn't awaken. The vicious marks were an insult. She turned her face to the side and her dark lashes flickered. A face that looked much younger than she had to be. No wonder playboy Frank Giacano had chosen her to be the one he came home to when he was bored with whomever his present girlfriend might be.

Sonnie should never have been exposed to a man like that. Chris felt a blaze of protectiveness. She had said, *"I won't die for you."* Die for whom? She'd said she wasn't sure her car crash had been an accident. But if she had any concrete reasons for thinking so, she'd given him no hint of them. *Die for you.*

She hadn't been joking when she asked him to move in here. And the damnable thing was that he wished he could.

Tomorrow morning early, the minute he was sure all was well, he'd be gone. And he'd work out a way to disengage from her.

He backed away, but instead of sitting in the chair where it was, he lifted it and set it down, very quietly, close to the bed.

As he lounged there, the hours slid by. He had turned off the light, but there was enough moonlight, then early dawning light, to allow him to see her clearly. She murmured from time to time, and turned her head from side to side.

When she rolled onto her back and came closer to him, he tried to make himself avert his eyes. Small she might be, but every line of her softly relaxed body affected him in ways that weren't new, but were uncomfortable just as they were arousing.

At last exhaustion fuzzed the edges of his mind. He rested his head on the mattress beside her hips. And carefully, so very carefully, he let the backs of his bent fingers rest against her ribs.

The room smelled of jasmine, but Sonnie was a lavender girl, fresh and clean and inviting—too inviting.

Consciousness fled, and in the last floating instant of comfort before sleep claimed him, he kissed her belly very lightly. And when he did enter the darkness, it was with his right hand spread over her middle, beneath her pajama top, and only a whisper from the gentle rise of her breasts.

Eight

There is a reason for everything. A reason why I wake up again when sleep is my only peace. A reason why I stay alive, want to stay alive. I do want to stay alive.

Sonnie's eyelids flickered. She didn't want to open them. As long as they were closed she could pretend—to herself and to the man whose presence beside her she felt—that she still slept and yes, she had a reason not to face another day quite yet.

Presence?

His very large hand covered her left breast beneath her pajama top.

A heavy, relaxed hand that probably felt nothing.

Sonnie felt so much that she fought against the cry that rose to her lips. Her heart beat fast and hard enough that it ought to wake him. She opened her eyes and looked down at Chris Talon. His face was turned toward her. Not a face a woman was likely to forget, even a woman who thought she'd never feel anything for a man again. She felt all right, and the sensation was definitely sexual. His other hand rested on her injured hip.

She liked the warmth that spread from his flesh into hers. He slept like ... like a man watching over a woman he cared about. Like a man trying to infuse his very life and strength into that woman.

Sonnie closed her eyes again. Loneliness and need and desperation could brew up a fine concoction of lies, of lovely imaginary foolishness. But she would forgive herself for her longing.

Very carefully, watching through narrowly slitted eyelids, she settled a hand on the side of his face, his ear. The tips of her fingers met his curly black hair and she was glad he didn't cut it short. She was careful to allow her hand to be as limp as his.

So there they were. And for as long as it took him to break from sleep, she would pretend she slept also.

Despite flamboyant bones that flared at his cheek and jaw and swept straight down his nose, except for the slight evidence of an old break, despite all that, his face was slender. Like a voyeur, Sonnie peered at his dark, arched brow, and at his mouth.

A mouth that must have kissed so many women.

She shut her eyes again. He would never kiss her. He wouldn't be touching her so intimately now if he knew what he was doing.

She didn't need him as a lover.

Just the word heated every inch of her skin.

She needed his help to prove whether she was right or wrong in thinking that out there, almost within the reach of her struggling mind, was a truth that would set her free. First it would make her heart as crippled as her body, but in the end it would set her free.

Chris Talon was going to do what she wanted him to do. . . . Why him rather than someone else? Because she felt connected to him. The more he protested that he didn't want to work for her, with her, the more she felt him struggle with the reverse conviction. And she believed what Roy said: Chris was a good man who had had some bad breaks, and he needed her as much as she needed him.

She would find out what had broken the man, what had brought him low enough to call himself washed-up. Then maybe, just maybe, and only as a friend, she could return the favor and help him.

If she asked Roy to do it, he'd kick Chris out of his little hideaway and then she'd . . . No, she couldn't, wouldn't. But she hadn't given up on getting him to stay here with her. After all, his virtue wouldn't be compromised.

She smiled and gritted her teeth. Her nipple became erect against his palm, and a sharp, aching reaction traveled its natural path. A moment, and then she wanted to press his other hand between her legs.

Sonnie thought about Frank, her husband. Until she heard otherwise she was married to him. Thoughts and feelings couldn't always be controlled. Actions should be.

His hand convulsed on her breast. He squeezed, then held still.

Sonnie dared another peek at him.

Sleepy hazel eyes blinked. That one visible brow shot down in a frown. He looked sideways at her slack wrist, then toward his hand on her breast, then upward. She made sure her own eyes were closed and that she breathed gently and evenly.

She thought he murmured, "Geez," but he didn't make any sudden moves.

They remained where they were, Sonnie knowing they both thought about the next move.

Chris slid his hand, millimeter by millimeter, from her breast, and Sonnie couldn't control the arching of her back. But she didn't open her eyes. The body could react in sleep, so she was asleep and reacting to a warm male palm, and very long, warm male fingers, sliding slowly over her aroused breast.

Too soon it was over, and she stretched in her "sleep" and turned enough to let her arm fall away from him.

Slitting her eyes once more, she studied him through her lashes. He held up his hands, studied them before letting them fall into his lap. The sheets were tossed aside and he studied her minutely from her feet to her face. With his head on one side and an unreadable expression in his eyes, his gaze settled on her face. He ran his fingers through his hair, never looking away. His nostrils flared and the breath he drew in was long, so long. He parted his lips and rested the tip of his tongue on the edges of his upper teeth.

That expression was so obvious, even to a woman who hadn't even thought about sex for a long time. He was aroused.

Why should that thrill her? It just did thrill her. She was only human.

Time to wake up, sleeping pretender.

She opened her eyes and looked directly at him—and almost smiled at the faint color that rushed across his cheekbones.

"Hi," he said. "Good morning."

She smiled and said, "Good morning. You slept in that chair all night?"

"I promised I would. I keep my promises."

"Oh, Chris, I'm sorry." She scooted to sit up, barely managing to grab her pajama bottoms before they slipped all the way off. With a sheepish grimace, she lifted her bottom from the bed and made sure she was properly covered.

His eyes remained in the region of her hips for a second or so too long.

"I'm really sorry for what I put you through," she said.

"You remember it? All of it?"

"I think I do. It gets clearer every time."

With his hands laced behind his neck, he stretched, and while he stretched he continued to regard her. No trace of sleepiness remained. "Have you ever spoken to the police about this?"

"About visions and voices? You used to be a cop, Chris. What would you have said to someone who came in talking about that kind of thing?"

He sniffed, and bent toward her so suddenly that she jumped. "I'd have offered them a ride home and suggested to whomever they lived with that a psychiatric evaluation was in order."

If he hoped the hard-nosed approach would get rid of her, he was wrong. "Okay. A fair answer. What if the person in question lived alone and didn't have anyone she could trust to get her some good help?"

"Then I'd just have to give the ride home and hope for the best. The cops aren't baby-sitters. And the law doesn't allow us . . . doesn't allow them to take people off the streets for being disturbed. Not unless they're creating a public nuisance of the threatening variety.''

More than once his attention went to places other than her face. But that was just a man thing. She was nothing more than a nuisance to him.

''What would it take to get you to work for me?''

''So blunt?'' He shook his head. ''I've already told you I'm not for hire.''

''To get you to work for me for free, then?'' She raised her chin. ''Or for whatever you need or want. You're alone; so am I. I don't want anything from you but an honest shot at helping me run down some information. I could look after you. Would it be so bad to have meals cooked? I'm a good cook.''

''I like the food at the Nail.''

''It's junk. And I'd look after your clothes and all the regular stuff.''

''I'm real good at the regular stuff. I manage to live in a small space and be the tidiest man alive.''

Sonnie Keith Giacano had a reputation for being quiet and unassuming. Time to blow that one. ''Keep your place at Roy and Bo's so you can get away whenever you want to. But move in here and have as much of the house as you want. No charge except a listening ear and an analytical mind. Roy says you've got the most analytical mind he's ever come across.''

''Roy thinks the sun shines out of my . . . head. According to him, I'm also Van Cliburn's successor, and a few other unlikely things. But that's what being brothers is all about. You love each other without reservation. Roy's a great guy. I couldn't have a better brother.''

''You won't get any arguments out of me. He's one of God's dearest people. He knew I didn't need a job. But he also knew I needed something, and he jumped in with a shot in the dark. And it was the right shot. I needed an opportunity to be around people, where I could listen and learn what was going on in Key West. One day, when this is all over, I'm going to think of something wonderful to do for Roy and Bo.''

His expression softened. ''I do believe you're a sweet lady.''

Those few simple words took her breath away.

"I also think you're generous and kind—and muddled as hell."

She drew up her knees and crossed her arms on top. Then she propped her chin and smiled at him.

"What?" His chin jutted. "What's with the grin? I call you muddled and you grin."

"What would you expect from a nutcase?"

"I need to go."

This time she was the one to make the sudden move. She shot out a hand and gripped his shoulder. "If I'm sweet and generous and kind, why don't you move in and help me? I've got a piano. I'll get it tuned."

He covered her hand on his arm, and Sonnie's stomach made a loop. "You ask too much, Sonnie, girl. I'm on the run and you want me to commit to a live-in setup with a lady—admittedly a lovely lady—but a lady who comes with more baggage than just about anyone I ever met. And why would my living with you be necessary anyway?"

This time she wouldn't lie even a little bit. "Because I'm very afraid. I don't know when I'll wake up in the night screaming again, and seeing sheets of flame, and faces telling me to die."

"You're doing a great job of persuading me."

She ignored the barb. "But I don't believe those things happen for no reason. I think the accident I had wasn't the way it went into the police reports. I believe someone will try to stop me from searching for the truth because I'd mess things up for them. What I don't know is why exactly I think that, or what the truth of it could possibly be."

"Maybe the truth of it is exactly what is in the books."

She shook her head. "Maybe it is. But if so, where do the voices come from, the threats?"

"What about all those reports from the time. Police? Medics? Fire?"

"They're there."

"But it was ruled an accident? No suggestion of foul play?"

"The reports say I was driving a Volvo station wagon, lost

control, and drove into a wall about a mile from the airport. They say I was doing about forty at impact and that I ought to be dead. I was thrown out." She swallowed, but wouldn't allow herself to stop. "I went to the airport to meet Frank. He'd called unexpectedly to say he was coming here on business. Then—so I'm told—he wasn't on the plane. It was poor Romano who came and told me Frank had been abducted. Because I was . . . I was pregnant, they think I snapped and that's how it all happened."

Chris watched her, unblinking. He took her hand from his shoulder and wound their fingers together.

"I was stabilized here, then airlifted out to Miami. There was so much swelling in my brain that they thought I'd never regain consciousness. Then my father brought in a surgeon who did a procedure to release the pressure, and I started to show signs of improving."

"You poor kid," Chris said. "I'm sorry about—"

"Yes, I know. Everyone was. But while I was recovering someone kept trying to send me back where I'd come from. Back along the path toward death."

"You don't know that."

"I think I do. You don't have to. Just prove the truth to me, one way or the other."

He stood up.

Sonnie kept hold of his hand. "Please. If I can't find someone to be on my side—all the way—I'm going to end up in a sanitarium."

"Your family won't allow that."

"They believe what professional people tell them. I think there's someone out there who has a really good reason not to want me to cast any doubt on the official story of that night. And I think they'll get at me through the people who love me most—my family."

He looked at their joined hands. His made hers look ridiculously small.

"Take a while to decide," she said, scrambling to stand beside him. "And you're not leaving this house without some breakfast."

"I don't eat breakfast."

"That's not healthy."

The expression that passed over his features unnerved her. Such sadness.

"At least have some coffee."

He tipped up his head and sighed. "That sounds great, but I feel like the bum I'm supposed to be. That's a bum rap because I'm a clean bum. I've got to shower."

"There you are." She indicated the bathroom. "Shower. I'll make coffee and then you can go on your way and I won't bother you again unless you tell me you've changed your mind and you'll help me."

His grimace made him look younger. "You don't know how to give up. Ma'am, I don't know whether I like that about you, or hate that about you. I'm thinkin' I should be grateful you're not an enemy."

"There are plenty of towels in there, and soap and shampoo. I'd offer you clean clothes, but mine wouldn't fit." She gave him the first impish grin she'd felt like giving anyone in too long.

"Okay. You win—but only the bit about the shower and coffee."

Once he was in the bathroom with the door shut, she combed her hair and put on some lipstick and mascara. Unfortunately she wasn't one of those women who could even pretend a scrubbed face looked wonderful.

Why bother to change out of her pajamas? He'd seen her in them. And felt her in them . . .

The glow she experienced when she went down the stairs wasn't all embarrassment, but she would have to get rid of any sexy thoughts with regard to Mr. Talon. He reacted as any man would, but she'd never be his type.

Sun shone through kitchen windows that rose to overhead skylights. The purple bougainvillea that grew from the side of the house and across the veranda roof made a canopy over the windows. The day was a sparkling, showy affair, and for the first time in months, Sonnie felt like singing.

Hitching repeatedly at her pajama bottoms, she started the

coffee, set out mugs, and cut up fruit. Then she assembled a bowl of yogurt, some muffins, and cream and sugar. She set them all on the black granite top of the central island, then found red floral place mats and napkins and set them side by side.

She heard a key turn in the front-door lock.

It took all her restraint not to call for Chris.

"Sonnie, you here? It's me, Billy. I've brought a friend of mine to meet you."

She made fists on the granite. All her life she'd walked in Billy's shadow, powerful, flamboyant Billy's shadow. This time she'd told her where she was going because she cared too much about her family to leave without a word. And she'd asked to be left alone. Already Billy had sent Romano here—Sonnie would swear to it. Now she'd actually ignored Sonnie's very definite wishes and followed her to Key West.

"Sonnie? You here?"

Sonnie went to the kitchen door and stood there until Billy revolved on the high heel of a gray suede Stuart Weitzman pump and saw her half-sister. "Well, there you are, Baby. Why didn't you say anything?"

"It's a little early, Billy." Sonnie held her temper in tight check. "As you can see, I wasn't expecting visitors. Would you mind getting a hotel room and calling me later? Perhaps we can have lunch."

"Baby?" With her chin jutting, her elegant black hair swinging, Billy approached with a wounded expression in her dark eyes. "I've come all the way from Denver to make sure you're okay. My bags are in the car. Of course I'll be staying with you."

"You're kind, Billy. Do you remember my asking you not to follow me here?"

"You're still sick. You shouldn't be alone."

"Do you remember what I asked of you?"

"Yes, but—"

"I meant it. I know you love me, but you smother me. You always have."

Billy's mouth opened and remained open. A simple red

cotton dress with a full, swirling skirt looked wonderful on her. "Come on in, Jim. Don't hover out there."

"*Billy.*"

"Oh, don't be silly. Jim's used to seeing women in their pajamas. Here, Jim. This is my poor little sister, Sonnie."

A tall, blond, slender man in a pale blue tropical-weight suit entered the hall. He looked upward toward the domed skylight before he turned his attention to Sonnie. He had a handsome face, but also a kind face—a nice smile.

Sonnie wished she could spirit herself upstairs, or simply manage to cover herself with something other than silk pajamas that didn't want to stay on her.

"Hi there, Sonnie," Jim said, approaching with his hand extended. "Nice to meet you. I'm Jim Lesley."

Fixing her left elbow at the waist of her pants, she shook his hand and said, "Hi, Jim." This must be Billy's latest significant male. They never lasted long, but there was always hope that one would stick. Billy had been married twice, both times very briefly to tennis players who weren't much more successful in the big time than she was.

"There's plenty of space, Baby, isn't there?" Billy said. "I promised Jim he'd get to spend time in your lovely house. I'll take the bedroom next to yours and he can have the one the folks use when they come down."

Only with effort did Sonnie manage not to gape. Separate bedrooms wasn't a concept Billy had ever embraced—not since she was a senior in high school.

"Carry in the bags, Jim; there's a love."

"Billy," Sonnie said, "this is a bad time."

"I *know.* That's why I knew I had to take matters into my own hands and look after you."

"No, you don't. Jim, I hate to seem inhospitable, but I'm still unpacking. I have a membership at the Sunset Golf and Tennis Club. It's very nice. In fact it's the nicest place around— to stay, that is. They don't have many rooms, but at this time of the year there shouldn't be any problem. Just drive over there; then call me when you're settled in." She had to make them leave. "Romano's already there."

"Absolutely not," Billy said. "I can't believe you could be so rude, or so ungrateful. I do have a life of my own, you know. The least you can do is be happy to see me and want me with you."

"How's the coffee comin', darlin' ?"

Billy, Jim, and Sonnie looked up into Chris's smiling face. Clad in his jeans, but no shirt, and with his feet bare, he jogged down the stairs, fastening his wristwatch as he came. His wet hair curled around his ears.

How easy it would be to sit down and cover her face and pretend none of this was happening.

"Sonnie?" Billy said when some of the shock had subsided.

"This is Chris Talon," Sonnie said, and actually gave herself silent congratulations for staying calm under fire. "Chris is a good friend of mine."

"The best," Chris said, reaching the hall. He took Billy's hand and shook it. "The Keiths make good-lookin' women. Wow." Then he turned to Jim Lesley and pumped his hand until the man winced. "Welcome to our island, Jim. It ain't exactly tourist season. Too hot, y'know. But you'll do well enough if you stay out of the way at the Sunset. Pretty good air-conditionin', they tell me. Not that they let the likes of me in." He laughed.

Appalled didn't cover Billy's expression. She turned her back on Chris and mouthed *Who is he? Get rid of him,* to Sonnie.

Promptly Chris put himself between Billy and Sonnie and said, "Smells like the coffee's ready, babe. We wouldn't want to cook it like we did yesterday."

Sonnie shook her head vaguely, and her gaze settled on what she hadn't noted before: the exact nature of his tattoo. Behind Chris's right shoulder, but with a tasteful chain trailing around the arm, lounged the image of a small but perfectly executed woman in manacles. A naked woman in manacles.

Chris gave the two latest arrivals a salute, took hold of Sonnie's wrist, and headed for the kitchen. "Watch out for my cycle, won't you, Jim? Never mess with a Harley man's cycle. Just a joke. Just a joke." *Cycle* became *sickle*. He guffawed as if he'd made a huge joke.

Pulled along, Sonnie hurried behind him.

She didn't catch her pajama pants until they hit her knees.

Nine

Romano remembered a saying: When you get lemons, you make lemonade. There was nothing about this time in Key West that fell in easily with his plans, but he had always been a resourceful man. He would turn what threatened to be a disaster into success, his success.

First item on his agenda: find out the identity of the man who was hanging around Sonnie. They weren't a matched pair. He was as obviously sexual as she was asexual.

Frank had never complained about being shackled to a colorless woman who, when she was naked, looked like a boy. Romano had spent enough time by her hospital bed playing the concerned brother-in-law to know how physically unappealing she was—certainly to him. He had dated her because she was rich. He liked a woman with plenty of flesh in the right places. The only thing Sonnie would be good for was curiosity. Perhaps that was what had kept Frank coming back to her from time to time—in addition to her money. Frank had been called a pretty boy all his life. Could be that all the women he fucked on the circuit were a cover for what he really was: a faggot who married someone he could pretend was a boy in the dark.

A compact man in his late thirties approached Romano's table in the Courts Café at the Sunset. He detested the third-rate club. He was accustomed to nothing but the best. The only elevated aspect of this place was its pretensions.

"Romano Giacano?" the approaching man said, grinning happily. His reddish tan went with his thick red hair, sandy brows, and freckles. The tan accentuated deep lines on his face. "As I live and breathe, it is you. What the hell, if this isn't the best piece of luck that's come my way in a hell of a long time. How the hell are you?" A large, callused hand grabbed Romano's and squeezed. "Don't tell me you don't know who I am, Cory Bledsoe. Golf pro and athletics manager. It's been a long time, but not that long."

Romano saw an ex-athlete still looking for some of the limelight he'd never earned. "Yes. How are you?"

Cory indicated the vacant second seat at Romano's table, and took it without being invited to do so. "Seeing you is making me feel just fine. Look, we've got a hell of a situation here. Our tennis pro took a hike with one of the wives—some weeks back. We've had no luck filling his place."

Lucky ex-tennis pro. Romano hoped the bitch was loaded.

Cory leaned out to slap Romano's arm. He wiped out the grin and replaced it with a somber frown. "Can't tell you how sorry I am about Frank. What a talent. What a loss."

"We haven't buried my brother yet," Romano said.

"No, no, of course not. But the worry. It's got to be like a nightmare that never stops."

"It is difficult. But we will not give up hope." In fact, Frank was really scaring him. Since he hadn't returned, and the business was growing too dangerous to pursue in some areas, money was showing signs of drying up. Without Frank to help replenish the Giacano fortunes, Romano must become very inventive.

"Look," Cory said, "I don't expect you to want to make a career out of this, but you're a hell of a coach. Everyone says Frank Giacano would never have made it without Romano Giacano in his corner."

Romano barely stopped himself from saying, "True." "My brother is an incredible talent." He was also an undisciplined, egotistical child with an insatiable appetite for dangerous thrills.

Cory clicked his fingers, and a white-jacketed waiter did an impression of a lone ballroom dancer as he slithered and feinted his way between tables. Romano was tempted to applaud when the man arrived, clicked his heels, and gave a short bow.

"A bottle of Dom Perignon, please, Godfrey," Cory said. "Very cold. And don't you have some beluga caviar hidden away somewhere?"

With a wink and a twitch of the mouth, Godfrey signaled that he did indeed have what Cory wanted.

When they were alone again, Cory laced his fingers together on the table and said, "Take over as pro for us, Romano. I'm not going to pretend. We need someone who can resurrect the program, and fast. Just your name would do it. If you can't commit to more than a limited contract, we'll understand. But you can name your price. Anything. What do you say?"

A bona fide reason to remain—and a way to make his moves on Sonnie and her money less obvious. And, despite the threadbare opulence of the Sunset, the club was the only place of its type on the island, and the reserves had to be beautifully deep.

"Romano?" Cory said. The man's anxiety made Romano want to smile.

"No contract."

The golf pro spread his hands. "That's a tough one. We need to cover—"

"Your asses will be covered by my word. If we can agree on terms, I won't take off with a member's wife. How's that?"

Cory guffawed and leaned back as Godfrey arrived with the champagne and caviar. "We'll work something out."

"Salary, and a percentage of the fees."

There was a slight but visible slippage in Cory Bledsoe's bonhomie. "Surely we can come up with a salary that'll make the other unnecessary."

The instant they had his name to throw around, the price of instruction would escalate enough to make his salary a pittance. "I'll want a cut. I don't work any other way. But if that's beyond your resources, I will understand. I did not come here intending to work. Perhaps we should forget it."

"No, no." Cory raised his champagne and waited for Romano to do the same. "Salary and a percentage."

They clinked glasses and Romano said, "Exact terms to be agreed upon."

His companion drank and looked at him over his champagne glass.

Romano smiled encouragingly and contemplated how much he'd screw out of this little arrangement—just until he secured more lucrative sources of funds.

He looked up and across the café. Speaking of screwing, coming toward him was the woman who did it the best—and demanded the most in return. Of all the foul luck. Billy Keith—as she called herself again since the last divorce—had located him in the softly chattering crowd and came toward him, the skirt of her showy red dress swinging with each undulation of those hips.

He got up rapidly, looked down into Cory's surprised face, and said, "I see my sister-in-law's sister looking for me. We have business to deal with. Please excuse me."

"Of course," Cory said, craning around to see Billy, who was also being seen by every pair of eyes in the room. "Ah, yes, I remember Billy Keith. Have fun."

Romano spared him an expressionless glance and went to meet Billy.

When they were within hailing distance, Billy's husky voice announced, "I couldn't believe you were here, darling. What a wonderful surprise. Jim Lesley's with me. You'll have to come and meet him."

Romano didn't have the faintest idea who Jim Lesley was; neither did he care. He was just moving within perfume range of Ms. Keith and already his dick was sitting up and begging. He would never understand how two women who shared a common father could be so different.

They met at midroom and Billy offered a cool cheek. Romano brushed it lightly with his mouth and restrained himself from whispering any of the things she'd undoubtedly hoped to hear.

He offered her his arm and she inclined her head while she

slid her hand around his elbow. Making small talk, they walked from the restaurant. They didn't stop walking until Billy reached her room. While she locked the door to the corridor behind them, Romano looked at the enclosed courtyard and pool beyond the sliding windows. When he turned back to Billy, the brilliant smile had fled.

"She's with a man. Why didn't you call me the moment you knew she'd hooked up with some biker on the make?"

Romano took off his silk jacket and tossed it over the back of a rattan chair. "I arrived yesterday—but you know that. You're the one who told me I'd better get down here."

"When did you find out about Talon?"

"What makes you think I did?"

"You went to the house?"

"But of course. Immediately."

"She wouldn't let you stay there, would she?" Billy asked. He shook his head.

"She also won't let me stay there, or Jim—Jim Lesley owns one of the most exclusive sanitariums in the country. He also happens to want me. That may prove convenient if it becomes necessary to send my dear sister away for a long rest."

Romano couldn't cover his surprise. "Sonnie wouldn't let you stay with her? She loves you, Billy. She trusts you."

Billy kicked off her shoes and sashayed toward him. "Evidently she doesn't trust me in the same house where she's living with a tattooed hunk."

"She's not . . . No, she's not living with him."

Billy's immediate response was to slip a disk into the player she never traveled without. Allen Toussaint's voice, and his magic fingers on the keys playing strictly New Orleans music, swung into persuasive action. Billy danced as only Billy could dance. Arms outstretched, shoulders lifting, fingers clicking, she moved parts of her body Romano doubted some people ever discovered in theirs.

"My little sister has the look of a satisfied woman," she said, getting closer. "I never saw her look that way. Your brother Frank spread himself too thin to have enough left over for her. Not that she could ever be his type. Chris Talon's got

to have plenty of what she needs. Whew. What a body. Now
that's the stuff of this girl's wet dreams.''

She had always thought her crudeness was a turn-on. He'd
never bothered to set her straight because he'd learned to shut
out the sound of her mouth. There were other things guaranteed
to make that easy.

''Are we likely to have a visit from your shrink friend?''

''Uh-uh.'' She shook her head. ''We have to talk.''

Not before he got what he wanted at the moment. ''It's been
a long time for you and me, Billy.''

She spared him a long stare from her very dark eyes. ''Business first, brother dear.''

''I'm not your brother.''

She stopped dancing. ''Let's sit down.''

''Let's not.''

''Oh, Romano, don't be so predictable. We don't have time
for any of that now.''

He was going to establish that he was in charge. ''I'll decide
what we have time for.''

''Don't try that approach with me,'' Billy said. ''We both
know I don't take orders—from anyone.''

That was the Billy he knew so well. He didn't like it, but
this wasn't the moment to fight with her. ''Let's get back to
business,'' he said. ''Unless we're a whole lot luckier than I
believe we are, there will be difficulties ahead for us. Your
tattooed hunk may have a lot of influence over Sonnie. If that
is so, the picture will change. She will be a problem to control.''

Billy put her hands on her hips. ''If Talon becomes a nuisance, well—he can't be allowed to become a nuisance, can
he?''

She had always had the ability to cool his blood. Billy Keith
lacked the one thing that separated a human being from the
rest of the animal kingdom: she had no conscience. A good
reason for him to control her at all costs.

''Can we?'' she repeated.

''I am not concerned about keeping a badly dressed, unedu-
cated moron in check, Billy. You may leave that to me.''

She took a breath deep enough to make it impossible not

to watch her breasts. "You and I will work together now," she said. "We will keep each other informed of everything, no matter how small. All we need is proof of Frank's death, and you become his heir. At least in all practical respects.

"How naughty of Frank to talk Sonnie into putting her money into his estate, and then to make it your job to administer everything if he died before her. My parents will be beside themselves when they find out." She shook a finger at him. "But don't forget that you must look after her. Frank stipulated that, didn't he?"

These were facts that were supposed to be known only to Frank and himself. Sonnie had been young, stupidly in love, and easily controlled after her marriage. She'd been persuaded to agree to what Frank described as a special trust.

"Romano?" Billy said. "What are you thinking?"

"That you are better informed than I realized."

She laughed. "Frank enjoyed telling me about it. We enjoyed a lot of things. Poor Sonnie. She isn't strong—in mind or body. When she has to be committed, you will become her guardian, and you will be even freer with her assets. Won't that be nice?"

She left him speechless. He had his own plans, but they weren't nearly as developed as hers.

"Won't that be *nice?*" Billy said again, taking another eye-catching breath. "Or perhaps I should say that it will be adequate until something even more permanent can be arranged. Come, we'll sit down and go over things more thoroughly."

The excitement she made him feel wasn't going away. "I'm going to love going over things with you, Billy. But first I shall love seeing you. Take off your dress."

She scowled. "We've already decided on business first."

"Fucking first," he said, keeping his voice even. "I have missed you. I will think so much better after we really say hello."

The anger remained on her face, but she stepped close enough for him to see the deep cleavage inside the zippered bodice of the dress.

First he undid her belt and let it fall. Next he unzipped her bodice as slowly as the pulsing in his penis would allow. Billy's clothes were made to apply rather than wear. Not a wrinkle showed anywhere.

When he reached for her, she batted his hands away and opened the dress herself. His jaws locked; so did his thighs. It was his turn to take deep breaths.

Billy prided herself on not owning many bras. She peeled the bodice aside until it framed the most amazing breasts he'd had the good fortune to enjoy. He didn't care how much she'd paid for them.

She wouldn't let him touch her. "Take off your clothes," she told him.

Ah, yes, how could he forget that she liked to play her little game of watching him strip before she took everything off?

He got rid of his shirt and his belt and started to unzip his pants. Billy stopped him. "I'd like a little attention first. Do you know another woman as big as I am who doesn't need a bra?"

"I do not. You are fabulous."

"Rub them with the hair on your chest. I like that."

He couldn't stifle a groan, but he managed to do as she asked without ejaculating in his pants. He rubbed her, and she rubbed him. No hands, just large, hard nipples and jutting flesh against a chest he was glad he kept perfectly defined. She dipped, raked herself over his ribs, then went to her knees and licked his belly.

"Billy." He moaned. "You're killing me."

She unzipped his pants and dropped them around his ankles. Then she stood and stripped off her lace-topped stockings and black thong panties. She'd always been able to surprise him— or shock him. A foot strategically placed behind his heels knocked him off balance, and, with his pants around his ankles, he couldn't recover. He landed on his back on the bed, his feet still on the floor and his knees bent at the edge of the mattress.

Billy straddled his thighs, then leaned over to fill his mouth with first one, then the other of her breasts. The instant he tried to clasp her to him, she pushed away, produced a condom from a pocket, and slipped it on him.

The hem of her skirt was stiff and she used it to play. Back and forth she swept the glazed cotton, repeatedly flirting with the head of his penis until his hips came off the bed with every pass.

"Billy," he pleaded.

She smiled at him, showing all of her sharp little teeth. "Okay, lover. This is for you."

She raised her skirts to show him her small, rounded belly and the triangle of black hair between her legs. She reached down to separate herself. He could see how ready she was without even touching her.

"For you," she said in a singsong voice, and impaled herself on him. The lady was strong. Her breasts bounced, once, twice, as she rose and fell on him; then he turned his head aside, incapable of stopping himself from pouring forth.

"Too damn fast, damn you," he said through his teeth. She'd already come to rest on him, shuddering with her own release. She opened her mouth to breathe deeply and tossed her hair back. A moment more and she left him.

"Billy, wait. I'll be ready again."

She zipped up her dress. "I won't. Looks like you've been hoarding, love. Better get that off before you make a mess. I promised I'd meet Jim now. We'll talk later."

Ten

She was a married woman. On her wedding day she'd taken vows she'd never intended to break.

And she hadn't broken her vows.

Cleaning the house, cutting bunch after bunch of flowers to fill vases for every room, keeping the washer and dryer rumbling away all day—no matter how tired she tried to make herself, how she concentrated on simple tasks, Sonnie couldn't keep her mind focused on anything but Chris Talon.

Would she sleep with him if he wanted her?

He didn't want her. He'd put on that crazy act in front of Billy and her friend that morning; then, once they had gone, he'd drunk coffee, eaten some of the food she'd prepared, and left.

She was back in Key West because the conviction that someone had tried to kill her here kept growing stronger.

What kind of person sent a woman who'd suffered as she had a box of calla lilies with a card to remind her of her child's death, and a not-so-subtle suggestion that she ought to join that child? Someone who wanted her to run away? Someone who didn't want her in Key West? Someone who wanted her dead?

She already knew the answers to her questions.

A gardenia floated in a crystal bowl on the wide parlor

windowsill. Sonnie flipped a forefinger through the water to make the bloom spin.

Billy told Romano to come here. Billy, who was their father's daughter by his first wife, had always overshadowed Sonnie, but she'd been kind, too. When Sonnie was hospitalized, Billy frequently slept in the room with her. Yes, Sonnie loved her sister and she wasn't proud of the way she'd treated her that morning.

The phone rang. Sonnie lifted it from the desk and put the receiver to her ear while she returned to the sunlight by the window. "Hello."

"Sonnie?" Chris had just enough of South Carolina in his voice to make him easy to recognize. "That you, Sonnie?"

Not that she wouldn't recognize his voice anyway. "It's me," she said.

"You're not much like your sister."

Hours had passed since he'd left. "You just realized that." Billy was gorgeous.

"No, ma'am. Noticed it right away. Forgot to mention it, that's all. Do you two get along?"

She squinted against the glare through the swaying fan palm fronds. "Of course we get along." Not that there hadn't been some disagreements.

"Doesn't always work out that way. But you trust her?"

Sonnie turned her back to the window. "You're making me feel strange. Of course I trust my sister."

"It was nice having breakfast with you."

"I'm glad." She perched on the edge of the desk and swung a leg.

"Great coffee."

He made her feel like a plain high schooler who just got noticed by the captain of the football team. "Thank you, Chris."

"You look cute when you sleep."

She almost dropped the base of the phone.

"Sonnie?"

"Thank you."

His laughter made her smile. "You're welcome, ma'am. Just thought you might like to know that."

"Well, it's the kind of information that could come in useful one day."

"Was it okay for me to interfere? Make sure your sister and her friend got out of Dodge?"

Trembling inside over a few trivial comments showed how lonely she must be. "I'm very grateful you did. But now I've got to speak with Billy and make sure she knows I wasn't myself when she arrived."

"You weren't?"

What was she supposed to say?

"You mean because you were in those wonderful pajamas—did I tell you how much I like those pajamas—is that why? You were in your pajamas, and you knew she'd think I spent the night with you?"

"Something like that."

"I did spend the night with you, Sonnie."

The cool cotton dress she wore wasn't cool enough. "Not technically."

His laughter lasted longer this time. When he caught his breath, he said, "Technically, yes, we did spend the night together. And *technically* we slept together, too. What we didn't do was . . . *know* each other, as it's written somewhere. But you didn't ask for all that explanation, did you? I'm sorry if you were uncomfortable because of anything I did."

"Thank you for what you did—and said," she told him hurriedly. "I've been pushing myself at you from the minute we were introduced. You've been very kind, and I know I've been a nuisance."

When the silence went on and on and he still didn't answer, she said, "I'm sorry about that."

He paused a while longer before saying, "Is Jim Lesley a friend of yours?"

"He came with—oh, you mean did I meet him before. No."

"And he's nothing special to Billy, as far as you know?"

She thought about that. "It's hard to be sure. When you look like Billy, men hover. I wouldn't expect her to be with him if he didn't interest her."

"There are a lot of ways to be interesting. You've given

me the answers I expected. I asked a few questions about Jim Lesley.''

''Why?'' She'd like to tell Chris that he interested her in lots of ways. ''How would you find out anything about a man you saw for only a few minutes? You wouldn't know where to start.''

He tutted. ''With so much faith in me, you must have been desperate when you asked me to work for you. I've got to go, Sonnie. But Jim Lesley is Dr. James V. Lesley. He's a psychiatrist and he runs an expensive, very *discreet* sanitarium. Sorry to rush. Maybe we'll talk later.''

The line went dead—not that she could have formed a response.

She should see Billy. Now. Ask her what she thought she was doing.

Calling Billy at the club, accusing her of bringing a psychiatrist to evaluate her sister, would be a bad move. Sonnie replaced the phone on the desk. She was fine, and she'd prove it without confronting family members who only wished her well.

The recollection of Chris in the kitchen, dressed only in jeans slung low on his hips—and a tattoo—made her grin. Billy might well be wondering about her mousy younger sister, but what the hell?

Sonnie went into the hall and through the open front door. The gardenia bush was to the right, and she picked another flower, this one to thread behind her ear.

A flash of orange and lime green alerted her to the approach of Just Ena. Using the gap in the hibiscus hedge to get into Sonnie's yard, the woman wiggled her fingers as she tripped forward in thongs that sported green rubber flowers.

''Hello, Ena,'' Sonnie said. It was time to make very sure everyone knew how pleasant and ordinary she was. ''How are you?''

''I'm just wonderful. It's you I'm worried about. Now you just tell me to go away and mind my own business if you like, but I wouldn't be a good neighbor if I didn't make sure everything's all right over here. I've been trying to decide what

I should say to you for hours. Of course, your friend was here. Then the man and woman visited. But—''

"My sister, Billy, and her friend. They came down from Denver to see me. I'm from Denver.''

"I knew that," Ena said. "I don't want that to sound as if I'm a busybody, but everyone knows you're one of the Denver Keiths. Beer. Your sister's as lovely as she used to look on television.''

Ena paused, and Sonnie smiled. She wasn't going to encourage her neighbor to discuss any of the very public facts she might know about Billy.

"It's a shame. Maybe she was too young to deal with that kind of high life. All the partying. The *drinking*.'' Ena's eyes let Sonnie know she was talking about Billy's drinking in particular, about Billy getting into trouble because of her drinking. There had been other, more destructive abuses, but their father had managed to intervene while Billy could still be saved.

"Yes, well," Ena said at last, "I was talking about that man—I mean the one who was here last night. He's not from Denver, is he?''

Nothing was going to get past Ena. "No, he's not from Denver. He's Roy Talon's—''

"No, no, I don't mean that great big man with the motorcycle. I was talking about the other one.''

Romano? "My brother-in-law?''

Ena's carefully made-up face registered irritation. "The other Mr. Giacano? No, no. I know who *he* is. Last night. Oh, I knew I should have called right away when I saw him, but I thought he must be someone you know. How would he get in otherwise?''

Sonnie gave Ena her full attention. With her every breath catching, she didn't realize she'd reached for the woman until she held her soft hands. "Please, Ena, be very clear. What time was this? Where was this man? Did you see his face—or anything that might remind me who he is?''

"I couldn't see his face," Ena said. "I was too far away. It was late, so I was inside. I don't even know what made me get out of bed and look out of the window. He was up there on the balcony. Not near your husband's rocking chair. Right outside those French windows. They were open, so I just thought he must have come from in there. But the more I thought about it, the more I worried. After all, that's your bedroom, isn't it?"

Sonnie glanced over her shoulder and said, "Yes. Where did he go?"

Ena squeezed Sonnie's hands. "You do know who I mean and you're afraid I'll tell someone, aren't you? Well, I won't, and that's a promise. A woman's got a right to her own business, that's what I say. I know you were home, and he went back in the bedroom. And you're looking much more cheerful today." She gave a conspiratorial smile. "Good for you, that's all I can say. You've been through a lot. If you can find some comfort, well then, I'd be the last one to criticize."

"Come on in, Roy," Chris said. His brother had let himself in and taken the only comfortable chair in the room. He stretched his legs, and tossed his hat on the handlebars of the Harley. "Yes, bro," Chris continued, "I insist you get in here and make yourself at home."

"I am at home. This place belongs to me."

"True enough. But I do pay rent."

"Not much."

"You won't take much. You never would. Let's quit fighting. What burr did you sit on?"

Hitching at his jeans, Roy sat straighter and fixed Chris with a hard stare. "Where were you last night?"

Roy's tone set Chris's teeth on edge. "I was doing a good deed. Okay?"

"And the recipient of the good deed?"

Pacing because he was afraid he might do something he'd regret if he didn't, Chris crossed his arms over his bare chest and trapped his hands beneath his arms.

"Chris," Roy said. "Were you at Sonnie's?"

"Back off."

"Were you?"

Chris swung around. "What the—what does it matter if I was? Yes. Yes I was at Sonnie's. That's one mixed-up woman you've got working for you."

"She's one special woman, and if you mess with her, you'd better be ready to find me in your face."

"When did you become her father? Or anybody's father, damn it?"

Roy ran his fingers through his red hair. He didn't take his eyes off Chris. "I'm not going to rise to that. Have you ever thought I might like to be someone's father?"

Chris felt himself turn red. "Forget what I said. Fate deals some bad stuff."

"Not so bad. You get the hand you're dealt, that's all. I've been a lucky man. I am a lucky man. Don't feel sorry for me."

Damn my big mouth. "No, I won't. I don't. I went over to Sonnie's because she called and sounded upset."

"I thought you didn't want anything to do with her. You turned her down, didn't you? Told her you wouldn't work for her?"

Chris looked speculatively at Roy, then went to make sure the door was locked. He pulled down the Murphy bed and smoothed the covers before sitting on the corner nearest the chair.

A massive frown ruckled Roy's brow and he leaned forward.

"You know I've told you how I get these *feelings* from time to time," Chris said. "Bunch of shit, of course, but still I do get 'em."

"You always did. Used to drive Mom nuts."

"No one ever believed me. They thought I was making it up."

"I believed you. You called it on the night when the cops came for Daddy the first time. And you knew about the baby. It—"

Chris held up a hand. "We're not going back there. Sorry. We're never going there again."

"No." Roy's eyes slid away. "But I've got faith in your feelings."

"I wish I didn't. Sonnie called me. She was crying. When I

answered, she said she'd dialed the wrong number, and she hung up. I went right over there and she was in some state. Nightmare. The kind we'd rather not have from the look of her.''

"And?" Roy had grown very still.

"She was exhausted. Sick. She tried to persuade me to move into that house with her.''

"She what?" Roy stood up. "I don't friggin' believe you. She's not that kind of—"

"Not that kind of woman? She surely isn't. And she wasn't inviting me to cohabit. She wanted me to take some rooms there. Fear is what's going on with her. She's scared out of her mind.''

Roy's magnificent frown returned. "What'd you say when she asked?"

"No. What else could I say? I sat in the room through the night while she got some sleep. I left this morning." He wasn't going to mention the family arrival.

"Why didn't you agree to move in?"

"Why, bro, you surprise me. A God-fearin' man like you. Move into a house with a woman who isn't my wife?"

"You smart-mouthed kid. She needs help and she trusts you. Don't ask me why—bad taste, I guess. But if that's what would make her feel better, that's what you should do.''

"I live here. I like it here. I don't do well in cozy arrangements. Remember?"

"That was different."

He didn't feel like discussing his defunct marriage. "She was like a drowned rat, Roy. Her pajamas were soaked with sweat. She had to take a shower.''

"That right?"

The innocent look on Roy Talon's face didn't fool Chris. The man had just turned two and two into five. "It isn't the first time I've slept in a chair. I was glad to do it. Sonnie's a nice woman, and I believe her that she's in trouble.''

"Do you? How long is it since you were with a woman?"

Chris bit back what he'd like to say. "I just told you. I was with Sonnie last night.''

That earned him an evil leer. "You know what I mean."

"If you mean what I think you mean, Sonnie Giacano is married. Her husband was abducted and we should all be hoping he turns up and looks after her."

"He never looked after her when he was here," Roy said. "Why would that change?"

"Doesn't alter the fact that she's not free."

"Big deal. She's unhappy. I think that egotistical bastard made her life hell. I don't know what she's looking for. But I'm not the cop."

"Ex-cop."

"Ex-cop, then. You're having feelings about her. The bad kind. And maybe the good kind, too. But if you're having feelings about Sonnie, I'd lay odds she's in big trouble and you've got a responsibility to look out for her."

"Like hell." He attempted a scoffing sound but it wasn't a good effort.

"Don't take your eyes off her for too long," Roy said, and his absolute sincerity wasn't in question. "From the way I look at it, only desperation would make her come back to the Keys alone. I've got it figured that she thinks someone might be after her and she's had the guts to draw them here because this is where it all started. Does that sound just way off?"

Chis wished it did. "I'm not taking my attention away from her for too long, Roy. Okay?"

"Yeah." Roy got up and embraced Chris. "Yeah. You don't know how much better that makes me feel. She doesn't have anyone—not really. She needs us."

Later Chris would fill Roy in about the brother-in-law and the sister—and the tame shrink.

The door opened without a knock and Bo stuck his head into the room. "Did either of you expect Sonnie tonight?" he asked.

Chris jerked to his feet and hitched up his sweatpants. "She's off tonight. Why?"

"She's come in. Doesn't look great, but she insists she's going to work. She wants to work."

"Then she works," Roy said. "You don't have a problem with that, do you, Bo?"

"Hell, no. She's a great gal. The customers think she's great. They talk about how they love the way she talks and how she's polite to everyone. Old Taffy wanted me to know how she treats him with respect. Seems respect has been something Taffy's missed."

"You'd better get back in," Roy said.

Bo nodded, but didn't leave. He and Roy exchanged a look and Roy followed Bo outside.

No more than a minute passed before Roy came back. "Look, I think I had a day off once, but I can't remember."

The kind of setup Roy aimed to pull wasn't hard to spot. "That's too bad," Chris said.

"Yeah. Man of my age needs to take better care of himself. Now, I don't trust many people to take my place, but if you were to offer tonight, I'd let you do it. Yes, sir, I'd be grateful and I'd step aside with a light heart."

"You expect me to saunter in there and tell Sonnie you just decided to take the night off because you're tired, so I'm stepping in. You don't think she'll see through that."

"Shee-it," Roy said. "Does it matter? Will she care why you're there when she's only here because she wants to see you?"

"You don't know that. Maybe she just doesn't want to be at home."

"Oh, well, that would mean she's really in fine shape, wouldn't it?" Roy pointed a long finger. "Okay, here's the scoop. Sonnie told Bo she *couldn't* stay at home. She said she thought she had a nightmare last night, but now she's found out that what she saw—some man—was probably the real thing."

With one eye on the door to the back, Sonnie set out a round of beers for a group of intrepid tourists, all wearing T-shirts covered with logos that read, *The Bars of Key West*. The T-shirts hung or stretched, according to the torso adorned. Each man was equally loud.

"Hey, hey," a man with a shaved head said, hammering a

fist on the counter. "Wassyourname? You, the little stuck-up one—wassyourname?"

Sonnie smiled at him and said, "I'm Sonnie. The coffee's great here. We're famous for our coffee."

"I don't want no fuckin' coffee."

"Not in front of the lady." Taffy, one of the men who fished off Key West, swung around on his stool and looked at the latest charm-school graduate. "Maybe you better do your drinkin' somewhere else."

"This your place, fat man?"

Taffy's toothless jaw set. Soft around the edges, but still bigger than he was fat, he got off the stool. "The Nail belongs to two of my best friends."

"The faggots who were here earlier?" the man shouted, bending double to laugh. "Figures. One asshole knows another, right?" He laughed uproariously at his brilliance.

Despite the warmth of the night, Sonnie felt cold. She felt even colder and much more horrified when Billy—wearing a leopard-print jumpsuit, a matching scarf over her head and tied around her neck, and huge, very dark glasses—sidled into the Nail and took a seat near the windows.

And that was the moment when Taffy brought his interlaced fists upward and under the loudmouth's jaw. The crunch that sounded rendered the whole bar silent. Groaning, the man folded. Blood ran from his nose and the corners of his mouth to the sawdust-scattered floor.

"Shit," one of his companions said in a loud whisper.

Bo came through the back door, surveyed the scene, and promptly positioned himself in the middle of the fray. A skinny man he might be, but he was wiry, and Sonnie knew how strong he was.

Sonnie prayed for Billy to leave, but she pulled out a cigarette instead and lit up, blowing a stream of smoke toward the ceiling.

"What started this?" Bo asked. "Taffy—"

"My fault," Sonnie said. "I mentioned coffee, and . . ." She turned up her palms.

Bo studied the swaying group and said, "We can see how

many more of us can end up bleeding all over my floor, or maybe coffee would be a good idea. What do you say, guys?''

There was a muttered, ''Flamin' faggot.'' But several others said, ''Sure.''

''You want to call the police?'' Bo asked the man who was down, and checked his mouth. ''Nothing broken. Your teeth went into your lips.''

''Fuckin' hurts,'' he said, sniffing and smearing blood from his nose on the back of an arm. ''No cops.''

''He swore at the lady,'' Taffy said. ''Don't no one swear at Sonnie.''

''No, they don't,'' Bo said. ''Maybe you should move on.''

''We ain't finished our beers.''

Bo nodded. ''Drink up and move on.''

Roy joined the grumbling assembly. ''Hey there, Sonnie. You're a workhorse. Thanks for coming in.''

He was the sweetest man. She batted his arm and kissed Bo's cheek—winning herself a bashful smile.

The beer was flowing down truculent throats, and while the beer went in, the bravado blossomed again. Finally the group shuffled in wavering lines toward the door. When all but the gentleman with the swollen nose and mouth were outside, he turned back and said, ''You better never let me catch you on your own, y'hear? I might have to show you what I do to troublemakers. You might have fun finding out, but you wouldn't walk for a long time afterward.''

It was Sonnie he pointed at. She grabbed Roy's elbow when he made to follow the man. ''Let him go,'' she said.

Roy put an arm around her shoulders and said, ''Yeah, you're right. Don't give that another thought. They'll be gone from the island soon enough, and by morning he won't remember a word he said tonight anyway.''

Sonnie would remember she'd been threatened with rape. She glanced at the back door—again.

Eleven

One day he and Roy might just have to revisit old times. Roy was ready. Chris wasn't. It was all clear enough in his head—his mother who was too gentle for the cruel man her husband had been, the perpetual rage, the fear, the inevitable destruction of two childhoods that never had a chance. The loss of a little sister who might have lived if there'd been any love in the Talon household. It was clear, but he couldn't face talking about it.

"God," Chris said aloud to a leaden night sky. They'd been helpless and trapped.

He walked slowly toward the back door of the Nail. All that was over. There was no changing any of it—there had never been anything he could have done.

Rotten, all rotten. Everything that could be good and true and special, got torn apart, beaten out of existence by an excuse for a man who used his fists on his wife and children rather than take responsibility for his own disappointments. And even that hadn't been the worst of it.

But Roy and Chris Talon had been tough, too tough not to fight back as soon as they were able. Up and out they'd gone. They'd both worked, often at more than one job, and made it through both high school and college. A year out of college,

Chris had applied to the police academy and was accepted. Roy got a big chuckle out of that. "Chris, soldier of justice," he'd called his brother. "The world's safe now it's in your hands." Chris had laughed himself, but he'd known his motives weren't too far from Roy's cracks.

The Talon brothers had helped themselves and, after their father dropped out of sight, they'd made sure their mother had enough to live the simple life she preferred without worry. They still looked after her. The old man had never shown up again. Just as well, since even gentle Roy said he'd kill him if he ever did.

Sonnie Giacano had lost her baby. She'd been hurtled through a window of her Volvo and thrown clear while the car crashed and burned. The woman had lived, but the baby had died. A little girl.

Irony had shown a tendency to like Chris's company.

He'd known despair.

He'd caused despair.

If he decided to take up Sonnie's cause, would it be because he thought he could somehow make the past right?

So much for his declaration to Roy that he wasn't taking any trips down memory lane. *Damn, damn, damn.*

More noise than usual came from inside the bar. He let himself in and used one of the skills his police career had given him—the ability to single out trouble, even in a crowd.

One small, fair-haired woman in a khaki bush shirt and matching pants had evidently managed to whip the anesthetized inmates of the Rusty Nail into something resembling frenzy.

Sonnie shook her head vehemently. Her face was visibly flushed.

Roy waved his arms and demanded, "Sit down, all of you. What the . . . Sam Hill do you think this is? The Old West? We don't do lynch mobs anymore, Taffy."

"The . . . Sam Hill, we don't," Taffy shouted through his gums. "Them fellas don't even live here. Foreigners, that's what they are. From somewhere up north."

"At least Georgia," Bo said.

Taffy nodded. "Like I said. From up north. They don't come

down here and get away with threatenin' a lady. We go get 'em. That's what I say. You with me, fellas?''

A discordant but assenting chorus went up. There was no progress toward the street.

"Please." The volume Sonnie managed opened Chris's eyes wider. "I don't want anyone getting into trouble. You're all so kind. You're real gentlemen. No way do you give those people the pleasure of knowing they've upset you. Come on. I'm going to buy everyone a drink."

Chris didn't wait to hear more. He pushed his way to the middle of the group. "What the . . . Sam Hill's going on here?" He gritted his teeth and said, "*Hell,* Roy. I leave you alone for half an hour and all *hell* breaks loose around here. Sonnie? You okay?"

She'd closed her eyes and he looked at the fish netting that drooped from the ceiling. Shit, now he was frightening her because he'd raised his voice a little. He glanced around at the clustered men. "Sit *down,* damn it. Can't you see you're scaring Sonnie out of her wits? Sit *down.* Set 'em up, Bo. I'm buyin'."

"You're the one whose scaring her," Roy said into Chris's ear. "Swearin' and shoutin'. You always did have a foul temper."

"What happened here?" Chris asked.

"Some jokers—tourists —wandered in. Evidently doing the rounds. We weren't early on the route. Sonnie offered them coffee and one guy got mad. He threatened her."

Chris felt the need to hit something, so he crossed his arms. "Threatened her how?"

"Let it go," Roy said.

"Like hell. Tell me."

Roy sighed. "I guess he threatened to do things to her if he ever caught her alone."

Chris dropped his arms to his sides. "How long ago did he leave?"

"Too long for you to catch up with him. The guy was drunk out of his mind, Chris. By tomorrow he'll forget he was ever here, let alone what he said to anyone. Let it go, will ya?"

He watched the patrons shuffle off to reclaim their stools

and chairs, all but Taffy, who patted Sonnie's back with an awkwardness that spoke of how unaccustomed he was to offering physical comfort.

Sonnie smiled at him and said, "Thanks, Taffy. I'm fine, really. Thanks to you."

"She probably shouldn't be here," Chris said. "She's not cut out for the kind of people you get here."

Roy bristled. "I can look after her, thanks. Bo and I would never let anything happen to Sonnie."

"No, I know you wouldn't. If you were there when some son of a bitch decided to take her apart."

Movement at a table by the window grabbed Chris's attention. At any other time he would have noticed the woman immediately—mostly because she didn't fit. But even if she weren't dressed like an escapee from a Hollywood set, an obviously affluent, unaccompanied woman wasn't a frequent late-night occurrence at the Nail.

Bo had started passing out the drinks, and Taffy leaned on the bar again.

"We'll keep a close eye on her, okay?" Roy said quietly. "Don't get her all worked up over something that'll probably never be a problem."

Sonnie remained where she'd been. She held her flattened palms against her hips and stared at Chris. The sheen in her eyes was no mystery. Tears were close. She'd been through too much. Last night she'd broken up over a dream. He'd seen how fragile she was. Whatever had happened here tonight could be sending her over the edge.

Chris said, "Look at her," to Roy. "She's too vulnerable."

"And you're fascinated by her."

Chris eyed his brother but he didn't argue.

"I don't blame you. If I were straight I'd be interested myself." Roy's grin demanded a grin in response. "Relax a bit about tonight. It didn't mean anything."

He wasn't so sure, but Chris nodded while Roy backed away, then turned to go to the bar.

The woman in leopard print and oversize dark glasses got up. Chris realized who she was. Billy Keith sauntered toward

Sonnie, and the annoyance he felt wasn't a good thing. Feeling territorial about Sonnie would never be a good thing.

He returned his gaze to Sonnie and doubted she'd ever removed hers. She looked straight back into his face. Billy gradually moved from the periphery of his vision, right into the central frame.

Sonnie walked toward Chris as if she hadn't seen her sister.

If everything he felt was in his eyes, he was in deep tofu—*shit.*

The limp was more noticeable when she moved slowly. Each step was a decision she made while she watched for a signal from him. She wanted him to encourage her to come to him.

She stopped.

Come on. Keep coming and maybe I'll know what to do when you get here.

What did he want? He wasn't a romantic, for God's sake. Chris Talon saw the bad old world through jaded eyes. He didn't want to take on her case. He didn't want to care about her. He *would not* care about her.

The lady was married.

"Sonnie," her sister said, sharply enough to make Sonnie flinch. "Look at me. I'm not here because I want to be. I'm here for you. I can't believe you're in a place like this."

Don't listen to her. Come on. Come on.

Caring about the client didn't automatically follow taking on a case. Not that it would necessarily be bad if it happened. She'd never said how she felt about Giacano—only that she wanted to know if she was his wife or his widow.

Her unblinking stare asked him all the questions he wasn't ready to answer. *Will you help me now? Do you want things to turn out for me? Has something changed between us?* And maybe there was more but he chose not to try putting it into words.

"Damn it, Sonnie," Billy said, and she was close enough to Chris for him not to have to strain to hear every word. "These aren't your kind of people and this isn't your kind of place. Do you even know what they are?" She indicated Roy and Bo, and Chris itched to answer for Sonnie and say, "No, what are they?"

"We're going to talk," Billy said. "Right now. It's my turn to be the stable one. I've got a car outside."

For the first time since the other woman approached, Sonnie gave her some attention. "I'm not leaving. Thanks for worrying about me, though."

Billy spread her arms. In the silky jumpsuit she might as well have been wearing a thin leotard. "This is just what I was afraid of when you said you had to come down here on your own. I'm moving in with you, Baby. I don't care how much you argue. Until I can talk you into going back to Denver, I'm going to stick to you like glue."

Chris felt like groaning aloud.

"If you remain in Key West at all," Sonnie said, her voice steady, "you will not stay at my house. You don't have the right to demand that. And I suggest you don't stay on the island. There's nothing for you to do here." She cast Billy a cold appraisal, and Chris knew she was thinking about his revelation that Jim Lesley was a shrink.

Billy turned on Chris. "I don't know how you managed to work your way into my sister's life, but you must have figured that she's not well, or strong, and that she's an easy mark. You've taken advantage of her. But that's going to stop. She's got family here now, and we won't stand for it."

"Chris is my friend," Sonnie said. Her voice was so much softer and less strident than her sister's, yet Chris had a hunch that Billy wasn't as tough as she'd like the rest of the world to believe.

"I'm worried about you, Baby," Billy said, and her mouth trembled. "You were always the one who never took a wrong step. This time I'm not the screwup. Let me take care of you. You owe it to me."

"Why don't we sit down," Chris suggested, "and keep calm. Sonnie knows how much you care about her." He met Sonnie's eyes again and hoped she read his message that she shouldn't mention Jim Lesley yet. "Let's have something to drink.'' He signaled to Roy, who hadn't taken his eyes off them since the little three way drama had begun.

Roy arrived at the table Chris chose. ''Evenin','' he said, focusing his considerable charm on Billy. ''What can I get you?''

''Grand Marnier over ice.'' She didn't return his smile. ''Make it a double.''

''You've got it,'' Roy said, turning to Sonnie. ''You okay, kid?''

''Great, thanks. How can I not feel great with you and Bo and Chris to look after me? And Taffy, of course. I'll have a dry sherry, please.''

Billy grimaced.

''The usual,'' Chris said.

Billy leaned closer to Sonnie and said, ''You know alcohol doesn't suit you. And you're still recovering from a head injury. You shouldn't mess with things like that.''

''I'm having a glass of sherry, not a triple martini. Where's your friend?''

Chris squeezed her knee under the table, and, when she met his gaze, he shook his head slightly. He kept his hand on top of her thigh and took pleasure in the color that rose in her face.

''Jim's a quiet man. He likes to read in the evening.''

Sounds like a real ball of fire.

He studied Billy Keith. She'd taken off her glasses. The scarf obscured her hair. The bones of her face were classic. She wore a considerable amount of makeup, but it was artfully applied. Her best feature was a very beautiful mouth with definite bowed upper arches. She cast frequent looks at Sonnie, and what Chris saw in those glances troubled him. He hadn't spent years on the force to learn nothing about body language combined with facial expression. She felt connected to Sonnie, but there was envy there. It would be interesting to find out why.

Worse things could happen than that he let the two of them talk alone for a few minutes. ''I'll go help Roy with those drinks,'' he said. ''Back shortly.'' He scraped his chair back. ''Either of you want something to eat?''

Both women declined and he left.

Sonnie gave Chris time to be out of earshot before turning to Billy. "What are you thinking of, following me around? I work here."

"That's pathetic," Billy said. "And you know it. There couldn't be a more unsuitable place for you. You need to come with me for a complete rest."

"Have you got a nice safe place in mind for me?" Sonnie said before she could squash the urge. She'd figured out that Chris didn't want her to mention what they knew about Jim Lesley.

"You'll be safe—and well looked after—at the folks'. I spoke with them today and they're worried sick. Your mom wanted to fly down here but I persuaded her not to—yet."

Sonnie didn't miss the threat. Billy wouldn't hesitate to bring Sonnie's mother running to Key West if Sonnie didn't do as Billy told her.

"Either you tell the folks that I'm doing fine, or I'll talk about Las Vegas," Sonnie said, being sure to keep emotion out of her voice.

"You'd never do that."

"You mean I'd never tell them how I found you—"

"You don't have to say it."

"Flat broke and dancing topless at some sleazy nightclub?" Billy blushed. "They wouldn't believe you."

"Want to try it out?"

"No."

"You're desperate for money again. That's what this is all about, isn't it?"

Billy wouldn't look at her. "No one in this family lets me forget that I made some unfortunate choices. I lived too high when I was married."

"Both times," Sonnie commented. "Twice you let immature men send you on the road to broke. Do you need a loan?"

"No." Billy narrowed her eyes. "You love being Mrs. Bountiful, don't you? Just because you've always been a dried-up, passionless woman. Well, you can have it. And you can choke on your money. What good does it do you? You don't get any pleasure out of being rich; you never have.

"You're afraid to let me take charge here. Just the thought of that scares you. You were Goody Two-shoes all our lives, weren't you? Each time I messed up, there you were enjoying the comparisons the folks made between us. Well, there was no way to outpriss you. But I was the athlete. I was the one people paid to see. A little more luck and I'd have gone a long way."

Sonnie smoothed the tabletop and weighed her choices. "It wasn't too little luck that ruined your tennis career." Avoiding the truth had never helped Billy before and it wouldn't now. "Alcohol and drugs—and bad company—that's what ended it."

"Damn you," Billy said, thrusting her face across the table. "You're jealous of me. That's why you enjoy dragging up my old problems. It's the only way you can feel better than me. I think you can even forget it was me who introduced you to Frank and Romano. I brought them home. They were my friends because we had so much in common. I could have married either of them. They both asked me. Frank only asked you because I wasn't ready to settle down."

Sonnie had long ago decided that whatever she did or didn't feel would always be a mystery to Billy. "Maybe you're right—about everything. Let's drop this before Chris gets back."

"Why are you bothering with him? He may be a stud, but he's nothing. And he's the kind you can't trust. Open your eyes, Sonnie. A man like that isn't interested in ... *subtle* women. Stick around with him and he'll eat you up."

Sonnie looked at her lap and thought there could be worse ways to go.

"What is he, other than a bloodsucker living on, what? His brother? You? Sonnie, are you giving that man money?"

"You can be so insulting, Billy. You don't even know Chris and you're making assumptions about him."

"A womanizer. Take it from me. He whips off that shirt and flashes his muscles and that disgusting tattoo, for God's sake, and women flock to get some."

"Don't *you* be disgusting."

"Still as prissy as ever. That's something else that makes no sense. Miss Priss and the local heartthrob. He probably collects women's panties."

"Stop it." She'd had enough. "You're working for Daddy and you hate it. You've always hated it when he could make you come to heel. That's when you turn on me. Why don't you marry some man who'll roll you in money and give you everything you want? You know you could come up with a dozen in twenty-four hours."

Billy had heard more than enough about her shortcomings. Sonnie was a boor, had always been a boor, but she never missed an opportunity to wield a little power. "Your lover's coming back," she said, taking in Talon's loose-limbed walk, the swing of his broad shoulders, the way his jeans fit narrow hips and long, muscular legs. All that with mousy little Baby! She didn't think so. Not without a real good motive, and it wouldn't be sex.

When he drew close, two glasses in one hand and one in the other, she waited for him to notice she was watching him, then sent him the kind of smile no man failed to interpret. She hooked an elbow over the back of her chair and crossed her legs.

He nodded.

Nodded.

Baby had found herself a thickheaded bike jockey who was too busy thinking about the way he looked to notice anyone else.

He arrived, set down the glasses, and passed them out.

Billy put her fingers over his on her glass and said, "Thank you, Chris. Are you here every night?"

"Oh, yeah," he said, and drank what looked like single-malt whiskey. "How's the sherry, Sonnie?"

"Good, thanks."

Billy swung her leg and sized Talon up from head to foot. He could be a problem. As of now she was certain he was the obstacle standing in her way of making sure Sonnie did whatever she was told to do.

"The Grand Marnier's good, too, thanks," Billy said, checking her watch, "but I've got to go. I've had the car waiting all this time and I didn't realize how late it had gotten. Chris, it's a real pleasure to get to know you better. Thank you for taking care of Sonnie. She isn't good on her own."

If Talon noticed the abrupt change in her attitude toward him, he didn't show it. She got up and retied the scarf more tightly. Then she kissed Sonnie's cheek. Passing Talon's chair, she put a hand on each of his very nice shoulders and bent to whisper in his ear, "I like a kind man." She *really* liked a man who smelled like the wind and looked—and felt—as if he were made of steel. "You don't have to spend time with a victim and we both know it. But I'm thanking you for that. I'd like to talk to you about how you think she is. I'll call you."

Without giving him a chance to respond, she waved to them both and hurried a block outside to the Cadillac with its black tinted windows. The driver pushed open the door and she slid into the buttery ivory leather interior and into open arms.

Twelve

Chris anticipated Sonnie's next question, and she didn't disappoint him. "What did Billy just say to you?"

He raised a brow. "Your sister wanted to thank me for spending time with you." The anger he saw in Sonnie didn't disappoint him.

She said, "Billy has trouble with her bitch factor."

He laughed, delighted at her show of spirit. "I'd say that's an understatement. You two are sure different."

"I'm like my mother. Billy's like hers. Daddy's been married twice. Actually Billy and I are both like Daddy in a way. Why didn't you want me to let Billy know I've found out about Jim Lesley?"

He lifted her glass from the table and held it to her lips, raising it until she was forced to take a sip.

"Medicinal," he said, passing the pad of his forefinger along her bottom lip, then placing it between his own lips and mumbling, "Tastes nice—nice medicine."

She started to speak, but seemed to forget what she'd been about to say. Instead she looked from his eyes to his mouth, then down to his chest where his shirt rested open for a long way.

Sonnie made his belly grow tight—and other parts of him

equally tight. Ms. Billy Keith thought she knew all about sex appeal. She'd missed just about every wonderful subtlety that had all the power over anything obvious. Her sister used them unconsciously.

"Sonnie?"

"Yes?" She raised her face and looked at him fully.

"Do you understand me when I say I think we'd better try to stay focused?"

"I do," she said quietly. "None of the rest of it's appropriate, is it?"

"Maybe not. But maybe. We'll have to find out—won't we?"

She passed a hand beneath her collar. "I don't know."

Slim she might be, but when the bush shirt pulled tight over a breast, there was no doubt that a small, shapely body could be the kind of turn on that made concentration a feat.

"You didn't answer me about Jim Lesley."

He looked around and got a sudden, uneasy feeling that he was getting sloppy about where he said what. "I think we should go somewhere we can be sure we won't be overheard."

Sonnie frowned.

"Don't get scared. It's just a precaution. We could go to my place if you're okay with that."

For several seconds a battery of expressions passed through her eyes. She wasn't sure she should be okay with going to his place with him, alone. She also wasn't sure she didn't like the idea quite a lot—or maybe he was stretching a bit there.

"Sure," she said finally. "Of course. That'll be fine."

He got up at once and held her chair while she joined him. When he ushered Sonnie ahead of him toward the back door, the patrons were sunk deep into a philosophical moment— mumbling comments about nothing in particular. But both Roy and Bo looked at Sonnie and Chris—while they tried not to look.

Chris reached around Sonnie and pushed open the door. She stepped outside and he followed her into a night with a rising wind, and moisture in the air.

"I like it here at this time of year," he said conversationally. "You're never sure of anything—except the heat."

"I've already told you I find it exciting."

"Watch where you step. There's not much light. Hold my hand."

Her cool fingers slipped against his palm and he gripped them.

He unlocked the guest house, flipped on an overhead light inside, and pulled her in behind him. Once he'd shot home the bolt behind them, he replaced the glaring ceiling light with a lamp that stood on the floor.

"Your bike's pretty," she said, surprising him. "Or elegant, I guess I should say."

"Thanks. We were partners a long time. Made us pretty close. You left most of your sherry. I think I've got something close. Like some?"

She hunched her shoulders and hesitation furrowed her brow.

"Good," he said. "Coming up." He poured a small quantity of cherry brandy. He'd have to make sure he had sherry next time.

That thought wasn't something he cared to analyze beyond the fact that he liked the lady, had begun to feel comfortable with her, and would be more than happy if she stopped by for a drink from time to time.

Oh, right. Maybe he should find out if it was too late to become a Boy Scout, too.

He gave her the drink and swallowed some of his own whiskey.

She hovered. "You hover a lot," he said. "Do you know that?"

Sonnie stood still. "Sorry."

"Don't be. Take the best chair, please."

"It's the only chair—apart from the stool in front of the computer."

"Exactly, the best chair, and it's yours." He patted the back. She sat down, looked up at him. "Thank you."

They studied each other a little longer than was necessary. He shouldn't be allowing any of this to happen. She wasn't the type to be comfortable with getting close to another man while she didn't know what had happened to her husband. Boy, would he love to ask her about him. Mostly he wanted to know if theirs had been a good, happy marriage.

She looked away first and tasted the cherry brandy. "Hmm. That's lovely."

"Glad you like it." He took his customary spot on the corner of the Murphy bed. "I may have to think about hiring an interior designer for this place."

She laughed aloud at that, then sputtered and put a hand over her mouth.

"It's okay," he told her. "That was meant to be a joke. But I may have to at least make things a little more inviting."

He was grateful she didn't immediately ask why.

"Okay, let's get to business. I stopped you from letting Billy know I found out about Jim Lesley. The simplest explanation is that I don't believe in playing any potential winning cards too soon."

She bowed her head, then looked sideways and up at him with her so very dark blue eyes.

And Chris remembered his hand on her breast while she slept. When he'd realized what he'd done he'd been disoriented, and intensely excited at the same time. He could remember the texture of her skin, the way her nipple had been hard against his palm. Her skin was soft; her flesh was firm—and as far as he was concerned, the quantity of that flesh was perfect.

His jeans weren't comfortable anymore.

"What is it?" she asked.

"I owe you an apology. While you were sleeping and I was sitting beside you, I ended up with my hand on . . . on your breast. Instinct, I suppose. I didn't mean to take advantage of you."

Her lips parted and he saw her struggle for breath.

"I must have done it in my sleep, and you felt so right, I stayed right there."

"Yes," she murmured. Her neck and face had turned red. "I'm sure those things can happen."

"I'm sorry, Sonnie."

"It's okay." She cleared her throat. "You think Billy's the one whose doing bad things to me. I don't. I think she's too obvious a suspect. The whole setup would be too obvious. And I don't think she'd really try to hurt me—not so vindictively— not when the chips were down."

"Well, well, you beat me to the punch. I'm thinking along the same lines. I wasn't sure how to approach it with you in case you panicked because we don't have much else yet."

"We," she said, cocking her head on one side.

He didn't respond to that.

"Billy has money troubles," she continued. "She went through her trust and she's had to go to work in the family business, which she hates. She's just angry because I haven't had her problems in that direction."

"Maybe she's angry enough to be figuring out a way to get her hands on your money. I'm just playing devil's advocate here."

"She might think about it," Sonnie said, "but she wouldn't do it."

"So how would you explain her boyfriend?"

She considered before saying, "Just as a boyfriend. He's attractive, and she's always been drawn to men who are well connected. Men with good positions. She married duds twice, but she's dated a lot of potential winners. The fact that he's a psychiatrist could be just a coincidence."

"Maybe. We're going to have to keep an open mind until something else happens, anyway."

Sonnie looked at him sharply. Her pupils dilated. He'd spooked her again.

"Try to keep calm. You aren't on your own."

Her eyes softened a little. "Do you mean you will help me officially?"

"That's all you care about?" And that was absolutely the last thing he should have said. "Getting my help?"

She shook her head. "All I care about?"

"You don't feel anything." Sometimes clearing the air was a good, if dangerous, idea.

"I don't understand." She looked puzzled. *"Feel?"*

"Forget it."

"No. I feel, Chris. What do you mean?"

"Nothing. You're convalescing. You should be at home in bed."

"I'm not convalescing. Still mending, maybe—and scars take time. But as far as I'm concerned, I'm past convalescence."

He swirled his drink and watched the pale liquor catch the light. He could smell its fine, pungent aroma. He felt Sonnie get up. She stood beside him.

Pushing back his hair, he looked up at her. He thought he saw a woman poised between wanting to flee and wanting to stay. Not sure what to expect, he pressed a hand to her stomach. Flat and instantly tense at his touch. Setting his drink aside to grip her hips came naturally. He smoothed his thumbs up and down the dips in front of each bone.

She pressed her elbows to her sides and held the glass with both hands.

"Stand closer," he told her, and eased her between his thighs.

She raised her arms higher, as if to protect herself.

"Relax." Why did he sound threatening, even to himself? "Say the word, and I'll put some space between us."

Sonnie didn't say the word.

He felt a fine tremor where he held her.

Chris slipped a hand around to the small of her back and rubbed his fingers back and forth. He took her glass and set it aside, then traced the scars on her face and neck. "They're fading," he said, and smiled. "If you were a man you'd probably think they added to your sex appeal."

She pursed her lips.

"Geez," he said, shaking his head. "I mean, men and women look at their own scars differently. I'm so grateful you were thrown out of that car."

"Are you?" Now she even sounded shaky.

Later he was going to wonder what he'd thought he was doing here. Later. "I'd have hated not to meet you, Sonnie. You make me feel calm."

"You're a strange man. Being around a woman whose skating a fine line herself makes you feel calm?"

"Yeah," he said, and knew his response was belligerent. "Yeah, it does. With you. I've skated that line, too. That's how I got here. Everything I believed in blew up in my face. In a way I crashed and burned. Maybe I should rethink that comment. I lost my focus; then I dropped out. I'm not sure I'll ever be ready to step back in again."

"It's easier to give up than it is to fight," she said quietly. "But if we all give up, what then?"

"I don't know. Or maybe I do and I don't want to think about it. I'm lucky; I've got Roy, and he never lets me forget I owe him. Gives me some focus. Why are we getting so deep here?"

She shrugged. "I don't know."

"You're being polite. You know I started it."

"I need a friend, too."

A friend. She needed a friend—preferably one with investigative skills—to help her. "You need a friend you can trust," he said. "But I don't appeal to you."

Instantly he felt her stiffen. She looked at her hands, then slowly set them along each side of his head. Her serious eyes regarded him so intently, he swallowed and heard the sound.

He didn't resist, didn't want to resist when she pulled his face against her and gently stroked his hair. "Is this what you mean?" she asked. "You don't think I've thought of holding you, and of being held by you?"

"I guess." His face rested on her ribs. She smelled faintly of lemons.

"You do appeal to me, but you shouldn't. And I shouldn't do anything about it anyway."

"You feel so good. I'm not—" No, he would not tell her he was more muddled than he remembered being, ever. "Can it be dangerous for us to find some peace with each other? Some comfort?"

She moved in closer and massaged his shoulders. When he made to raise his head, she pushed it to her again. "You know the answers to your questions," she told him. "It's dangerous, Chris."

"Do you care?"

One of her knees pressed where he might like it to press, but not where it did anything to help him think clearly.

"Do you care if this is dangerous, Sonnie?"

"I don't want to analyze what I feel, or what I think. It would take too long to tell you all about my marriage. And even if it wouldn't, I'm not ready. This is strange. You and I don't match. At least, I don't think we do. You're a man who should be with someone . . . someone like Billy, I guess."

He put both of his arms around her and hugged. "Oh, no. Shows what lousy instincts you've got. I know my type, and she's not it. You are." Maybe if he'd met her . . . if he'd met her years ago, she'd have been too young for him, and he wouldn't have been ready for her.

"So strange," she murmured. "Frank was—is a good look-ing man, but I know why he chose me. What he needed in a woman—no, a wife—was different from what he needed. . . ."

When she didn't finish what she'd begun, he let her be. He could figure out the rest on his own. Frank Giacano's reputation with women was a legend all its own. Chris held her even tighter.

She held him firmly, yet gently.

"You need comfort," he said. "That's what this is all about. I can give you that, so take it."

She leaned away enough to urge his face up. Her first kiss skimmed his forehead softly. Before his eyes had completely closed, her lips touched his. When he could think straight again, he'd tell her that any man who didn't find her sexy was beyond help. She opened his mouth slightly, passed the tip of her tongue along the underside of his upper lip, and breathed in an uneven rhythm that made him sweat.

Chris pulled the bottom of her shirt out of her pants and smoothed her skin. He felt the raised edges of intersecting scars, and she froze with her mouth fused to his.

He removed his hands and held her upper arms instead.

He'd be happy to die with this kiss on his lips. He didn't want it to stop.

It didn't stop, but Chris knew the instant she felt how hard he was. Gripping his shoulders, she dug in her fingertips and was careful to keep her legs still.

When she paused for breath and he could see her face and her blush, he said, "Sorry about that," and grimaced.

She said, "I'm not sorry, but I don't know what to do about it."

He didn't feel like laughing, but he laughed just the same. Time to do some kissing of his own. With a hand behind her neck, he kissed her hard enough to be pretty sure she wasn't thinking what she should do about anything. And while he kissed her, he undid her shirt and tucked his fingers into the cups of her bra. A little skin to skin in there and she forgot to hold still. If he didn't want to forget himself altogether, he'd better be careful.

"You're something," he told her, and pressed kisses into the delicate swell of her breasts above the bra. The small, heart-shaped locket rested against her faintly freckled skin. He fingered it briefly, then delved a little deeper inside her bra. "Is this okay?"

He couldn't see her face, but she said, "Mm."

Once more he put his hands on her back. She jerked away.

"Okay," he said. "Let's get this out of the way." He took hold of her waist and spun her around. Before she could do anything to stop him, he tossed up her shirt.

She struggled to break free.

"Stop it," he told her. "Stand still and let me look. I guess if that window had been all the way open you'd be less messed up, but you'd probably have hit your head a whole lot harder."

"Please don't."

"Grow up," he said, and regretted each word. "Sorry. That wasn't anything I wanted to say. But stop overreacting, will you? You've got a lovely body. You turn me on, just looking at you. Scars and all." And he tried to prove his point by mapping those scars with the tip of his tongue and his lips.

And he shifted his hands to her ribs, then around to cover her breasts.

The glass in that window had left a wide swath of wounds, healed to bumpy red, over the left side of her back. And he didn't give a damn.

"I never look at it," she whispered. "It's not important, but I know it isn't pretty. Please don't touch it. I don't want you to feel . . . You're a good man, Chris Talon, but no man wants to touch that. He certainly doesn't want to kiss it. But thank you."

The anger he felt unnerved him. He rested his brow on her spine and worked at stopping himself from snapping at her.

"Chris?"

"For this moment . . . I know we shouldn't do anything about it. At least not now. But for this moment could we stop second-guessing what we think and just enjoy being with each other? You feel so good to me. And you look so good to me."

He didn't care if she answered him. He stood up and pulled her shirt from her arms. Then he unhooked her bra and tossed it aside. Her breasts fit into his hands like dreams. Kissing the back of her neck brought him too close to the edge for comfort, but he kept right on inching closer.

Sonnie raised her arms and reached back to put her hands behind his neck. She rested her head against his shoulder and arched her back.

"Yes," he said, passing his thumbs over her nipples, "this is you, isn't it? The real you. And I'm the lucky schmuck who gets to be with you when you come alive again."

"I never was alive before," she said. "Except for Jacqueline."

"Jacqueline?"

She stayed where she was, leaning against him, but grew so still. "No one you know. I don't know why I said that. We'd better stop."

Why, oh, why? He wanted to keep right on going. "If that's what you want."

"It's not what I want. It's what's got to be."

"Okay." Chris turned her to face him and managed not to

smile when she showed signs of wanting to cover herself. "What a pretty lady. What pretty breasts. I'd love to kiss them, but I guess that doesn't come under the headin' of stoppin' this."

She met his eyes. "No, it doesn't."

"Think you'd like to start it again soon?"

"What I'd like and what I'm going to do are two different things."

He lifted one corner of his mouth. "I expected you to say that." She had dimples in her cheeks, close to the corners of her mouth, and he tapped each one. "But you won't try to run away from me, will you?"

She took a deep breath. He was just a man and he appreciated seeing her small breasts rise. God, give him the strength to resist.

"If we can forget what we just did, I'd really like us to be friends. I like you, Chris."

He managed a cheery smile and didn't say the first thing that came into his head: that he was never going to forget the way she looked, naked to the waist in front of him. He also wouldn't say that the only thing that would be better would be to get rid of the rest of her clothes—and his—and stretch her pale body out, beneath, beside, on top, or any other way as long as it was against his on the bed.

"Chris?" With one fingertip, she touched first one, then his other nipple. She pinched lightly—and looked surprised when he sucked air through his teeth. "You don't believe me, do you?"

Concentrating didn't come easily while she finger-combed the hair on his chest.

"You don't believe there's really anything for me to be worried about. You think I'm still messed up from the accident. In my head, I mean."

He took firm hold of her hands, held them up, and kissed each palm. "If I thought that, I wouldn't have decided we're going to work together on figuring out what's going on, would I?"

Sonnie checked out his eyes. Right now they were more

green than hazel, and they were concentrating so hard on her that she found it hard not to look away. "You're going to take me on."

His one-sided grin brought a flush to her skin—her naked skin. "Thank you," she said, and tried to figure out a graceful way to retrieve her bra and shirt. "I don't know how to thank you enough."

The grin was there again. He was laughing at her. She tried to scowl, a warning scowl. *Don't say what you're thinking,* was the warning.

"Okay," he said. "Don't worry about thanking me—yet. Let's see how things progress first, shall we?"

Before she could even attempt a smart comeback, a scrabbling came from the door.

Chris crossed his arms. "Killer."

In the act of sweeping up her clothes, Sonnie faltered. "What did you say?"

"It's Killer. Alias the moocher. He's adopted me."

He went to the door and Sonnie managed to get into her bra and start putting on her shirt before a rangy orange cat erupted from the darkness, bringing a strong gust of warm wind with him.

Sonnie heard a voice call, "Chris, Chris. Hold it right there."

Chris looked at her and she struggled to finish putting on her shirt and stuffing it into her pants. He smiled at her, and her legs, predictably, felt weak.

"We've got a lot of talking to do," he told her. "Can I take you home and get started?"

She'd be a smart woman to say no. "Sure." If being reserved and alone was smart, then she'd been too smart for too long. Look where it had gotten her.

"I hung up and said I'd come find you," Roy said, bursting into the little guest house. "We've got to get a move on. I'll drive."

"Hey, bro," Chris said mildly.

"Can it," Roy said, looking not at Chris, but at Sonnie. "Got a call, Sonnie. There's a fire at your place."

Thirteen

Roy met them across the street from Sonnie's house. "What the Sam Hill took you so long?"

"You know I don't believe in breaking laws," Chris said in what sounded like a strained voice.

Still sitting behind him, and hanging on to his jean jacket, Sonnie felt too wobbly to move. The helmet she wore was too heavy and caused every sound to reach her through a fuzz. Chris had also insisted she put on one of his jackets for the ride. Even rolled up several times, the sleeves covered her hands.

Firemen, their heavy coats flapping, scuffed between hoses that stretched from three trucks to lie like discarded umbilical cords. Little groups of people stood watching and whispering. A searchlight shone on the upper right area of the house where the stucco was charred black and peeled away in chunks from the timbers beneath. The tiled roof sagged at the corner, and a jagged hole had opened to the sky. Pieces of burned and shattered wood protruded from what had been the storage room window.

Keeping a hold on Chris's back, Sonnie climbed from the Harley.

Her knees began to buckle and Roy grabbed her by the waist.

"Does that ever happen to you?" she asked him. "You can't feel your legs when you get off?" She giggled.

Roy gathered her up, pulling her hands from Chris's jacket. "It doesn't happen because I'm not fool enough t'get on that fool thing. You should have come with me. Take some deep breaths, Sonnie. You're all shaken up."

She didn't remind him he'd told Chris to bring her, and rushed away. How strange to want to laugh when a big chunk of your house was destroyed, much of it lying in a pile of rubble on the front lawn. Hysterical? Oh, she wasn't going to admit to that. No. Absolutely not. She couldn't catch her breath.

"Hold on." Chris had kicked the bike stand on. He took her from Roy and bent to look into her face. "We need to go over and talk to the folks, then take a look-see at the house."

"Bad luck," she said, smiling up at him until her eyes watered and his face blurred. "Everything I touch is bad luck. No, that sounds like a bunch of self-pity. And it's not true, I've had a lot of—"

"We need to talk to the firemen."

"I've had good luck, haven't I? Is everything as much of a mess as it seems?"

He held her by the back of her neck and shook her gently. "You've had good and bad luck. More bad luck than could possibly be good for one woman. But I don't think the mess is so bad. I . . . I want to help. I've told you I will."

"You have?" Roy sounded outrageously bright. "Well, hell, if that isn't the best news I've heard in a long time."

"Swearing, Roy," Sonnie said. "And you're jumping to conclusions."

"So," Chris said, "my first inkling about the cuss code at the Nail."

Sonnie didn't get it, but neither did she ask for an explanation.

"You said you're gonna help her," Roy said to his brother as if Sonnie didn't exist. "That means you're taking on her case? Does it?"

Chris shot an arm around Sonnie's waist and all but carried her across the road. "That's what it means," he said over his shoulder. "But if you say a word to a soul about it, I will cut off parts of you that will hurt and . . . Well, Sam Hill, we just won't like you very much anymore."

"My lips are sealed and my legs are crossed," Roy said. "I think this man coming is the one who was asking for you, Sonnie. He's a big son of a gun, but don't worry; Chris and I can take him between us if we have to."

Boots scraping gravel, a fireman who'd discarded his coat approached in a rubberized bib overall. Soot smeared his face, and in the white light of the giant lamp his eyes were bright blue. "Don't suppose you're Sonnie Giacano?"

"She is," Roy said. "She works for me at the Rusty Nail. You know the place—on Duval."

"I know it, sir."

"Bring all your boys by. The drinks'll be on me."

"Thank you, sir. I'll do that."

Sonnie didn't need a translator to figure out that Roy was making sure the fireman didn't have any more questions about why she was getting home so late. "It's pretty bad, huh?" she said.

"Could have been a whole lot worse. I guess you stored a lot of stuff in that room. Fire started there. We don't know why yet. Destroyed that, and the small bathroom next to it. The other side of the house is pretty much untouched. Up and down."

Sonnie felt suddenly cold, and she looked upward. "The skylight over the entry hall? Did it break?"

"I don't know." The fireman turned around and shouted to one of his men.

"Yoo-hoo." Just Ena's familiar voice—ratcheted up a notch or three or four—preceded her arrival by a second or so. "Oh, Sonnie. Oh, my dear, dear friend. When is it going to be enough? One might think the Fates were against you. You must come and stay with me. I insist."

Sonnie smiled at her and leaned closer to Chris, who wasn't listening to Ena.

The second fireman came at a rustling trot. "I think we've got it, Chief. Just punching a few holes."

Sonnie squirmed at *punching a few holes.*

"Skylight over the entryway?" the chief said. "Did it blow?"

"Er—no, no, it didn't. Not enough heat built up. Lucky we got the alarm so early."

"I called in," Ena said cheerfully. "Couldn't sleep as usual, so I was taking a turn around my yard and I saw smoke puffing out of the open window. Rushed inside my place and called."

The chief's white grin made his filth-streaked face very appealing. "You're Mrs. Fishbine? I'd say you saved the place. In fact, I know you did."

Glancing in all directions, Ena simpered with pleasure.

"Did you lose something, ma'am?" one of the firemen asked.

Ena shook her head. "Just surveying the scene. Isn't that what you people do sometimes, survey the scene?"

The man laughed and said, "Always, ma'am. You'd better watch out. Get too familiar with the lingo and we'll have to sign you on."

Ena batted his arm and smiled. Some women, Sonnie thought, would never stop being coquettish.

"I want to go inside," she said. "Is that okay now?"

"Nope," she was told. "Probably won't be okay till tomorrow. We'll want to check everything out thoroughly, make sure the fire doesn't break out again. Then there's the question of security. Wouldn't want you living in the place till everything's battened down again. Do you have somewhere to go, or should we—"

"She'll come to me," Ena said.

"You're a good woman," Roy said, and Sonnie didn't miss the glance that passed between him and Chris, "but Sonnie's always got a place with my partner and me. Her own suite of rooms. We make her keep them lived in, anyway, so this'll fill her obligation for a little while. But thank you anyways."

Ena's smile had evaporated. "Did I ask you, sir? No, I did not. Friends stick together and I insist."

"Sonnie's a good friend of ours," Roy said, as if patience was costing him a good deal. "Of course, it's up to you, though," he said, as if just remembering Sonnie might have an opinion.

"You're a dear, Ena, but it'll be easier for me to be at the Nail. This is a strain, and my life will be simplified if I stay there."

Chris's hand spread to hold her side. He squeezed, but when she looked up at him she wasn't sure he even knew what he'd done.

"Well, of course," Ena said. "I understand perfectly. I just want you to know you aren't on your own here."

The arrival of a white Jag with very dark windows was a blessed diversion.

"Hey," the fire chief called out, bearing down on the driver's window. "Not there. No. No! Goddamn it, not in the driveway, you moron."

"Arrogant . . ." Chris pointed. "Will you look at that? He's gonna park right in the middle of the driveway."

"Oh, Romano," Sonnie said. "He's not thinking."

"He's a pushy son of a bitch," Chris murmured. "I don't believe this. He's determined to drive right over those fu—"

"Hoses," Roy said rapidly. "He can't drive over them. Even if he makes it, it won't do his fancy car any good."

Romano parked, head-on, between two fire trucks. With the front end of the car partway on the sidewalk, and the rear sticking out into the street, he threw open his door and a stream of Italian poured forth.

Another siren sounded in the distance, growing closer by the second. Then Sonnie heard another, and another. She groped for Chris's hand. "Is that more fire vehicles? Why, if the fire's out?"

"Not fire," Chris said. "Police. But I doubt if they're coming here."

"Sonnie," Romano yelled. "Get over here now. Tell this man to remove himself from my face. He is in my face. Tell him who I am."

Chris showed signs of restraining her, but she said, "Best

if I go. I'll be fine," and walked across the street. "This is Romano Giacano, sir. My brother-in-law."

"I am also an internationally renowned tennis coach," Romano stated. "I am a busy and important man. I am in Key West to take care of my sister-in-law, whose husband, my brother, is missing. She is not herself and requires my assistance. Now I wish to inspect the premises."

Four firemen now stood in a line across the driveway. In response to a shout from the house, the chief had left

Chris and Roy ambled up with Ena trotting in their wake. They stood at a short distance but the two men radiated hostility.

"Sonnie, my pet, we cannot allow these fire people to interfere with our wishes." Romano spoke as if she were a child.

"These people just stopped my house from burning to the ground," she told him. "They responded fast enough to do a great job of limiting the damage."

"It doesn't look to me as if there is so little damage. Sonnie—oh, no, I will not plant seeds."

"What?" she said, inclining her head. "What seeds?"

He lowered his voice. "Did you start smoking again?"

"Smoking?" Completely bemused, she frowned. "I don't smoke."

"No, my dear, at least I didn't think you had started again."

"I never smoked, Romano. What are you talking about?"

"Ah." He sucked in his lips, then shrugged. "Forget I mentioned it."

"No. What do you mean?"

"You have forgotten that you smoked until . . . I don't wish to bring up unpleasant memories, but you smoked until you were pregnant."

"I *didn't*."

He sighed. "Very well, you didn't. It is of no importance, anyway. I just wondered if you could have had a little accident up there."

"She hasn't been here," Chris said. "And she doesn't smoke. Anything else?"

Romano jutted his chin and moved close to Chris. "You

are not needed here. This is a family matter. This is my brother's house.''

Chris stepped around him.

''And my house,'' Sonnie said, and managed not to wilt under Romano's shocked glare. She looked away from him and at the damaged area of the house once more. ''That room again,'' she murmured.

Chris's breath against her ear was warm, clean, intimate. ''Don't say anything else, please. Okay?''

She nodded, and avoided Romano's stare.

''Good girl. Keep cool and we'll get through this. I'm with you. But we keep what I was and what I do under our hats. Remember that.''

She nodded again, and touched his jaw.

Romano took hold of her arm roughly. ''You are not yourself. I will take you back to the club with me.''

''I don't need this,'' Sonnie said.

The sirens were no longer distant. Revolving lights swept across the houses on either side of the street. The first vehicle belonged to the fire department, but was different from any Sonnie had seen before. This was followed by three police cars. Men spilled forth and formed huddles with some of the firemen.

''Hah,'' Romano said. ''Such a provincial place. They have nothing to do so they *all* come to a fire that is already, *poof*, nothing.''

Roy cleared his throat and said, ''What d'you think, bro?''

''Trouble,'' was all Chris said. ''Arson team could be routine here for all I know. But we've got a lot of cops on the scene, huh?''

''That's what I thought.''

''You're going to upset Sonnie,'' Romano said, then seemed to notice Ena for the first time. ''You should stay back, madam. With the rest of the crowd.''

Ena said, ''Twit,'' very succinctly and remained where she was.

Sonnie grinned at her, and received a gleeful smile in return. Sonnie told Romano, ''This is my friend Ena. She lives next door. And she reported the fire or there probably wouldn't be anything left of the house."

Carrying equipment and followed by the entourage of police, the man and three women from the first vehicle trudged up the driveway and into the house.

But for sounds from onlookers, minutes passed in silence for Sonnie. None of the others spoke.

A police officer appeared on the front steps once more. He began unwinding crime scene tape across the veranda steps.

"Why would he do that?" Ena said. "It's to make people stay out, isn't it?"

"They must think it's arson," Sonnie said slowly. Fire. It could have been another attempt to frighten her away.

Or to kill her.

Spinning around, she walked into Chris's chest. Sounding almost impassive, he said quietly, "I'm asking you to keep it together. Don't give anyone any ammunition. We don't want to give some whiz kid—or someone with an agenda—an excuse to say you're acting strangely. I've got a hunch some people would just love to pin that little fire on you, then use it as an excuse to get you to a place where no one even heard of Key West. For your own good, of course. To rest. And just to remind you, whatever happens, do *not* say I'm an investigator of any kind, or that I'm working for you."

"They're putting that tape everywhere," Ena said loudly. "Will you look at that? I bet that kid never got a chance to use the stuff before. Looks like he's playing cat's cradle or something."

Ducking the tape, a man in a suit and a straw fedora ran down the front steps and made straight for the group beside the Jaguar. He pointed to the car and said, "I want that out of the way. Now."

Roy said, "I'd do it if I were you, Romano, old buddy. You're lookin' at the law—I can recognize it, y'know, had practice—and he's prayin' one of us gives him a reason to slap us in irons."

"Move it," the man demanded, and snapped his fingers.

Romano's nonchalant walk to his car must have taken willpower—he was definitely jerky. He got in, gunned the engine, and backed up.

The man in the straw fedora reached Roy, Chris, Ena, and Sonnie. He pushed the hat back on his head and smiled, showing a wide space between his two upper front teeth. "Mrs. Giacano?"

"That's me," Sonnie said.

"Detective Kraus," he said. "I need a word. Alone, please."

She nodded and followed him under the tape that crossed the end of the driveway now. He took her by the arm and led her closer to the house.

"The fire's out," he said. "I understand you've been told to spend at least tonight elsewhere. That's a good idea. You may want to make that more than a night. Because of the odor, if nothing else."

"I've already made arrangements," she said, starting to relax a little.

"You've only been here a few weeks, is that right?"

"I've only been back a few weeks. I lived here for three years before—"

"Your accident. Yes, we have all that information. Recovered any memory of the event, have you?"

Nausea flowed in, all but overwhelming Sonnie. "No." She couldn't explain the bits and pieces that almost came clear.

"Okay. Sorry for your trouble." Before she could thank him, he continued, "Living here alone, are you?"

"Yes."

"You sure? We don't shock easy, Mrs. Giacano. And we don't judge. You need company, that's your business."

"No," she said, and knew she was protesting too loudly. "No, Detective Kraus. There's just me here."

"Think carefully. You didn't let someone stay for a few days? Someone who was passing through, maybe?"

She remembered to breathe. "No. Why are you asking me these questions? You're making me nervous and defensive."

"Well, ma'am, if you're telling the truth and you've got nothing to hide, there's no need for any of that, is there?"

Sonnie didn't like him. "I guess not."

"Okay. I'll get to the point. We're going to need you to come down to the station on Angel Street with us."

She needed to sit down. Sonnie cast around, then looked at the grass.

"Sonnie?" It was Chris who shouted. He jumped over the tape and sprinted across the debris-scattered lawn. "I'm the lady's friend," he called to the detective.

To Sonnie's horror, Kraus produced a gun and leveled it at Chris. "Hands up. Keep 'em where I can see 'em. And back away," Kraus said.

Instantly Chris's hands went up.

"This is my friend," Sonnie said, "and I want him with me. Put that nasty thing away, please."

"Stay where you are," Kraus said. "Gimme your name."

"Chris Talon."

"From?"

"Most recently, Duval Street. Sonnie's a good friend and she also works for my brother."

"You don't say. Okay, but keep your hands where they are."

Chris followed directions and stood beside Sonnie.

"I'm waiting for another officer to join me. Then we'll be driving Mrs. Giacano to the station."

"What the hell for?" Chris asked.

Sonnie heard Romano's voice, raised again, but he showed no sign of following Chris onto the grounds. For that she was grateful.

The officer Detective Kraus was waiting for arrived, breathless and leafing through a notebook, stopping to scribble a word here and there.

"Whatcha got?" Kraus said.

"It's affirmative. Corpse under the cave-in. Poor bastard never made it out of his sleeping bag."

Fourteen

Officious little punks.

Had he ever been like that? That pumped up? Capable of picking on a woman he didn't know and pushing her around even when he could see it was like pushing a kitten, or a kid—a one hundred percent one-sided confrontation?

Had he been like that?

Maybe. At least once, even though the situation had been so different.

He couldn't go back there, not tonight. Tonight he'd made promises he had to keep.

They'd put her in the back of a vehicle for the drive to the station. No, they couldn't let her come in on her own. *Shee-it.* Big men protecting themselves against one dangerous unarmed unknown quantity—approximate weight, 110. Record? Zero.

And now he had to go in there—fast—and keep his head. If he lost it, even for a second, he'd lose any advantage he might be able to use for her. *Bumbler.* Yeah, that was a good one. Not-too-bright bumbler. Cheerful . . .

"Who's there?" He'd been too engrossed in watching Sonnie taken from the car into the building, too engrossed in talking himself down, to sense what he should have sensed at once. Someone was nearby, watching him.

"A friend," said a familiar voice. "Don't you know how to stay away from these places even when you don't belong there, schmuck?"

Chris glanced from the lighted windows to the rangy figure that stepped from the shadow of a wall. "Flynn? For . . . What the fuck are you doin' here? I don't have time to argue with you now."

"Ah, ever the grateful, charming Talon. Keep it zipped a second, you ace schmuck, and I'll get a chance to say you worried me when you called, so I decided to take what miserable little R and R I've got coming and use it on you."

"Touching. How'd you find me?"

Laughing, Flynn came closer, his teeth white in the darkness. "I drove. Thanks for asking. And yeah, I left a few hours after we talked. And you're welcome. I figure we owe each other more than one or two good ones. And your brother's too good for you. I know what's going down. I don't know why you're going out on a limb for the woman, but that's your business. You're going in there now, aren't you? How're you going to handle it?"

The reason they'd made such a great team was because they'd developed the magic some cops only dreamed about. They knew each other's minds. "Cheerful, bumbling buddy, I thought. No way do they find out who I used to be."

"What you are, you mean? Okay, okay, save the violent thoughts till you need 'em. Let's go."

"You're not coming."

"The hell I'm not. I can be a bumbling charmer."

Chris slapped Flynn on the shoulder. "Look, friend. I'm glad you're here. Or I'm sure I will be in time. You'd confuse Sonnie—not that it might take much. Roy's gone back to the Nail. You know your way. I should have remembered that. Wait for me there, huh?"

Flynn didn't waste time arguing. He grunted and turned away. "Make sure you don't forget to bumble," he said. "You're right. Letting the local boys get a whiff of NYPD might be a nasty idea. See ya."

"Sure," Chris muttered, already on his way to find Sonnie.

The initial shock of knowing Flynn was around had passed. It couldn't hurt to have official access to information.

But Flynn and the other—the stuff that had to stay gone—they were tied together. That *could* hurt.

Inside the pink stucco building he had to stop himself from looking too at home. He followed arrows pointing to "Detectives" up flights of stairs to a floor artfully tiled in pink and turquoise. Tiled a long, long time ago. Sure, the place was pedestrian compared to what his slice of law enforcement had been all about, but the air held the same heady aroma of dust, sweat, aggression, and hopelessness. Hell, where was the vast used-furniture warehouse that must supply crappy standard issue to every precinct in the country? How come the voices sounded the same no matter the city or cast of characters? Cussing, whining, sniveling. The great universal language of trouble.

He arrived in a tiny anteroom where a wooden half door separated him from whatever action was in play.

"Hey," he said, stuffing his hands in his pockets and waiting for a cop with his heels on a cluttered desk to move his face from behind a copy of *True Crime*.

After the required period of silence, the guy lowered his magazine and looked at Chris through a pair of wire-framed glasses with lenses that were just big enough to cover his pupils. "Hey, yourself," he said, deadpan.

"Is it always this busy in the middle of the night?" Chris asked, repeating a question he'd heard too many times. "Just joking." He heard the law at work, but only the policeman was in sight.

The officer concentrated hard on ripping another strip from an already punished thumbnail. When he'd examined his efforts, he said, "Is there something I can do to help you, sir?" and whipped Chris's cynical superiority away. "Works best if you just ignore all that back there. Takes all kinds, and we get all kinds. You learn not to notice."

When Chris collected himself, he said, "Sounds like good advice." Then he remembered he was supposed to be not very bright, but pleasant. "I'm lookin' for a friend of mine. A lady.

Her house caught on fire. I don't really understand why, but they said she had to come here so they could talk to her about it.''

The cop, whose name tag identified him as Guntrum, swung his feet to the floor. He kept on smiling, but the almost gentle expression on his face sharpened. "Your name, sir?" he asked.

"Talon," he said, "Chris Talon." He just had to hope they didn't dream up a reason to run any checks on him. He wasn't about to assume any names—not anymore.

"Don't I know that name?" the cop said.

Chris managed not to groan aloud. "Roy Talon's my brother. The Rusty Nail on Duval? He and his partner own it."

"Oh, sure. Roy. Good guy. Let me go see if I can find out what Detective Kraus's up to."

Chris watched him walk away. So much for thinking anyone had heard of Chris Talon, supercop—superscrewup.

Several familiar officers came in and filed past Chris. The men were familiar because they'd been at Sonnie's house tonight, and they would soon be huddled, putting pieces of their puzzle together and deciding who would do what, how, and why.

Guntrum returned. He wasn't smiling anymore. "Seems the detective's got a burr up his ass," he said conversationally. "He certainly knows where he'd like to see my ass—and everyone else's. Guess he hasn't had a whole lot of sleep lately."

The son of a bitch was losing it around Sonnie. Chris stuffed his anger far enough down to say, "That can be hard on a person, Officer," with all the Southern charm he'd never learned at his daddy's knee. "I surely would like to be with my friend Sonnie. She's a sensitive little thing. I'm kinda like her brother. She relies on me."

Guntrum frowned and nodded. He came around his desk and patted Chris down. "She doesn't look great. I mean, she doesn't look too well. Nice-looking woman." He checked over his shoulder and lowered his voice. "Corridor on the right." He inclined his head. "Office at the end. I must have stepped out. You're just looking for your friend, okay?"

Chris could have hugged the man for his common sense—and his decency. "You've got it, Officer," he said. "She hasn't been arrested, has she?"

"Not as far as I know. I can't see any reason she can't have a friend with her. I'd sure do what you're doing if she were my friend."

Yeah, no doubt. "Thanks." Chris ambled toward the corridor. He felt a stab of irritation at the thought of Officer Guntrum being attracted to Sonnie. But she was attractive, damn it, and Chris Talon didn't have any right to feel proprietary toward her.

Most doors were open to the offices that lined the corridor. Not the one at the far end, the one that didn't do much to soften a raised male voice on the other side.

Chris set his teeth and speeded up, prepared to be stopped at any moment.

He made it to Detective Kraus's nameplate and knocked.

"Yeah?" The guy would make some marine sergeant. And bumbling was getting a whole lot harder for Chris.

He opened the door, stuck his head inside, and looked straight at Detective Kraus. "There you are, Officer."

"Detective."

"Oh, yeah. Sorry. Detective. Geez, it's tough to find someone in here. I never had any idea how many people a guy like you commands." *Command* should be a word Kraus relished. "Kinda found my way. All those little rooms those guys work in look like jail cells. Hey, there, Sonnie. How's it goin'? Need some company?"

She appeared almost transparent, and no blue eyes had ever been that dark—not that he'd seen. She held out a hand to him. "You okay, kid?" he said, planning murderous things for Kraus. A dark night, a quiet place, and the little Nazi would never look the same.

"Get out," Kraus said. "We got an investigation going on here. You'll be given your moment. But not here and now. And for your information, this used to be the jail and those offices *were* jail cells. They're plenty big enough."

Sonnie's hand remained outstretched and Chris took hold

of her cold fingers. He smiled at her and rubbed her icy skin. "Don't you worry, okay? The officer doesn't understand. This is probably what they call circumstances. You live in a house that had a fire and a poor man died in the fire there. The officer's just asking routine questions. Right, Officer?"

"Detective. I don't need your help here. What was your name?"

"Chris. I was there at the house with Sonnie. I brought her back after she heard about the fire."

"Nice of you. Now get out until you're told someone wants to talk to you."

Chris frowned. "But I was told it's okay for me to be with Sonnie now. She hasn't done anything wrong, so you're just talking to her, right? She hasn't been well, you know, Officer. She had a terrible accident—"

"We know all about that. We know about that and a lot of other stuff. Mrs. Giacano isn't living a simple life."

Sonnie ground their fingers together, but when he studied her face, although he saw she was scared, he also saw she was determined.

"I want you to stay with me. I'm not arrested, am I?"

"Not yet," Kraus said.

"This is what's called cooperating with the police," Chris said. "I've read that lots of times. That's why they could put you in that car, I suppose, although I don't know why I couldn't have brought you."

"You don't have to know," Kraus said. "Wait out front."

"If he goes, I go," Sonnie said, standing up. "Chris is my friend. I trust him. You didn't do any of that rights business. Should I get a lawyer? What would I say you're charging me with?"

The asshole had the grace to turn red.

"We're not charging you with anything yet. It's just easier to talk one-on-one at this point. Iron things out nice and easy. Casual. Friendly."

Friendly like a poisonous snake, Chris thought. Keeping his act up wasn't easy, but Sonnie was worth it. "You're so right," he said to Kraus. "I always say there's a nice way to do things, and a nasty way. Nice is nicer—cleaner.'' All suitably bumbling affability, he sat in a chair beside Sonnie's and grinned engagingly at Kraus. "So what's the theory? Who was that poor guy? How'd he get into Sonnie's house?"

Kraus's red face turned slightly blue. "Look, I'm trying to be understanding here, but you're pushing me. I'm the one who asks the questions. Got that?"

"Oh, yes. Oh, I surely do, Officer."

The detective rolled his eyes but didn't bother to correct Chris again.

There was a knock at the door and a detective entered. He dropped a file on Kraus's desk and said, "Preliminary, but interesting," before retreating.

Kraus opened the file and tipped his chair back. He leafed through papers, and Chris was almost sure the guy would like to smirk. "Where were you this evening, Mrs. Giacano?"

"I already told you that."

"Tell me again."

"I worked at the Rusty Nail on Duval Street."

Kraus looked at her. He unwrapped a toothpick and gripped it between his teeth. He chewed, and each time the pick worked its way into the gap between his front teeth, he used his tongue to work it out again.

"When the call came in, Roy—that's my brother—Roy told us and I drove Sonnie to her house."

"So I've been told. Mrs. Giacano, how about the time between when you stopped working and when you showed up at your house, ma'am?"

Sonnie still held Chris's hand and her grip grew tighter and tighter. "What do you mean?"

"You left the bar about an hour before we got the word from the fire department that there could be something we needed to look at. Where were you in that hour?"

Chris felt the moment when Sonnie stopped being totally intimidated and became angry instead. "How do you know all that? How would you know when I left the bar and for how long?"

Kraus smiled. "We have our sources."

"You mean you've got someone with nothing better to do than watch a woman who should be of absolutely no interest to you?"

Chris started an inner mantra: *Patience, patience, patience.* His lady had cottoned to his act immediately. They would do fine as long as he didn't blow it.

His lady?

Kraus had assumed a pained but tolerant demeanor. "I know this must be difficult to understand. Police work is very complicated and precise."

Shee-it. Chris chewed his tongue.

"We have many kinds of sources. We got a tip. We rely on tips a great deal. This was a call saying that someone was afraid you should probably be watched but that they didn't know just where you were."

"Watch Sonnie?" Chris said. Forrest Gump would be proud of him. He looked at Sonnie and leaned a little closer. "I wouldn't blame anyone for wanting to watch Sonnie, but not because she's some sort of dangerous person. She's the best, Officer. Absolutely the best."

"I'm sure she is. What do you do for a living, sir?"

Chris lowered his eyes. "I'm kinda between gigs. Unless you count playing at the Nail now and then. I'm a pianist."

"Real go-getter, huh?"

"We all have hard times," Chris said, managing a petulant tone. "Sometimes things get slow and I come down to be with Roy for a few weeks."

"You live with your brother?"

"I live in the place he's got out back of the Nail."

Kraus made a few notes. "Where were you between the time when you left the bar and when you arrived at your house, Mrs. Giacano?"

Chris was going to enjoy thinking about where she'd been, but for now he had to think of some words to form an alibi without giving Mr. Personality an excuse to leer. "Sonnie was with me. I was in the bar and invited her back to my place to talk. We talk a lot, don't we, Sonnie?"

He wished the soft face she turned on him was for real rather than an act.

"We do," she said. "Chris helps me see things clearly. He makes me forget some of the things that are on my mind."

"I'll just bet he does."

Bastard. Chris didn't say a word.

"Oh, he does," Sonnie said, still studying Chris.

She really did have a mouth that made a man want to feel it on his. Particularly once he'd already felt it on his.

"Then Roy came to tell us about the fire and we went over there. That poor man. I just can't think where he came from or who he might be. But I've got to tell you something, Detective Kraus."

"You do?" He leaned way forward over his desk. "You can say anything to me. You just take your time."

"Well, it's just that it feels horrible to think of a stranger being able to get into your house and set themselves up in your storage room. Why would someone do a thing like that?"

Chris wouldn't advise Kraus to play poker. Disappointment made his shoulders sag. "We don't know yet, but we will. Did someone see you go with Mr. Talon?"

"Oh, I'm sure lots of people saw us leave the bar," Sonnie said.

"And you can prove you were in his—wherever he lives— the whole time that's unaccounted for."

Chris couldn't remain silent a moment longer. "The time wasn't unaccounted for. We already told you, Sonnie was with me, and Roy found us there."

Kraus returned to the folder. "They're doing an autopsy now."

Sonnie shivered. "He died in the fire. Maybe he was a vagrant who got inside somehow."

"We don't think so. We think he wanted to be there, and he intended to sleep, but there's nothing about him to suggest he's a bum. You're surrounded by a mystery, Mrs. Giacano. Your husband . . . well, he disappeared under suspicious circumstances."

"He was abducted by terrorists."

"So they say. No ransom demands, though?"

"No."

"That qualifies as strange. These people may not be big at returning victims, but they're real big on extorting money for corpses."

"That'll do," Chris said before he could stop himself. "You're out of line. She doesn't deserve this."

Kraus's gaze became speculative. "Would I be wrong if I suggested your friendship with the lady goes beyond sharing cookies and warm milk?"

"You'd be wrong if you suggested anything about our friendship," Chris said. "It's none of your business. You're out of line."

"He's just doing his job, Chris," Sonnie said, quietly and calmly enough to shame him. "We've had a bad night, Detective Kraus."

"We all have," the man said with no shred of graciousness.

A commotion outside erupted into the entrance of Billy Keith with Dr. Jim at her shoulder. Chris looked at the ceiling and prayed the woman wouldn't put the lid on any chance of getting Sonnie safely away from all this.

"That's my sister," Billy said, slurring her words slightly. "I'm Billy Keith. I should have been called. What's going on? What's she done? I'm the one who looks after her, aren't I, Jim?"

Chris couldn't believe what he'd just heard. The leopard jumpsuit had been discarded in favor of a short, tight, black dress with skinny, rhinestone-studded straps that had to go a long, long way down to support a straight-cut bodice that only just kept the woman from public indecency. She wore black hose, and every move showed their lace tops. Her backless satin shoes had heels encrusted with more rhinestones. She barely kept her balance—without Dr. Jim's steadying arm, she'd probably fall.

"Billy," Sonnie whispered. "Sit down, please."

"I don't wanna sit down, thank you. Are you ever going to stop being a pain—being a nuisance? If I'd wanted kids, I'd have had my own. What'd you do this time?"

Sonnie looked at Chris, who said, "Sonnie hasn't done anything. Did you see her brother-in-law? He made himself scarce when things got tough."

"When she was taken in by the police, you mean?" Billy shivered with feigned delicacy. She crammed her elbows against her body with the result that her nipples were responsible for hanging on to the top of the dress. "Romano did the right thing. He came back to the club to tell me and discuss with me what would be the best thing to do."

"Hello, Ms. Keith," Kraus said. Chris assessed the trajectory of the man's stare. It was an easy study. "Do sit down. We're really glad to see you. I wasn't aware Mrs. Giacano had any relatives here."

"Oh, she wouldn't tell you," Billy said, staring pointedly at Chris until he got up and held the back of the chair while she sat down. Dr. Jim went solicitously to her side and rubbed her neck. "This is my good friend, my *very* good friend, Jim Lesley. Dr. Jim Lesley. We're here to do everything we can to help you and my sister."

Chris sensed that Kraus was considering Billy Keith, and he'd stopped looking at her like a perfectly cooked steak. Maybe the detective had even decided he didn't feel too sure of his feelings for Billy. Just the idea sent the man up in Chris's estimation.

The door opened yet again and the same officer as before dropped another file on Kraus's desk. "They rushed this over," the man said, raising his eyebrows significantly. "Thought you'd want it right away."

Kraus read quickly, turning pages and sweeping the text while he ran a blunt-tipped finger down the typed lines.

At last he looked up and seemed to consider what to say. He picked up his phone and asked for someone by name. Until a tall, dark-haired woman arrived, Kraus went back to reading his files as if he were alone.

The woman took a chair from a corner, sat down, and placed a recorder on Kraus's desk. She gave the date, then opened a notebook and sat, evidently bored but ready to write what needed to be written.

Chris wanted so badly to say this was unorthodox, but held his tongue. It could be that they'd need a friendly technicality before too long.

"This is an informal conversation," Kraus said. "I've asked for a record of our discussion in case any of us has difficulty recalling what was said." He didn't fail to glance at Billy, who, even over her perfume, reeked of liquor, and who wobbled on her chair.

"Feel free to comment at any time," Kraus said. "Looks like our unidentified victim may have been asleep when the fire broke out. There was the butt of a cigarette inside his sleeping bag—but the arson squad's having difficulty believing that's what started the fire. If it had, the body should have been severely burned—particularly after it had been in the area while the fire was totally involved. Apparently he tried to get out of the sleeping bag, but for some reason—maybe smoke inhalation—he didn't make it." He read some more. "There's nothing else here that's relevant right now."

Chris stood behind Sonnie. *Nothing you want to talk about. If that's the light artillery, the big guns are going to be scary.*

Billy started to cry and Jim bent over her, talked softly into her ear. She waved him aside. "She's my sister and I'm going to look after her. I've been afraid of something like this." Sobbing without making her mascara run, she leaned toward Kraus. "She's my sister, do you understand? I love her. She was in a serious accident and had a terrible head injury. She's unbalanced. If she set fire to her own home, she can't be blamed."

"Billy," Sonnie said with more calm than Chris was sure he could muster at this point. "Listen, a man died in the house. In the room where I store things. Aren't you listening? Can't you see where this is heading? The police are trying to decide if I had something to do with the death. With wanting the man to die, that is. By *killing* him."

Chris didn't know whether he wanted to applaud her approach or clap a hand over her mouth to stop her from saying anything more.

Billy turned sideways in her chair and commenced to cry loudly. She sobbed and sobbed.

Dr. Jim instantly dropped to his knees and drew her into his arms. No matter how she fought him, he had no difficulty holding her close. "Would you be kind enough to give me that bag?" he asked Chris, who hadn't noticed the little black bag the man had set inside the door. Dutifully Chris retrieved it and handed it over.

"Hush," the doctor told Billy. "Just hush and I'll make you feel better, my dear."

"Help Sonnie," she wailed. "Has she killed someone? My God, I've got to know."

A syringe was produced from the bag, and very shortly Billy was much quieter. She leaned on Jim Lesley and her eyes took on a glazed quality.

Yet again the other officer arrived, this time with an envelope. He handed it to his boss and left again without any comment.

Kraus slid photographs onto his desk, photographs most human beings ought never to see. Chris shook his head. He was helpless to stop what was happening, but he was grateful that at least Billy seemed too out-of-it to threaten more crying.

The door, opening once more, startled everyone in the room who was fully conscious. In slipped Ena. Her face ashen, she said, "I was told you might want to know about . . . I've got something to tell you. It's probably nothing, but I'm so worried." She nodded at Chris, but looked at Sonnie as if she were looking at her only friend. "Sonnie, what are we going to do?"

"We'll do the best we can," Sonnie said. Brave words, but beneath Chris's fingers, her back was damp. "Ena, you should be in bed. Get a ride home and I'll talk to you in the morning."

"You don't understand," Ena said.

"Well," Kraus said. "Come one, come all. Kindly stand over there and be quiet, ma'am. This isn't a group therapy session we're holding here."

Billy Keith had passed out on Dr. Lesley's shoulder and he said, "I'll stay until I'm sure Sonnie's okay. Billy would want

me to. But then I'll have to get Billy back to the club. This
has all been too much for her.''

"Mrs. Giacano,'' Detective Kraus said, ''this is difficult.
Please understand that I sympathize with your inexperience in
such matters. Bear with us and we'll help you if you need help.
Would you please look at these photographs? They're of the
man who died at your house tonight—last night now.''

"Damn it,'' Chris said. ''Do you have to do this now?''

"Yes, I do,'' Kraus said, but with no particular animosity.
"We need to move as quickly as possible on this. We may
have something really complicated here. Can you handle it,
Mrs. Giacano?''

She nodded and shifted forward to look at the shots Kraus
spread on his desk. ''It's possible that the fallen tiles—while
they inflicted injury—may have helped shield him from some
of the fire. It's also possible the fire actually started either in
the space between the ceiling in the room and the roof—or
elsewhere entirely. According to preliminary reports, the cause
of death isn't yet definite. May take a day or two for forensics
to get through.''

Chris could see the stark pictures, and he could feel the
waves of trembling that shook Sonnie. She stared at a body
half in and half out of a sleeping bag and surrounded by charred
debris.

Sonnie covered her mouth and retched.

"Oh,'' Ena cried out, stumbling to the edge of the desk.
She began to gather the photographs, clasping them one after
the other to her breast. When she'd collected them all, she
turned to Sonnie and said, ''Edward. It's my lodger, Edward.''

Fifteen

Aiden Flynn sat sidesaddle on Chris's bike and watched the big man pace. Chris had done a lot of pacing in the past twenty-four hours, and Aiden had done a lot of watching.

A hot wind wrapped itself around palms in the courtyard of the Banyan Inn. Chris paused to stare toward the unit Sonnie had moved into. Aiden uncrossed and recrossed his ankles. He'd like to tell his buddy that he wasn't thinking with his usual scalpel-like precision. In fact, he was being an ass. Prowling around a woman who was running scared just about guaranteed the reverse reaction to the one Chris wanted. Aiden hadn't been formally introduced to Sonnie Giacano, but he'd lay odds she knew Chris was patrolling her present pad, and that his fanatical determination to be with her—whether she wanted him or not—was making her crazy.

Giving his opinion wouldn't win him any points. On the other hand, you couldn't buy much with points. "Yo, Talon."

Chris waved a hand but didn't turn around.

Aiden raised his voice for the next "Yo, Talon."

"What?"

"You're going about this all wrong, man." But then, taking a few points away wasn't going to hurt him, either. "She's sending you a message. 'I'm going it alone.' That's what she's telling you.''

''Save it, Flynn.''

''She's already running scared. You're making it worse.''

''Can it. You don't know Sonnie. She's scared of something, but it isn't what you think.''

''What do I think?''

''Hell, how would I know what you think? There she is—you stay put.''

''D'you think there's going to be a hurricane? I've never been in one.''

Chris waved again and strode away.

''Okay,'' Aiden said into the wind. ''Brush me off, but you'll be back.''

Chris's shirt billowed and flattened to his back by turns. One big, good-looking son of a bitch. And hardheaded as they came.

With bulging sacks in each hand, the woman walked—or limped—around the perimeter of the courtyard. A man came from a walkway between buildings and swiftly approached her. She looked up and stood still. The man gestured, and Sonnie turned back and started to run.

Aiden couldn't hear what Chris shouted but assumed it was her name. The stranger spun to look at him, and took off between the nearest buildings. Chris paused, clearly deciding whether to go after him, but Sonnie set off for the street again. When she saw Chris, she actually sped up and passed him without looking at him.

''Uh-uh. I warned you,'' Aiden muttered. Sonnie Giacano's story wasn't entirely new to him. He was aware of her husband's abduction. But he wanted to know more about what she was looking for here in the Keys.

Chris let her go. He gripped his upper arms and watched her. She left the hotel grounds, passing close to Aiden, and crossed the street. She looked desperate, but not frightened.

Swinging his arms again, Chris returned to Aiden. ''Who was the guy?'' Aiden asked.

''I don't know. You saw how much talking she did.'' Chris

stood at the curb until Sonnie went around a corner; then he set off after her.

Aiden followed Chris. He followed him all the way to the front windows of a crowded Laundromat and stood beside him. Inside, Sonnie had dropped her sacks to the floor while she fed coins into a detergent dispenser. Her face was flushed, her movements jerky.

"Some might make a case for harassment here," Aiden said. "Will you tell me one thing?"

"If it'll shut you up."

"She's let you know she doesn't want you around. Why don't you leave her alone?"

"Because that's not what she wants."

"Really? You mean she really *does* want you shadowing her?"

"The minute she gets things started in there, I'm going in. I'm going to make her talk to me. She wore me down until I wanted—until she made me agree to help her. Then, when I'm too far in to want out again, she gives me the cold shoulder. I want to know why."

"You want the woman," Aiden said, checking out his fingernails. "You've fallen for her." He was fussy about his fingernails.

"Now that would be a really stupid move, wouldn't it?" Chris said. "In case you've forgotten, she's married."

"To a man who isn't around anymore—hasn't been heard from in months."

"She's crippled."

"Don't try to fool me. You don't give a damn if she limps. She's cute—in a different kind of way."

Chris stared at him. "You aren't her type, so don't get any ideas."

"Geez, sometimes there's no winning with you."

"I'm going in. Go back to the Nail if you like."

"When I came all this way to spend time with my old buddy? No way." He indicated his car, which happened to be parked within his sight. "And I want you to enjoy my pink pony for a while. You haven't felt power till you've held her in your hands. I'm telling you, Chris. . . ."

Sonnie felt the instant when Chris decided to come into the Laundromat. The other man followed him. She'd made a mistake and now she didn't know how to back out of the terrible mess she'd made.

Next she felt silence form in the middle of all the hum and clank of machines. She didn't have to check around to see what had caught the awed attention of the predominantly female customers. Her entourage would silence just about any crowd. She ought to feel lucky to have two dynamically handsome men following her around. What she felt was quite different. *Trapped* would be a better term.

For the first time since the accident, she wore shorts. The police had taken her into the house to collect clothes. The only things that didn't reek of smoke were in boxes on shelves in a backyard shed. There she'd found shorts and several outfits that would do until she got the washing done. All morning she'd watched Chris and his friend from a gap in the hotel room blinds. She'd watched, and waited for them to leave. In the end she'd given up.

There were two empty washers. After pouring in the little boxes of detergent, she divided the clothes and stuffed them inside the front-loading doors.

"Says not to overload the machines," Chris's friend said from behind her. "Those are overloaded."

She ignored him. Every other washer was in use and she wanted to get through and go back to her room.

"You won't get anything clean. The way all that stuff stinks, that wouldn't be a good idea."

A snicker from nearby was quickly cut off. Sonnie checked out the other patrons. Several young moms with toddlers winding around their knees and babies in their arms. A woman wearing a crocheted hat from which large sequins hung and glittered, and who might well benefit from her own turn in a washer. And several men wearing only undershorts and playing cards while they apparently washed the rest of what they'd been wearing. Gaunt bodies suggested they could use a good meal, not that lack of food had inhibited the growth of their hair—including straggling beards and mustaches.

"What d'you think would happen if you put goldfish in one of those?" Chris's friend asked. "In cold water, of course."

"They'd die," Chris said.

"Even if you set it on delicate? And you wouldn't put in detergent."

If they'd planned a way to make her even more nervous, it was working. She'd leave while her clothes washed, only she didn't really have any place to go other than back to the hotel.

"Salmon swim upstream, don't they?"

"Your point?" Chris said. He sounded explosive, as if he was so close to the edge he was barely hanging on.

"Well, can't be as tough to take a whirl in a washing machine as it would be to fight all those currents."

"We're talking goldfish here, not forty-pound salmon."

"Ah, a lot of those salmon aren't anywhere near forty pounds."

Sonnie spun around and studied first one, then the other man. They were seated side by side, on green plastic chairs. Chris's expression was solemn. The other one, the one built with the lean lines of a tall quarterback, and who had startlingly blue eyes, and lashes that ought to belong to a woman, smiled until he finally accepted that she wasn't going to be amused. He shrugged and bent forward to rest his forearms on his knees.

Without a word, Chris moved one seat to his right and patted the chair he'd vacated. "Sit down, Sonnie," he said, "before you collapse. Who was the guy with the shaved head who tried to talk to you?"

"The man who threatened me at the Nail that night."

"Damn it. Why didn't you give a sign? I'd have run him down."

"I know. That's why I didn't. He asked me to forgive his behavior. I was too shaken up to stay calm."

"You should have—"

"I didn't. End of topic."

"I want you to sit down," Chris said, raising his voice. "It's my job to look after you."

Sonnie turned hot. She avoided checking reactions from the cheap seats and did as she was told. Promptly she closed her eyes.

Pressure against her side, Chris leaning close, was almost enough to make her cry out.

"Sonnie," he said into her ear, "why did you run away like that last night?"

"I didn't run away."

"What would you call it when someone excuses herself to go to the bathroom and doesn't come back?"

"I had to think about Roy and Bo."

"What the . . ." He breathed heavily, angrily. "What does that mean?"

"I don't have any right to take my trouble into their lives."

"They want you there with them. That's why they asked you to stay. They wouldn't have insisted if they hadn't meant what they said. There'll always be a place for you with them."

The butterflies in her belly sickened Sonnie. She couldn't remember the last time she'd felt like eating. "Why don't you go back and apologize to them for me? Tell them I'll be in touch." He was choosing to forget how he'd embarrassed her by announcing that he'd stay with her while his friend used the cabin.

"Nope," he said. "I'll go back when you come with me."

She opened her eyes and looked at him. "You're making a fool of me."

Chris assumed the same forearms-on-knees pose as his friend.

"We didn't have a chance for a formal introduction this morning. I'm Aiden Flynn. Pleased to meet you."

The large hand that was thrust before her demanded attention. Sonnie tried to touch palms quickly with Aiden Flynn, but he was too fast for her. Immediately her fingers were enveloped in a strong grasp.

For the first time she exchanged a dedicated examination with the man. He might put on a flippant act but he was one serious guy. "Hello, Aiden," she said. "I didn't hear where you're from."

"All over," he said, and the directness in those eyes didn't invite deeper questions on the subject. "Chris and I go way back. We've lost touch recently. I decided to put that right."

"Great timing," Chris muttered, apparently engrossed in the card players. "Nothing like dropping in on very busy people."

"He's always had a charming way about him," Aiden said, still holding her hand, still not smiling. "But he's a hell of a good man to have around. Resourceful. Determined. Bad tempered. Arrogant. Good body. Winner of the best manacled-woman tattoo contest—"

"Stow it, Flynn," Chris said, looking at them over his shoulder. "And you can quit holding hands. How long is this going to take?"

"What?" Aiden said.

"I wasn't talking to you. How long does it take to wash the clothes?"

"You got a maid or something?" Aiden said, undeterred. "You never used a washing machine?"

They had the attention of everyone in the place—including the card players, who had breasted their hands and turned their chairs for a better view.

"Can I get a straight answer?" Chris said. "In case you've both forgotten, we've got places to go and things to do."

Sonnie caught the eye of the woman in the sequined bonnet and saw . . . pity? An old irreverent streak that hadn't surfaced much of late chose that moment to return. Sonnie shook her head and cast her eyes heavenward.

"They're all the same," the woman said. "No good, any of 'em."

Sonnie nodded. "But you try making one of them believe that," she said. "They think every one of them's a gift."

"*Men,*" said a woman with four children who might have about eight years between them.

Sonnie congratulated herself on remembering a universal language guaranteed to create a diversion.

"Cute," Chris said, while one woman after another joined

in a comparison of annoying male traits. "How did you do that?"

"Please go, Chris," she said, as quietly as she could. "I'm trying to work out what to do. When I do, you'll be one of the first to know."

"Damn it all," he said, silencing the women instantly. He looked around at them, then aimed a winning grin at a little boy who appeared close to tears. "Have you started your Christmas list? Hope so. Takes a long time to write down all that stuff." The child might not know much of what Chris was talking about, but the conspiratorial tone won out and produced a giggle.

"See," Aiden said. "I told you he was resourceful."

"Ma'am," Chris said to the woman in sequins, "are you going to be here for a while?"

"I'm the attendant."

"Ah." Somehow he managed to sound enlightened. "So you'll be here."

"I'm paid to be here."

"That right?" He worked his wallet from his back pocket and took out a clump of bills. "When our stuff's ready, we'd be very grateful if you'd take it from those two washers and put it in a dryer. If that's okay, we'll stop back for it later."

Our stuff? Sonnie sought about for something to say but came up empty.

"That'll be fine," the woman said. She pointed to a scale of fees on the wall, counted out several dollars, and handed the rest back to Chris. "I'll be here all day. If you don't get back before closing, I'll lock your things in the back room."

Chris thanked her and gave her another dollar—and held Sonnie's elbow while he stood up. She had little choice but to stand with him. Aiden got up on her other side, smiled all around, and walked out of the shop.

Aiden continued to walk ahead of Sonnie and Chris. She was too aware of her left leg, of how much thinner it was than the right—and too aware of how she was being manipulated by a forceful man she'd been the one to pursue until he decided to be caught.

The street was all but deserted. To the right the ocean was visible, and a purplish haze hung on the horizon. A desolate atmosphere had slithered in to fill the landscape. Only here had Sonnie ever felt the presence of disaster borne on gardenia-scented air.

"Storm coming," Aiden called back to them. "Think we're going to get that hurricane?"

"Could be," Chris shouted. "You'll know it if we do."

She'd been too preoccupied to follow the weather forecast as closely as people usually did down there.

"You and I need time alone," he said to her. "You've been through a lot, but trying to turn me off now doesn't make a whole lot of sense. You need me more, not less."

"No. No, you're wrong. I've been thinking for hours. I'm not sure what I ought to do, but it's going to be different from what I've been doing."

"You've decided you don't want to know what really happened when you crashed?"

"I crashed. That's it. Time to accept it."

"I see. So what does that mean?"

"Just what I've said. I've done enough damage already. And I've been warned about it. Sometimes you have to accept that you're not going to win and move on."

"Run away, you mean?"

She tried unsuccessfully to pull her arm from his hand. "You ought to know about running away," she told him. "You've already admitted that's what you're doing."

He didn't even flinch, but the last thing she expected was his light kiss on her lips. She caught at his shirt to steady herself. The kiss stopped as quickly as it started, but they didn't step away from each other.

He crossed his arms around her and studied her face. "You're right," he said. "Mostly. I was running away—past tense. You stopped me, and I'm not going to run anymore. Not as long as I've got something to stay put for."

"You can't make me responsible for your actions."

"Can't I?" he asked, bending to kiss her again. This time for much longer. The thought came and almost instantly left that she was a married woman standing on a public street and kissing a man who wasn't her husband. His hands were in her hair, caressing her neck, the sides of her face. And she leaned on him, and wished they were somewhere private, somewhere that would allow them to go wherever the moment took them.

They paused for breath and Sonnie rested her face against his chest.

"Are you ready to tell me everything now?" he asked.

For an instant she felt disoriented. "I've told you."

"No, you haven't. You've barely begun. I want to know about your husband—all about him. What happened the last time you were together? Why was he away so much when you were pregnant? He wasn't even playing most of the time."

"Don't," she said. "Please don't."

"Too late. You came here because you don't believe what you've been told to believe. There have to be reasons for that, and you surely haven't shared much about them with me. Vague comments, but not much more."

"I know I more or less begged you to help me." His fingers on her mouth distracted her. "I know I did. But I shouldn't have. It's too dangerous. If I don't give this up I really believe someone will get hurt. Someone else."

"Nothing doing."

She frowned at him.

"You're trying to get rid of me. I'm not going. You'll have to get a restraining order to stop me from following you around. You prepared to do that?"

He was making this too hard. She'd . . . She was never going to forget him, but she owed it to him to cut loose now. "I'll do it if I have to."

"No, you won't."

A hint of sunlight played over the hair and skin at the open neck of his shirt. Sonnie watched skin move over bone and touched it before she could stop herself.

"No, you won't," he repeated.

"No, I won't," she agreed. "But I'll find a way to keep you safe. Being around me isn't safe. Where's Aiden?" She turned her head.

"He's playing with the Harley," Chris said. "It's not his thing. Look behind you. See that pink monstrosity?"

"The pink Mustang? Isn't it beautiful?"

Chris groaned. "Not you, too. It belongs to Aiden. Do *not* encourage him to talk about it." He picked up her locket and turned it over. He snapped it open and said, "Who's Jacqueline?"

She couldn't explain, or even tell him he had no right to pry.

He looked more closely and said, "Ah. You had a little girl, too."

"Too?" Despite the heat she turned cold. "You had a little girl, Chris?"

He laughed. "No such luck. Slip of the tongue. I was thinking about something else. But this was your baby, wasn't it?"

"Yes." Sometimes it was easier to be straightforward. "I like thinking about her. This makes me feel I'm still carrying her with me."

"This isn't the time or the place, but I . . . You're very important to me. You know what I almost said then, but I'm not ready to say it, and you're not ready to hear it. You may never be. But you asked me to stand with you in whatever comes and I agreed. We didn't sign any contracts, but we might as well have. D'you understand?"

She nodded. "But I'm going to make you see that it was a bad idea from the beginning."

"Good luck. Even you aren't that persuasive. Let's move before we manage to draw another crowd. The intrepid few will be on their way to Mallory Square shortly. Not that there's going to be much of a sunset."

Sonnie wasn't sure what to do next. "I'm probably going back to Denver."

"I don't think so." Chris held her hand and they strolled back toward the Banyan Inn. "Have the police told you when you'll be free to start putting the house back together?"

"They said within a few days. What do you think Edward was doing in that room? In a sleeping bag?"

He didn't want to scare her, but neither could he pull punches anymore. "I think he was waiting for you. Ena said he'd mentioned liking you and how kind you were to him. Maybe not too many people were kind to Edward and he wanted to spend time with you."

She shuddered. "He waved to me and I waved back. That was it. I never met him. Was he planning to attack me in the night?"

"I was never in his head, kid. I'm sure the cops are doing their stuff and finding out as much about his background as they can. That'll give us a clearer vision of what kind of guy he was."

They reached the motel and approached Aiden, who sat on Chris's bike again. He saluted. "I'll stick around the Laundromat and bring back Sonnie's things, if you like."

"Good man," Chris said. "You comfortable at my place?"

"Cushy," Aiden told him.

"Good. Bring the laundry to Roy and Bo's then. Sonnie can't go back to her place until it's secure anyway."

Sonnie felt herself being drawn into a web that was only partly of her own making. "I should probably go to the club," she said. "This place is nice, but Billy and Romano will make my life a misery if I don't make an attempt to smooth things over. I will have to stay long enough to deal with the house; otherwise I'd head back to Denver right now." She tried to avoid Chris's eyes. When she gave up, what she saw shouldn't please her so much. He didn't want her to leave him. Very soon she'd have to find a way to remind him that she wasn't free, and she'd have to make him not want her.

For the first time in her life, she'd found a man she responded to as a mature woman, both a thinking and a sexual woman, and she had no right to him.

"If you want to go to the club later, okay. But would you come back with me first? To put Roy's mind at ease? And so we can talk? Please? Alone and for as long as it takes?"

So that he could wear her down and wipe out her resolve to break away from him? She wasn't strong enough to refuse. "Okay. But I can't stay."

"I've got to take my car to Roy and Bo's," Aiden said.

She glanced at him. Just as she'd already noted, he was built like an athlete. But his slender face with its high cheekbones and sensitive mouth had an irresistibly intense quality. Relaxed on his thighs, his long-fingered hands bore scars on their backs, but they were hands that invited touch, and would probably invoke a longing to be touched in many women. He had to be in his mid-thirties. Another man who shouldn't still be alone.

Chris gave Sonnie one of the two helmets that hung on the bike. "You've probably got time to do that other thing we talked about and still be back in time to get the laundry," he said to Aiden. "What d'you think?"

"Wally Loder's on the case."

"Efficient man, Wally," Chris said. "See you later, then." He mounted the bike and waited for Sonnie to settle herself awkwardly behind him.

Aiden Flynn was already walking away.

"Who's Wally Loder?" Sonnie shouted from inside the hated helmet.

"Keep your voice down," Chris told her mildly. He half turned on the bike and leaned into her. "For reasons we'll explain when the time's right, Aiden is sometimes Wally Loder. And he needs to be while he's down here—at least in some instances. Our job is to keep that straight."

"Being here is dangerous for him?"

Chris raised his eyebrows. "He's used to danger. Aiden does what has to be done. I wasn't happy to see him, but I'm getting used to the idea of having him with me. You'll get used to him, too."

"We won't spend enough time together for that to happen."

He settled a hand on her thigh. "Kiss me, Sonnie."

She parted her lips, and he wasn't sure if she'd do as he asked, or cry. She bent forward and kissed his jaw. He had to plant his feet more firmly on the ground on either side of the bike.

When he could speak again, he said, "I'd like to take you riding across the country with me. Leave everything behind. One day we'll do that."

She let her head fall back, and he figured she was making sure any tears went back where they came from.

He put a knuckle under her chin and took her bottom lip gently between his teeth. The way she sucked in a breath made him feel more than good.

"Mmm," he murmured. "I'm only saying this once for now, but I'm surely thinking that loving you would be easy."

Sixteen

Romano let Billy into his room. He checked the corridor before closing the door and turning to face her. "What are you doing here? I told you not to come again."

"And I told you not to tell me what to do. We're in this up to our necks. Both of us. That means you don't get to hand out orders."

As long as he'd known Billy, since she was a self-destructive kid on the tour, she'd been impossible to control. The best approach was the placating approach. "If it got out that you and I have something going, it could cost us everything."

She gathered her hair into a bundle on top of her head and secured it with a band she took from one wrist.

"Billy," Romano said, clinging to patience. "We can't look as if we're involved with each other. Do you understand that one slip could ruin all I've worked for?"

"You haven't worked alone, but I understand."

"Good. I'll call you."

"She's in some motel or hotel," Billy said, swaggering in a neon orange string bikini. "Banyan something. We've got to bring her here where we can keep an eye on her. And the sooner she's back in Denver, the better. We must have my father's cooperation. He's got to be convinced she's a danger to herself, and needs care she can't get at home.''

He agreed, but he wasn't about to let Billy think he respected her opinions. ''My first priority is to find out exactly why that man was in her house. He doesn't fit.''

''Of course he doesn't. He was a coincidence, that's all. And he's brought a lot of attention that could mess things up for us if we're not careful.''

He laughed shortly. ''Don't be hysterical. I won't allow any interference.''

She stretched out on his bed and stacked her hands behind her head. The effect she achieved was no accident. ''Cory Bledsoe's sniffing around. He thinks he should teach me how to play golf. And he's making noises about my helping you coach.''

''What the fuck does that mean?''

Billy smiled at the ceiling and settled her bikini-clad curves more comfortably. ''He'd like to keep me company, of course. But he could also be curious about what brings both of us down here like this. He's probably right in thinking I'd be an asset, and he just likes opportunities to look at me.''

Romano seethed. The vain bitch thought every man was drooling over her. ''He knows Sonnie's here. He also knows the story about how very close our combined families are. How we look after our own. Unless we make a stupid mistake and disillusion him, Bledsoe won't have any reason to think anything different.''

She hummed.

''Right?'' he said.

''It's possible Cory's a little smarter than you think. There's talk. The big, strong Harley rider isn't a man who doesn't get noticed. Cory wonders if there's something going on that's making us nervous. Like Sonnie wanting to forget she's got a husband—or may have a husband.''

''Shut *up*,'' he told her, and his hands itched with his desire to take hold of her. ''The next time you suggest my brother may be dead, I'll make you wish you hadn't.''

''So masterful,'' she said, winding her body from side to

side. She kicked off her sandals and ran the sole of one foot up and down the opposite calf.

"You are such a willful child," he told her, but it was impossible not to look at her nipples through the open mesh of her bikini top. "Will you never grow up and stop using yourself like a whore to get what you want?"

She jackknifed to sit up. "I don't have to take that from you. If looking at me disgusts you, don't look. Let's hurry up here. I've got a date."

"With whom?"

"That's my affair."

"Are you telling me Bledsoe's been asking questions about Sonnie? About you or me?"

She wouldn't look at him. "That's what I'm telling you," she said.

Alienating her could be very dangerous. "I'm sorry I'm edgy. It's all coming down to this, Billy. What happens here and now in Key West. Sonnie's forced our hand."

Billy's expression softened a little. "She behaves as if she's better than me. Holy. But she's catting around." She looked at him. "She's catting around behind Frank's back."

He knew she was only pretending she didn't think Frank had been murdered. "Yeah," he said. He was convinced Frank was still alive.

"Call this Banyan place and ask to speak to Sonnie. Be sweet, Romano. You're good at that when you want something. Tell her how worried we are about her and that I'm beside myself. Say Jim had to sedate me again today, and tell her I need her with me."

"I must have time to think first. We don't move until we know exactly where we're going. There can't be anything messy."

Billy got up and walked slow circles around him. "Perhaps you're thinking too much. Perhaps you should do what you'll do in the end anyway—whatever I decide I'll allow you to do." Her arrogance was wearing his nerves to nothing, but she was doing exactly what she wanted to do: turning him on.

He'd ignore her bait. "We've got to keep up the image that

we are family, Billy. Nothing more than family. Your friend, Dr. Lesley, he is here to help us keep up that little charade, yes? Your current boyfriend happens to be a psychiatrist, but his only interest is in you.''

She began to dance. ''I like Jim. He's not as boring as you think he is. Not nearly as boring. Especially in bed. He'll do anything to help me.''

''That's nice.'' He grew more heated by the moment. ''Let's go over our plan just one more time. Then you will promise me never to come to me like this again.''

''We'll go over the plan, lover.''

Always so difficult. ''This is simple. As long as we both do our parts. With Sonnie out of the way, I hold the purse strings. I shall be very charming to you and your father—and Sonnie's mother. They won't be happy, and you will convince them you are not happy either. After all, they know you are jealous of your little sister. If they get even a hint that you might benefit from the tragedy of Sonnie's unfortunate mental illness, they will cut you out of their will.''

''That won't happen.'' With her hands on her hips, she continued to dance, but with less abandon. ''You will help me make sure it doesn't.''

''But of course. I'm trying to do just that. After all, my dear, it is bound to be a very big will. So be careful about your *dates*. Or should I say, be careful what you say to your dates. You have a history of becoming drunk rather quickly, and the drunker you are, the more you talk.''

Romano didn't see the blow coming. She hit his face with the flat of one hand and followed with a slap from the other hand that knocked his head to one side.

He stumbled, but regained his balance.

She breathed hard and squared off to hit him again. ''I'm not a drunk. That's what you're suggesting. That I'm a drunk. And that I talk too much. I won't listen to any of this from you. A few words from me and you're finished. I could talk about what you ship from your warehouses. The way you milk people.''

While she paused and eyed him, Romano worked to keep

his anger from erupting. Billy was a strong woman. His face stung.

"You can't afford to make an enemy out of me," she said. "I know everything, remember?"

The room grew warmer. Romano took off his jacket. She could sometimes be frightened into submission—if that was a game she wanted to play. He threw the jacket on the bed and unbuttoned his shirt.

"Don't bother," she said, her voice flat and hard. "Touch me without permission and I'll scream. Now that's a risk you ought to run, don't you think?"

She was bluffing. He took off his shirt.

"I can get you arrested," Billy said, and she walked directly at him. When she was close enough, she shot the stiffened fingers of her right hand toward his face. "There's nothing you can say or do to defend yourself against me."

The fingers darted toward his eyes, and he flinched, flinched and stepped back. "That's enough," he said. "I don't have time for this."

"No? But you have time to give orders, and to show me what a big man you are."

He made a grab for her hand and missed—walked backward some more and thudded into the wall.

"There are people in high places who would love to talk to me about you. You would go to prison until you're very, very old."

For an instant he felt disoriented, but only an instant. There was no way she could know everything, was there? "Go to prison because a jealous woman suggests I cheat foreign markets by charging too much for surplus goods?" He laughed, and his jaws ached. "You little fool. Charging what the market will bear has never been a crime."

"Maybe you're right. But maybe you're wrong. Do you want to take that risk?"

This wasn't going as it should. "Look, Billy, you should go now. Just be careful what you say and everything will be fine." The look in her eyes actually frightened him.

She shot out her hand again, but this time she went for his

throat. Her hard little fingertips pressed into the flesh on either side of his windpipe. "I will go when I'm ready to go." With her free hand she batted his face lightly, first in one direction, then in the other. "There is always the time for drawing lines in the sand. Isn't that what they say? Now is the time for our line."

"Yes. You're absolutely right."

"You want to kill me, don't you, Romano? You could. But that would be the end of everything—for both of us." Her laugh was an ugly sound. "You want to kill me so badly you're afraid even to touch me."

"You're sick. Yes, I could kill you, and that ought to warn you to go away, to go away very quickly and quietly."

"It would warn most people, but I'm not most people. And I know you so well. You and your brother. Neither of you has any guts."

The feverish light in her eyes was unmistakable. Danger had aroused her. Once more she tapped each side of his face— and she began to pant. Her breasts rose and fell and her stomach sucked in flat.

"You are mad," he told her.

She tightened her hold on his throat.

Romano stared into her face. "Take your hand away," he said.

"Not yet. Not until you tell me you'll do whatever I tell you to do."

"Never," he said.

He didn't see her next move coming until her knee connected with his crotch. Doubling over, he heard his own yell. Too late he remembered the vulnerable back of his neck. Billy's two fists landed there and sent him slipping and sliding down the wall. The next sounds he heard were from the radio she turned on loudly.

Then she was upon him, shrieking and laughing, pummeling and tearing at him.

They fought, rolled across the carpet landing blows where they could, and the mad ecstasy in Billy's cries testified to how much she reveled in the violence.

Somewhere in the struggle she lost the bikini. Her delight in her own body showed in the pose she made of each move.

"Tell me what you want now," she said in a breathy voice, and grew still. Stretched out on her back on the floor, she said, "You can have anything you want."

Sitting beside her, he inclined his head to see her face and wished he could also look inside her head.

The door slammed so loudly the walls vibrated.

Billy clapped a hand over her mouth, and her eyes opened wide.

Holding still, Romano waited. Slowly he turned his head and saw Cory Bledsoe's ruddy, grinning face. The man came toward them and dropped to his knees beside Billy's shoulders.

"Romano," Billy said softly. "We wouldn't want to spoil a lovely friendship, would we?"

He didn't understand but said, "No."

She narrowed her eyes and said, "I'm glad we agree. Let's invite Cory to join our game. He's a friend, after all. We believe in sharing with our friends."

Her deliberate coldness struck at him as fiercely as any of her blows had done. Now he knew what she intended. "Of course we do." It would be pointless to argue with her.

Billy sat up and shot her hands around Cory's neck. "This is what you want, isn't it?"

Swallowing visibly and passing his tongue over his lips, Cory Bledsoe nodded. He looked at her breasts and turned bright red before he touched them.

"That's right, Cory," Billy said. "Romano, let's show Cory how right it is."

Seventeen

The scent of salt from the ocean had grown stronger. It was hot, hot, hot, and the wind that constantly blew didn't cool Chris's skin. Even the locals were staying indoors this morning.

"We should have ridden over," he said to Sonnie. "You shouldn't be walking in this heat."

"I need to walk," she said. "You don't have to come."

So she'd already told him—several times. "I want to come. How can I help you if I'm not with you? It's time to ask our own questions and demand answers. Why not see if Ena can give us some hints? This Edward can't be the total mystery the local boys insist he is. The poor devil has to have come from somewhere."

Sonnie tried not to look at him, but failed. She wanted to tell him she was afraid something would happen to him because of her, but she didn't dare. Admitting she cared about him that much was too personal.

"What are you thinking?" he asked. The intense colors of the day emphasized his tan, the darkness of his hair, his brows, the sharp hazel of his eyes. A blue-mauve day that tinted him brilliant.

Sonnie turned her face away. "I'm not thinking." This was a flirtation with an exotic male whose attention she should question. "Except that you ought to have better things to do than hang around with me."

"I don't have better things to do."

"Because you have no ambition? You're drifting? That ought to bother you."

He figured she was trying to goad him. "You'll have to do better than that," he told her, but the words had stung.

"How long do you think you can hide?" she said. "Don't you worry about waking up one day and realizing the only one you've been fooling is you? What then? You'll have to stop whining about being washed-up. You'll have to do something with yourself—with the rest of your life."

He'd have to face the past again, what he'd caused, then run away from. He stopped walking.

Sonnie carried on.

The distance between them widened.

She felt herself getting farther from him with each step. Tears stung her eyes—and made her mad. She had no right to draw him into her troubles in the first place, and no right to want him so. And she had no right to insult him for his kindness.

She stopped and bowed her head, turned back—stared at him.

Damn him anyway; he was smiling at her. Not one of his dazzling, color-your-heart-happy smiles, but a smile stripped of any pretense. What she'd said had hurt him; it had actually made him hear what he didn't want to hear—that while he was following her, he was avoiding himself.

"I'm not ready," he said, and despite the distance between them she heard him clearly. "My turn will come. For opening all the cupboards. But not now. If I did it now I'd die under everything that fell out. Do you understand?"

"I understand that you play games. You pretend to be something you're not. You are not a simple man, Chris Talon."

How did a man live with so much wanting? How did a man who had vowed never to need another soul as he'd once . . . How did a man forget his vows and allow himself to fall for a woman he'd probably never be able to have?

When she started back toward him, he couldn't even stand

where he was. His feet helped close the space between them, and there was no way he could have done anything else but go to her.

"Are you here because you're bored and you need something to be interested in?" she said.

"Oh, no."

"Why then?"

He ran the fingertips of one hand down her bare arm. "I'm here because I want to be with you. You're a very complicated lady, and I want to know everything about you. And I want to help you. You're not the hysterical type, but you're working so hard to hold yourself together. Something caused that, and I want to find out what it was. Or who it was."

"There could be eyes on the other side of every window on this street, Chris. Maybe I should carry on and see Ena because she needs someone. Later I'll tell you what she says."

His fingers hovered over the back of her hand. He'd never known such a need to be able to reach for someone and feel her. "Later? When you've run for cover again?"

Was that what she intended, even without thinking what she'd do next? "I don't know where I should go—where I should be. I was grateful to be at Roy and Bo's again last night, but it isn't right for me to take advantage of them." An urge to cry all but overwhelmed her. She breathed through her mouth and struggled for composure. "I am dangerous. I'm sure of that now. Otherwise why would a man I didn't even know die in a freak fire in my house? Other than as a nodding acquaintance, I had no idea who he was."

"That freak fire was started. I don't know how yet, but I will, and so will you. How could the fact that a disturbed man became fixated on you make you dangerous?"

What did it matter who watched them? She walked into him, clasped his shoulders, and buried her face in his chest.

She made him feel peace in his heart, and happiness, and at the same time she wounded him so deeply he felt disoriented. Her need was huge, yet she fought not to need at all—not to need him. But she wanted him. He wasn't fooling himself about

Sonnie's feelings; she was at war and he was both ally and enemy.

"Hey, hey, kid, what say we stop asking ourselves all the questions for now?" He would not let her drive him away. "We could just take things an hour at a time. How about that?"

She moved her face and he felt dampness soak through his cotton shirt. She cried. When had her body become familiar? Her scent familiar? The texture of her hair against his palm familiar?

"Okay," she mumbled. "An hour at a time. But you can't pull the big-man act on me."

He almost laughed. "Big-man act? Me?"

"Yes, you. If an hour comes when I decide I've got to make you go away, you'll go." She raised her face, her unforgettable face, and said, "I won't want to. It'll be because it's the way it has to be. Promise."

Sonnie saw his struggle. She saw how he sorted through responses that would allow him an escape. "I promise I'll respect your opinion," he said, and she analyzed exactly what he meant.

"There, you have your promise. I want to get you out of the sun. You're too fair for this heat." He hadn't lied, only given her a promise that wasn't exactly the one she'd requested.

Truman Avenue looked as it always looked. Stucco houses gleamed startlingly white or pink beneath the sun's rays, and the vegetation looked lush despite a layer of dust that had gathered on leaves and flowers. Lawns had begun to turn crisp. A good rain—and that rain was rarely far away—would wash away the dust and green the lawns again.

The one difference in the landscape was the presence of a cop who shaded himself beneath Sonnie's poinciana tree, and managed a prizewinning bored demeanor.

Holding Sonnie's hand, Chris turned sharply at Ena's driveway. He assessed a house that had started as a cigar maker's three-room abode, but which had been built onto over the years. The result was a whimsical concoction of wood and stucco, of gingerbread moldings over doors, and cutout wooden shutters at the upper-story windows. Ena grew cacti in an endless assortment of old cookie jars, cachepots, brass pots, sawed-off plastic milk bottles, and even a discarded round sink she'd sunk into the earth near the stoop.

"What time is it?" Sonnie asked.

He saw her studying windows covered by closed blinds—every window in the house as far as Chris could see. "Eleven," he told her. "Maybe her air-conditioning doesn't work so well, so she's trying to shut out the heat."

"Maybe." Sonnie didn't think so. Ena seemed almost to bloom on sweltering days. "She could be mourning."

Chris mounted the front steps, but the door opened before he could knock, and Ena looked out at them. Her face crumpled and she turned her back. Chris glanced at Sonnie for guidance, but she was already hurrying up the steps and taking Ena in her arms. "Come on," she said. "We're here now. It's okay, Ena. We'll help you with this."

Ena let herself be led into the house, but she said, "It's nicer on the back porch. I've got iced tea in the icebox."

"You go out," Chris said. "I'll bring the tea."

Chaos abounded in Ena's kitchen. Charming chaos, it was true, but overwhelming to Chris, who spent his days streamlining his life and getting rid of anything he didn't absolutely need.

Cats were Ena's theme. Ceramic cats. Pewter cats. Papier-mâché cats painted unlikely colors. Kitchen spoons with cats on their handles and stored in a crock shaped like a marmalade cat with a big grin. Stuffed furry cats. Cats dressed up in Halloween costumes. Already a cat or two sporting red velvet Christmas caps.

Chris focused on the refrigerator and found the iced tea—in a large jug painted with green cats. The discovery of glasses that were free of any decoration was a relief. He carted his haul out to the back porch where Ena—still sniffling—sat with her feet up on a swing. Sonnie had taken a place on a sagging wicker couch draped with a floral sheet. He put the jug and glasses on a metal table stamped *Cinzano,* and sat beside Sonnie.

She looked significantly at Ena, who fluttered a bamboo fan

before her face and occasionally wiped her eyes on a white-spotted red handkerchief.

"I'll pour," Sonnie said. She wanted to do something, anything. Ena's abject misery wasn't something she'd been prepared to face. "You need to drink plenty when it's like this, Ena."

Ena flapped the handkerchief and offered a watery and wan smile. But she accepted a glass and drank thirstily.

"The police were here?" Chris said.

Sonnie glared at him. Men could be insensitive—even sensitive men like Chris.

He shrugged and drank some tea.

"They've been all over the place," Ena said. "Poking and prying. I told them I'd show them whatever they wanted to see, but they had one of those warrants and they ignored me."

"Bastards," Chris said. He cleared his throat. "Sorry, ladies. I get angry when I see bullheadedness." The moments when he didn't quite recognize himself were getting closer together.

"Thank you," Ena said. "I was wrong about you when I first saw you. I thought you were one of those awful biker types. Molls, and those terrible rally things when they all get naked together—or the women, anyway. I saw that in the paper."

Chris's mind went blank.

He was finally struck silent, Sonnie thought, and smiled sweetly at him. "Imagine anyone thinking things like that about a shy man like you," she said. "Ena, Chris would probably run the other way if he saw naked people hanging out together."

"Sturgis," Ena cried. "That's it. Sturgis. North Dakota, or South Dakota, or somewhere. And the women take off their shirts for some sort of contest. What kind of contest that would be, I can't imagine."

"A contest I wouldn't win," Sonnie said softly, offering Chris a mischievous grin.

He attempted a scowl but grinned back just the same. "I wouldn't know anything about those things," he said. "I don't get out much."

"Tattoos, too," Ena said. "Obscene, some of them."

Chris had been waiting for that. He'd also been waiting for Sonnie to mention the little monstrosity he'd acquired as part of his tough disguise. The more time that passed before she did ask, the better. He wasn't prepared to tell her his entire history yet—might never be.

"Ena," Sonnie said gently, "would you tell us about Edward? I saw him only a few times. Didn't even meet him, really, just saw him close enough to wave. He seemed such a nice man."

"I think he was a nice man." The woman's tone toughened and she sounded defensive. "The police told me off for renting to him without knowing more about him. But he said he knew a cousin of mine in Miami. That's where I'm from. Not that I've spoken to her—my cousin—since we were in our twenties. I never liked her. But she's family and that counts for something."

"Yes," Chris said, and felt the sinking sensation that came with the conviction that he was dealing with a difficult witness. "I expect the police here have made arrangements to speak with your cousin."

Ena drank more tea and her expression became closed. "I don't know where she's living. I told them that. They got angry with me again. Said I wasn't cooperating, but how could I tell them what I don't know?"

"But Edward knew her? He'd seen her recently enough to give her as a reference?"

"Well . . . it wasn't exactly like that. He'd met Janice some years back and they'd gotten into a conversation about the Keys. She told him she had a cousin down here. Said since it's a small place he should be able to find Ena Fishbine if he needed to, and that I used to let rooms. Though, now that I think about it, how she knew that I can't imagine."

"Janice Fishbine," Chris said. "And you think she's still in Miami."

"Fishbine's my married name," Ena said, and sniffed. "There's still a Mr. Fishbine but I couldn't say where he is at the moment. And I'm sure I don't care. But he'll be hugging a bottle, I can tell you that. I don't know what Janice's last name would be. Edward mentioned she was married, but I never thought to ask her name. Wasn't interested."

This was great. All roads leading to nowhere. He would risk a more direct approach. "Do you suppose we could look at Edward's room, Ena?"

She frowned at him and pursed her heavily painted mouth. "The police have turned it upside down. Don't ask me why. There's nothing in there but all that magic stuff."

Sonnie blinked and caught Chris's glance before it slid away. "Edward was into magic?" she said, and once more felt vaguely nauseated. "What did he do for a living?"

Ena's chin rose. "He paid his rent regular. I'm not a nosy type. I don't believe in poking around in other people's business. He was a very good magician. All he needed was a break."

"So he didn't find much work," Chris said. "That's tough."

"Oh, he found work okay. Just not real regular and not any that paid a lot. But he paid me in cash and he paid me the minute he was paid. And the fun I had when he did tricks for me! He could do anything. Make things disappear. Swallow swords and lighted torches. He wanted to cut me in half only I wouldn't let him." She giggled. "I was afraid he would forget how to put me back together again."

"You liked him," Sonnie said, wishing she could read Chris's impassive expression.

"Yes, I did. He talked about doing magic for children in the hospital. A good heart, he had. Even if he did have those pictures the police made such a fuss over."

Chris's impassivity slipped a little, but he recovered quickly. "What kind of pictures?"

"Oh, I don't know. I suppose they were like the ones on his walls. I did mention them to him once, but he laughed and said they were a joke."

"Did the police take them all?"

"Not the ones on the wall," Ena said.

Chris got up. "You don't have to move, but it might help us understand a bit more if I took a look. Just tell me where to go."

Her expression shutting down, Ena got up and said, "I'll

take you. But you'll have to be quick because I was told not to let anyone near that room. Not that I care what those nasty people say. Don't care a bit about what happened to Edward, they don't. I'm going to bury him, you know. They can't find any family or anyone at all who knew him. So I'll put him in the ground. Come along.''

Reluctantly Sonnie followed them into the stuffy house and up a dark flight of stairs. A second flight rose to the attic floor, where a large space with sloping ceilings had been turned into a bedroom and living room combined.

''His bathroom's a floor down,'' Ena said. ''But he doesn't mind. Didn't mind.'' She sighed. ''See what a mess they've made?''

Assuming Edward had been a tidy man, the police certainly had made a mess. Every visible drawer had been emptied. A trunk pushed into a dormer window stood open to reveal many items that must be part of Edward's magic supplies. Bedding was strewn.

Hooks lined two walls. Brightly colored silk scarves hung there, and capes, whips, hoops, lengths of cord in different thicknesses, and braces of rubber birds. Jumbled on a table were several top hats, a jeweled turban, silver-tipped canes, boxes of playing cards, ropes of glittering beads, and a profusion of items so tangled Sonnie couldn't identify them. Looking at the trappings, she experienced some of the mystery of childhood encounters with magicians.

Chris wasn't examining the glitter. Rather he stood before an array of photographic posters, each one displaying a scantily dressed or naked woman contorted into what seemed a painful pose. Real knives, each one driven into the genital area, helped spear the pictures to the wall.

Sonnie shuddered.

Chris didn't miss her reaction. He didn't want her here, but getting her out of the room might cause Ena to order them both away. As it was he saw how the woman looked frequently and nervously toward the stairs.

''Did the police say they'd taken everything they needed?'' he asked her.

"They didn't say they hadn't," Ena said. "We mustn't stay long in case they come back. They can get mean, y'know."

"I know," he said. "The photographs they took away—they were photographs, weren't they?—did they look like these on the walls?"

"Some of them, I think." She shrugged. "People have their funny sides. So he liked nasty photographs. There could be worse things."

Like lying in wait for a woman and planning to do who knew what to her when he got her alone? He held his tongue and went back to studying the posters. "Did he know these women?"

"How should I know? I wouldn't think so. They obviously aren't very nice."

"Edward must have thought so, too. Why would he stick knives in them otherwise?" *Because he hated women.* Chris had dealt with his share of perverts. Some never acted out their fantasies. Others did. . . .

"He said they needed to be punished," Ena said, but her confidence had fractured and she wouldn't meet his eyes. "That's why he put knives in the pictures like that. He was really a very moral man."

"Oh, yeah," Chris said solemnly.

Sonnie's palms sweated. Evil lived in this space.

Ena sighed. "He used to have little Wimpy jump through those hoops. It was so funny to watch. Do you know why Edward called him Wimpy?"

Sonnie had forgotten the tiny dog. "No."

"Because he loves hamburger. Like Wimpy in *Popeye.* Edward always bought him hamburger. Jump through one of those hoops when Edward set fire to it, Wimpy would. Just as long as he could see the hamburger on the other side."

Slowly Sonnie turned to Chris and found him studying her hard. He shook his head slightly, obviously warning her to save what was on her mind until they were alone.

She nodded. "Chris and I had better get along. But I plan

to move back into the house just as soon as I can. Could be as soon as tomorrow. I've already found a contractor who says he can close up the outside in a few hours and make sure I'm secure. He can take his time redoing the inside.'' She would not allow herself to be frightened away from her own home.

"I can't tell you how happy it makes me to hear you say that,'' Ena told her with tears in her eyes. "I feel we've become friends. We've shared a lot. I'll be here for you. All you have to do is call. And I'll check on you every day.''

Sonnie managed not to wince. "I'm sure I'll settle in quickly.'' She went to the stairs and started down. When she halted, Ena bumped into her and laughed. "Sorry,'' Sonnie said. "I forgot all about that dear little dog. Where is he? You didn't . . . Well, you didn't get rid of him, did you?''

"Oh, my,'' Ena said. "Oh, *my*. Wimpy. I didn't even give him a thought. He went everywhere. . . . Oh, no. He went everywhere with Edward. Edward wouldn't let him out of his sight. He must have . . died in the fire.''

Sonnie faced Ena and started to speak, but she caught Chris's eye and he shook his head vehemently. Mr. Talon was very good at nonverbal communication, Sonnie thought, vaguely irritated.

Finally they were outside again, having left by the back door to the porch. "You go ahead and take a look around your gardens if you want to,'' Ena said in response to Chris's comment that Sonnie missed her place and wanted just to sit on the veranda—at least until some officious cop turned them out.

Sympathetic Ena ushered them toward another space in the shrubbery between the two houses, this one near the very end of the properties.

Sonnie waved to Ena and followed Chris into her own garden.

He waited silently and listened. "I think she's gone inside,'' he said at last.

"Does it matter?'' Sonnie said. "She's so sad, Chris.''

This lady who fascinated him so much had a heart soft enough to kill her if he didn't keep a close watch.

"She is sad," he agreed. "And confused. But we have to be careful what we say to her, Sonnie. She wouldn't mean to, but she's very capable of repeating what she's told. Not out of malice. Just because she wants something to say, something intimate enough to draw people to her."

Sonnie thought about that. "You've probably got great intuition," she told him, and thought that his intuition was only one of many things that were great about him.

"We're not going to find anything here," he said. "But I still want to look. If I decide to enter, I'll want you to leave the area."

"You still talk like a cop."

"Sorry. I'll work on it." Some things were harder than others to stamp out. "I'd like to know how he got in. You kept all the doors locked, didn't you?"

"Yes. Always."

"So there should be some sign of a break-in."

"Wouldn't the cops have found that?"

"Maybe, but they aren't going to share their information with Joe Blow, alias Chris Talon. See if you can find some cover where you can watch the guy out front without him noticing you. I want to check the doors and windows at the back."

Sonnie's heart fluttered too hard. "What will they do if they catch us?"

"This is your house. You want in to get something. You decide what it is, just in case."

Keeping close to the veranda, she hunched over and crept forward.

Scratching sounds brought her fluttery heart into her throat. She caught at a veranda railing and looked for Chris. He was watching her, an unreadable expression on his face. She waved at him, and gestured toward the veranda.

Quickly and quietly he came to her. "What is it?"

"Listen."

He raised his head and narrowed his eyes. "I don't hear anything."

She caught at his sleeve. "There it is again. Someone's under the veranda."

Chris bent to look under the pilings that supported the structure. "There isn't room. At least not for some*one*. I hear it though. Probably an animal."

Instantly she knelt down and peered into the darkness. At first there was no sound and nothing to see. Two gleaming eyes appeared quite suddenly, so suddenly Sonnie jumped and almost cried out.

"Don't make any noise," Chris told her. He wished he could stop her from being so antsy. She reacted to anything and everything. "It's nothing. Probably just a rat."

He barely got a hand over her mouth to stop her scream. "I am a fool," he said, trying to sound matter-of-fact. "In some ways, I always was. Open mouth, insert foot. Come on. Go keep watch for me."

The scratching became a rustling.

Out from the gloom beneath the veranda popped the round head of a very small black dog. Its eyes resembled bulging golden marbles—only with the saddest expression Chris remembered noting in an animal. The creature's coat—or what could be seen of it—shone like that of a wet seal.

"Wimpy," Sonnie whispered. "Oh, you poor little guy. You must be starved. Chris, he's been here for days. Come on, Wimpy. Come to Sonnie. I'll look after you."

Dropping his belly close to the ground, Wimpy crawled forward. Slowly he brought all of his ten or twelve inches of length—from nose to tip of tail—into the light.

Holding out her hands, Sonnie encouraged him to come to her. Wimpy spared her a glance, but went to Chris, who picked him up and sucked in a breath when the dog whimpered.

"He's burned," Sonnie said, barely remembering to keep her voice down. "All over his tummy." Never mind if he'd shunned her attentions; she didn't blame him for trusting Chris. "It must have happened when . . ." She looked upward at the house.

"I think our troubles are over," Chris said, confusing Sonnie completely. "Let's get out of here and think a few things through. I need you to remember exactly what happened that night when you called me over. After the nightmare.''

He put Wimpy inside his shirt, held a hand out to Sonnie, and pulled her to her feet. ''It's going to be okay. This could have turned out to be really nasty, but I think we got lucky. If I'm right, you're safe now.''

Eighteen

Café Orange occupied a three-story house with an outlook that promised there could be no better sunset view on the island. Not that there was likely to be a visible sunset tonight. Sonnie eyed the purplish afternoon sky and the shadows cast by sullen clouds upon an eerily calm sea. A storm would be a relief, a long, cleansing cloudburst complete with lightning and the satisfaction of great thunder to follow.

She thought of her house and the holes that were not yet permanently sealed. By tomorrow they would be; the contractor had promised. On this coral rock one hundred and fifty miles to the south of its motherland, yet only ninety miles north of Cuba, devastating storms that changed even the shape and size of the land were accepted, expected. Those who called Key West home took its capriciousness in stride, including repeated threats to their own safety and the safety of their homes. No matter how long it took, Sonnie was only passing through, and the prospect of a hurricane—and all that would mean—ripped at her nerves.

She sat at a table on the second-story veranda, nibbling at the straw in her daiquiri, and contemplated possible reasons for painting a restaurant called Café Orange pink.

Chris had done everything short of ordering her not to accept

Billy's invitation to meet her—alone—to stop Sonnie from keeping this appointment. ''Why,'' he'd asked, ''if she has nothing to hide, would she be so insistent that you leave me behind?''

Sonnie had told him, ''She didn't even mention your name. She wants us to be together and feel free to talk. We're sisters. Family. Is that such an unusual request?''

He'd shaken his head, but there was anger in his eyes, and tension in his flared nostrils and the white line that formed around his mouth.

Billy should have arrived by now, but she was invariably late.

A tree of purple orchids rose halfway up the veranda railings. This, too, was still, as was a mass of hauntingly sweet-smelling frangipani. Sonnie's cold drink frosted the outside of her glass, and wherever she touched it, another rivulet of water wound its way downward to the stem and, eventually, the pink tablecloth.

She wished Chris were with her.

She wished she never had to go anywhere without him ever again.

She was, in fact, in a hopeless mess.

And brilliant Mr. Talon was all wrong in his optimism about her future. What he didn't understand yet was that the events that had happened since her return didn't impact her reason for coming. Tonight she would tell him the truth, all of it, and if he told her, as had already been suggested, that she had a form of post-traumatic stress syndrome and needed therapy, she'd have to find a way to make herself tell him good-bye.

''Sonnie!''

She half turned to see Billy approach. Billy with Dr. Jim. He looked abashed, as he should. Sonnie faced the view again and seethed. At least if it had been Romano there might be an excuse.

''Darling,'' Billy said, bending to plant a kiss on Sonnie's cheek, ''this place is so *hokey*. In fact this entire island is hokey. I can't understand why you and Frank came here in the first place.''

Sonnie didn't say, *Neither do I,* but, ''He loved the climate and the atmosphere. It may not be your thing, but it's unique. You never know for sure what you'll encounter next." That was true, and there were times when she enjoyed the madness.

Billy sat on Sonnie's left, and Jim Lesley walked around to take the chair at her right. Something close to suffocation assailed her. "Family chat, hmm, Billy?" she said. "Since you're making a party of it, where's Romano?"

"He's gone for a couple of days. Up to the course at Marathon, evidently. Filling in, he said." She made much of smoothing her short blue skirt over her bare thighs. "Jim is my friend. I asked him to come because he's such a voice of reason, and I'm hoping you can come to trust him as much as I do."

Sonnie averted her face from Jim and gave Billy her entire attention. "Chris is my friend. I find him very reasonable. At your request I asked him not to come today." She turned to the doctor. "Please forgive me for saying these things in front of you. My sister has left me no choice. My argument is with her, not with you."

He smiled and some of her irritation dissolved. Jim Lesley had a really nice smile and such kind eyes.

"Don't suggest there's any similarity between Jim and that man," Billy said. "I don't need to point out the differences. You know them. And you also know that _I_ don't have a husband. There's no reason why I shouldn't be involved with a man who means a great deal to me."

Jim reached across the table, narrowly missing Sonnie's glass, and wound his fingers around Billy's.

"I am delighted for both of you," Sonnie said. "Let me know when you're ready to name the day. I'll look forward to that. Chris and I are just friends. Obviously, even if we wanted to be something more, that isn't possible. Please don't be insulting enough to remind me of my marriage again."

"Oh, _God,_" Billy said, letting her head fall back. Her hair was gelled close to her scalp. The style showed off her beautiful features. Her enjoyment of her own physical drama was visible. "Sonnie, you're making a fool of yourself. I've told you already that even if he is an unemployed drifter who likes to mooch off of people, he's gorgeous and he's the type who goes for flashy women. No disrespect, but you aren't flashy. You're pleasant to look at—the little-girl-next-door type. Don't you think there's something odd about—''

"Billy," Jim said, and when Sonnie glanced at him she was surprised to see that his face had become pale, his posture stiff. "There's no need to continue with this. Sonnie's a lovely woman. I don't think she cares what I think about her but, for what it's worth, Sonnie isn't the obvious type, and there are many men who really don't want what you call flash. Shall we order something? Late lunch? Early dinner?''

"I'm not hungry," Billy said, pouting. "I want a Grand Marnier over ice. Make it a triple. It goes down so quickly in this ghastly heat.''

Jim didn't look happy but he signaled a waiter.

Billy stared at Sonnie until she said, "What's the matter?''

"Can't you wear your hair over the scar?" Billy said. "And make sure your neck's covered?''

"They're just scars," Sonnie said, but her heart beat harder. "It's too hot here to cover up.''

"Exactly so," Jim Lesley said.

"I wasn't talking to you," Billy told him. "I don't want to sound unkind, but most people who are disfigured try to disguise it. They don't want everyone who looks at them to be disgusted.''

Sonnie's sister disgusted her. "Drop it," she said. "If it bothers you to look at me, don't look.''

"You're impossible," Billy said. She peered at the sky. "I think there's going to be a hurricane. They keep saying the two that are way south won't hit here, but they're cutting down the coconuts and clearing away any fallen ones. They don't do that unless they're afraid a hurricane will turn them into projectiles, do they?''

"I don't know," Sonnie muttered. And she didn't care.

"The sooner we all get out of here, the better. I suppose you've noticed that half the population's gay. And other things. Honestly, who wants to watch men prancing around in drag?''

Sonnie detested bigotry. "It's a free country—supposedly. You don't have to watch, and you're certainly not the audience they're looking for. I find it works for me if I don't judge what I don't understand.''

"Well, I think they're all scary.''

In spite of her annoyance, Sonnie laughed. "If they did notice you, they wouldn't find you scary. They aren't interested in you at all.''

"I like it here,'' Jim said, and pretended not to notice Billy's scowl. "Diversity's good for provincial souls. I wouldn't even mind a hurricane. At least it would be different.'' He wrinkled his nose. "As long as it's really mild and no one gets hurt.''

Billy's Grand Marnier arrived, and Jim's gin and tonic. He told the waiter they weren't ready to order a meal.

"Enough small talk,'' Billy announced. "This isn't a discussion. I'm taking you home, Sonnie.''

As usual, Chris had been right: she shouldn't have come— at least not alone.

"Do you understand that I mean what I say?'' Billy said.

"*You're* making a fool of yourself,'' Sonnie said. "You have no right to tell me what to do, and you know it. Thank you for caring about me, and I believe you do, but if you want to help me, allow me to work my way through a difficult time the best way I can.''

"I told you,'' Billy said to Jim. "She isn't rational.''

That heated Sonnie's blood. "I think I'd better go.''

"Your limp is worse,'' Billy said, loudly enough to get the attention of other patrons. "Don't tell me you aren't aware of it. You were told you might need more surgery, and you do. You must be in pain. That foot—oh, dear. Why not admit it and throw yourself into getting well?''

"I am well.''

"You walk like a cripple.''

Sonnie swallowed. "I am a cripple.''

"Yes, but why not minimize the obvious?''

"Billy,'' Jim said. "You sound so cruel, and you're not cruel at all. Be careful what you say, and how.''

"I didn't ask your advice,'' was Billy's prompt reply. "This is harder on me than on anyone. I'm the only one with the guts to tell the truth and do something about it. Look at her face.

It's awful. You're a doctor. Don't pretend you don't see that it's past time for more plastic surgery.''

"Apart from the initial wound closure, I haven't had any plastic surgery,'' Sonnie said through lips that had turned numb. "There's plenty of time. The more healing that takes place beforehand, the better.''

"Jim?'' Billy said, her eyes wide. "Help me.''

"Don't do this to him,'' Sonnie said. "I intend to get some opinions soon. Just as soon as I feel I can leave Key West.''

"You can leave *now,*'' Billy said. "Why wouldn't you be able to? There's nothing keeping you here, is there?''

Only a need to look for the reason why I lost control of my car. I'm not the panicky type. When I was told that Frank had been abducted, I'm sure I felt bad for him, but it wouldn't have upset me for myself. I wouldn't have had an accident because of the news. I didn't love him anymore. He made sure of that. I don't love him now, and I don't know why I ever thought I did.

"Sonnie? Answer me. Is there anything keeping you here?''

"Don't interrogate your sister like this,'' Jim said.

"I've got to look after the dog,'' Sonnie said. "He isn't well enough to travel right now.'' Desperation could make a person say really dumb things, Sonnie thought, and turned hot.

"Dog?'' Billy said. *"Dog?* What dog?''

"Oh, I forgot to tell you I got a dog, didn't I? He's such a dear little thing, but he hurt his stomach and needs to heal. He needs a lot of attention right now.''

Billy leaned close and patted Sonnie's cheek. "Dear little Baby,'' she said, "dear, wounded little sister. I've got to help you face up to the truth. You just want something to love, and a dog is the closest you can get to what you want most. Your baby died, Sonnie. You can't replace a dead baby with a dog.''

Darkness edged into Sonnie's mind. She stared, but the scene faded. Billy was talking again but from a great distance. All feeling had left Sonnie's body.

A gentle shaking—Jim shaking her shoulder very carefully—slowly dispelled the protective shield she'd closed around her. He was smiling at her again. "You're frail,'' he told her. "Why wouldn't you be? You've been to hell and back and you're doing so well. Will you allow me to say a few things to you?"

Sonnie stared at him and nodded.

"Your sister is a sweet, gentle—completely undiplomatic woman. I'm a man who doesn't make decisions easily, but I've fallen in love with her."

Billy said, "You say dreadful things, then make me cry. You're a beast, Jim Lesley."

"Try to sit quietly," Jim told her, "until I've finished telling Sonnie what I see here. Or maybe until I tell her something about myself that could help her. I'm not your doctor, Sonnie, but I am a doctor. A psychiatrist." He gave a breathy laugh. "I don't know much about scheduling plastic surgery, but it seems you should probably get an evaluation soon. Does your leg hurt?"

"Yes. It probably always will. My tolerance for the pain increases, though."

"Brave girl," Jim said. "Anyway, regardless of my medical training, I'm not *your* doctor. I can't advise you as a practitioner unless you ask me to, but I can speak as a friend, and as a man. I'm on R and R, Sonnie. I've got a private clinic. It's very successful, and it demands almost everything I've got to give. A day came when I knew that if I didn't get away and regroup, I was likely to be occupying one of my own beds. The task I've given myself is to decide what's really important. That means I've got to face up to where I am in my life, and why, and if the answers add up to a situation that's injuring me, I've got to change course. Scary as hell, but no scarier than risking burning myself out.

"Does any of that sound familiar to you—as if I could be talking about where you are today?"

She could tell him none of it was applicable, or she could say that if she examined what she was doing in Key West, she might find out she was hurting herself. Only she wouldn't tell him that because, unlike him, she wasn't prepared to change course.

"It's the biker," Billy said, producing a small mirror and

checking her makeup. "Not entirely, but mostly. She's unbalanced—or not herself anyway—and he's taking advantage of that. Why else would he give her any attention, especially now? He sees an easy meal ticket, and she's leaning on him because she's lost. I'm going to contact her doctors and ask advice."

Stiff from sitting too long, Sonnie pushed to her feet and gripped the edge of the table until her spine loosened up.

"Sit down," Billy said. "We're going to order a meal soon."

"I hope it's good. I'm going to have to beg off. I hope you'll excuse me, but I've already been here longer than I intended to be. It's time to feed Wimpy."

Billy snapped her compact shut. "Wimpy?"

"My substitute baby."

The last time Chris had been in Key West, Mallory Square Sunset had been a place to avoid. Street entertainers had reached combative terms with each other and often fought over prime spots where the tips were best. Beggars had passed the quietly insulting phase and were openly aggressive. Bad jugglers and worse magic acts had abounded, and the crowd frequently included those—both men and women—who shed clothes to show off body piercings. A young man might lie on a bed of nails with a concrete slab on his lap and request volunteers to break the slab with a hammer.

Overall the vibes became malignant. Chris had had enough trouble with his own internally generated "bad feelings" and avoided the place completely for years.

Eventually the powers that be had cleaned up "Sunset," and the wowed gawkers had returned to take photographs of the sinking sun, photographs soon destined to be forgotten.

If Bo hadn't been down to a merchants' meeting near the square this evening, Chris wouldn't have known where to look for Sonnie. In truth it might have been some time before he realized she wasn't still with her sister.

The sunset hour was upon them, but there was no sunset. The unholy calm that had pressed down on the area in midafternoon remained. All that seemed to move was the gradually encroaching darkness.

He crossed the red brick-paved square to a walk that edged the water. A few staunch photographers—no doubt visitors for the day determined to get a shot of something they could point out as the sunset—craned their necks to see past a moored cruise ship. A vendor hawked conch fritters in a tone that never changed, at intervals that never varied, while stray cats feasted on scraps.

At the farthest point to his right, past an evangelist who was the sole listener to his own lesson on the meaning of sin, Chris saw Sonnie. She sat with her legs hanging over the water, and gazed toward the Gulf and the lights on Sunset Key. From a distance she seemed completely motionless.

A bad feeling didn't come close to what was going on inside his head, his body. Was she preparing herself to tell him she intended to leave Key West? How would he respond to that? What would he do? Would he do anything?

Or was he feeling something else, something he'd persuaded himself was over: that Sonnie was in danger?

At first he hurried toward her, but the closer he drew, the slower his feet moved. When he could actually see her profile, he could hardly move at all. Remote and lovely, with no particular expression, she still conveyed sadness.

That sister of hers had done something, said something to hurt Sonnie.

He arrived behind her.

"You found me," she said. "How did you manage that?"

"I'd like to say I closed my eyes and knew you were here. Bo saw you."

"Dear Bo."

"Yeah, dear Bo."

"I've got to make up my mind—about what I should do."

Chris settled a hand on her shoulder. "I thought that's what you might be doing here." Deciding whether to stay or go. He wanted to figure in her calculations, but feared he didn't. "May I sit with you, or would you rather I left you alone?"

She covered his hand on her shoulder. "Sit with me."

He did as she asked, trying not to feel too exhilarated. "You sad, kid?" He put an arm lightly—and, he hoped, nonthreateningly—around her shoulders.

"Maybe." Her gaze remained fastened on the seascape. "I cry too much these days. I never used to cry at all. Not as far as I can remember."

"Tears have a purpose. Good for you. They say if men cried more, they'd live longer."

Sonnie looked at him, and the look stole his breath. She searched his face as if she were trying to see inside him. Her smile was a relief. "Start crying, then," she said. "Cry a lot. I'll buy the tissues."

All the years of hiding what he really felt had left him unprepared for moments like this. Offering her his hand, he waited until she placed her palm against his, and he took her fingers to his mouth. Never looking away from her face, he kissed each one. The faintest blush rose in her cheeks.

In the silence that followed, they sat holding hands and facing the hot, thickening gloom.

"The tissue bit," Chris said, "did that mean you wish me a long life?"

"Of course."

"Why?"

"Best not to fish. You might hear something that'll frighten you."

And that, Chris thought, could mean a number of things. "Right," he said. "What were you thinking about when I found you? You said you were trying to make your mind up."

"I've decided I trust you. Really trust you. It's not because I've learned much about you. But I think you care about me, although you didn't want to. You tried very hard not to care about me."

"That was before I got to know you."

"You don't know me."

"How can you say that? We're not strangers." He resumed kissing her fingers, and she gave him a reproachful glance. "What was that for?" he said. "I'm only telling the truth. We've spent some pretty significant time together."

"Significant?" She shook her head. "Now you're a diplomat. I'm not safe, Chris. You were wrong when you said I might be."

Gripping her hand tightly, he frowned. "Want to enlarge on that, darlin'?"

"It's quite possible that the dreadful thing that happened with Edward Miller had nothing to do with what frightened me into coming here in the first place."

"On the night you had the nightmare and called me, you saw fire, and you saw a face behind the flame. Isn't that what you said?"

"Yes."

"You tied that up to other nightmares. Other unexplained things that have happened to you."

"I did then. I know what you're getting at. It was probably Edward who produced the flame and looked at me through it. He was dark haired —like Frank—and I made Edward's face into Frank's."

He tucked her hand around his elbow. "I'm sure you're right. When Ena talked about him making Wimpy jump through hoops of fire, it all came clear. The guy was psychotic. For some reason you became his fixation. But he's dead and you're not. It's not going to happen again."

"Maybe not that, but something probably will."

"Sonnie—"

"Listen to me. From the start I told you I thought someone wanted me dead. That was before the fire thing. It started in Miami—in the hospital—when I wasn't conscious much. There were voices. They told me to die. They said I *should* have died. I must join my baby. They said I should join her because that's what I wanted to do. And I did, Chris. I was so broken. I began to wish myself away. But then the pressure in my brain was reduced, and although I was so broken, I stopped wanting to die."

She might make him feel like crying some of those tears she'd mentioned. "Okay," he said, "I'm more grateful about that than I can explain. But you could have been hallucinating when you were in the hospital."

"No." She pulled her hand away. "That's why I never told anyone. I knew what they'd think."

"I didn't say it's what I think. I just mentioned the possibility."

"One day there was a lot of commotion because a nurse came in and found one of the tubes out. One of the tubes into my body. I don't know what it was for, but everyone started running. Afterward I heard them talking about how I must have pulled it out, only they couldn't figure out how I'd managed it.

"I'm sure I didn't pull it out, Chris. Someone else did. Someone who wanted me dead."

"Hell," he murmured. "But you can't say for sure that you didn't pull it out."

Sonnie rubbed her hands down her face. "No, I can't. Or I can't say it and hope to be believed. I heard those voices, soft and in whispers, telling me to stop fighting, telling me to die. Over and over they told me to die. And when I started to get a little better, the doctors said how they'd spoken with my family and that everyone believed Frank's abduction had caused the accident."

"Is that so far-fetched?"

"The plane came in," Sonnie said. "I was told all this—I don't remember much. The Giacano plane came in, but it was Romano who got off, not Frank. Frank had called from Miami. He asked me to meet him at the airport that night. He said he'd be in a hurry and needed me to do something for him. He rarely traveled by commercial plane. Romano arrived and told me Frank had been kidnapped. I was so shocked I got in my car and drove wildly until I hit a wall. I was thrown free but no one noticed that until the emergency crews arrived. The car caught on fire, and Romano—he'd tried to follow me— Romano thought I was still inside."

Chris had read the official reports of the accident. They pretty much matched what Sonnie said. "And now I believe in angels," he told her. "Angels who save good people like you for rotten people like me."

She bent forward to peer at the water below. "I believe,

absolutely believe, that I was supposed to die in that crash. I'm not saying Romano knew that. He probably didn't because . . . because the person who wanted it to happen would probably keep Romano in the dark. So he could say all the right things later.''

"Sonnie," Chris said gently. "How would someone try to pull off something like that?''

"I don't know. By doing something to my car? By giving me drugs—a shot, maybe. I've tried to find any airport personnel who were on duty that night. All I've reached is one dead end after another. It seems as if several people left shortly afterward and no one knows where they went.''

He rubbed her back. She was a very intelligent woman, but hunches didn't make the grade if they couldn't be proved. "Wouldn't that mean your brother-in-law was involved?''

"No. *No.* Romano has always been so good to me. I do think he's having business difficulties now—and he may even be afraid I intend to talk out of turn about Frank. Romano adores Frank and he'd protect him at any cost.''

Chris rested a forearm on his thigh and leaned his head as close to Sonnie's as he could. His next question had to be carefully posed. "If you talked out of turn about Frank, what would you say?''

She turned until she could look at him. "I won't talk about Frank. I don't even know if he's alive or dead. I've got to respect him until he can defend himself.''

What she said—if she said anything—wouldn't be so great. So he felt good about that? He was only human. "Give me something else to go on.''

"I'm asking too much of you, but stick with me, Chris. Be with me. How can a person explain something they feel in their gut? You asked me once about going to the police. Now you see what a waste of time that would be. I just have to keep my eyes open all the time, keep waiting for someone to make a move on me. I talk about being well and strong, but I've got a way to go before that's completely true. You've said you'll help me. Now I want to make this a business arrangement, the way it should be. I'll pay you a salary. You can have your own rooms, just like I suggested. You'll be my bodyguard and my extra brain—you'll at least try to help me keep myself alive.''

A flash of anger fizzled under the fear she struck into him. He didn't ask permission to gather her hair at her nape and pull her face to his. When his mouth met hers, Sonnie's eyes were closing and she panted lightly. His own eyes were shut tight when the thought occurred to him that this was a first. He hadn't kissed a woman this many times without doing a lot more since he was a kid and afraid of getting slapped.

Sonnie left him in no doubt that she liked being kissed by him. She found her way inside the neck of his shirt and played with the hair on his chest. The tips of her fingers touched every feature on his face as if she was fascinated by the form of him. Chris's grasp went to her waist and narrow rib cage. The sensation that he could swing her up into his arms and bear her away intrigued him, made him feel strong and protective. He liked the feeling.

Slowly, taking his time to land hard little kisses as he did so, Chris parted his mouth from hers. ''Okay,'' he told her, breathless. ''I'll be your eyes and ears. But you're going to have to sit through the kind of interrogation you've never sat through. I've got to know everything. I've got to know things you didn't know you knew. And you won't be able to hold back.

''I'll live in your house. My rooms will have to be very close to yours.''

Sonnie still stared at his mouth. She touched it softly and leaned so close he felt her breath on his lips.

''Are you listening to me?''

She nodded.

''Good. I'm going to be asking questions all over this town, and I may turn up things you'd rather no one ever found out. You understand?''

He got another nod. She inclined her head and brushed his hair back.

''That means I'll be asking about other people's impression of your relationship with Frank Giacano.''

Her eyes met his, deeply sad but resigned.

"And if nothing else happens, you'll be able to stop worrying and carry on with your life."

"What life?" she asked, and frowned. "I shouldn't have said that. Of course I'm going to have to get on with things. What I can't even think about now is how I'll go about that."

"Because you may still have a husband?"

"Partly. Partly because I got married before I was ready to take care of myself if I was alone. I don't have any real skills."

"Women go back to school all the time."

"If they know what they want to do."

He'd never had a conversation like this. "You don't know what you want to do?"

She plucked at her beige linen pants. "I do know. I always did."

"So it's going to be easy."

"Is it?"

When she raised her eyes to his, she tightened every muscle in his body.

"I want to be the wife of a man who really loves me. And I want to have his children, and look after his house, and plant things in the garden. I guess I'm either a throwback or I don't have any ambition."

He didn't remind her that she'd accused him of that sin. "I think you're wonderful. And you're going to be the very best at it."

"Once I thought so."

"Think so again."

"Not with Frank." She sucked her breath in through her teeth and made to get up. Chris stopped her. He pulled her face against his shoulder and just held her.

She made no attempt to move away; rather she settled there and burrowed her forehead beneath his chin.

"This is a strange relationship we have, love. Or some people might think so. Can we put it in my job description that I have a responsibility to comfort you whenever I think you need it?"

"If you like."

He'd like. He'd like very much. "Do you want Frank to come back?"

Her arms went around his waist and she held him tightly enough to hurt.

"Sonnie? Do you?"

"I want him to return alive. Of course I do."

"Return to you?"

"I . . . Don't ask me that question. Chris, Frank didn't want the baby. He found pregnant women ugly—disgusting, even. That's why he left me so quickly when I'd asked him to come home. I asked him because I was so excited about the baby and I hoped the news would make him change."

"No good, though?"

"No good. He liked the excitement of being on the road—of the tournaments and all the attention he got. He said he'd come back for what he called 'the proud papa' pictures. He said they'd play well. His words, not mine. I came to wonder why he'd married me in the first place. Billy would say it was because she'd refused him. That could be true. She brought him home—and Romano. Looking back it was as if she pushed me at him. They were the close ones. They laughed together. Stopped talking if I found them. That sort of thing. I don't know. He was losing, you know. He'd been losing for some time before he disappeared, but he still went out there and lived the kind of life I would have hated. Parties, gambling—drugs, I think."

Chris wanted to call the man a fool, but knew better. "But if he comes home you'll try to be a good wife to him? You'll be here for him?"

"When the accident happened—that was when he was supposed to come back again—I think he was only coming because he needed money. Maybe a lot of money. I don't believe he was coming because he missed me."

"You could be right. But that still isn't any reason to think someone wanted you to die that night."

"If I'd died, Frank would have inherited everything, including my trust fund."

"What are you really suggesting?" Chris held her head

away so that he could see her face. "Don't play with this anymore. Are you saying you think your husband wanted you dead so he could inherit everything?"

She ran her tongue over her lips. "I'm saying it's one motive someone could have. And I think I'm right where I started when I got here. I believe Edward decided I was one of those women he needed to punish. He'd know from Ena that my baby died. Maybe he blamed me for that, and for something happening to Frank."

"The guy wasn't balanced," Chris admitted. "He obviously hated women."

"He set me up to be scared. Who knows what he intended to do that night? I don't want to think about it."

They regarded each other for a long time. Doubt nagged at him. She'd suffered a head injury. He wasn't an expert, but those things could mess with a person's mind, and no matter how much another person wanted it to be otherwise, he supposed paranoia could be the result—and it didn't have to be curable.

She peered past his shoulder. "Don't we know someone who bought a car from a *Playboy* bunny?"

He didn't immediately make the connection. When he did, he grinned and twisted around to see Flynn's pink Mustang parked under a light in the deserted parking lot. "What can I tell you? Flynn regards that as a work of art. I didn't know he'd told you it was probably a gift to a *Playboy* bunny. Runs like a Rolls, so he tells me. He's had a thing for cars like that as long as I've known him, and that's a long time."

His old partner's long legs covered ground fast. He bent forward at the waist, peering into what had become almost total darkness.

"He thinks we're here," Sonnie said. "Roy and Bo must have told him."

"You can bet your boots they did. They're all in cahoots."

"About what?"

And that, Chris thought, was not an appropriate topic to visit this evening. Sonnie was the subject of the day, not Chris Talon. "They're following what's happening to their favorite friend—you. You've really found a way into my brother's hard heart—and Bo's.''

Aiden Flynn had broken into a run and arrived, silent in tennis shoes, in an amazingly short time. ''Bo said—''

''You'd probably find us here,'' Chris finished for him, but without rancor. ''Join us. We're watching the sunset.''

''Huh?'' Aiden looked over his shoulder and across the Gulf. ''There isn't going to be any sunset tonight. It's too late, anyway.''

''Is it?'' Chris managed to sound surprised.

Aiden cuffed him playfully across the ear. ''I need to talk to you, Chris. Our friend Wally was busy today. Let's get Sonnie somewhere safe and have a chat.''

''You won't be having any chats without me,'' Sonnie said, scrambling to her feet and grabbing Aiden's sleeve while she bent and stretched her left leg several times. When she put her full weight on her right leg, she screwed up her eyes momentarily. Chris glanced at Aiden. She'd really been beaten up in that crash.

''Why not take it easy at Roy and Bo's?'' Chris said.

''This is all about me, and I want to know anything you've found out.''

Chris's instinct nudged him to find a way to stop her from hearing whatever Flynn had to say.

''Okay by me if it's okay by Chris,'' the ever-helpful Flynn said.

''It's okay with Chris—isn't it?'' she said in a tone that dared him to argue.

''Sure,'' he said. ''There's a bench over there. I doubt if there's anywhere much more private. Lead on, Flynn.''

The man went to the bench and flopped down at once. He popped up again as Sonnie approached and waited until she sat to join her. Chris remained standing.

''I'm worn out,'' Flynn said. ''Would you believe I haven't eaten in hours?''

''No. We'd better do something about that—after you spill whatever you've dug up.''

Flynn cleared his throat. ''There's no make on Edward

Miller. Not a damn thing outside what the police found at that place next door to Sonnie's. They're furious. Kinda enjoyed that. The gent appeared on the earth in Miami—fully grown and apparently in his forties. That's all. Not another thing.''

"Shit," Chris muttered. "I'd feel better if we could trace him."

"Wouldn't we all? I didn't say I'd give up."

"What else?"

"Wally got to go talk to the local Medical Examiner this afternoon. He was in the mood to discuss his work. Seems he had a notable customer recently."

Chris heard Sonnie make a soft sound. He'd rather she didn't go through this, but she'd been determined not to miss anything. "You can explain how you managed that later. Anything interesting?"

"I saw the record. Some really impressive candid shots, too. Apparently fairly healthy white male. Won't bother you with the preliminary stuff. Standard *T* opening—"

"Cut it out," Chris said.

"The Medical Examiner had done that, and it wasn't pretty, I can tell—"

"Don't tell us. It's time you grew up."

"You're terrible, Aiden," Sonnie said with an unconvincing laugh. At least she restored a little of Chris's confidence. He didn't want a fainting female on his hands.

"Not a'tall," Flynn said. "Just revealing all, like himself told me to. Okay, me darlin's, Edward Miller was supposed to burn in that fire. I don't know exactly what went wrong, although there is talk of a gas can being found. Probably supposed to make a really good job of the barbecue."

Chris gave up trying to control Flynn. He'd always been a sick bastard in these situations. His way of dealing with what was beyond acceptable, some had said.

"The fire was started—or so they're almost sure—above the ceiling in that room. Apparently they found evidence to that effect in the attic. The intention was that when it reached Miller, it would shortly make contact with the gas and there you are. Toast. Only something went wrong, and although the cigarette they left alight in the sleeping bag did some damage, the gas was never touched by the fire.''

"Couldn't he have crawled out?" Sonnie asked. She breathed hard. "Or did he die from the smoke?"

"Nope," Flynn said, finding Chris's face in the gloom and raising his own brows. "Amazing what those pathologists can find. He probably went in willingly. He had friends who helped him, but they didn't fill him in on all the details they had in mind. You got a cigarette, Chris?"

"You don't smoke anymore." Flynn used to smoke until he saw a pair of blackened lungs at the autopsy of a Harlem pimp.

"So I don't," Flynn said. "Even toughies like me get jumpy sometimes. Edward Miller was a smoke screen. At least that's my take. The question is, whose smoke screen? Medical Examiner found evidence of intravenous shots. Backs of Edward's arms where he couldn't have done them himself. Bruises, too, so he struggled. No smoke in the lungs. Tissue samples should be back soon, but they're already convinced Edward Miller was murdered.''

Nineteen

Aiden recognized impending tragedy when he saw it. The man sharing a table with him at Captain Tony's showed all the signs of misery in the making. Chris Talon had made his share of mistakes, but his biggest had been to believe that by ducking out on what had been his chosen life, he'd turn himself into someone different.

People didn't change; they only became more of what they already were. Chris had never talked about his childhood, but Aiden figured the man was a graduate of something tough. The next piece of amateur psychology Aiden had pinned on his buddy was that he'd gone into law enforcement because he was committed to justice—because he hadn't known much justice himself. And Chris was a man who had loved once, lost that love, and vowed never to put himself in the way of that much pain again.

Tonight Aiden sat with Chris Talon who, although he might not be in love, was certainly moving in that direction, and with a married woman who, if her husband showed up again, would probably go to him regardless of her feelings for Chris. Strike two for Chris. Aiden really didn't like thinking about where his friend might decide to go from there.

"I sure as hell don't like it when you stare," Chris said abruptly. "Makes me think you're analyzin' me. You're the one who still has the problem. I got rid of mine."

"Bullshit," Aiden said, and felt angry all the way to the little hairs on his toes. He also felt caught. "You're sinking fast and we both know it. We're not even going to discuss what you think you mean about me. If it'll make you happy I'll be glad to go there with you. Later."

Chris downed the dregs of his second whiskey. He'd informed Aiden that the only patrons were locals. Talk of hurricanes had grown louder. Tourists were thin to nonexistent. Even some of the natives were rumored to be getting ready to abandon ship if necessary and go north.

"It's too damn hot," Chris said. "Wind's picking up again, too. We could be in for it."

"Forget hurricanes," Aiden said, bracing for whatever might come. "This is some common sense you need to hear and act on."

"Save it." Chris got up and went to the bar. Business cards tacked on top of business cards, names on names, stories on stories covered every inch of wooden pillar and beam. Donated bras flapped like freeze-dried bats—memories of old hangovers. Captain Tony's decor was classic clutter with a dash of cozy sleaze thrown in.

A woman who sat at the bar left her stool and walked to stand between Chris and a man with an iguana on his shoulder. Aiden figured she was the right side of forty, and nice on the eyes—if you liked blond, blue-eyed women with good figures and killer smiles. Aiden had a thing for red hair.

Shoot. Sonnie had, well, fair hair and blue eyes. She was little, but her shape was sweet. Nothing was likely to be sweeter than her smile, though.

He watched the blond with fresh interest, or he watched Chris's reaction to the blond with fresh interest. She said something to him and he turned, looked down at her.

That man never changed. He remained a straight-backed, obviously powerful, and apparently magnetically *male* male. Aiden had been told by trustworthy sources—female members of the force—that visions of Chris Talon kept a lot of women awake at night. The blonde was mature enough not to drool, but from where Aiden sat, she looked close to doing so. She leaned on Chris's tanned forearm and raised her face to his as if she were in the presence of perfection.

Smiling slightly, Chris listened to her. He bent toward her and inclined his head to hear her over the singing guitarist's gravelly roar. When the woman had finished and waited, her lips parted, for whatever Perfection might say, he smiled at her, and Aiden wondered, since Chris had a glass in each hand, if she'd faint and fall on the floor—uncaught.

Chris spoke.

His words brought disappointment to the lady's expression, but she inclined her head and responded before returning to her stool.

"What did she say?" Aiden asked as Chris sat down. "She's cute."

"She wanted to buy me a drink."

Aiden puffed up his cheeks.

"I thanked her but said I'd already paid for these. Then I told her she's very lovely, but I'm already involved."

"Damn," Aiden said with feeling. He put his elbows on the table and propped his chin in his hands. "You're the only man I know who has knockout women offering to buy *his* drinks. And you turn 'em down?"

"Drink."

"I haven't forgotten what I want to say to you."

"Drink."

Aiden did drink, and he reached to grip one of Chris's wrists. "Now," he said when he wasn't thirsty anymore, "this is the way I see it. Sonnie's a nice person. You respond to nice people, and this time you've convinced yourself that what you feel is something bigger than usual. Yeah, well, that wasn't supposed to sound that personal."

Chris grinned and Aiden warmed to his topic. "You're not in yet, so it's a breeze to get out, isn't it?"

"I don't follow," Chris said. He sniffed his drink.

"Sure you do. You aren't really *in* with Sonnie yet, so making sure you don't get in shouldn't be a problem. Frankly, I'm worried about her anyway." He held up a hand to silence Chris. "Hear me out. She's a sweetie."

"She is *not* a sweetie, Flynn. Little kids are sweeties. Sonnie isn't a little kid."

"Yeah, well. Right. Sonnie's easy to like—a lot. But she's got trouble, and I'm not sure how much of it is outside her mind. And she's married." He raised his voice to override Chris's protests. "And that's the truth, schmuck. She isn't available. Maybe that's what appeals to you—she's already attached, so you can play with the idea of loving her without ever having to do anything permanent about it."

"Aiden."

"Or you could really be in love with her. Hell, how should I know? But if you are and her husband comes back, what d'you think that'll feel like? She's the kind who'll think loyalty means she has to go back to him—even if she's in love with you, too, and she doesn't love Giacano anymore. Look at it this way: you've got to be strong for both of you. Break it off. I don't mean you shouldn't be kind to her—you would be anyway—just quit sleeping with her."

"Goddamn it, Flynn. You're running off at the mouth."

"So you are sleeping with her." Suspicion One confirmed.

"I'm sitting at this table, on a rotten Conch Republic night, wide awake. Sonnie's asleep at my brother's place."

"Don't be facetious. What's Conch Republic?"

"A Conch is someone who was born here. Conch Republic is what some of them would like this island to be. Don't say another word about Sonnie."

This was more dangerous than Aiden had expected it to be. Even more dangerous. "Have you slept with her?"

One by one, Chris pried Aiden's fingers from his wrist. He placed Aiden's hand on the table and brought a fist down on top.

There was more than one hard man present. Aiden winced, but didn't make a sound.

"None of your damn business," Chris said, "but no, I haven't—not in the way you mean."

Aiden stopped himself from asking what other way there could be. "That's something. Don't. You'd both hate yourselves in the morning. She's doing a great job of holding herself together most of the time, but I'm not so sure she doesn't have some kind of mental problem." He braced himself for onslaught. It didn't come. "You're worried about that, too, aren't you?"

Evidently the smell of Chris's whiskey grew ever more irresistible to him.

"I'm not saying she wasn't in a terrible accident or that she hasn't lost just about everything that really mattered to her. Husband, a chunk of memory, and a baby she wanted. But the world already knows all that. They also know how and why it happened. So what's the mystery? Why all the talk about there being something deep and dark and evil that she's got to find out? Edward Miller got knocked off at her house. Probably. For all we know, whoever did him made a mistake. They could have meant to off him at Ena's place but got the address wrong. Any way you look at it, what could he have to do with Sonnie? Which brings us back to a big, fat nothing. Be a friend to her if you think you've got to, but don't let her suck you into believing her story, and don't—*don't* do anything that's likely to make you feel responsible for her. You've got to be able to walk away, man."

"Finished?"

Aiden sat back in his chair and propped his ankles on the corner of the table. "Yeah."

"My mother was right about you. You're an opinionated bastard."

"Your mother never met me. And my father is married to my mother."

Chris leaned across the table. "I've only got your word about your folks. And if my mother had met you, she wouldn't have liked you. But I'm patient. I've heard you out and now you're going to hear me out."

Aiden sank his chin on his chest, but kept an eye on Chris.

"You don't know everything that I know. You don't know everything she's told me."

"Any witnesses to what she's told you?"

"You can believe what you want to believe. You weren't there when I went to her house after she called me. She was almost unconscious with fear. You didn't have to listen to a description of what she'd seen.''

"According to her.''

Chris's eyes narrowed to slits. "You didn't see the box of calla lilies some sicko sent her—with a card that talked about her baby's casket. Sonnie detests calla lilies—she's always found them funereal, and the person who sent those lilies knew it.''

"Those would be the lilies paid for in cash by someone no one at the florist's remembers. And Sonnie knows she doesn't like those lilies.''

"She didn't send the lilies to herself.''

"Prove it.''

"Goddamn it, Flynn. I'm going to rip your throat out. When she was in the hospital after the so-called accident—''

"It *was* an accident. I've seen the records.''

"I've seen them, too,'' Chris said. "Since when did you believe everything you read in a police report? The whole thing could have been staged. And the local boys believed what they were supposed to believe.''

"See those little green men, Chris, the ones diving into your booze?'' He looked into Chris's glittering eyes and decided he could possibly back off an inch or so. "It could have happened that way, but it didn't. You know it and I know it. Don't you at least have some doubts about Sonnie's stability? You told me yourself that the guy who came down with her sister's a shrink. The sister seems real worried about her, and she's known Sonnie a little bit longer than you have.''

"Is it my turn?'' Chris asked.

Aiden breathed in deep, coughed on smoke, and said, "Uh-huh.''

"Good. You're a logical guy. Every word you've said could be exactly the way it is. And I can't be one hundred percent certain Sonnie isn't having some emotional problems. She *is*. I just don't know if they're making her irrationally afraid. However, in my gut I believe something really weird went down with her, and until I prove I'm wrong, I'm going to keep on trying to prove I'm right—that she's right.

"I'd bet my Harley that she didn't buy herself lilies and have them delivered, that she heard noises in her house because there *were* noises in her house, and that Edward Miller's body was supposed to be found exactly where it was found. I don't have any way to be certain about her sister's motives, either for being here when Sonnie doesn't want her, or for bringing the shrink, but two more unlikely half-sisters I never met."

"Do I get the Harley if you're wrong?"

"If you felt what I feel for Sonnie Giacano, you'd can the jokes."

"What do you feel for her?"

Chris got up from the table. "She's the best thing that ever came my way. It's just possible she's made me think there's something worth making a life for. Tomorrow she gets to go back to that house. I'm going back with her. Uh-huh, I'm going to live there with her. Before you ask, we'll be sleeping in separate bedrooms. But as long as she wants me, she's got me. I've got a tough piece of investigation ahead of me, but I used to be pretty good at that."

"You still are," Aiden muttered.

"If there's something to find, I'll find it. With Sonnie's help. And in case you've wondered, she does have guts. For someone who was looking into the grave only months ago, she's amazing."

Under his breath, Aiden said, "Infatuation."

"I'll ignore that. I'm staying with Sonnie because I want to and because I believe in her. If it turns out that things happened the way they're recorded, and she's suffering from some sort of post-traumatic disorder, I'll still stay with her. I'll stay until she tells me to go."

The fight went out of Aiden. "I was afraid you'd say something like that. Are you ever going to think you've atoned for past sins—so-called sins? None of that was your fault, you—"

"No, no, no," Chris said. "That's off-limits. Permanently. You're a good friend, Flynn, and I'm grateful to have counted you as one of mine. Maybe my only friend outside of Roy and Bo. I could have used your connections, but I respect your opinions. You have to do what you think's right."

Chris straightened and said, ''Thanks for coming down. I know it was a long drive.''

''I didn't say I was going anywhere.''

''You said you've already made up your mind about Sonnie. You can't believe her innocent until proven guilty. You've already tried her and found her guilty of insanity.'' He emptied his whiskey into Aiden's beer. ''An extra one for the road. Give my regards to Harlem.''

Twenty

"I'm not going in there," Roy told Bo.

"She's gonna wake up. I'm telling you, she'll wake up and walk right out that door. It's after ten. I can't believe she's slept this long."

Roy looked at the door to the outside stairs.

"Why look at the door? Is looking at the door gonna stop her from using it?" Bo got up from his favorite wicker rocking chair, hissed at the creak it made, and tiptoed to peer down the hall toward the bedrooms. He closed his eyes and aimed one ear in the direction where Sonnie had better still be asleep.

"If she wants to get up and go somewhere, we can't stop her," Roy said.

"Take her shoes away."

He had to smile. "No, I'm not going to take her shoes away. I'm not going into her bedroom, period. I think I'll go downstairs and see how Pep's doing."

"You're not leaving," Bo said, hurrying back into the living room. "I promised Chris we wouldn't let Sonnie go anywhere without him."

Roy made sure he wiped off his grin. "So you said. And I know you take your promises seriously. You might want to hold back on promising Chris anything in the future, though. Sometimes he asks too much.''

"He's your brother," Bo said. "What I do for your brother is never too much.''

For eighteen years, Bo Quick had been the best thing that had ever happened to Roy. They ought to be taking each other for granted by now, but Bo made that tough when he kept showing one more way in which he was gentle and loyal. "Okay," Roy said, "but I've got to look after you. If I don't, who knows who'll take advantage of a good heart? Chris could be hours, and there's no way we'll get Sonnie to hang around for very long. Come on, we'll both go check on Pep. She's probably—''

"It's slow and you know it. If she needs us, she'll call us. I'm not leaving, and neither are you. I've got it; I've got it!'' His smile showed off crooked white teeth that were part of his character, one more special part. "We fix her door so it won't open. Then, when she wakes up and can't get out, we make a big show of trying to rescue her, but we take forever.''

"That's a nice shirt, Bo. You look good in green. Shows off your tan.''

"I don't have a f—friggin' tan. I never go outside.''

"I meant it shows off your eyes.''

"Yeah, right," Bo said. "Chris is in a bad space. So is that lovely Sonnie. We gotta help them. And they're good together. You said that, and I can see it, too.''

"You're a romantic," Roy said, and thought he heard a sound. "Lower your voice; she could be coming.''

Bo crossed his arms and bobbed on the balls of his feet, a sure sign of real agitation. He was older than Roy by several years, but looked younger. Small and thin, he had the manner of an enthusiastic teenager tempered—most of the time—by a wisdom that was a constant reminder of why Roy respected him so much.

Roy put a finger to his lips. She was definitely opening her door.

"Don't mention *murder*," Bo whispered.

Enveloped in Bo's best white terry bathrobe, Sonnie emerged

from the hallway. She'd brushed her hair back into a tail at her nape, and, discounting her expression, she looked about twelve.

"Good morning," she said. "Afternoon, soon. I never lie in bed like that. What's the word on the storm?"

"Looks like we're lucking out again," Bo said. "It's getting weaker as it comes this way. You're very tired. I'll make you a little breakfast; then we want you back in bed. You've had too many shocks."

Roy tried to catch Bo's eye and send some warning to be careful what he said.

"It isn't every day some mad magician gets murdered in your junk room. That Aiden Flynn is some detective. I bet he and Chris made one hell of a team, and . . ." At last he turned to Roy with something close to horror on his face. Roy shrugged.

Sonnie told herself that the time would come when she'd be able to think of what had happened on Truman Avenue and not shiver. She had a way to go on that. "I just came out to say good morning—which it's not—and thank you very much for letting me stay again last night. I'm embarrassed. You've done way too much for someone who's almost a stranger."

"You're not a stranger," Bo as good as yelled. He rubbed his hands together and started for the kitchen that stood open to the living room. "You're one of our family now—just like Chris is. We want you both to be happy."

Sonnie heard Roy groan and looked sharply at him. He smiled at her and said, "One of the family," and she heard false cheer in his voice.

"I've got breakfast all planned," Bo said. "In fact, Roy and I put off having ours so we could keep you company."

Roy managed to swallow another groan. They'd eaten stacks of pancakes only a couple of hours earlier. "You sit yourself down, Sonnie," he said. "C'mon, over here on the couch. Put your feet up and take it easy. Bo's a great cook, and I'm no slouch. But I agree with Bo—you need more sleep."

Her eyes were bright and clear. Although her face was pale, her mouth was determinedly set, and she was definitely a woman with action on her mind.

"A mimosa and a nice little fruit compote to start," Bo said, walking backward and stepping sideways behind the kitchen island, "followed by bagels, cream cheese, lox, and more mimosas. And fragrant herbal tea—my own mix, and guaranteed to soothe you. Roy, the mimosas."

Sonnie didn't move from the middle of the living room, but Roy sprang into action. He took orange juice and a bottle of champagne from the refrigerator, and poured more of the latter than the former into a tall juice glass. He dropped in a maraschino cherry and slapped a slice of orange on the rim of the glass. "Voilà," he said. "Quick and Talon's perfect mimosa."

If ever there was a woman who didn't want what he was offering, it was Sonnie Giacano. Fortunately she was exceedingly polite and took the drink. Roy hovered over her as if watching for her reaction to a masterpiece. She took a sip and said, "Mmm," before setting the glass down.

"The fruit is fabulous this year," Bo said, hurrying to place three bowls of fruit compote on the dining table. "Nothing like a few stewed prunes to keep you regular."

While Roy decided to give up on Bo's finding a shred of diplomacy, at least this morning, Sonnie sat at the table and waited for her hosts to join her.

"Keep her company," Bo said, waving a bread knife. "Eat, eat. There's plenty more fruit. I could whip up some eggs Benedict. You like eggs Benedict, Sonnie?"

"Er, no. That is, no, thank you, Bo. In fact I'm not hungry at all. I really need to get ready and go over to my house. I've got to see what the contractor's up to, and whether the police are still holding court. I intend to move back in today."

"Not a bit of it." Bo rushed forward with a plate of bagels, cream cheese, and lox. The portion of lox was large enough to overhang the edges of the plate. "Chris said he's going with you. He just ran out to do a few things. He'll be back before we know it."

Sonnie didn't need a confession to figure out that these two were trying to keep her here. And she was pretty certain the idea had come from Chris. "What's Chris doing?" she asked, not caring if it might be rude to pry. He'd brought her here last night, then left with Aiden Flynn. She hadn't seen him since then. "Is Aiden with him?"

Bo rescued her mimosa from a ledge in the living room and put it beside her plate. "I didn't see Aiden today. Chris only said he had things to clear up. Whatever that meant. Look after her, Roy. I'll go back and make sure her bed's comfy."

"No," Sonnie said. Chris had definitely placed the burden on Bo and Roy to make sure she didn't leave. That made her angry. "You're both off duty now. No more baby-sitting Sonnie. Not even if Chris has told you that's what you ought to do. When did he say he might be back? He had to give you some idea."

From the way Roy and Bo looked at each other, she doubted Chris had done any such thing.

"Aiden's car's still out back," Roy said, and the uncertain way in which he tapped his fingertips together was out of character. "They were out together last night. At Captain Tony's. Didn't get back till late. They could be together now."

Bo made two more mimosas and brought them to the table. "Okay, let's come clean and throw ourselves on Sonnie's mercy. All this pussyfooting around is wearing me out. Sit down and drink this, Roy. Back me up with Sonnie before she eats me alive."

"If there are two people I won't be eating alive, you're it," Sonnie said, but her temper was getting shorter by the second. "Just tell me what Chris said. Tell me where you think he is and why he wants me to hang around until he decides I can do something else."

Both men shrugged. Bo said, "He told me he was going out to the airport and it might take a long time. That's all. Honest. And you're to wait for him because you're not up to being out and about on your own." His voice relaxed and she could tell he was warming to his topic. "Chris is protective of you. And that's not his usual thing, is it, Roy?"

"Not his thing," Roy agreed. "My brother's a good man. He's been through a lot, but we think he's ready to join the rest of the world. You're doing that for him. He needs you.

And because of the kind of man he is, he needs to think he can give the orders. He . . .''

Roy met her eyes, and his lips remained parted while she saw him search for a way to rephrase what he'd just said.

"You mean he's a chauvinist who hasn't figured out how to pretend he's not a chauvinist?" She clucked and shook her head, then left the table to go and get dressed. "Poor Chris. It's time for him to learn a lesson, isn't it? Thanks for giving it to me straight. You've got my permission to give it to him straight, too."

"Now see what you've done," Roy said when Sonnie was out of earshot. "You said too much."

"*I* said too much?" Never able to sustain annoyance, Bo lost control of his frown and laughed. "Who told her Chris needs to think he can give orders? You blew it and he's going to give you hell."

The carpenters hammered all afternoon. They had temporarily closed the hole in the roof, and framed the walls where charred wood had been removed. They assured Sonnie she didn't have to worry about a thing. She'd be secure enough tonight, and tomorrow they'd continue to work.

Ena hadn't put in an appearance. The curtains next door remained closed. When Sonnie arrived at the house there had been no sign of the police, and a call to the station rewarded her with a disinterested response.

"They don't care if I'm here or not," Sonnie told Wimpy. They were in the parlor, where Sonnie had taken a bucket of soapy water, a mop, and some sponges. "They've already forgotten about poor Edward."

His popping brown eyes glistening, Wimpy followed Sonnie's every move. He'd been waiting on the veranda when Sonnie opened the door.

The smoke had left every surface in the house filmed with smelly black grime. The fire department had done a good job with ozone spray, but the mess was everywhere. "The insurance company would pay for this to be done," Sonnie told her perfect listener. "But it's good for me, isn't it? Keeps me busy and gives me exercise." In fact she was achy and should probably stop.

Footsteps clattered on the stairs. One of the carpenters popped his head around the door and said, "That's it for today, Mrs. Giacano. It's tight up there. Nothing to worry about. We'll be back tomorrow."

Sonnie smiled and nodded. It wouldn't do to say she didn't want to be left alone. The front door slammed and she hurried out to make sure it was locked.

Outside it was growing dark. The latest hurricane might be blowing itself out, but the wind was strong enough to bend the palms, and rain fell at last.

Not a word from Chris.

Devoid of enthusiasm for food, she nevertheless went to the kitchen and took an apple from the refrigerator. She poured a cup of the black coffee she'd brewed after she arrived. It was thick and tasted burned, but she drank it anyway.

The phone rang. In her hurry to pick up the receiver she almost dropped her mug. "Hello."

"Sonnie? It's Billy."

She slumped onto a chair. Feeling disappointed at the sound of her own sister's voice might be a disgrace if that sister hadn't been so cruel. And she was disappointed not to hear Chris on the phone. "Hi, Billy." She made sure to sound cheerful. "Having a good time?"

"Wonderful." Sarcasm dripped. "This club just hops. Even Jim's getting tired of relaxing. How long are you going to hold out on us?"

Same stuff. "I'm in my home and I'm staying here. The question is, how long do *you* intend to hold out?"

"I'll ignore that. Jim wants to know if you'll let him talk to you."

In other words, Jim Lesley was missing his professional life and wanted to keep in practice by grilling her. "He's a very nice man. I'm glad you've found each other. I'd be delighted to talk to him. When I've got some time. At the moment I'm busy cleaning off soot."

"Yuck," Billy said. "I'd offer to help, but the smell would make me sick."

The work would make her sick, Sonnie thought. "Thanks anyway," she said. "I'll give you a call tomorrow. Did Romano get back? I bet if you ask nicely he'll give you a private lesson on the courts."

Billy hung up.

What hurt Sonnie so deeply was knowing that Billy really did find her disgusting to look at, that her injuries represented the thing Billy feared most—loss of physical beauty.

Wimpy whined and Sonnie turned to see him come into the kitchen. From his teeth trailed a long green silk scarf. Sweat popped out on Sonnie's brow. She dropped to her knees and scratched the little dog's head while she gently removed the scarf. It was the kind she'd seen in Edward's room. He must have had this one with him when he got into her house. "You're not supposed to go in that room," she said, and felt cold at the thought of the darkness at the top of the stairs and in the destroyed room. The police had stripped it of everything, but they couldn't take away the atmosphere that remained.

Sonnie turned the scarf over. It was smooth, pristine. It couldn't have been in that filthy room.

Where else had Edward gone when he had sneaked in here? Where had he dropped the scarf? Why would he carry silk scarves with him?

Wimpy whined some more and Sonnie stroked him. With a small thud, the dog flopped to his side and rolled over until all four stubby legs stuck into the air. "Oh, no," Sonnie said. "No wonder you're crying. Your poor tummy's a mess." Where he'd been burned, sores suppurated. They needed to be cleaned and have something soothing applied. "I'll take care of you, baby. Don't turn me in to the SPCA. I was having some troubles, honestly I was. And I forgot I should check you."

Wimpy stared up at her with adoring eyes, and Sonnie scooped him into her arms. "Poor baby. Upstairs we go." She couldn't avoid going up there again forever.

Where was Chris?

The darkness was becoming deeper. Maybe he'd had enough and retreated back to his original stance with her. She didn't want to be left alone. She didn't want to be without him.

"Please come," she murmured, and looked at the phone. She could call Roy and Bo and ask if they'd heard from him. They'd be relieved to hear her voice.

She couldn't call them.

The entrance hall lights were low. With her arms full of little Wimpy, she didn't try to turn them up.

"Hush little baby, don't you cry. . . ."

The song again. Sonnie's stomach clenched. Had she heard someone sing the words, far away and in a brokenhearted voice? Or was the voice in her head? Yes, it was in her head.

Was she going mad, just like her family thought she was? They did think she was. Mom and Dad never said it, but they watched her with frightened faces, and Billy had already voiced her suspicions loud and clear.

"Keep it together, Sonnie. Up the stairs with you and find what you need for Wimpy. Poor baby." She stopped halfway up the stairs. *"You can't replace a dead baby with a dog."* This was silly.

Schizophrenia had been mentioned.

A lot of questions about voices had been asked. One psychiatrist had gone so far as to talk to her parents about the applications for cognitive therapy in schizophrenic cases.

There was nothing wrong with her head other than what her enemies had tried to convince her was wrong.

But who were her enemies?

With his trusting golden brown eyes on Sonnie, Wimpy lay supine in her arms. Deliberately averting her face from the end of the upper hall, where evidence of the fire showed, Sonnie went quickly into her bedroom and threw on every light. The curtains were already drawn.

Her medicine cabinet yielded nothing useful.

"Hush little baby, don't you cry. . . ."

"Stop it." She held Wimpy to her face, and the dog licked tears from her cheeks. "I'm jumpy is all."

The nursery, which she hadn't entered since the day of the

accident, was next to the master bedroom. What she needed for the dog was in the changing table that had never been used.

There was a sound of rhythmic tapping but it didn't come from the bedroom. With a heart that hammered painfully, she crept back to the upper hallway where the sound was louder. The carpenters had closed the door to the room where they were working. The tapping came from the other side. Why wouldn't there be tapping or banging, or the flapping of Visquine? The place was under repair.

The time for self-indulgence was over. Sonnie turned the knob and went into the nursery. In the shadows she could see the antique bassinet she'd been so excited to find and cover with white eyelet frills. A rocking chair was a still shape near the room's one window.

With a hand that shook, she fumbled to put on a little lamp atop a chest of drawers. The lamp shade was covered with miniature versions of the frills on the bassinet, and the chest bore the carefully stenciled lambs Sonnie had applied. More lambs cavorted along the tops of the walls. The ceiling was bright blue with unlikely, fluffy white clouds painted freehand by an artist she'd found working in the courtyard near the Hog's Breath off Duval.

The sight of it all struck her hard, harder than she had expected. She set Wimpy down on the changing table, kept a hand on the dog, and wiped tears from the corners of her own eyes. The locket at her neck felt hot, and she lifted it to look at the inscription on the back. In time the grieving would pass. If the baby had been lost under different circumstances, perhaps the healing would have been faster. Sonnie doubted it. She found a jar of medicated pads, opened it, and turned Wimpy upside down again. The little animal cried when the antiseptic stung his injured belly, but he never as much as showed a tooth. Rather he licked Sonnie's hand whenever it got close enough.

The ointment that should have been used on a baby's bottom would probably work well enough on Wimpy's sores. Sonnie slathered on a thick coat and saw the animal relax. "There you are, babe," she said. "Isn't that better?"

Fluffy lambs hung from a mobile attached to the back of

the changing table. Sonnie wound it up and smiled sadly at the tinkling notes of "The Cat and the Fiddle."

"You can't replace a dead baby with a dog. . . ."

She snatched up Wimpy and held him tightly. That wasn't what she was trying to do. This was convenient; that was all. And there was certainly no other use for any of this. "Down you go," she said. "Better go eat." There was dog food in the kitchen now.

The dog scuttled from the room, and his claws clicked on the stairs where the carpets had been taken up and sent out to be cleaned. Time to push aside the goblins and gremlins and get ready for bed.

Where was Chris?

Her breath grew short. What if something had happened to him? She squelched her natural reserve and picked up the phone. "Roy," she said when he answered, "Um, just checking my schedule. I'm on tomorrow, aren't I?"

"You surely are, little girl. And don't you be late."

"I wouldn't dare. Um, how are you guys doing?"

"Good, good. How are you doing?"

"Good, too. Roy—have you heard from Chris?"

She listened to reggae for a long time before Roy answered. "Isn't he with you?"

The slow revolution of her stomach sickened Sonnie. "You said he had errands to run."

"Uh-huh. I did, didn't I? Must have been a lot of errands."

"Roy." Her voice sounded small in her own ears. "I'm worried about Chris. Why would he take so long?"

The man let out a sigh. "My brother gets preoccupied. One thing leads to another with him. Don't worry about him. He'll come walking in here with no idea he's put anyone out. O' course, when the two of you—if the two of you come to some sort of agreement, you'll have to lay out your feelings on things like that. I recommend no tolerance, take it or leave it. He'll take it."

"Thanks, Roy," Sonnie said, too freaked out to continue talking. "Of course he'll show up." She hung up again.

Dragging her feet, she left the nursery, deliberately without shutting it up, and returned to her bedroom. Should she get ready for bed? There were things she and Chris needed to work out about his staying here.

If he came.

Where was he?

"Hush little baby, don't you cry. . . ."

She had to fight against tears. Schizophrenics heard voices, and they couldn't usually differentiate between whether the voices were real or imagined. Was it a male or a female voice that sang? She didn't know. She didn't even know if it was her own voice she heard.

A madwoman. Madwomen got locked away. She'd be sent to a comfortable place where they would keep her peaceful, probably with drugs, and speak to her like a difficult child. And if she tried to leave, they'd put her in one of those jackets. In summer she'd sit in the gardens surrounded by flowers— and mad people. And in time she probably would be mad herself.

After locking herself into the bathroom, she took a rapid shower and toweled off as quickly as she could. Already too hot, she put on a cotton nightie and robe and combed her hair back. The scars on her face showed up livid. She'd grown even paler since she'd been here. Her bottles of perfume were still on the counter, and she selected Cartier's So Pretty to spray on her wrists.

The phone was ringing in the bedroom.

Sonnie tore open the bathroom door and rushed to answer. "Yes. Sonnie, here."

"Where have you been, *cara?* I tried to reach you earlier."

She wound the phone cord so tightly around her hand it hurt.

One of the French doors swung outward and crashed against the wall.

Sonnie jumped. "Romano?"

"Oh, don't tell me you think I'm Romano, my sweet one. You will destroy me." For some time there was only the sound of breathing.

Sonnie felt her way to sit on the edge of the bed.

"Do you hear me?" the voice shouted abruptly. "Answer at once. Do you hear me, Sonnie Giacano?"

"Yes," she whispered.

"Good. I will not tolerate stupidity from anyone. Least of all my wife."

She slid from the bed to sit on the floor. Even that had no substance. When she plucked at the carpet, she couldn't hold the pile. "Frank?"

"Who else would it be? Listen to me. Listen to me very carefully. Within a few days I will be leaving Miami and coming into Key West. Be ready because I will be in a hurry. When I call, it will be time for you to get to the airport. I'll be looking for the Volvo. Do you understand me?"

All the same words, the ones he'd said before—about nine months before. Sonnie shook so fiercely she couldn't focus her eyes. "I understand. Where have you been?"

"Been? You are not yourself. You know where I've been. Busy. The tournaments keep me very busy. I will need your help and you will give it to me. Do we understand each other?"

"Yes. But you were kidnapped by terrorists." She must not scream.

His laughter sent spasms into the muscles of her back. "You have quite the imagination, *cara mia*. Have you been plotting against me? Is that what all this is about? You don't want me back so you have tried to get rid of me? Well, you have failed."

"I don't want that, Frank. I wouldn't do anything to hurt you."

"Good. Then I shall see you soon. Wait for my call."

"Yes, Frank." Everywhere she looked, objects swelled and shrank. The phone was slippery in her hands.

"That's very good, Sonnie. I have to go, but before I do, one question—do I have a son or a daughter?"

She cried out, but he'd already hung up.

The whole room swung. She crawled to the bathroom and threw up.

Who would believe Frank had called? No one. If she spoke of it, they'd have another reason to say she was mad, another reason to lock her away.

The bathroom floor was blessedly cool, but it wasn't solid beneath her knees. She clung to the toilet bowl. What if he called again? He'd said he would call again.

"No." Her voice echoed. Chris would understand. He'd believe her. No, he'd say he did, but he wouldn't. She'd see pain in his eyes, maybe even fear. Chris wanted to help her. He wanted her in his life, but he'd be driven away in the end.

She managed to pull herself up to the sink and turn on cold water. Sluicing her face and neck didn't make a difference to the heat inside her.

Romano needed to know Frank had called.

But would he believe it?

Her legs wouldn't hold her. On her hands and knees again, she made it back beside the bed. Tears fell. She was mad. She had to be.

Call Romano. Whether he believed her or not, he had a right to be told.

She dialed his number at the club. When he picked up she almost fainted with relief. He would help her.

"Hello," his distinctive voice said.

"It's Sonnie," she told him. "You've been gone."

He didn't answer immediately. Then he said, "I took a job here. It's keeping me busier than I want to be. I don't intend to stay long."

She wasn't interested in his job.

The other French door flew outward. The two took turns clattering against the walls. A hot wind swirled into the room.

"Sonnie?" Romano said. "What is it?"

"Frank," she said, choking on her own tears. "He called me."

"What?" His shock was palpable. "What the hell are you talking about? Frank called?"

"He did. And, Romano, he said all the things he said when he called and said he was coming before. The time I had the accident."

"No, Sonnie. Look. Billy's right on this one: you need help. Where are you?"

She shouldn't have called him. There was no help anywhere.

"Sonnie? Answer me. Where are you?"

"In my house." She would not give up. "And I haven't lost my mind. The phone rang and it was Frank." She wouldn't tell him what Frank had said about the baby. Romano wouldn't believe her for sure if she did. Frank would know the baby was due many months ago. And he'd never shown any interest in their child before.

"I should come to you and bring Jim Lesley."

"If you do, I won't let you in. And I'll call the police to have you kept away."

"You won't do that."

"If you try to force my hand, I will do it."

Romano made a sound as if he smothered a curse before he said, "Put Talon on the phone."

As if he could be sure Chris was there. "Chris isn't here."

"Oh, yeah? What happened? He get bored?"

"He's busy elsewhere." Why would Romano talk about Chris now? "Didn't you hear what I said? It was Frank, I tell you. That means he's alive and well."

"If it were Frank, he'd already have called me."

Romano had stung Sonnie more than once with talk about how much closer he was to Frank than she could ever be. But Romano was good to her, and she mustn't forget that. He didn't often show his concern in gentle ways, but that was because he didn't know how. "Okay," she said. "Sorry to bother you."

"You're not bothering me, except because you frighten me. You need help, little one. And I'm going to make sure you get it."

She couldn't argue, not now. "Good night, Romano. I feel better already. We'll talk tomorrow maybe, huh?"

"Absolutely. Get some sleep. And Sonnie—Frank didn't call, sweet, so start deciding to let me help you. Sonnie, think of it. Frank and publicity are blood brothers. Don't you think that if he'd been released from captivity every news staff in the world would already know? He'd be lining up interviews—and endorsements." Romano laughed. "There are things about Frank that never change. 'Take care of business first' is his motto."

Once more she hung up the phone.

Raindrops flew in from the night. She ought to close the doors.

Instead she crawled on top of the bed and curled up whcre she could watch both entrances to the room. A scrape and a tinkling sounded. The tinkling happened again.

Wind chimes? That was what it sounded like, only it was inside the house.

A crash came from the lower floor—probably the hallway. Clamping a hand over her mouth, Sonnie got to her feet and stumbled to the landing. She looked over the banister to the open floor below, and she screamed. Facedown, his arms and legs at unnatural angles, lay a man in a sequined black cape that spread wide over the tiled floor. Draped on the back of the cape was what looked like another silk scarf, this one brilliant yellow.

Gasping through her open mouth, Sonnie made slowly for the top of the stairs. She'd find the strength to help him. She held the banisters with both hands and crept down several steps. Her angle on the figure changed, and she saw what had been invisible from above: the scarf was pinned to the man's back by a knife, a knife driven in to the hilt.

If she could catch enough breath, she'd scream again. She glanced around and up, searching for where the man had fallen from. A crystal chandelier hung from the center of the domed skylight. The chandelier swung gently to and fro. Long, slender prisms glinted. A little more motion and they'd tinkle.

She took another step, and another.

Blond hair, grown long, rested in curls against the floor. She couldn't see a face.

In one hand was gripped a long-stemmed calla lily.

From the kitchen came Wimpy. He trailed a multicolored silk scarf from his teeth.

Shaking so violently she couldn't keep her teeth together, Sonnie continued on down.

The lights went out, and she slipped.

Banging each step, she slid sideways and crumpled to the stairs. She hit every remaining tread on the way down until

To start your membership, simply complete and return the Free Book Certificate. You'll receive your Introductory Shipment of 3 FREE Zebra Contemporary Romances, you only pay $1.99 for shipping and handling. Then, each month you will receive the 3 newest Zebra Contemporary Romances. Each shipment will be yours to examine FREE for 10 days. If you decide to keep the books, you'll pay the preferred subscriber price (a savings of up to 20% off the cover price), plus shipping and handling. If you want us to stop sending books, just say the word… it's that simple.

If the FREE Book Certificate is missing, call 1-800-770-1963 to place your order. Be sure to visit our website at www.kensingtonbooks.com.

FREE BOOK CERTIFICATE

Yes! Please send me 3 FREE Zebra Contemporary romance novels. I only pay $1.99 for shipping and handling.
I understand that each month thereafter I will be able to preview 3 brand-new Contemporary Romances FREE for 10 days. Then, if I should decide to keep them, I will pay the money-saving preferred subscriber's price (that's a savings of up to 20% off the retail price), plus shipping and handling. I understand I am under no obligation to purchase any books, as explained on this card.

Name _____

Address _____ Apt. _____

City _____ State _____ Zip _____

Telephone (___) _____

Signature _____

(If under 18, parent or guardian must sign)

Offer limited to one per household and not to current subscribers. Terms, offer and prices subject to change. Orders subject to acceptance by Zebra Contemporary Book Club. Offer Valid in the U.S. only.

CN093A

Thank You!

lll..l..lll....lll..llll.l.l.l.l.t.l..lll.l..l..ll.l..lll..l

Zebra Contemporary Romance Book Club

Zebra Home Subscription Service, Inc.

P.O. Box 5214

Clifton , NJ 07015-5214

PLACE
STAMP
HERE

she lay on the cold slate tiles at the bottom. "Help," she said, but knew no one heard. Softness passed over her face and hair. Silk.

But she wasn't mad. Not feet from her lay a man who must have fallen from above, a man who had no right to be there at all.

"Hush little baby, don't you cry. . . ."

At last her voice returned and she cried aloud. Cried for help, cried for Chris. "Help," she cried again and again. Her hair had come free of the band and hung, wet, in her face.

"Die. Go to your baby. You know you want to. It's time, Sonnie. Go to your baby." The voice was faint, but clear.

The softness met her face again. She got to her feet, only to walk into hands, hands that pushed her, hands that caught her and pushed her back again, and hands that stroked her. Her face, her neck, her shoulders, her breasts. The hands evaded her futile attempts to ward them off. "Stop it. Please stop it."

The last shreds of control spun away and she screamed afresh and turned in circles, punching at air and stamping her feet. She turned and turned until she thought she would be sick again. Laughter sounded. All around her, then gradually climbing as if it rose into the air.

"Stop it. Stop it, Sonnie."

Another voice sent to torment her. She struck out again and met solid flesh and bone. "You won't kill me," she said. "You won't because you'll get caught this time. I'm not mad. I'm not."

She was released.

The lights came on and she threw out her hands, ready to ward off the next attack. She stared at the middle of the hall floor.

"Gone," she said. "No, no, he can't be gone. I didn't make him up." She burst into tears. "He was there." She pointed to the empty floor.

Strong hands grasped her elbows from behind and slammed her back against a solid body.

Sonnie felt her face crumple, her mind close down. She was falling.

Twenty-one

She fought him.

"Who?" he said. "Who was here?"

With her hair hanging in her face, Sonnie struggled until he had to let her go or hurt her.

The sounds that came from her throat had to be painful. She was wearing herself out while he watched. "Sonnie, it's okay," he told her. "Sonnie, be still. Look at me."

She kept on coming. Her fists didn't do any damage, except to their owner. He let her pummel his forearm. "Sonnie. It's me, Chris. Look at me."

He hadn't closed the front door completely. It blew open and leaves slid across the tiles.

"I will not give up," Sonnie said, her voice hoarse but clear. She scuffed her bare feet backward, pushing her hair from her eyes as she went. Her short cotton nightie didn't make her look any sturdier, but Chris surely found her appealing in simple, flimsy things.

He reached to push the door shut. "You won't give up," he said. "Nope. You will not give up, Sonnie. Neither will I."

Her eyes were closed.

"It's Chris," he told her very clearly. "Sonnie, it's me."

The roaring in Sonnie's head faded. *Chris.* She opened her

eyes. "Where were you?" That hadn't been what she meant to say. "You weren't here." Not that, either.

"I thought you'd stay at Duval Street. Roy said he'd told you I wanted you there till I got back. Bo, too."

"You said you agreed to my offer." Her arms and legs ached and trembled inside. And she was so sore from falling on the stairs. "You would help me. That's what you said."

"Yeah, I did."

Panic had receded a little but it inched back. "You changed your mind, didn't you?"

"If I'd changed my mind, I wouldn't be here. You need to sit down. Or lie down."

"I don't want to sit down." Why did everyone insist on coddling her, telling her she was weak, trying to stop her from doing what she must do?

"You're watching me," she said. "Why are you watching me like that? Like there's something wrong with me?"

He shook his head, and every few seconds he looked in a different direction.

She followed his gaze. "What are you looking for? Don't you believe me?"

"Believe you? You haven't told me anything new, have you?"

"They've been talking to you, haven't they?"

Again he glanced from place to place in the entry; then he looked upward.

"Someone is trying to make me look crazy. They're trying to drive me crazy, Chris." Deep burning in her hip took her breath away.

"Tell me who you think I've talked to about you."

If he had talked to Billy and Romano it would be dangerous to mention their names. He might tell them what she'd said and they'd say she was proving them right, that she needed help because she imagined they were against her. And they'd only be saying what they believed, but she'd lose Chris's help. If they all got together they'd probably find a way to make her leave Key West.

"Sonnie," Chris said, "will you explain what's happened to you?"

"Why are you here now?" Suspicion mounted. "At this exact moment?"

He took a step toward her. Sonnie moved farther away.

"Okay, okay. We'll stand here and talk in circles. Until your legs give out and you fall on those nice hard tiles. What's with your foot? The right foot. It's swollen."

"Crushed," she muttered. "The toes got crushed when they tried to kill me. They swell sometimes."

His blank expression terrified her. "In the car," she said, working for each breath. "When I . . ." She spread her arms and looked down at herself. "All of it."

"Let me hold you, Sonnie."

Hold her. She wanted him to hold her, but she couldn't relax until he understood what she needed him to understand. "And when I saw him"—she pointed to the floor—"I fell down the stairs. A black cape with sequins. It spread wide on the floor. And he had long curls. Blond curls. One of the scarves, a yellow one, was on his back. He'd been stabbed. The knife went through the yellow scarf." The rooms that opened off the entry were in darkness. "He must have dragged himself somewhere."

Chris held out a hand and she looked at it. "I want to hear all about it," he said. "In the kitchen? I'll pour us a drink."

"You took so long to get here."

"I really thought you'd stay at Roy's."

"You could have called to find out."

"I got pretty involved. But I did call in the end. Then I came here."

Such easy answers. "I kept looking outside for you. I listened for you. It was scary here. Wimpy brought one of Edward's silk scarves and it wasn't dirty. I don't know where it came from. I cleaned, but there was soot everywhere. There's still soot."

He smiled. "I wield a mean scrub brush. Tomorrow I'll help."

"You don't understand. I'm telling you the scarf wasn't

dirty. That means it was brought into the house after the fire, and after we'd been to Ena's and seen Edward had them. They knew we'd seen them and it would frighten me. I'll show you."

"You're hurt. You've got marks on your arms. We'd better be sure you haven't broken anything."

"Don't change the subject." He didn't want to hear what she had to say. Well, that was too bad. "Somewhere in this house we're going to find an injured man. A stabbed man. He fell from up there." She pointed to the chandelier. "I heard the glass clinking, then the fall."

"There's no blood," Chris pointed out. As far as he could tell there was no sign of any seriously injured man. A man who had fallen a long way from a . . . chandelier without pulling the thing down with him? "The police searched this house. All of it. From the attic down. Stay put. I'll check." He jogged from room to room, switching on lights, knowing he'd find nothing. When he returned, Sonnie hadn't moved from her spot. "Nothing," he told her. "If there was someone here, they've left."

"I think he was dead," she whispered, and went to the middle of the floor, immediately beneath the chandelier. "His legs and arms were twisted."

He didn't point out that a mortally wounded man should have left traces of blood. There were none.

"Okay." She tucked her hair behind her ears, rubbed her hands over her face, and took a deep breath. "I'm feeling better now. I'm just going to tell you the whole thing. First there was the singing again, or whispering or whatever it is. Then the scarves. Wimpy brought one of them." She bent to pick up random leaves and pieces of white gravel.

"He could have gotten it from Ena's house."

"He *didn't*, I tell you. There wasn't time. And Wimpy didn't sing a song to my baby, or tell me to die, or put a man on my hall floor, then help him get away. He didn't turn out the lights and push me, and . . . and *touch* me. And it was Frank who called, not Wimpy."

Sonnie didn't want Chris to narrow his eyes like that. As if he was deciding about something. "*Frank* called? Sonnie—"

"The man had a calla lily in his hand," she said, remembering, and buying time before she'd have to talk about Frank's call again. "When there's singing, they sing 'Hush little baby, don't you cry.' And it comes from high up. Up by the ceiling. It floats."

"Up by the ceiling? Floats?"

She was too hot. "Yes." Her skin flamed. She blinked her eyes because they stung. Rain tapped hard at the fanlight. "The doors in my bedroom are open. They just flew open on their own. They need to be closed. The rain will come in."

"Sure. I'll see to that."

So why didn't he move? "Do something," she cried. "Don't just stand there. Do something."

She had no time to prepare before he lifted her into his arms and took the stairs a couple at a time.

Struggling would be useless.

"I went into Jacqueline's room to rub ointment on Wimpy's tummy. He's got sores from being burned. But I went in there. I hadn't been able to do that since my baby died—until tonight. Do you think I'm getting better?"

"I hope so. Bed; then I'll get you that drink. I think we're having a brandy moment."

He took her into her bedroom and stood her on the floor while he turned back her covers.

"I'm not ready for bed," she said. "I've got to show you some things."

Chris took his arm from around her waist. "Look at yourself."

"I know what I look like," she said, angry that he should say such a thing. "I can't change that."

"If you want to do something, brush your hair and wash your face. You'll feel better."

Embarrassed, she started toward the bathroom. "I know I'm a mess. Sorry."

"I don't care how much of a mess you are. I just want you to feel as good as you can. Hey." He barely caught her before she hit the rug.

"Stupid," she said. "I'm okay. My hip does that sometimes."

"Sure it does. You're exhausted and strung so tight it's a wonder you don't snap."

"I'm okay." The irritation she tried to muster was without conviction. "Let me get a robe. I'll show you which bedroom's yours. Where are your things?" Her next glance speared him. "You didn't bring them, did you?"

He was so grateful to be able to give her a smug smile and say, "They're on the Harley. I just wanted to make sure you hadn't changed your mind before I started moving stuff in. Are you sure you're going to be comfortable with this? With me living here, more or less?"

"I asked you to, didn't I? I don't change my mind. Go get your stuff."

"Not till I see you settled." He remembered something she'd said and looked over his shoulder.

"What is it?"

"Nothing."

"Don't do that to me." She braced her feet apart and took breaths through her mouth. "It is something. Tell me."

He raised his eyebrows. "Guess the doors must have blown shut again." They weren't standing wide open to the weather as she'd said they were.

"They didn't blow shut." Her eyes shifted toward the doors, then away again. "What can I be thinking of? Of course they did. I got a bit confused, that's all."

"Sure you did."

Sonnie didn't need him to spell out that he didn't believe her.

He went to the doors, caught hold of a handle, and pushed. He rattled it and tried again. It didn't budge. Bending over, he pulled up a long bolt that fitted into a hole in the threshold. A second bolt fitted into the wooden frame above. When he'd freed them both, he opened the door and walked onto the balcony.

They were setting her up. His mind would be made up. She was a freak, a crazy. The body she'd told him about was gone.

Now the doors she'd insisted were open were not only closed, but locked.

Make light of it. Don't protest. You'll only make yourself seem more troubled.

Chris came in and bolted the door again. "No sign of anyone now." He didn't meet her eyes. "They had plenty of time to get away."

"You're humoring me." There was no stopping the tears that sprang to her eyes, or the sore tightness in her throat. "You think I'm . . . You know what you think. Well, you're wrong. I don't know what's going on, or why, but what I told you is true." She shouldn't have said that.

"I don't know what's true or not true," he told her. "That's the honest truth, Sonnie. You can't blame me for wondering. You said Frank called, but you didn't mean Frank, did you?"

She knew what she must do. "No, of course I didn't. I meant Romano." She turned from him and went to lock herself inside the bathroom.

The sound of running water reached Chris. He sprinted from the bedroom and downstairs. Outside he retrieved the saddlebags from the Harley and carried them inside. In the kitchen he located a bottle of brandy and two glasses and turned to carry them upstairs.

The ugly little dog from next door eyed him from beneath the oak table. "Hey, Wimpy," he said, snapping his fingers.

The dog yawned and made chomping sounds with small, prominent teeth.

"Oh, you are a beauty, aren't you?" Chris said, grinning at the pop-eyed face. "Where do you think you're spending the night? You'd better go outside."

"Chris?" Sonnie sounded as if she was standing on the stairs. "Are you talking to Wimpy?"

"I am. He's ignoring me."

"Maybe he's got good taste."

He grimaced. "Thanks. I'm going to put him out for the night."

"No! What are you talking about? He can come up here."

Wimpy grinned, definitely grinned. Chris curled his lip at him.

"Do you hear me?" Sonnie said.

"I hear you."

"Chris?" Halting uncertainty loaded that word.

"Yeah."

"On the counter there's a scarf. A green silk scarf. Bring it up, would you?"

"Okay," he said, although—as he'd figured—he didn't see any scarves.

He didn't know how he'd tell her there wasn't one thing to substantiate what she'd told him, and yet still convince her he believed in her. The damnable thing was that he did believe in her—even if he was being forced toward thinking she was a sick woman. What he believed was that she was right when she said someone was backing her into a corner where she could easily be painted as insane.

Later he'd wrestle with what it would take to pull off such a thing.

He hadn't taken two steps toward the entry hall before Wimpy dashed ahead and led the way upstairs. He nosed his way into Sonnie's bedroom and stood there, looking back as if waiting for Chris to catch up.

With her fingers laced together, Sonnie hovered near a chair. "Where is it?" she said, craning her head forward.

"No green scarf," he said. "We've got our hands full, but people who play this kind of number always leave tracks. We'll find 'em, kid. Into bed with you."

"I want to help you look for clues."

"Not now, you won't. Do as I ask you."

She shook her head, and started when Wimpy took a leap onto the bottom of the bed, where he sat displaying his prominent teeth and panting.

Chris smiled. "We've got one happy customer present. He likes us."

"I can't keep still," Sonnie said. "I feel as if things are crawling around under my skin. Jumpy."

If he suggested they got her something to calm her down

she'd never forgive him. "Me, too," he lied. He held up the bottle and glasses. "Talon's fix-all. Now I don't want you thinking I spend a lot of time drinking my worries away." And that wasn't a complete truth, either. He'd cut himself off from the booze when it had looked like it was becoming a problem, but not before a few mornings when the hangover made him wish he didn't have a head—and what he remembered of the night before was unclear or nonexistent.

Sonnie whipped past him so quickly, so unexpectedly, that he didn't have time to try to stop her. She limped rapidly along the hallway, turned past the room where the fire had occurred, and went into a room on the other side. "Come on," she called. "This is yours."

He took the time to pour two brandies and leave them on her bedside table before following.

"What kind of beans did you have for dinner?" he asked. It wasn't funny, but it was the best he could do.

"No beans," she said. "No dinner."

"I meant because you're jumping all over the place. This is great. Bedroom, sitting room, bathroom. Suite fit for a king."

"Nothing would be too good for you." She colored. "I mean, I wish it was cozier. This was the first place I cleaned, though. The sheets have been changed and everything's vacuumed. Where's your stuff?"

She frowned so deeply, he flexed his hands to stop himself from reaching for her. "Downstairs," he told her. "Won't be a minute."

Sonnie looked from the balcony into the entryway while Chris ran down the stairs and out of sight, to return with the leather saddlebags from his motorcycle over one shoulder. In his denim shirt and jeans, with his lean, tanned face turned up to hers, he reminded her of a cowboy. Not that she'd ever seen a real cowboy.

"Do you ride horses?" she asked. If he didn't already think she was bizarre, he wasn't too observant. "I mean—"

"It's the saddlebags." He grinned. "Hopalong Talon comes to town. I like to ride but I don't get a lot of opportunities."

He dropped the bags at the top of the stairs and extended a

hand to Sonnie. She came to him slowly and he led her back into her bedroom, where Wimpy waited patiently.

"In you go," he told Sonnie, propping up her pillows. When she did as he'd asked, he gave her a glass of brandy. "Sip that slowly. It'll relax you and help you sleep."

She sipped obediently, then pointed past him.

Wimpy turned circles on the bottom of the bed and finally flopped down. He arranged a paw over his stubby nose and studied them with his shiny eyes.

"Guard dog," Chris said. "Or just an opportunist, is more likely."

"Sit with me," Sonnie said. "I've got to do something to prove I'm not losing it. I'm not, Chris. Really, I'm not."

Tipping up his own glass bought a little time to think. "Whoa, that sterilizes the tonsils." He coughed. "You don't want to talk now, sweetheart. Sleep. We'll go over everything in the morning. Meanwhile, remember I'm going to be near enough to hear you breathe. And I'm a rough, tough guy. You don't have a thing to worry about."

"You talk a good story, but you're not rough and tough." She swallowed more brandy and he actually saw her face start to relax. He mustn't forget that she didn't weigh much. A little strong liquor would go a long way with her.

"I'm tough," he told her. "If you don't believe me, I can find a bunch of people to convince you." Not that he was proud of that not anymore.

"I'm not ready to go to sleep yet. Talk to me."

Talking was something they needed to do, but he wouldn't take out any bets that she'd want to touch the subject he had in mind.

"Sit here." She patted the bed beside her.

Uh-uh, Chris. Pack up the hormones and sit in a chair while you still can. Without commenting, he got a chair and sat close, but not too close. The cotton nightie gave his imagination a boost. His fascination with Sonnie's small breasts didn't make much sense when he thought about his supposed taste in women. Not that there had been anything wrong with the women he'd known before her. No, sir, not a thing wrong with them.

"The brandy's good," she said, looking into her glass. "I think it tastes better as it gets warmer or something. You think that's it?"

It tastes better the more you drink of it. "That could be it. I bet you had real pale hair when you were a kid."

Her eyes were wide, her pupils dilated. "When I was a kid? Mmm—pale. White. Billy was the colorful one. I was the colorless one. That's what people used to say." She giggled. "I'm glad because it made her happy. She lives in the world. I live in my head. That makes me happy."

"That doesn't surprise me. Are you sure you don't want to go to sleep now?"

"Sure," she said, frowning. "I couldn't sleep yet. I want to talk."

Okay, so she wanted to talk, Chris thought. "I went out to the airport today. And to Stock Island. Asked a lot of questions. I've been to the police station and talked to a few people. I tried to find out what they're thinking about Edward's death."

Sonnie raised her shoulders. Chris couldn't stop himself from looking at them. Smooth. And her arms were so slender. He'd like to pass his palms up and down, up and down, and settle her on her back, and cover her mouth with his, and . . .

"What did they say about Edward?"

"Oh, they didn't say a whole lot. They got the tissue samples back. I found that out from my friend at the desk. Intravenous shots of local anesthetic. Procaine and lidocaine. A lot of it. Caused cardiac arrest."

She was quiet at that.

"But the police aren't killing themselves to do much about it. I suppose they'll get to it. They talked about his being a druggie. Don't ask me why. And don't ask me if they think he was a contortionist who gave himself shots in the backs of his arms, shots almost guaranteed to kill him."

"Ena's still shut up in her house. I didn't see her all day. She's taking this hard."

"Yeah. Sonnie, you met the plane, didn't you?" Catching her off guard might work. It was worth a try.

"Met the plane?"

"The one Frank was supposed to come in on."

She licked the rim of her glass and said, "I don't remember." She had to tell him the truth about the phone call. "I lied about who called me tonight. You won't believe me but I'm going to tell you anyway. It was Frank, not Romano. It was so strange. I got sick afterward. He said all the things he said the other time. When it happened."

The back of Chris's neck prickled. He didn't respond. Better to let her continue.

"He said I was going to have to meet him at the airport in the Volvo. The Volvo was wrecked." She raised her eyes. "But you know that. He told me I had to be ready to go there in a hurry because he needed my help. Just like before. He got angry with me."

Chris flexed muscles in his jaw. "How come?"

"I don't know. Maybe because I was too shocked to say the right things."

"What would the right things be?"

"Whatever he wanted me to say, of course." The brandy might be making itself felt.

"Did he frighten you?"

"Frank likes to frighten me." Sonnie covered her mouth and shook her head. She whispered, "I didn't mean that the way it sounded."

"How did you mean it then?"

She pressed her lips together and averted her face. "What am I supposed to do? I told Romano and all he wants to do is get me what he calls 'help.' If I've lost my mind, I know it— I didn't think that was the way it was supposed to be. I don't even dare call the cops. I know I won't find a single person who'll take me seriously. Can you even imagine how that feels?"

"I think so." Time to come at this from another direction. "You did go to the airport. That first time—when Frank had called you and told you to be there."

"I don't know."

"After the plane landed, you had a conversation with Romano, didn't you?"

She shook her head. "I don't remember."

"Try."

"I can't."

"Can't? Or don't want to?"

"Can't."

The anger was something he'd learned to press for during interrogation. He didn't like doing this to Sonnie.

"You got in your car and drove. You drove faster and faster."

She threw back the covers and pulled up her right foot.

"It still hurts," he said, remorseful. "I should get you some ice."

"It jammed under the gas pedal. I was lucky it didn't stop me from being thrown out on the sand."

Chris looked at her sharply. "I thought you didn't remember."

While she rubbed the foot, she showed the smooth underside of her leg all the way up to the lace edging on her white panties. "I don't remember. They must have told me."

"Didn't I read that they avoid telling amnesiacs any details they want them to remember for themselves?"

"I don't know what you read."

"Frank frightened you a lot, didn't he?" It was a shot in the dark, but that was all he had—shots in the dark.

She didn't answer him. With her head bowed, she played with strands of hair. From time to time she paused and smoothed two fingers up and down her cheek.

"Tell me all about it," he asked her. "I'm only here for you. I don't have one thing I owe anyone else."

"You don't owe me," she said quietly. "I've asked too much of you."

"Was your husband abusive?"

She shook her head almost violently.

The admission that they'd tolerated abuse often shamed women—or men. "Did he hit you sometimes?"

Gripping the glass in both hands, she emptied it and held it out for more. He didn't want to refuse, but rather than pour more, he gave her a little from his own glass.

So he wouldn't push that any more for now, but he thought he had his answer. "When you left the airport, you drove along South Roosevelt. At Bertha, you missed your turn and hit the wall. That curved wall. Smathers Beach is right there. That would be the driver's side of your car."

"No." She shut her eyes. "No, I don't know."

"You were told some of this. You said you were."

"But I've forgotten now."

He could push a woman until she broke. He ought to know, he'd . . .

She covered her eyes with one hand and took the glass to her lips with the other.

"The report said you were going too fast. Gathering speed rapidly."

"Don't remember."

"Then you hit that wall. The car caught on fire and they thought you were still inside. You were thrown a long way and you landed on rocks on the beach. They couldn't see you there at first."

"I won't listen to you." The hand that had covered her eyes went to her stomach. She spread wide her fingers and pressed them to her.

Thinking about the baby. He detested himself. "You weren't wearing a seat belt. Why wouldn't you? Especially at such a time."

She pointed at him with a shaking forefinger. "You stop it right now. Who told you to do this to me?"

Damn, damn. He took her glass, and she didn't try to stop him. "You're wonderful, know that?" If he could smile he would. He couldn't. "You've got guts. I do believe you, Sonnie. There's so little we have to work with, but so much out there to find. Patience and luck—and Sonnie's brand of guts. That's what we need."

She rested her forehead on her knees. "Thank you. It's . . . You feel so helpless when you're afraid you won't be believed. And when you can understand why people wouldn't believe you."

Chris stroked the back of her hair.

He trailed his hand over her back, across her shoulder.

The nightie gaped at the neck. He looked elsewhere, but not before he'd seen what made it difficult to keep his pants zipped.

"I'm going to bed," he said abruptly, and stood up. "We've got a lot to get done tomorrow. Or a lot to get started on. Call if you need me."

He left the room without looking back.

A cold shower didn't calm him down, or shock his body into submission. By the time he slid, naked, between the sheets, he pulsed in every vein. Heat tormented him and he threw the sheet off. He quickly thought better of that and covered himself.

The moment had come when he'd been convinced that Sonnie's missing husband was a violent man. Why else would she so often use the word *scared* or *frightened* when she spoke of him? And when her hand had gone to her face, he could have sworn she was remembering blows.

If the bastard showed up, God help him if he ever set another finger on her.

Sure, and what could another man do about it if the woman suffered in silence and didn't come to him for help?

Sonnie and another man? Even if he was her husband? Chris doubted he was completely sane himself tonight. He turned off the light. With his eyes closed, holding his breath, he listened. No, he couldn't hear her heart beating. Now who was losing it? He felt her heartbeat. That was it. He placed a hand on his own chest and could swear there was an echoing beat to his own. A lighter beat. Hers.

He'd feel so much better if she were with him.

That brought him a smile and some relief. At least he still had some sense of humor left. A man didn't have to be real smart to figure out that he'd feel better with a woman in his arms—in his bed—especially if he'd been fantasizing about just that from the night they met.

"Chris?"

Now he couldn't breathe if he wanted to. *Be strong.* He kept his mouth shut and shut his eyes.

"Chris?"

What if something had happened? "Hmm? What is it, Sonnie?"

"Um, I . . . Can I come in?"

No. "Sure. What's the problem?"

"Well, I wanted to talk some more."

He stared toward her in the half light from the upper hall. That statement was a lie. She didn't want to talk. "Okay. Give me a minute to get decent and we'll go downstairs."

"Couldn't we talk here?" She stood beside him, looking down. "Would it be all right if I got into bed with you?"

Fate could be a joker, Chris decided. "Are you sure you ought to do that?" And he would soon be up for sainthood.

"If you don't want to talk, I won't keep you awake. I'll be very still and quiet." A long, expelled breath sounded loud. "I'm tired, too, but I just don't want to be alone. You could move over a bit, and I'll lie on the very edge."

Safe in the dark, he rolled his eyes. But he obediently moved to the far side of the bed. She slipped in, barely moving the mattress, and did as she'd promised.

"There's more safe room than that," he said. "You'll fall off there."

She bumped a couple of times, but didn't move perceptibly closer to him.

He put a hand behind his head and stared at the ceiling. One piece of cotton the thickness of a tissue was all that separated her skin from his.

Gritting his teeth, he tried to will his penis into retreat. He rolled his hips slightly to the right, just in case she fell instantly asleep and got too close.

"Are you asleep?" she whispered.

Chris didn't answer.

"Asleep," she whispered. "You should sleep. You're good, Chris Talon, a good man."

Would she feel the way his heart had speeded up?

She sighed and turned on her side, the side that let her face him, he thought.

Some time passed. She must have fallen asleep herself.

Her hand settling on his chest made him doubt she was other

than very much awake. There was a sound and he knew she'd moved again. He became convinced she was looking at him and kept his eyes shut.

The backs of her fingers connected with his jaw, and touched his neck. More bumpy action on the mattress followed. She'd shifted closer, and he'd bet his life she was watching him.

When she rubbed her flattened hand over his chest and passed the tip of a forefinger back and forth over first one, then his other nipple, he felt winded. His thighs hardened, and his buttocks. The tension in those muscles raised him higher from the bed—all of him.

Her touch on his stomach was unlike anything he'd ever experienced. Devoid of any demand. The gentle touch of a woman drawing strength and prepared to give it back. She tended him, soothed him. She cared about him.

Delusions. A place between soft sheets with a sweet woman who was everything he'd probably dreamed about, when he dreamed about having someone who would be that "helpmate" he'd been told to look for a long time ago.

He was naked. Sonnie hardly dared shift for fear of what she might touch.

His skin, the hair on his skin, aroused her. And she was wrong to be here—to be here touching him, taking advantage of his kindness. Billy had told the truth: he was gorgeous, and Sonnie wasn't the type of woman he would want. But could a woman be blamed for taking the chance to be with him, even for a little while?

His arm was behind his head. The faint light that seeped from the hall showed the sharp line of his profile and neck. Against the white pillow, the muscles in his shoulder and upper arm were flexed. She wanted to feel those muscles, and touch the skin on the inner side of his hipbones—to rest a hand on his thigh. Most of all, she wanted to put her head on his shoulder and lie against him. If she could do that without his waking up and making her move away, well then, she'd sleep.

Her hand was warm, and he didn't jump when she tucked her fingers beneath the covers and, oh so cautiously, rubbed his hip. The skin on the inside, at the edge of his belly, was smooth, but the slightest reaching brought her into contact with hair again, hair with the changed, coarse texture of pubic hair.

Only with great effort did she keep still long enough to get over wanting to pull away. His thigh shocked her. So hard it didn't give at all, the muscles felt massive and absolutely rigid.

Her breasts stung. They were tender, and that tender, constricted sensation found its way between her legs. She had no right, but she wished, so desperately, that he would make love to her.

Remembering to breathe, she drew closer. Inch by inch she brought her body close enough to touch his. Her thighs rested against his buttock. Sonnie gritted her teeth. *Ecstasy must be like this.* Did such things have to be forbidden to be so exquisite?

Waiting for Chris to set her firmly back where she belonged—if he didn't make her leave altogether—Sonnie lowered her head to his shoulder.

He didn't wake up.

She put an arm over him and settled herself close at his side.

Time passed. Her neck was at an awkward angle. Wiggling to get more comfortable, she turned to lie partly on top of him, with her cheek on his chest and her breasts flattened to his ribs.

Repeatedly she drove her teeth into her bottom lip. The moment should never stop, this moment. Drawing herself higher, she settled her face into the hollow of his shoulder, close to his jaw, embraced his still body, and put her knee on his belly.

She panted lightly and couldn't stop, and couldn't listen to the reason that warned her to leave him at once.

The calf of her raised leg was where it should never be. The base of his penis pressed against skin and bone.

She gasped. He was erect.

But she only clutched him harder. Clutched him, kissed his jaw, raised her face until she could press her lips to his cheek.

"Sonnie," he said quietly. "For God's sake, Sonnie. What . . . Why are you doing this?"

Twenty-two

Sonnie rolled away from him, and he prepared to grab for his shorts and go after her.

She didn't leave the bed. Rather, she turned on her other side and put as much distance between them as possible.

Chris looked at her back, at the tumble of hair and pale shoulder picked out by faint light from the hallway. "Come back here," he said.

"I'm sorry," she told him. "I only wanted to get as close to you as I could. I wanted to feel you because you're alive and strong. I shouldn't have done that."

"I want you back where you were. Because you're alive and strong and I want you as close as I can get you." He settled on his side, too, where he could see any move she made.

"You think I'm disgusting."

He snorted. "Oh, I surely do, darlin'. Disgustin'. May every man be cursed with a woman as disgustin' as you are. This world would be a peaceful place filled with happy men."

That didn't buy him any answer. "Why would you expect me to think you're disgusting?"

"You know. I don't have to tell you."

"I'm afraid you do."

Her elbow angled up and she gathered her hair on top of her

head. He'd forgotten just how special small, intimate moments could be, the kind of moments a man and woman shared when they weren't studying every move.

"I'm not the kind of woman who cheats."

"You think I haven't figured out how honorable you are?"

She rested the back of her hand on her temple. "Some of the things I've thought—and done—aren't very honorable."

He wanted to hear her tell him about the things she'd thought. "You don't have a thing to feel guilty about." Sometimes you had to be patient and hope you'd be told what you'd like to hear—eventually.

"You don't know what goes through my mind. My mad-woman's mind."

"You aren't crazy." He rose to an elbow and propped his head on his hand. "Don't say that about yourself." Strange how a time like this could feel better than any other time he remembered.

"I . . . When I got in this bed I . . . I had notions I have no right to have."

He was a weak man. "You want to share those notions? So I can make you feel better about them?"

"I'll tell you. Just so you understand you've got to be careful around me because I get wild ideas. As long as you don't let me go anywhere with those ideas, I won't make a fool of myself, or put you in a difficult position."

Come on. Come on. Spill it all, sweetheart.

"I mean, I've got to stop it. It's not right and I know it, but it keeps happening."

What keeps happening? He had to let her tell it in her own way and time or she might back off again.

"I shock you, don't I?"

"No." But he'd like her to, Chris decided. He'd really like her to finish telling him her dreadful truths, too. Preferably before the sun came up.

A tinny rendition of the opening bars to the *William Tell* Overture brought a curse to his lips. Fortunately—thanks to his brother's recent lectures on being appropriate around ladies, and Sonnie in particular—he'd already learned to swallow such vile words.

"What is it?" Sonnie asked as the notes played again. She sounded anxious, damn it.

"Just my cell phone," he said, and reached for the bedside table. "I thought that was a cute ring until now. Sorry." He hit the answer button and put the phone to his ear. "Yeah?" If his tone didn't get rid of whatever slime called at a time like this, nothing would.

Nothing did. "Chris Talon?" A man's voice.

"You've got him."

"I apologize for disturbing you so late." The formality, and the accent, gave the caller away. Chris didn't allow himself to say Romano's name aloud. The less Sonnie knew about this conversation would probably be better.

"Chris? May I call you Chris? This is Romano Giacano."

"Yeah."

"Where are you?"

"None of your God . . . None of your business. Good night."

"Don't hang up. I must speak with you. It's about Sonnie."

Evidently, Chris thought, the fact that he was more than a little interested in the lady wasn't much of a mystery. "Make it quick. I need my beauty sleep."

Romano gave a short laugh. As quickly as the laugh had come, it faded. The man cleared his throat. "This is awkward. I, er . . . I have had some difficulty." He made a sound that was suspiciously like an effort to hide emotion. "A great deal has been happening. I haven't wanted to go to Sonnie yet because she is so deeply disturbed. But now I must let her know what I know."

"What do you know?" Chris's body hadn't made the slightest move toward neutral. He inclined his head to look at Sonnie again. One tiny piece of encouragement and his gears would be racing.

This was taking too long. "Let's get this over with."

"Very well. I will start with the first matter. Please, you must keep your counsel on what I say to you. My greatest fear is that Sonnie will run again, and this time we may not be so fortunate in finding her quickly. You understand?''

''I understand.'' They might not be so fortunate. Fortunately for Chris, tracking people down was one of his major accomplishments.

''I have spoken with Jim Lesley. He is highly respected in his field, and because he's in love with Billy, he's more than willing to help Sonnie. Will you assist me in getting her to agree to go into therapy with him?''

''You ask me that out of the blue? Hell, no, I won't.''

''Because you don't believe she's in trouble.''

Sonnie turned on her back but didn't look at him. He wanted to reach out and pull her against him. ''I didn't say that,'' he told Romano. ''But your interpretation of trouble and mine are different in this case.''

''There are things you don't know. I talked to Jim about Sonnie's call to me earlier tonight. She called from her house and sounded near collapse. Terror. That's what I heard in her. She insisted Frank had called her.''

''Oh, yeah?'' He'd better be more surprised. ''Oh, come on. You're not serious, are you?''

''I do not joke, my friend.''

''Why call me about this?''

''Because I can tell she trusts you. You are a strong man. Sonnie has always needed a strong man to take care of her. She is nothing on her own.''

Chris really didn't like this man. ''I can't respond to that.'' She'd admitted that what she wanted most was to be a wife and mother. And he'd bet she'd make a fantastic job of it.

''My brother needed a different kind of wife. I tried to tell him, but''—Chris could almost see the other man shrug—''who is the one who listens to reason when he thinks he's in love? At first he enjoyed her adoration, her dependency. But it became boring to him.''

''Was he into punishment?''

''What do you mean by that?'' Romano asked softly.

''I think you know.''

''Sonnie likes you. I'm glad. She needs friends.''

Chris thought being Sonnie's friend was a dandy idea. Being her lover was a downright stimulating thought. He pursed his lips and blew out a long breath. He'd better rein himself in before there was a disaster.

"You understand that I mean what I say. She has always been unbalanced, but so worth helping. And her whole family wants her to have that help, including me. I am a member of her family also." He made a choking sound.

"You okay?" Chris asked reluctantly.

"Yes." Romano didn't sound okay. "I am sad tonight. You will understand such things."

Chris frowned. Was the guy saying he knew more about him than he ought to? "Are we finished?"

"No, no, please. I must plead for my brother—for his reputation in your eyes. I have said Sonnie is unbalanced. That is not new. Frank stayed away as much as he did because he couldn't deal with her anymore. I did not condone that behavior, but . . . well, Frank was afraid he might do things he would hate himself for doing."

Chris stiffened. The hair on the back of his neck rose—a sure sign of one of his bad feelings coming on. "A violent man, huh?"

"I didn't say that."

"But you meant it."

"It's over now. I will not speak badly of him. Life must go on, and the time comes to put such things behind us. A great many women have admired Frank. How can you blame him for succumbing to what they offered? They wanted him as their lover and they wanted to do things for him. Many wanted to give him a great deal. No, you cannot blame him."

"Maybe you can't. I can. I'm just an old-fashioned boy and think someone should have shaken him up. Pointed out what he had, and whipped the shit out of him if he didn't get the message." So much for lady-appropriate language.

"I will not allow you to say such things about my brother."

"I just did."

"Please help me to finish what I must say. There is a great deal to be done and none of it is easy."

Chris thought about that. "I can't help you do anything. But I can listen if you think you're ready to get this over with."

"Sonnie did not get a call from Frank tonight—late last night."

It was true that midnight had come and gone. "Go on."

"She told me he gave her all the same instructions as he gave on the last occasion he called. That was before we were due to fly to Key West on that terrible night."

Chris wasn't going to do any prompting.

"It is senseless for her to suggest Frank called and said all those things."

"Maybe not. What about the Volvo? He asked her to be ready to drive it to the airport. It was junked months ago but evidently he didn't know. That would fit with his being abducted and finding a way to escape later."

"It might if he were alive."

At the mention of the Volvo, Sonnie had sat up in bed and was looking at him. "What do you mean?" Chris said.

"Is it so difficult to understand?" A clear sob broke from the man. "I have taken my business into near bankruptcy in order to pay some exclusive people who know how to find things out. Very difficult, sensitive things. I paid them to search for my brother. They tell me he died only hours after he was kidnapped."

Chris also sat up. "You're sure?"

"Would I lie about such a thing?" The words were barely audible. "It is my worst nightmare come true."

"I'm sorry." He considered what Romano had told him. "What proof do you have that you've been told the truth?"

"Why do you care? Isn't this what everyone has thought, that Frank is dead?"

"Maybe."

Romano said something in Italian; then he told Chris, "My brother wore a medallion. A gold medallion. He never took it off. It was his good luck, he said, his reassurance. I am holding that medallion in my hand. It was taken from his body."

Chris said, "I'm sorry," again. What else was there to say?

"I ask you to do one thing for me, please. Sonnie is close to you."

"You don't know that," Chris responded at once.

"That was not a criticism. I am glad. She does not feel kindly to me at the moment. Please tell her about Frank. And tell her that when she's ready, we will talk and deal with matters that must be dealt with."

Tell Sonnie her husband was dead, killed by kidnappers? "I don't think that's a good way to do this."

"I think it's the only way." Romano's voice rose. "She will not let me comfort her. You, yes, I think she will allow you to give her comfort and to calm her. I ask you to prepare yourself, then tell her. And be ready to help her. She must go into intensive therapy to deal with the great traumas that have happened. We are all ready and anxious to make sure she gets the very best attention."

Now wasn't the appropriate time to engage in further discussion. "Okay," he said. "I'll do my best. And I'll be in touch." He'd be in touch to try to figure out exactly what was afoot with the Keiths and Romano. If they trotted out a plan to incarcerate Sonnie at Jim Lesley's clinic, he'd have a battle on his hands.

"Thank you," Romano said, distant and formal again. "I shall await your report."

"You do that." Chris switched off the instrument and set it aside.

He scooted higher in the bed and arranged the pillow behind his back. On her thin strip of mattress, Sonnie did the same.

"Who was that?" she asked. "Romano?"

There would be no lying to her. "Yes."

"How would he get your cell number?"

Chris held very still. *Good point.* How would Giacano get his number? "You should go into detective work. I hadn't even thought about that. I don't know."

"You didn't give it to him?"

More conspiracy theory. "No, Sonnie. I'd have no reason to do that."

"Then how would he get it? Who knows it?"

He reached for her hand, but she pulled it away. "You think I'm doing things behind your back. You couldn't be more wrong. So Roy has my number, and Bo and Aiden." He considered before saying, "And you. Yes, that's it. I can tell you without a doubt that no one else has it—or they shouldn't. Roy, Bo, and Aiden would never give it out."

"But you think I might?"

"I didn't say that."

"I wouldn't and I haven't. You're a private man and I wouldn't do anything to intrude on that."

He smiled a little. "Thank you."

She fussed with the sheet, rubbed her face, adjusted her nightie on her shoulders. "I'm not very good at remembering numbers."

"You're not alone. A lot of people have troubles like that."

"Do Roy and Bo?"

"Not that I know of."

"They wouldn't write the number down somewhere so they wouldn't forget it?"

This could be leading somewhere. "They wouldn't do that because I've told them not to. Aiden's got a photographic memory."

"Lucky Aiden," she murmured. "I . . . I have to write everything down—if I want to remember at all."

"You remembered mine once." He picked up the phone again and played mumblety-peg with it on his knee.

"I don't know why," Sonnie said. "It was a fluke. Oh, Chris, it's on the dry-marker board by the kitchen phone."

"That explains it," he said. "Lighten up. So Romano decided to help himself just in case."

"He hasn't been here since I put it there."

"So Billy did it and passed the number on. It doesn't matter, does it?"

"Billy hasn't been here either." Her tone grew higher, more agitated. "I want to know whose been snooping around. I don't like it."

"You're making too much of this. I'll ask Romano where he got my number. Will that make you feel better?"

"No. Don't ask him anything. If he's gone to such lengths to get your number, he may be up to something."

"Okay." He held his tongue then to give her some breathing time.

"Chris?"

"Yep, sweetheart?"

"I've got your number written in the book beside my bed, too."

"I'm glad. I hoped you would make sure you could find it easily, just in case you wanted to get hold of me."

Sonnie said, "What if one of those people who got in here saw the number? In my book or by the phone downstairs? If they gave it to Romano it would mean he's involved in all this somehow."

From the moment Chris met Romano, he hadn't liked him. And he'd also come to wonder just why the man was hanging around Key West when his sister-in-law had made it clear she didn't want him there. He had no right to force himself on her. He could be involved in something, although Chris doubted it. "Don't imagine things about Romano, Sonnie. He seems to be genuinely concerned for you."

"Why do you always accuse me of imagining things? I don't unless there's a reason."

When should he break the news about Frank? "I'm sorry if that came off sounding wrong. I think it's natural to imagine things around here, although I think my being here is going to put a crimp in the style of anyone who thinks it's cute to torture you."

She sighed. "Yes. If you don't decide you have to leave. Not that I expect you to change your whole life for me," she added rapidly.

"I'm here because I want to be here. I wouldn't go if you asked me to. You'd have to throw me out, and I don't think you could manage that."

She sighed again, but didn't sound sad.

"Sonnie, there's something I need to tell you. It won't be easy. First I want you to promise me you'll be calm. But if you want to get mad or cry or something—do it, but do it with me and let me help you.''

Her face came his way and within a second she was on her knees beside him. ''What? What is it? Did something happen to my parents? Is one of them ill?''

''This has nothing to do with your parents. It's your husband.''

She put her hands to her cheeks. ''What about him?''

''Romano asked me to tell you some sad news. Sonnie, Frank died only hours after he was kidnapped.''

Her hands remained on her cheeks. He could see the glitter of her eyes in the almost-darkness.

''Your family will all be ready to help you. Romano asked me to tell you that. When you're ready, they'll want you to tell them what you need.''

Sonnie shifted sideways to sit down. ''I don't know what to say. What am I supposed to say?''

Whatever it was, those two questions didn't seem appropriate. ''I can't tell you that.''

''I suppose I'm shocked.''

''Of course you are.''

''Not the way you mean.'' Unconsciously, she smoothed her nightie up her thigh and massaged her hip where the leg of her panties was cut high.

''You loved him,'' he told her. ''You're bound to be shocked.''

''You don't understand. I'm shocked to hear about it, but . . . I'm not sorry about Frank. Chris, I'm not sorry he's dead.''

''You are in shock,'' he said. ''I'll go get some more brandy.''

''I'm wobbly inside. It's unbelievable. Maybe I'm sorry he's dead for his sake, but not for mine. He was never kind to me. I don't know why he married me. He didn't want our baby. He told me pregnant women were ugly and he didn't like ugly women. He used to say he wished I would die because he was tired of having the responsibility for me. Even though he really didn't. I looked after myself.''

Chris didn't try to stop her. She needed to let it all flow out.

"I sound selfish and cruel." Her head hung forward. "What kind of woman thinks about herself when she's just been told her husband's dead? Some sort of a monster. That's what I have to be. He was Billy's friend first. Then it was almost as if they planned for him to marry me. That's stupid, a stupid thing to think. Billy encouraged it, but that made me happy. She wanted me to be happy, and she thought Frank could do that—make me happy. I don't feel anything."

"Will you let me say what I think, Sonnie?"

"I suppose the family's waiting for me to be a grieving widow. Oh, what do I do now?"

"You let someone help you."

"They'll help me right into a sanitarium."

His thoughts exactly, although he couldn't be sure he wasn't just looking for reasons to snatch her away from the family and friends he'd met so far.

He wanted her for himself. "You've had nearly nine months to think. In that nine months you've gotten accustomed to the probability that Frank wouldn't be back. He wasn't a good husband. You've admitted as much. And you feel some relief in knowing he won't be able to hurt you anymore."

"Is that it?" she asked. "Maybe it is, but I don't want to be a hard woman."

"You aren't a hard woman, Sonnie. You're so gentle it almost hurts to watch and listen to you sometimes. Stay put. I'm going for the brandy. I think I need some myself." He got out of bed, and remembered his shorts too late. He grabbed for them and pulled them on, hoping she hadn't seen more than she ought to.

In her bedroom, Wimpy had abandoned the foot of the bed in favor of burrowing under the sheets and settling down with his head on a pillow. Chris pulled a sheet up to his chin and was rewarded with a one-eyed stare before the animal snuffled and shut him out. He took the glasses and the bottle and returned to his own bedroom.

Sonnie had turned on a lamp.

She confronted him—naked.

Twenty-three

"I've never been"—Sonnie tried to moisten her dry mouth—"I've never been impetuous."

Chris looked at the glasses of brandy in his hands as if he'd forgotten they were there. Or as if he were buying time to think.

"I've made up my mind. I'm going to get started on plastic surgery. They say they can do wonderful things now." She stood with her right side toward him, hiding as many of her scars as she could. Laughter bubbled into her throat. She swallowed. "I'll always limp, but I won't look so—"

"Stop it. Don't say another word. Please."

He was shocked. He'd already let her know he didn't want her advances.

Advances. She wasn't the kind of woman who made advances. She struggled to pick up her nightie from the bed without turning around and giving him a full view of her back.

"My God, you don't know anything about me," Chris said.

She reached the gown and yanked it on over her head. "Yes, I do. Honestly. I don't know what got into me." Once she was covered she turned to search for her panties but couldn't locate them. She couldn't stop a short burst of laughter. She faced him again. "Don't leave. That's all I ask. Forget this. Forget my delusions about you. And stay. I'll never embarrass you like this again.''

''You're in shock,'' he said.

''That's it,'' Sonnie said. ''In shock. Not myself.''

Dressed only in black shorts, he loomed even larger than usual. He drank from one of the glasses, but never took his eyes from hers.

''Yes, well, I'm sorry. I already said that, but I am. It honestly won't happen again.'' She calculated the space between him and freedom and made a dash for it.

She made it through the door, and heard shattering glass. He was throwing things. . . . Sonnie clutched at her throat and felt Chris's fingers close on her upper arm.

''Don't you move another step. Got it?''

''I'm sorry,'' she whispered. ''I'm so sorry. Oh, what have I done?''

''You're a fool,'' he told her. ''Maybe you do need major treatment, because you don't make a whole lot of sense sometimes. You make a move based, I assume, on something you feel. Then you don't trust your feelings and you gibber. I hate it when you gibber. You're smarter than that.''

''Yes. Thank you. I'm sorry.''

He shook her. ''You say *sorry* one more time and I won't be responsible for my actions. You've been through too much. Why are you sorry? What are you sorry for?''

''For putting you in a terrible position. For doing what I did, not just once, but twice. Forcing you to confront a woman who was offering herself to you. I know I'm not your type. I probably sicken you.''

She attempted to pull away from him. ''We both need to get some sleep.'' She managed a smile. ''Wimpy will wonder where I am.''

''I just broke two brandy glasses in there.'' Chris aimed a thumb over his shoulders. ''Your fault. You shocked me, but not the way you think. Does that look like I find you sickening?'' He pointed to his crotch.

Sonnie glanced down, and quickly away.

''Does it?'' he pressed her.

"No."

"Talk to me. Tell me what's going on in that complicated head of yours."

Did he really want to know? "Women dream about being alone with men like you."

His smile wasn't really convincing, but he said, "Who can blame them? Do you dream about being alone with me?"

She felt the blood drain from her head. "Yes."

"How could you suggest you're mad? Obviously you're very sane and all your thought processes are in perfect tune."

"You're making fun of me."

"I'm making fun of both of us. If I don't, I'm likely to turn into an animal, and I doubt you're quite ready for that."

Light-headedness came, but she willed herself not to give in to it. "I was going to tell you something. Before Romano called. I was going to tell you I've thought about you making love to me, and that I wanted you to."

His eyelids lowered a fraction and his eyes turned darker. He held her by the arms. "Past tense? You don't still want us to make love?"

"What kind of woman wants to make love when she's just heard her husband's dead?"

His lips parted. "A woman who fell out of love with her husband a long time ago? A woman whose husband was cruel? I can't give you the perfect answer, but I don't think you're a monster to want to be alive again. Who sets the rules for what's appropriate? How long you wear widow's weeds? When you can stop expecting to be gossiped about if you've decided not to leap into the grave after your husband?"

"Let me go."

He moved in closer, backed her to the wall, and spread his legs to trap her hips between them. "That's a *no*."

This was what she'd wanted, wasn't it? Her pulse hammered. She felt it throughout her body. "No. Yes. This is my fault. You're trying to help my ego. That's not fair to you."

Using his forearms to keep her shoulders still, Chris kissed her. This was another new kiss. A faint growl came from his throat, and she was helpless not to answer with her own moans.

Holding her face in his huge hands, he kissed her so deeply she felt he was drawing her into him. He was eating her, and she liked it.

His fingers hurt her scalp.

His erection probed her belly, and her own moisture needed him right there between her legs, right now.

The night was hot and getting hotter. Standing against the wall with Chris, Sonnie was afire and wild, and she didn't care about all the questions anymore.

A shift and his palms were on her breasts, flattened, rubbing circles that caused her knees to weaken. He looked down at her. "If you want to stop, say it now. Another second will be too late."

She shook her head and kissed his chest, flipped the tip of her tongue over a nipple until she heard his sharply indrawn breath.

He nipped at her neck and found the raised scars at the back of her shoulder. He smoothed them as if they stimulated him, drew him to her. Once again he kissed her, opened her mouth so wide her head tipped against the wall. Their breathing soughed together, and her breasts rose against his chest. Where her nipples touched him, the intense searing began.

"No." Struggling, she tried to free herself. She reached a hand sideways along the wall and fought to escape his weight. "No. This isn't the way it should be."

"What isn't the way it should be?"

He sounded as she'd never heard him sound. "Chris— standing here like this. As if we're out of control. Oh, my God, Chris." Another sideways push sent her stumbling beneath his arm. She began to fall but caught her balance.

"Out of control is just the way I want it," Chris said. And he grabbed her by the back of her nightie. "You had your chance. I told you it was going to be too late. It is." He caught the neck of the nightie and ripped it apart down the back.

Heat and need and lust. Even while she tried to run, she lusted for him.

Chris shot an arm inside the tattered cotton already slipping from her shoulders. He spun her around, picked her up by the waist, and lifted her against him. Her feet dangled free of the floor and she was once more all but naked.

He bowed his head to her breasts and she screamed. The sound shocked her. This couldn't be her. She'd always been reserved, careful of her reactions and emotions.

With his arms wrapped around her waist, he held her higher and used his mouth on her breasts. He moved his lips in circles that never quite reached her nipples. "I want," she said, "I want." But she couldn't put into words exactly what she wanted.

He licked a nipple and took it into his mouth.

Sonnie pushed a leg between his thighs. She wasn't gentle. Rubbing him, she grinned at the way he widened his stance to give her plenty of room.

Lowering her feet to the floor, pinning her to the wall, he sank down, and his tongue darted into the folds beneath her pubic hair. Her heart missed beats. She rose to her toes and flattened her hands behind her. All that remained of her nightgown was a destroyed piece of cotton that hung from one elbow.

She was going to climax. Right here in the hall, with Chris on his knees before her, she would climax like some desperate partygoer grabbing release in a darkened corner.

"Chris." She pulled at his hair. "This is wrong. We've got to stop."

This time her effort to get away landed her on her hands and knees.

Chris covered her instantly. With the fronts of his thighs against the backs of hers, he bent over her back and reached beneath her to hold her breasts. "This is *not* wrong. I don't know who twisted your view of sex, but it's going to get untwisted. Now. You are so ready for me, and baby, I am ready for you."

He removed one hand and she heard him pulling down his briefs.

"What are you going to do?" She sweated, reached back to try to feel him. "Chris, what . . . *Chris.*"

He entered her from behind. First he thrust into her vagina;

then he rocked back and forth, grunting with each sweeping inner caress.

Any resistance fled. Sonnie planted her hands and knees and fell into his rhythm, driving against him, feeling him far inside.

Too soon for Sonnie, he ejaculated, and the sound he made was high and uncontrolled. But he continued to rock into her until she dropped her head to the carpet and held still.

Against her back, his jaw was rough and wet with sweat. He kissed her, kissed her scarred hip again and again.

"Why are you doing that?"

"Just kissing it better," he said breathlessly. "Sonnie, oh, Sonnie, I can't say anything else."

He came out of her and she dropped completely to the rug.

Chris rolled her over and sat astride her hips. "Did that hurt?"

"Yes. I liked it."

"You may not when you wake up in the morning. You're going to be sore. But I guess it's been a long time."

She didn't want to think about that. "A very long time."

"I'm so glad we did that," he said, and raised his face toward the skylight. "Thank you, all the good powers that be."

"I thank them, too," she said, wondering how she would extricate herself gracefully.

Chris looked into her face. "Good. I think you're finally learning to be yourself."

She did believe she'd pleased him, and she smiled. She was so grateful.

"No regrets, Sonnie?"

"No regrets. Whatever happens now, I'll have you to remember."

His smile vanished. He retrieved what was left of her night-clothes, found a corner of cloth, and used it as a weapon of torture. He passed it over her sensitive nipples, tickled the corners of her mouth, and finally, efficiently, tied her wrists together with it when she tried to fend him off.

"Sonnie, as long as I'm still breathing, you aren't going to need much of a memory about me. I intend to be within grabbing distance at all times."

Twenty-four

Billy Keith was spoiled. Spoiled, self-obsessed, and dangerous. Romano watched the tip of her pointy little tongue connect with a drip of ice cream on the end of her spoon.

She'd ordered him to meet her at Half Shell Raw House, and she'd hung up the phone before he could begin to argue. When he'd arrived at what she'd called "the last place anyone would ever recognize us," it was two in the afternoon, and he doubted the glass of red wine in front of her was the first, or even the second.

So far she'd refused to reveal her reason for wanting to see him.

"Where Margaret Street meets the Gulf," she said in a dreamy voice that didn't impress him. "The perfect spot for an authentic Key West tradition, and this restaurant is a tradition. This area is the real thing, the heart of this island. This is what makes it tick. Fishing."

He was agitated. "Fish feeds the tourists. Tourists make the island tick. And every day the shopkeepers light candles to the cruise ships."

"You don't have a romantic bone in your body."

"I am in the very best of company."

Billy took a mirror from her lime green straw purse and

checked her lipstick. Apparently pleased with what she saw, she returned the mirror and snapped the bag shut. "You are mean to me. If you weren't such fun to fight with, I'd leave you."

Such good fortune was unlikely to come his way, he decided. "I have things to do, Billy. May we get this over with, please?"

"So polite. Romano was always the polite one. Unlike that nasty little prick, Frank. I don't like those purple clouds. What do they mean?"

"They mean the clouds are purple. I know nothing of such things."

"It's bad for my nerves here," she said. "One day a hurricane is supposed to be coming. The next day it's not coming. Then there is enough wind to tear out trees and they talk about abandoning the island. Then they say the storm won't hit here. Exhausting."

Romano didn't like the threat of hurricane any more than she did, but he didn't intend to commiserate with her. "If you don't have anything else to say to me, I will go now. Please make sure I can reach you."

"It's not time for you to go. I don't know how anyone could eat that," she said, eyeing what was left of his squid appetizer. She abandoned the ice cream for more wine. "Make sure you practice your poker face."

He set down his iced tea. "Meaning?"

"Isn't this a great place? All the locals come here."

"What was the 'poker face' comment about?"

"I'll get to it. First I want you to relax. Look at the water. Smell the brine."

"I have looked," he told her. "And I can smell the sea. I know lots of locals eat here. And it's got a great, authentic feeling because it is a great authentic place to eat. Love these trestle tables and benches. Love being within spitting distance of the fishing fleet. I love the fish these people serve, and the squid was wonderful. I'll be back for oysters—alone. And we couldn't be more obviously trying not to be obvious if we tried."

The lenses of her dark glasses obliterated her eyes, but they were definitely aimed in his direction. The downward turn of her lips spelled out her mood loud and clear.

"In case you haven't noticed, just about everyone comes here," Romano said. "You and I should not be seen having cozy afternoon trysts. If I could have trusted you not to do something foolish, I would not have come."

"You don't get to call the shots, *darling*." Her lovely face came nearer. She pushed the bowl of melted ice cream aside and leaned even farther across the table. "Do you want to talk about Cory Bledsoe?"

"You—"

"Ah, ah. Poker face, remember?"

"Bitch," Romano said, but rolled a cigar between his fingers and held it to his ear. Too bad she would remain a necessary nuisance. Not that she wasn't frequently enjoyable.

She laughed. "Very good. I do believe I admire you sometimes. Chris Talon is a liability."

The cigar lost its appeal. "Don't be a fool."

With her right index fingernail, she made whirlpools in the wine. "Did you say you wanted to talk about Cory Bledsoe?"

"Shut up," he told her. "You're as guilty as I am."

"Am I?" The glasses came off and he got the full force of her extraordinary eyes. "Who would believe it? After all, how was I to guess he'd walk in like that. But that's not the point. I think you're losing your nerve and that won't do. Not now."

"Losing my nerve? I have everything in perfect control. Soon it will be time to go to Sonnie and talk. Today, I think. Talon told her what I told him to tell her. It was perfect. They think I asked him to break the news because we accept him. She called me and she doesn't sound herself. Whatever that is. She is almost ready. We will persuade her that we need to get away from this place. Together. We will soon have everything we want."

"Not with Talon glued to her." Her wine-soaked fingertip came to rest on his lips. "I told you they were getting too cozy. They've been together since last night. Like Siamese twins. Every moment since last night. I assume you understand what I'm telling you. He's trouble, I tell you. I've asked around. He was a hotshot detective. New York. Narcotics. Chris Talon is a hard, hard, man and for some reason he's decided to stick to my sister like superglue. God, what a waste."

There were times when Romano detested Billy's cruelty to Sonnie. At least for him there was nothing personal about what he had to accomplish with his brother's wife. "A waste because you wish he was fucking you instead?"

That nail jabbed into his lower lip and she snatched her hand away before he could grab it. "First I intend to try talk therapy," she said. "I'm going to do my best to convince that lovely man that he's wasting good time on a sicko he can't save."

Panic rushed to his head. "You won't go near him. You won't say a word. You'll give everything away. If he is this hotshot narcotics detective you say he is, he will not be easily fooled. And if we are really unfortunate, he will turn his policeman's eyes on us because he will wonder why you would speak so of your sister."

"You forget how often I've been told I'd make a great actress."

Romano tasted blood on his lip. "You were told, a long, long time ago, that if you played tennis as well as you made a fool of yourself on court, you'd be a great champion. Apparently you've chosen to interpret those embarrassing statements differently."

Her face paled. "I hate you. I hate you and I'll make you pay for what you just said."

"Do not lose focus, my dear. Not yet, or we will fail. If we fail . . ."

"When will you get together with Sonnie?"

"You don't want to face possible consequences." There was no satisfaction left in taunting her. "We must both go to her. That is the appropriate way. We will discuss the news and beg her to come north with us. After all, we must stay together in our grief. We must suffer together, cry together."

"Throw up together."

He smiled, but the taste in his mouth was bitter. "I think you forget that I loved my brother."

"You don't know he's dead. Not for sure."

"If he were alive," Romano said, "I would have heard from him by now. And I didn't lie when I said I got a call, a tip, that Frank died soon after he was abducted."

Billy gave a theatrical sigh. "What a pity, what a shame. Call the waitress."

"I have also received proof of his death. You've drunk much more than enough."

"I'll call her." She waved her glass in the air. "You will get Sonnie away and talk to her. At the same time, I'll be with Chris Talon, persuading him to move on."

Romano had never felt more threatened. "How do you think you will do this, Billy?"

"Why, Romano"—she chucked him under the chin— "don't you trust me? First I thank him for looking after my little sister; then I point out that there's someone much more worthy of his attention."

"Call me—do do do—im-pet-u-ous. Oh, yeah, I'm—do do do—im-pet-u-ous."

Sonnie paused beside the piano at the Rusty Nail and screwed up her face at Chris. "Cute," she said. "You ought to write songs, but you might want to put them to original music. You can really play, Chris. I love listening to you."

He reached up and crossed his wrists on top of the piano. "I love everything about you. Top that."

Frank might have been dead, yet she was enjoying the attention of another man. Yes, she was enjoying every moment of it. And *attention* was a weak word for what they'd shared last night. "I don't think we'll hold a contest here."

"Aha. But we will hold one somewhere else?"

"I'm supposed to be working. And the day's more than half over. Shouldn't you be out asking some more questions?"

"I will be, boss. I'm waiting for some calls. One call, to be precise." He wasn't joking around anymore. "Sonnie, while I'm gone you have to be where I can be sure you're safe. Roy and Bo can take good care of you if you'll let them. Will you?"

"You frighten me. I can't stay—" A man on the opposite side of the street caught her attention. His impressive gut had nothing to do with the feeling he'd given her. His absorption did. He was watching her through the open shutters of the Nail. His head was shaved.

"What is it?" Chris asked, whipping around to see what she was looking at. "What?"

"Nothing."

"You can cut the lies, lady. We're dealing with serious stuff."

The man had been completely still, but he turned away and was lost in the surging crowds along Duval. "I think I just saw the man who threatened me that night. The drunk. He turned up at that motel."

Chris got to his feet. "And you stood there without telling me again?" He came from behind the piano.

"He's gone now. You'd never find him."

Chris curled his tongue over his upper teeth. What he was thinking didn't need to be said.

"I know I should have said something at once, but I'm afraid to heap on any more supposed *events*. If you don't already think I've got an overactive imagination, I don't know why. He's not important. Just a man at loose ends. I thought he'd have left Key West by now."

"You hoped he would have."

Snapping his fingers to a rhythm only he heard, swinging an imaginary partner, Bo danced toward them. "Okay if I ask a question?" he said.

"You will anyway," Chris told him.

"Most certainly. You haven't spent much time in your luxury quarters of late. Any comments about Aiden's limousine being parked out there? And there being no sign of Aiden? Did you send him on a mission?"

"Nope."

Sonnie looked sharply at Chris. "Did something happen between you two?"

"Don't worry about it."

She persisted. "Chris. Why is Aiden's car out back if Aiden isn't anywhere around?"

"Maybe he wanted to give me his pride and joy as a sop to his conscience."

Whatever spoke to Bo's musical tastes set his head gyrating from side to side. "Don't know why you put up with this bozo, Sonnie," he said, closing his eyes. "He's mean and tough. He alienates his friends. He doesn't appreciate having the best brother in the world."

"I don't know where Flynn is, okay? I told him to get lost and apparently he complied."

"Why would you do that?" Sonnie said.

The way Chris's lips pressed together didn't inspire warm sensations.

"We had a disagreement," he said. "Bo, I need to follow up a few leads. I've asked Sonnie to stay with you. That means—"

"What leads?" she asked when she recovered from the casual way he mentioned them. "What have you found out?"

"Later, ma'am. Bo, without wanting to send too much fear into anyone around here, this lady must *not* be allowed to leave this place. Not until I'm with her. Do we understand each other?"

Every inch of Bo moved to his music. "I've got it. Roy'll get it, too. Our Sonnie may say she doesn't intend to get it at all."

"I want to know why Aiden would leave his car behind," Sonnie said. "He loves that thing. Chris, I'm worried about him."

"Don't be. Ornery SOBs like Aiden have more lives than a cat."

"I distinctly heard that boy say he'd already used up eight lives," Bo said. "That could mean he's on his last one. I agree with Sonnie. We want to know where Aiden is."

"Shee-it."

"Ladies in the house," Bo said, still dreamy. "If Roy hears you, I'll pity you."

"Phone," Roy yelled from behind the bar. Pep, the small, golden-skinned woman who helped out during the day, ducked out with a cordless in hand. She trotted to give it to Chris and said to Bo, "I'm off now. Got to feed that man of mine. So long, Sonnie. Don't take anything from these guys."

"I won't," Sonnie told her.

Chris listened and injected occasional "Yeahs." He clicked off the instrument and set it down on top of the piano.

"Get that back over here," Roy shouted, letting them know he was watching every move.

Picking up the phone again, Chris angled his head to indicate they should all go to the bar. "Give me a few minutes, will you?" he said when both Bo and Sonnie had joined Roy on the other side. "I won't be more than a few minutes. Honest. I gotta check that pest Flynn's vehicle."

"Why?" Sonnie made fists on the counter. "What was that call about? Don't keep anything from us, Chris."

"I need a few minutes on my own, okay? I'll come back and fill you in."

"Chris—"

"Please, Sonnie. We're wasting time here, and I don't think that's a luxury we can afford."

"Go," she said, but she could scarcely stand the suspense.

Chris didn't argue. He left by the back door.

Bo let out a huge breath and slumped with his elbows on the bar. "That man will be the death of us all. So much goes on inside him, yet he is still so secretive."

Sonnie's thoughts exactly. She didn't want to hang around waiting for Chris to come back when he felt like it. "It's quiet this afternoon," she said, striving for nonchalance.

"Not that quiet," Roy said promptly. "Not quiet enough for you to find an excuse to slide out of here. So if you've got any ideas, forget 'em. Right, Bo?"

"You got it. Sonnie, Chris wants the best for you. He cares about you, and that's something we haven't seen in a long time, not since—"

"Not in a long time," Roy put in. "And if you leave, I'm just going to have to go with you."

She took glasses from a dish crate and slid them into the wooden racks overhead.

"Sonnie?" Roy said.

"I'll stay put. Thank you for caring about me."

"We do," Bo said. "And we think we're lucky to get the opportunity. Nasty weather forecasts coming in again. What d'you think, Roy? Are we gonna get hit this year?"

Roy ducked his head to squint outside. "I've got a feeling we may. I always feel the storms are playing with us. They try to make us careless, then sock it to us. We'll just have to keep an ear to the ground. Anybody ask that guy over there what he wants? Too good to serve himself, I guess."

Grateful for the diversion, Sonnie took the man's order for a beer and a tequila shooter. He was tall and bleached blond, his eyes hidden behind dark glasses, and dressed entirely in black leather—including a black leather jerkin unzipped almost to his navel. His chest bore an impressive array of tattoos. One ear was edged with at least a dozen rings, a small cross dangled from another piercing in his eyebrow, and there were two rings in his right nostril. He gave the impression of not welcoming small talk, so she didn't give him any.

"Sonnie," Roy said when she was back behind the bar, "how much has Chris told you about himself?"

The question caught her off guard and she blinked several times.

"Not much?" Roy said. "That doesn't surprise me. You think he's a hard son of a . . . beechnut, don't you? He's had some hard knocks, but his real problem is that he's too quick to take the blame for other people's actions. Not that he'll listen to anyone who tries to tell him that."

Sonnie checked the bar. Despite Roy's protests to the contrary, the place was all but deserted. A couple sat near the windows, and the blond man occupied his table with evident surly uninterest in his surroundings. "I don't think Chris would like it if he knew we'd talked about him."

"To hell—he isn't here, so he doesn't know what we're talking about," Bo said. "And Roy and I have decided he needs help. He needs to stop hiding from himself. No way can a man come to terms with himself as long as he pretends there's nothing wrong with him."

"He's a hell of a detective," Roy said. "They fought to keep him in New York, but the man's got concrete between his ears when it comes to listening to what other people think of him. He blames himself for something that wasn't his fault, and he won't listen to anyone who tries to make him more objective. You sure he didn't say anything about what happened in New York?"

Sonnie shook her head. She glanced repeatedly at the back door. "I think Chris has to decide to tell me himself, if he ever wants to."

"He won't decide," Roy said.

"Because he won't forgive himself," Bo added.

"We want you to know this because it'll make it easier for you to understand when he gets real moody," Roy said. "He was on a case. Called into a pusher's place on a domestic violence complaint. Chris had been aching for a reason to go in there. The pusher had beaten up his wife and scared his kids—if they were his kids—into gibbering balls in the corners.

"The wife's sister was there—and her boyfriend. Evidently the boyfriend and the pusher were real tight. The sister didn't look so hot, either. She had a face that had probably looked a whole lot better before it needed so many stitches.

"Chris rounded up the guys—while the women begged for them to be released. Why would any woman behave like that?" He shook his head and obviously didn't expect an answer. "Chris got the handcuffs on. He'd called for his backup—who was Aiden Flynn—and Aiden got in at a trot. Then Chris went in a back room. The place was filthy. Stank. On the floor between a bed and the wall he found an unconscious baby, about six months old. The kid was covered with bruises. Chris went mad. He loves kids. He wanted his own, but Beatty was never quite ready for them. Beatty was his wife. When he saw this little guy who'd obviously suffered so much, he just lost it."

Tears slid down Sonnie's cheeks and she didn't do anything to stop them. "I don't blame him." Chris had never mentioned that he liked children.

"Neither do I," Roy said. "But he turned into a vigilante

and all but conducted a trial on the spot. Outcome? Seemed the mother had beaten the kid to silence so her old man wouldn't get even madder. Chris left the pushers to Aiden and hauled the woman off. Got her charged in night court and threw her in the pokey.

"She had excuses. Explanations. She admitted hitting the kid, but said he was okay when she left him. He was asleep.

"Chris didn't believe her, and he didn't have any difficulty finding support for his theory. Long story short. The baby died. The mother was convicted of murdering her own child and sent up."

"And she got out on some technicality," Sonnie said. "I don't know how anyone can be a conscientious policeman. They can't get the courts to keep criminals behind bars."

Bo and Roy looked at each other. "The woman died in jail," Bo said. "Hanged herself with a bedsheet. And it turned out she was covering for her sister and the boyfriend. They were occupying another bed in the same room with the kid. When he cried, they made sure he shut up."

"And they didn't come forward with the truth?"

"Not until the mother died and the sister finally found some remorse. Anyway, Chris blames himself one hundred percent. That's why he left the force. He says he murdered that woman. That was over two years ago. The moment he said he was getting out of NYPD, Beatty divorced him. Apparently she found being a cop's wife glamorous. Wife of a washed-up cop didn't appeal. She remarried within a few months. Another cop. This one had been helping Beatty for some time. He kept her company through the lonely nights when Chris was on duty."

Sonnie passed the backs of her hands over her eyes. She didn't know Chris had returned until his arm settled on her shoulder and his deep voice said, "I just got the end of that. There was no reason for you to know any of it. I'm sorry Roy and Bo opened their big mouths and spilled my business."

His tone chilled her. She looked up in time to see his cold face and the angry eyes with which he regarded Roy and Bo. "When I got down here I was pretty shaken up. If I hadn't been, I wouldn't have unloaded on you. I'm trying to forget. I didn't want Sonnie to know any of it. Not ever.''

"You hypocrite," Sonnie said. Anger hadn't been the feeling she expected. "You want to know everything about me and I've confided in you. But you've got to be the big, strong guy who can deal with his own ghosts. You don't need anything from anyone."

Roy touched her arm and said, "Go easy, Sonnie. I spoke out of turn."

"You did not," she told him. "You love your brother and that's why you told me. You think I can help him. You're wrong. He'd never let me." And she wished she could be far away without having to deal with what she felt, the disappointment, the embarrassment at her foolishness in thinking he'd begun to rely on her, to want to be with her.

"Now see what you've done, bozo," Bo said. "The best thing that ever came your way, and you're managing to turn her off."

"I do want to be with you," Chris said, ignoring Sonnie's resistance and turning her toward him. "I would have told you when it seemed right. You're going through heavy times. We've got to deal with you, not me."

"Too easy, Chris. Too quick. Don't you know anything about me? I don't want pity. I want help, yes, but not pity. And maybe it would help me if I knew you had bad things to cope with, too."

Roy and Bo drifted away.

Chris leaned to drive a thumbtack deeper into a postcard on the burlap-covered wall. "I'm sorry," he said. "But I repeat: until tonight it hasn't been about me. I did tell you I'd dropped out. You must have known I had a reason. I'm a shit. That's the reason. Because of my hard head, a woman died. It wasn't enough that she'd lost her baby. I had to hound her, drive her into a corner until she'd have said anything to shut me up. So I got a confession. And it was a lie. I killed her, and I'm never going to forget it. I'm trying to forgive myself—at least enough to carry on. And you're helping me with that."

She could scarcely swallow. "How could I have known

what you're going through? Chris, I'm sorry. Let me in. Let me be here for you. I need you; you know that. Would it be so bad for you to need me, too?''

His hands came to rest on the sides of her face. He leaned his brow on hers. "I do, Sonnie. I thought you knew that by now. I don't even want to think about not having you where I can get to you."

"You weren't to blame," she told him. "You weren't, Chris."

He shook his head. "Let it be, darlin'. I appreciate what you want to do, but let it be."

Sonnie placed her fingers on his mouth. Her body quickened just because he was near. "Will you let me know when you're ready to deal with it?"

"I'll let you know." He kissed her. She felt air currents from the fans whirring overhead, and smelled Chris's clean skin. And she stood on her toes to kiss him more deeply.

His hands were on her bottom, holding her against him. She wasn't the only one aroused.

"What does it take to get a drink around here?"

Sonnie slowly lowered her heels to the floor, slowly allowed their mouths to part. And when they had, she looked at his lips and wanted right back where she'd been.

The sound of a glass banging on the bar opened Chris's eyes. Sonnie grimaced at him and he showed his teeth in a silent growl before turning around. "You got a problem?" Chris asked the blond man who had managed to find enough energy for a walk to the bar. "Where I come from, interruptin' a lady and gentleman at a time like this wouldn't be considered respectful behavior. No, sir. I think you should apologize; then we'll talk about a drink."

"Well, I'm mighty sorry if I've offended you," the man said. "I surely do ask you to pardon me, sir. Now, get me a goddamn beer and join me at that table. You too, Sonnie. If we don't have even more trouble than we thought we had, then my name isn't Wally—Aiden Flynn, to you."

Twenty-five

These were the moments Aiden lived for. "You're losing your touch, partner," he said when Sonnie was seated in the booth and Chris was in the process of sliding in beside her. "You looked right at me. Geez, I know I'm good, but wasn't there anything familiar about me?"

"I did wonder about the smell, but we Southerners set great stock in good manners."

Sonnie aimed an elbow at his ribs, but she also grinned. "I didn't suspect it was you, Aiden. The disguise is fabulous."

"He's like a kid," Chris said. "Halloween is his idea of heaven. But you're right, he's dam—darned good at it."

Aiden knew better than to persist with the ribbing—at least not at a time like this. "Thanks. And don't worry, Sonnie; I rarely choose something this flamboyant. For the past couple of days I'd definitely have been missed in any crowd."

Bo and Roy arrived with drinks that hadn't been ordered. Oysters followed, and baskets of French fries and onion rings. "Just to keep your strength up," Bo said, sliding several pieces of Key lime pie on the table. "Nibble here and there. That's what I do when I've got a lot on my mind."

"Thanks," Aiden said, and refrained from mentioning that nothing Bo ate went to his waist.

Bo hung around.

Roy returned with a bottle of champagne and five glasses.

"What the hell's that for?" Chris asked.

"Language," Roy said. "It's just in case we might want to celebrate something. Okay if we join you?"

"Hell, no," Chris said.

"Hell, yes," Sonnie said, and Bo laughed, slapped his knees, and cackled.

"This is business," Chris informed everyone. "There isn't goin' to be any celebration today, and the fewer people who know what's goin' on here, the better."

"Ooh, but he does get so Carolina when he's mad," Bo said. "I love that lazy sound."

Roy looked at the ceiling. "In case you haven't noticed, bro, you seem to need our help. Bo's and mine, that is. Is it just possible we'd get better at making decisions where Sonnie's concerned if we knew more? Hey, say the word, kid, and we're outa here. We'll still do our best because she's our best girl, but it might be nice not to be handicapped by ignorance."

Enjoying himself thoroughly, Aiden slipped all the way into the booth and slapped the seat beside him. "You're right. Sit down. Maybe we'll celebrate a little common sense around here, huh?" He looked very deliberately into Chris's hard hazel eyes. At the moment they were real hard and showed the shade of green that got mixed in when he was boiling at being crossed.

At last he said, "Pull up a chair, Roy. Don't take what I say too personally."

"Never have," Roy said comfortably. "You always were a pigheaded little varmint. I don't know how anyone could stand being your partner anyway."

"Drop that," Chris said. "Fill us in, Aiden. Everybody keep both eyes open for approaching ears."

"Gotcha," Roy said, and Aiden took great pleasure at the sight of Sonnie pressing her lips together to stop herself from grinning again.

Chris jabbed a forefinger at Aiden. "Before you wow us with your incredible detective efforts, answer me a question or two. It took a bit, but I finally got a call back from Ballsy in Records.''

"Ballsy?" The chorus went up from everyone but Chris and Aiden.

Chris waved a hand. "Don't ask. If he weren't invaluable, he'd have been out on his ear years ago. You, Mr. Flynn, are on an indefinite leave of absence. I told you to get lost, and you promptly got the sergeant to believe you're all stretched out and need a looooong break. Now, if I'd asked him for that kind of privilege, he'd have laughed me out of his office. But good ol' Flynn doles out a sob story and he gets all the time he wants. How come? Something between you and the sarg I don't know about?''

"Watch him, Aiden," Bo said. "I know it seems unlikely, but this guy might be questioning your sexual preferences. Now, I'd be one of the first to welcome you to the family, but if that isn't your scene, I'll get the ice bags and you can flatten him.''

"I won't need the ice bags," Aiden said, chuckling. "He likes to push. If he pushes too far, he'll get his, but I won't be offering TLC. I got the leave. End of story.''

"Where have you been?" Chris said. "I even went out to look over that blot on the landscape you call a vintage automobile. I figured you might have been sleeping in it and I just didn't notice. It leaks so badly it's always fogged up anyway.''

"Oh, no." Aiden covered his mouth. "Don't tell me I forgot to make the bed.''

Sonnie turned a slice of pie around and around and finally attacked it with a fork. She rolled her eyes with ecstasy and got real serious.

Aiden couldn't resist revealing his latest personal acquisition. "I'll be putting the pink pony in mothballs soon. Just wait till you see my new baby. I got a 'fifty-nine Cadillac Sixty Special four-door hardtop.'' He actually clapped his hands.

"Cadillac?" Chris said.

Flynn nodded. "Time I got versatile. Bought it at auction. Sight unseen, but who cares? One-hundred-thirty-inch wheelbase. Overall length''—he paused—''two hundred twenty-five inches. Torpedo-shaped dummy air swoops. And those *fins*. It's got to be taken all the way down, but—"

"Paint it chartreuse," Chris said, rubbing his head.

Aiden pointed at him. "You've got it. Chartreuse. I love it."

"A zoo," Chris said. "We're supposed to be conducting an investigation, and the rest of you are having a party."

"Got to eat sometimes," Sonnie said around a mouthful. "Congrats, Aiden."

"Thanks," Aiden said. "All right. Down to business. I've lucked out, Chris. First, I don't think Sonnie is delusional."

"Thanks," she said without looking up.

"Sorry if I gave that impression," he said, and he was. "It was just that there didn't seem anything to substantiate your claims. Cops are boring about stuff like that. Judges don't listen to hunches, so we've got to keep going after evidence that can be seen, heard, and preferably touched."

"Like dead bodies," Chris said. Apart from the occasional French fry, he was too engrossed in Aiden to eat or drink. "Any idea why KWPD's so nonchalant about Edward's death?"

"They'll probably get less nonchalant in time. Especially now. One of my visits yesterday was to the funeral home. The assistant medical examiner's a nice guy. Very professional.

"There's no doubt the tissue and blood samples turned up heavy doses of local anesthetic. But there's something else. And this is really stupid on behalf of whoever did it. Edward was unconscious when those shots were administered. Speculation is that he was stuffed into his sleeping bag. He tried to get out and hit himself a good one on the side of the head. There was a nasty hematoma and a lot of swelling. He would have been unconscious. So giving him those shots was a piece of cake. But they really screwed up using the backs of his arms. Somewhere he'd have been capable of reaching himself would have been so much better. Then there would have been some thought about suicide. Good news is that he was out cold before the fire started. He had some nasty moments, but not as nasty as they could have been."

"Thank God," Sonnie said quietly.

Roy and Bo said, "Amen," in unison.

Chris said, "If I could be sure the bastard didn't intend to do something to Sonnie, I'd be lighting candles to him. The jury's out on that. What else?"

"Moving right along," Aiden said mildly, picking up his beer and taking several hefty swallows.

"Why don't you have a meal before we go on?" Sonnie said. "I'm so grateful for everything you're doing. So's Chris. Aren't you, Chris?"

He looked sideways at her and Aiden's jaw tightened. His old buddy had a bad case. Now they'd better pray the bottom didn't drop out.

"I'm grateful," Chris said finally. "You want to eat, Aiden? It's okay with me."

"I'm doing fine, thanks to Bo and Roy."

"This is dangerous stuff, isn't it?" Roy said. "You're right to be closemouthed, bro. But don't think you can't trust us to be careful."

"I don't. Aiden?"

"I've been polishing up my pilot's license. Got to get in my annual hours."

The expression on Chris's face showed that he expected this announcement to have bearing on the case.

"Went up with a guy from Island City Flight Service. Nice folks. Casual but good. And helpful. The first guy I went up with didn't respond to any of my hints. The second guy was full of information. Sure as hell doesn't like the Giacano brothers. Said they were assholes—"

"Language," Roy said predictably. "And you're talking about Sonnie's relatives."

Aiden smiled sheepishly. "Sorry, Sonnie. This guy said he knew someone who was at the field the night you had the big bang up. Evidently there was a miniexodus afterward. Several guys left for various reasons, so there aren't many people to talk to."

"Come on, come on," Chris said, beckoning with four fingers. "What about this guy who had all the information?"

"I'm getting to that. He said this other guy, the one who was at the field that night, said he couldn't figure out why Romano went back to the airport after the accident—on foot—and rented a moped when he had that fancy Jag. Romano said he'd left the Jag where it was because the police didn't want anything moved, but he had to get messages out to Sonnie's family, and do a whole lot of other things."

This time it was Chris's turn to pour down some beer. "Unless the Jag was involved in the accident, there'd be no reason for it to be kept there. Romano would have to testify to what he saw, but that . . . well, maybe there's something we don't know. I'll get out there and talk to the moped outfit. Could be something that'll help. Where do I find the loudmouth? The guy who talked about Romano renting the moped?"

"We're not having a lot of luck with witnesses," Aiden said with that old frustrated sensation he knew so well. "Deep-sea fishing was his thing. Matter of days after Sonnie's accident, the man drowned in high seas. They never found him."

Every time the phone rang, or someone came through the door of the Nail, Sonnie jumped. Roy had insisted on opening the champagne and pouring each of them a glass. "To celebrate that they were alive and kicking," he'd said. Sonnie was alive, but kicking might be out this evening.

Another customer walked out of the sultry evening, and Sonnie jumped yet again. She was still expecting Mr. T-Shirt to pop up again. He troubled her, and she knew he troubled Chris, too.

The man approached her directly and she rubbed her eyes. How could she have failed to recognize Romano immediately?

"Hello, little Sonnie. How is my girl doing?"

"Fine." Snapping back that she wasn't his girl would be childish. "How are things at the club?"

He wrinkled his very straight nose. "Frankly overwhelming. Seems Cory Bledsoe has taken lessons from the previous golf pro and ducked out. Not a word. Just packed up his things, put them in his car, and left. Which means that since I have a sense of responsibility, I'm doing my poor best to fill his place, too, and I'm interviewing prospective replacements. I'm not having any luck. But that isn't what I came here to talk about.''

I'm sure it wasn't. Sonnie was too tired. The day had been long and tense, and she didn't like it that she couldn't be sure where either Chris or Aiden had gone. Mostly she just didn't like Chris being gone at all.

"Roy," Romano said suddenly. "I am Romano Giacano. Sonnie's brother-in-law.''

Dislike thinned Roy's mouth, and his expression turned flat. "Is that so?''

"Yes. We have been a very close family but we have suffered a great deal. Did Sonnie tell you that we have had word that my brother Frank—her husband—is dead?''

Roy made sympathetic noises.

"I haven't spoken of it," Sonnie said, disturbed at the realization. She hadn't as much as considered telling Roy and Bo about Frank's death. "There hasn't been a right moment.''

"Ah, I see. But Chris did explain what happened—my call to him? You think highly of him, and I thought he would break the news kindly.''

"Yes." She looked away. "He did." Her mind revisited the upper hallway at the Truman Avenue house and she felt muddled.

Romano took something from his pocket and slid it across the counter toward her. "Would you wear this? It was Frank's. But you know that. I know he would want you to have it.''

Frank's medal. He never took it off. "Where did you get this?'' she asked.

"I . . .'' Romano fumbled to sit on a stool and closed his eyes. He propped his elbows and buried his face in his hands.

"Romano?" She no longer knew what to believe about him, whether he was friend or foe, but she knew he was suffering now. "This hurts so much, doesn't it?''

"It was delivered to my room at the club. Can you imagine that? They must have been afraid it would be traced if they shipped it to me. It was on the floor outside the door. Just like that.''

"I'm sorry," Sonnie said, and she was sorry for his pain.

"I'm sorry for both of us," Romano said. "We both loved him. How will we go on?"

Guilt made an ugly companion. "I wish I could say something to make you feel better."

"You make me feel better just by caring. Wear his medallion, Sonnie."

Sonnie picked up the heavy gold chain with a religious medal attached. Frank had been his own god. Just touching the gold sickened her, but to let her true feelings show might be very unwise. Keeping her eyes lowered, she put the chain over her head. She was careful to wear it on top of her cotton shirt rather than against her skin. "Thank you," she said. After all, Romano would expect her to find his gesture touching. "I'll look after it."

"He may come back, Sonnie."

"You're the one who said he's dead." He could only be speaking his longing aloud, and she pitied him.

"I had to report what I'd been told—and what that medal signifies. But in my heart"—he looked up and beat his chest—"I feel my brother is still alive. You and I need to talk. You are the closest I shall ever come to having a sister of my own, and I need you. Will you help me through this? As I will help you?"

"If I can," she said without thinking. "Yes, of course I will."

"Thank you." He bowed his head again. "Thank you, my dear sister. I haven't always been as understanding as I should. Forgive me for that, please."

"Forget it." The least she could do was comfort him. "I'll never forget how kind you were to me at the hospital. We've got to put the past behind us."

He nodded slowly, but his face remained strained. "Will these gentlemen allow you to leave for a few hours? I need you, Sonnie."

The thought of Romano smothering her with his emotional outpourings terrified her. "I'm working."

"Roy," Romano said promptly. "I should like to take Sonnie with me and to have an opportunity to talk things through with her. Would that be agreeable?''

Roy and Bo glanced at each other. ''Sonnie,'' Roy said. ''You know what Chris said.''

Sonnie looked from Roy to Romano, who clung to the edge of the bar and pleaded with his eyes.

''We'd better see if we can get Chris,'' Bo said. ''Make sure he isn't coming back for you like he said he might.'' The lie didn't sound comfortable on the man's lips.

''Of course,'' Romano said. ''You have other arrangements. Forgive me for intruding.''

She felt trapped. But perhaps she could turn the time into something useful. She'd talk to Romano about the night she'd been injured. He'd explain about his reason for walking back to the airport—and he might well tell her other things that would be useful. ''I'll come, but only for an hour or so,'' she told him. ''Roy, if Chris calls, tell him I'm with Romano and we'll be back in two hours at the outside. Will that do?'' she asked Romano.

''A great deal can be accomplished in two hours, my dear.''

The last prop plane from Miami set down late after its twenty-five-minute flight to Key West. It arrived just before midnight. Chris was aboard. Zipped into the inside pockets of his jean jacket were sheafs of papers, copies of documents. He'd sweet-talked a medical records clerk out of them at the hospital in Miami where Sonnie had fought her way back to life.

He ran down the rickety metal steps from the plane and hurried to the arrivals and departures building, where an illuminated sign announced that he was back in ''The Conch Republic.''

He barely made it inside one of the doors when Billy Keith popped in front of him. ''Hi,'' she said, showing a lot of white teeth, and a lot of other things. ''Isn't this great? I couldn't believe my luck when I saw your Harley out there.''

His Harley wasn't where the casual onlooker would stumble

over it. "Hi to you, Billy." He made to move on. His bike was inside the tall wire fence at a separate area of the airport, an area used by the passengers and crews of light planes.

Billy showed no sign of going on her way. "I came out to pick up an Airborne shipment." She brandished a pack as proof. "But you're a big bonus."

Moments when Chris became aware of a woman looking him over—the way Billy Keith looked him over—were rare. *Sizing him up* was the right term. The sensation wasn't flattering. "Nice to run into you, Billy," he said. "I'd better go bail out my bike."

Still she didn't move. Her gray linen dress might be minimalist, but it was perfectly cut—for a perfect figure. He was no sartorial expert, but the lady knew how to put herself together. Low-heeled gray sandals showed off bright red toenails that matched her lips and fingernails. She'd pulled her hair away from her face into some sort of sleek thing at the back of her head.

Yep, Billy Keith was a showstopper, but Chris avoided women he couldn't like.

He looked past her toward the street side of the building. "Well, nice to see you, Billy. I'd better get on."

The big smile disappeared. "Running into you like this is a sign. I've got to talk to you and I can't put it off any longer."

Chris wanted to get back to Sonnie, and he wanted to make some plans with Flynn. "It's late, Billy. Don't think me rude, but I've got to get some sleep before I try to make sense talking to anyone."

She pushed a hand behind his left biceps and held on. "I've got to throw myself on your pity." Leaning, she raised her face to his. From his angle he was presented with one too many scenic choices. Keeping his attention on her face took restraint.

"Chris?" she said, her voice husky. "I don't care how tired you are. Listen to me, will you, please? Just come to the club and listen to me."

All systems went on red alert. "The club?" he said, and felt like an ass.

"I've got a beautiful room there. You can stretch out and relax, and just listen until you're ready to say what you think."

He'd been offered a lot of dessert trays. This one was higher class than most, but he wasn't tempted—much. "It's too late." He checked his watch. "I really have to get back, but thanks for the offer."

Anger hung at the back of those very dark eyes. "It's about Sonnie," she said. "There's a lot you don't know. If you're going to do your best for her, you've got to have all the parts of the puzzle."

He hesitated. "Tell me now. Here."

"Don't be a fool." She clamped her lips together and he heard the breath she drew into her nose. "You know we can't discuss something like this in public. My room is private. We won't be disturbed."

Chris walked and she had no choice but to let go of his arm, or trail along with him. She trailed. "I'm partial to the café here," Chris said. "It's dead this time of night. Come on."

He led the way past the ticket counters and into a hallway that led to the neon-lit café. Billy had to run to keep up.

The odd mechanic or pilot had staked claim to a varnished table. The windows were filmed with condensation, and a jungle of green plants showed their appreciation for the growing conditions. Chris led his sulking companion to a table beneath a wall-mounted propeller—the real kind.

"Cute," she said, turning down the corners of her mouth. "I bet they think Grand Marnier's a ski run in the Alps."

"Which Alps?"

She ignored him and snapped her fingers at the woman tending the bar that occupied a good percentage of the room. Chris got up and ordered, and used the time while the drinks were made to prepare himself for whatever was likely to come. He had plenty of reasons to be very careful with Billy Keith.

He returned to the table, put a Grand Marnier in front of her, and sat down with a cup of coffee. "Okay, fire away."

Sipping the Grand Marnier she appeared to be deciding if the drink would do. "I can rub people the wrong way," she said. "I do it all the time. It's a hazard I have to live with.

That's my way of apologizing if you think I come on too strong, or say the wrong things, or whatever. I'm sorry. My main reason for waiting around for you was to thank you for everything you've been doing for Sonnie. Obviously you're a very kind man.''

And what, he wondered, did she really mean by that? "Sonnie's special.''

"I know." Billy flashed another smile. "She's a sweet little thing. Always has been. As long as I can remember she's attracted strong people who want to take care of her. Of course, with all the scars and the limp and so on, well, she's pathetic, but in a very appealing way. I still don't think a lot of men like you would spend time on her. You're different.''

Never having been a high school girl, he hadn't learned what it was that could make some women so openly catty. The woman who sat beside him was a perfect example of a high school Miss Popularity who'd never grown up.

"Sonnie is a brave woman," he said, choosing to study his coffee rather than his companion. "She's been through so much, but she never complains. And she's always more interested in what she can do for other people than what other people can do for her." He glanced up in time to see Billy grimace.

She recovered at once and said, "You're right. I've got an idea, Chris"—she put a hand on top of his—"and I want you to at least think about it. I've known Sonnie since she was born. I know *all* about her. You're trying to help her find peace with what's happened to her, aren't you?''

"Yeah." The waters were getting very muddy.

"That's what I thought. But you can't be sure that what she tells you is exactly right, can you? You don't know if a lot of what she says comes from her imagination. I do. Why don't we work together to help her?''

He barely stopped himself from laughing. "What a great offer. Thanks, Billy, but I'm a loner when it comes to this kind of thing.''

"I can help," she said. The studied hoarseness dropped from her voice. "I know I can. And I need you as much as she does. I've suffered through everything Sonnie's suffered through.''

Disgust made it hard to look at her. He said, ''Really? You weren't in the crash, were you?''

''No, of course not. But my life's been turned upside down by what happened. My father and step-mother are grieving because their youngest child is crippled and disfigured. They loved Frank dearly, but he's dead. You know that from what Romano told you.''

''Yes.'' And he'd bet neither Romano nor Billy spent many lonesome hours in their respective rooms. ''How's the doctor? He seems a nice guy.''

''He is a nice guy,'' she said, sounding impatient. ''And he's as good a psychiatrist as they come.''

''That's great. I'm sure he's being very helpful to you.''

''He is. Now I want you to help get Sonnie to see him.''

''Does she need a psychiatrist?'' Two could play the amateur actor. ''She seems fine to me.'' Where Billy was concerned he had no choice but to lie, at least until he understood more of what was in the documents he carried.

''How can you say that?'' She downed the drink, got up, and went to the bar.

Chris made no attempt to go after her. In Sonnie's records it was noted that the patient's brother-in-law and her sister took turns sitting with her around the clock. One of them had always been at her side.

Billy came back and settled in again. ''I'm going to be blunt. She's fooling you. You get one face; we get another. Sonnie calls either Romano or me constantly. She tells the wildest tales. Hobgoblins coming out of the walls. Things that go bang in the night. Fire. Distant singing. Even phone calls from Frank. *Frank.* The tales go on and on. We're exhausted and frightened. She needs the best help we can buy her.''

Once more Billy was holding his hand and leaning against him. ''Sounds to me like you're trying to take away Sonnie's responsibility for herself,'' he said.

''We've *got* to before it's too late. You've been with her, haven't you? A lot?''

Her meaning didn't have to be spelled out. "Sonnie and I are good friends."

"I'll bet," Billy said, and didn't bother to look embarrassed. "She must think she's died and gone to heaven."

"If that's a compliment," Chris said, "it's not welcome."

"It ought to be." The real Billy had stepped up to the plate. "Help her. I want you to do that. But don't get so sucked in that you think you have to keep her warm at night."

"I've got to leave," Chris said. "Let me see you to your car."

Billy didn't move. "Have you seen any evidence of these things she keeps telling us about? Have you heard voices *up near the ceiling?*"

He had chosen to believe there was some form of eerie noise in Sonnie's house. And Flynn was now convinced that they weren't wasting their time helping her.

"Well, have you?"

"Time to go home," he said, extricating his hand and standing up. "I know you've been through a lot. Sonnie has told me that you and Romano have been very good to her."

That bought him a sharp stare. "She has?"

"Of course. Why don't you make a note to get in touch with me if you think of something that might help Sonnie deal with her past? And I'll tell her we've spoken."

"No. No, don't tell her that. She's always wanted to try being independent. Why not let her think she is, at least for a little while?"

On the walk to the airport drive, he contrived to keep himself out of holding range.

"I could leave my car and ride back with you," Billy said. This one didn't know when to give up.

"I've never been on one of those Harleys."

"You're not dressed for it," he said. "And I don't have the passenger seat on anyway. We'll save it for another time."

Her sandals clacked as he walked her to her car. A tomato red Porsche, it was parked beneath a light in the lot. Chris held the door while she got in, then slammed it and ducked down to say, "Good night. We'll be talking."

"You can bet your . . ." Her smile was sly. "Just bet on it."

She gunned the engine.

Chris laughed and yelled, "Eat up those roads, tiger. And get someone to wash that thing." He slapped his palms together to dislodge dust.

He waited just long enough to see her turn onto the highway before leaning against the lamp standard and taking out his cell phone and dialing.

While he listened to the ring, he brushed the pale dust from Billy's car off his jeans and studied the angle of South Roosevelt.

It was Roy who answered. "Is that you, Sonnie?"

Twenty-six

"Driving," Romano said, "calms me down. It always has. There was a time when I thought I would race, but responsibility got in the way. I am a better tennis coach than I am a race-car driver, and my brother needed me."

Although she could see little but dark, sucking water on either side of the overseas highway that connected Key West to the rest of the Keys and to Miami, Sonnie kept her face toward the passenger window. "Yes," was all she could think of to say. They'd been gone for hours, many more than the two hours she'd mentioned to Roy, yet she didn't dare ask Romano to take her back. He drove alternately incredibly fast and at a crawl.

"You see how it is here," he said. "So easy to be cut off from everything, to become lost to the world. One long road and so many little islands. I wonder how many people are supposed to be living on those islands when they are either far away or dead."

"You think of the strangest things," she said, and forced a laugh. "Such an imagination. You should write books."

"True," he said. "I've thought the same thing. When I can spare a few days, I will do that."

He had driven her all the way to Miami and back, stopping

time and again to point out some remote key. He hadn't mentioned what he'd said he wanted to discuss with her, and there was a recklessness about him that cautioned her not to cross him.

"This is Marathon," he said, as he had when they'd crossed the island on the way north. "The main golf course is here."

He'd also mentioned that. She couldn't see much in the dark. Midnight had come and gone. She couldn't bear to think of Roy and Bo worrying, and probably Chris and Aiden by now. But at least Romano was on his way back to Key West.

"We should talk about Frank," she said tentatively. "I know it hurts you to think about him, but you said—"

"I know what I said. Why would I speak with you about my brother? What did you ever know about him?"

She turned her face away again.

"I worry about you all alone in that big house," Romano said, his voice unnaturally soft and distant. "Frank would not want that for you. You need people around you."

Her ribs didn't want to expand. The spaces between the bones went into a spasm. "I'm very fond of the house."

"But it frightens you. When you are there you see and hear things that come from your mind. I've put off confronting you with your irrational behavior, but now we're out of time. You must take responsibility for your behavior. And you must do what is best for your family. I am part of that family."

He held her captive in his luxurious car, captive with the onslaught she expected to start now.

"Answer me," he said sharply. "I am not that policeman gone soft. You think he is a big, strong man to lean on. He is a failure. He could not do his job, so he ran away."

"You don't know him," she said, unable to choose her own safety over defending Chris.

"I know far more than you think. Be silent. Do not contradict me; is that understood? In the Giacano family, women do not argue with their men."

"You are not my man."

He slammed on the brakes so hard the car fishtailed back and forth across the road for many yards. Despite her seat belt,

Sonnie was thrown from side to side. In the past hour, the wind had picked up to the highest velocity she'd seen since she arrived, and seawater roared over the roadway, leaving it wet and slick.

"See what you do when you make me angry?" Romano said. "You make me forget myself. Remember, I know everything about you, *everything*. I know you were a terrible wife for Frank but that he championed you against all odds. I know your family has spoiled you, coddled you, allowed you to have your own way even where you are unfit to make any choices for yourself."

She took short breaths and struggled against rising nausea.

"You argue with me, just as you argued with Frank. You were the wrong woman for him. I should not have allowed them to play such a dangerous game."

"Them?" He confused her. "What game? I don't understand."

"Of course you do. Billy and Frank played with you. She was disappointed by her career, her failures, but she peaked early. And the alcohol was poison to her. It still is. Alcohol pushed her out of the game in the end.

"She and Frank were too well suited. At least they knew that. And they didn't have enough money to satisfy themselves. But they needed each other, and you became the game they played together. He married you because they decided he would. You were their bank, my dear. When Frank looked at you he didn't see a woman; he saw a bank.

"Your sister would sit with us and laugh at your foolishness. She has always needed power. It thrills her—fills her hunger. She could have her lover marry her sister to provide for her own needs, and Frank's. You see, she was in control all the time."

Sonnie crowded against the door, putting as much distance as she could between them. Great gusts buffeted the car, and she felt Romano work to hold the vehicle steady.

"All of that silliness is behind us. Now you will play your part and do everything you can to help me," he said. "Is that understood?"

She shook her head. He wanted her to be terrified. He wouldn't get his way—or know he'd gotten his way. "No. I don't understand you at all, Romano. You said you wanted to talk to me. You've said almost nothing that makes sense, and we've driven over three hundred miles. You said you needed me, but I don't know what for, especially when you say I'm useless and you don't know why Frank married me—except for this fantastic story you've invented about Billy and Frank."

"Fantastic?" He turned sharply toward her. "Why do you think he married you?"

"Because we were in love." She had been in love, and Frank had declared his love over and over.

Romano laughed. To Sonnie's horror, he stroked the side of her face and tangled his fingers in her hair. He pulled until she was in pain and tried to pry him loose.

He dropped his hand lower. From her shoulder, he moved to run a forefinger over Frank's medal where it hung between her breasts. And he made sure the contact was intimate.

"Please don't," she murmured. "What have I done to you?"

"Nothing. That's the whole problem. You have done nothing for me or to me. You have shunned me. You consider yourself too good for me." With that he undid the top button on her blouse and pushed his hand inside, and then inside her bra to cover her naked breast. He laughed again. "I'm trying to make myself believe the old saying: The closer to the bone, the sweeter the meat." He pinched her nipple. "Perhaps I can learn the wisdom in that after all."

Very firmly, Sonnie grabbed his wrist. For a moment he showed her how incapable she was of making him do anything he didn't want to do. Then he took his hand away. He looked her in the face, then administered a light but stinging slap to her cheek.

Tears burned her eyes and she shrank from him.

"Don't bother to tell anyone I did that. They'll never believe it. That's the beauty of an impeccable reputation. You are with me now, Sonnie. I am in charge and you will do only what I tell you to do. I'm even thinking of marrying you. After all, my brother would approve. He'd like the idea of my looking after you, don't you think? Of my teaching you how a woman should behave toward her husband?''

"Frank called me again," she whispered, desperate to shock him back to reality. "I didn't imagine it was his voice. I am sure he's being kept captive. What he said was so close to what he said before he was to come to Key West the last time. But there were other things he would have said only if he knew nothing about what had happened to me."

"Shut up," Romano said, slipping the car back into gear and driving away. "Nothing would please me more than to think my brother would return. My sources say that will not happen, and they have no reason to lie. Now I want you to talk to someone. He is waiting. He's been waiting for some hours."

"Don't do this to me," Sonnie said. "You're frightening me. Why would you do that? What have I done to you?"

"You have complicated my life," he said shortly and in the toneless voice he'd used almost from the moment she'd gotten into the car and he'd locked the doors from his controls. "You have not done as you were told. You have put yourself first. You sicken me, but I will try to save you. If you do as I tell you now, I will make sure you are comfortable and very, very safe. And I have made up my mind, yes. I will make you my wife and give you my protection." He settled a hand high up on her thigh where the edge of his small finger rested in her groin.

"I want to go home," she said, no longer able to hide the fact that she was falling apart.

"Which home would that be? With the fairies on Duval Street, or the haunted house on Truman Avenue? Not a very good choice, hmm? I think I shall take you back with me. I will soon make you forget the muscle-bound policeman. Despite the things that would turn some men off, I can make you a happy woman."

She must find a way to keep calm. Showing him how badly shaken she was would only fuel his confidence and make him more dangerous. "You'd do anything for Frank, wouldn't you?" she said.

"My brother's responsibilities have become my own." He

changed gears, and promptly returned his hand to her leg. "You need to be where you can have therapy. Both mental and physical. With physical therapy, this withered leg will improve."

She didn't argue with him. She didn't point out that she'd been using her injured leg from the day she was told it would take her weight and that, although it was thin, it wasn't withered.

He pinched her so hard above the knee that she gasped.

"Ah, there is plenty of feeling in the leg, hmm? I must remember that. Stimulation is undoubtedly good for it."

He wouldn't be able to hold her captive. Would he?

"First we must make the call. Then I have certain other things in mind."

He pulled onto what felt like a sandy lay-by, switched off the engine, and dialed a number on his cell phone. "You were waiting, Bob," he said promptly.

In the faint light from the dash, Sonnie could see his unpleasant smile. "My father?" she said aloud, and her hopes immediately soared. "Let me speak to him."

Romano turned until his angle allowed him to clamp a hand over her mouth. "Yes, yes, Bob, of course I'm in touch with her. Rachel's with you?" He looked so like Frank. She could almost imagine Romano *was* Frank.

"Oh, Mama." Sonnie moaned into Romano's steely tennis-player's fingers.

"Hello, Rachel," Romano said. "You should have gone to bed and allowed Bob and me to deal with this. You are not to worry. We have things well in hand." He ground harder against Sonnie's face. "I absolutely agree with you. She has to leave this place. You won't believe this, but it's even more unsuitable for a delicate woman like Sonnie than it was before. No, she's not here. I decided it would be best not to make her anxious over anything. I'm sorry to tell you this, but she is extremely agitated. That will stop as soon as we get her somewhere safe. Tell me what I should say on your behalf."

He listened for some time and made noises of agreement now and again. Then he said, "Yes, hello, Bob. You and Rachel are absolutely right. And I'm going to make sure we follow your wishes. You know Billy is here with her friend, Dr. Lesley. A fine man. A very fine man. And they seem very fond of each other. With their assistance I will bring Sonnie home.'' He paused before saying, ''Soon, very soon. Now that I have the terrible news about Frank, there's nothing to keep Sonnie here. It's my responsibility to look after her, for Frank and for you and Rachel. Yes, sir. Of course we'll keep in touch. It won't be long. Good night.''

He rang off and took his hand from Sonnie's face at the same time. Panting, she tried to grab the phone. ''Let me talk to them.''

''Do you think I'm mad?''

''I won't tell them about you. I promise I won't.''

''Tell them what? More lies. Do you think that would help you? Or would it just possibly make them even more convinced that you've lost your mind?''

Calm, stay calm. The only defense you have against this man is to make him look ridiculous by being so normal that no one would ever question your sanity.

He put the phone between his seat and the door, where she had little hope of reaching it. ''Now, let's get back to Key West, shall we? I'll be taking you to the club, so save any protests, because they won't get you anywhere. When we arrive, I'll have you make a call to that place on Duval Street. I will give you a script, so you won't have to worry your head about what to say.''

''If you say so,'' she told him. ''I'm very tired, Romano.''

''You'd better sleep for the next few minutes then. We've got a lot of ground to cover before I tuck you into my bed.''

Only with super control did she stop herself from shuddering at the thought.

''I didn't expect you to fall apart when I told you Frank had been kidnapped, you know.''

Sonnie didn't answer, but goose bumps flourished on her skin.

''Your behavior was out of character. Or perhaps it was in character, but I just hadn't seen that side of you before. Out of control. Completely out of control and obsessed with what

Frank's disappearance might mean to you. You showed no concern for him.''

''I have no recollection of what was said to me, or how I reacted.''

''Don't you?'' With one hand on the wheel and the opposite arm spread along the seat behind her, he drove easily now. ''I don't think I believe you anymore. Oh, it could be that you've done a great job and buried some details, but it's all there somewhere, isn't it?''

''No,'' she said, and her heart began to hammer. ''I don't remember anything, except . . . no, nothing.''

His fingers curled around her shoulder, and the car traveled a little faster. ''Except? Come on, Sonnie, if you're going to be really well again, you've got to get this out.''

''Nothing,'' she insisted. ''I just had an impression for an instant, but it's gone away.''

''Concentrate on that impression. Tell me anything. I'll take whatever you say seriously.''

''No, nothing.'' She paused. ''Fire.'' No, she hadn't meant to say that.

''Fire?'' Romano said. ''What fire?'' He cracked the windows a little, and the smell of seawater slipped in on the wind that lashed the car. ''Fire that night?''

''I don't know.''

''Sure you do. The Volvo caught fire. It wouldn't be too unusual for you to think you remember something about that. It didn't start until after you'd been thrown out, of course. But you might have seen it.''

She drew her heels up onto the leather seat. ''I couldn't have. I was already unconscious.''

''You can't be so sure of that.''

Her hip ached, and her feet. She rubbed at her right foot.

''They said you must have caught your shoe on the gas pedal and trapped the foot. There are a lot of little bones in a foot, and you broke just about every one of them.''

''I don't want to talk about it anymore.''

''Were there any sounds?'' he said. ''Anything at all. Maybe you heard the gas exploding. Or glass breaking. Do you think you may even have heard a voice, or voices?''

She trembled steadily. "I don't remember anything. I was thrown a long way and I was unconscious for days afterward.''

"So the reports go. You didn't have your seat belt on. Didn't you ever wear a belt?''

"Of course I did. I don't know why I didn't have it on that night.''

"Because you were so upset at what I'd told you about Frank?''

"No. I mean, I don't think that was it.''

"You didn't love him anymore, did you?''

She dared to look at his face. The expression he turned in her direction was amused, evil and amused.

"You don't have to answer that. It's not important. What is important is that you allow yourself to get in touch with what happened in your head that night. We know about your body, but I want to be sure we're not missing any useful clues from Sonnie the woman.''

At last he emerged from the overseas highway and made a left turn from Stock Island onto the oceanfront on Key West. Romano moved swiftly through the gears, and the powerful vehicle shot past the airport and along deserted South Roosevelt.

To keep herself from being sick, Sonnie breathed through her mouth. He showed no sign of slowing down.

"Stop,'' she cried, finally unable to restrain herself. "Please, oh, please. Not this. Not again. Stop.'' She screamed, and the sound went on and on until Romano hit her across the mouth.

Sonnie screamed afresh. "Don't hit me,'' she shouted, tasting blood. "Don't hit me anymore, Frank. Please don't hit me. I can't change anything. It's too late.'' She felt herself slipping away.

Faster and faster. On the right, buildings were a blur; then there was open ground. And, finally, the wall loomed. That wall. Each time she'd been forced to come this way since her return, she'd contrived to look elsewhere. Tonight, in the heavy darkness, the headlights of the Jag drew her eyes to the hard, curved surface, and she couldn't do anything but stare at it.

Her next scream lodged in her throat. She felt the wheels lock. They shot forward like a downhill bobsled out of control. She covered her face and head.

A sound—screeching. It went on and on. The windows slid down and the violent wind, torn inward by velocity, pinned her against her seat.

"Now what do you remember?" Romano yelled. "Tell me, Sonnie. What do you remember?"

"My head," she said. "Don't hit me again."

"What else?"

"Noooo—my foot. No. No, my foot. The brake. I can't reach the brake. Stop it. The brake. Stop it. It's too late." She closed her eyes and wrestled to undo her seat belt.

The screeching sound didn't stop.

She felt the Jag's wheels turn normally. Fast, but not locked.

The car stopped. Sonnie lurched forward but the seat belt stopped her from hitting the dash. She expected the air bag, but it didn't deploy.

The sound of laughter broke the last threads of her control and she twisted in her seat. Romano grinned at her, his eyes, eyes so like Frank's, crinkled with hateful, malicious mirth. "You are not, how do they say it, tightly stitched."

She wouldn't set him right. "I'm fine. As fine as any human being would be after what you just did. I'm going to the police." At once she knew her mistake.

"I don't think so, my dear. There is not one person alive who will believe you once I have told the story of this evening, of your madness."

Sonnie's cotton shirt was soaked. Her windswept hair clung to her head and neck. He thought he had won whatever it was that was so important for him to win, but he was wrong. She did not believe Chris would turn against her.

Lights flashed before her eyes. Dancing lights. Her face hurt. There was pounding in her ear; her right ear and the bones in her face ached on that side.

She grasped the door handle.

Romano brought the back of his hand against her mouth

again. "Do as you are told. The door is locked, but you annoy me that you try to escape me. You will never escape me."

Her lips swelled. She felt the tissue puff up, and the renewed drizzle of blood into her mouth.

"Don't think anyone will believe you if you say I struck you. You struggled with the wheel and almost sent us into the wall. You are obsessed with that wall. It is your craving to die there and take someone with you. Tonight it was me. You hit your mouth when you struggled with me. So you see, you cannot outdo me. I am too clever for you. Now you can get out."

"I don't want to."

"But only a moment ago you tried to get out. Now I insist." He opened his own door, unbuckled her belt and his own. He dragged her across his seat and out onto the verge near the wall. The front of the Jag had stopped only inches away.

"Why are we here?" She could scarcely hear her own voice for the bellowing roar in her brain.

"You know that amnesiacs are encouraged to reclaim their own memories. With as little help as possible."

"Yes. But to bring me here? And to do what you just did?"

"What *I* did? My dear, it was what you did. Slamming your foot on mine to drive us at this wall, then fighting with me to stop me from interfering with your death wish."

"I didn't do that. I have no death wish. You lied to me— and to Roy. You told us you needed my company, to talk to me. I didn't want to come, but I agreed because I felt I should."

"How touching. But how will you deny the evidence of your behavior? Am I known as a man who hits women?"

"I don't know. Are you?"

He raised a fist, but gradually returned it to his side. "That's where the Volvo hit and exploded," he said, pointing. "You were fortunate. You were thrown through the window and onto sand. If there had been no sand you would be dead for sure— as your baby is dead."

Sonnie staggered. Hysteria hovered so close to the surface of her body and soul that she threw out her arms as if she might ward off whatever came at her.

"Good," Romano said, advancing on her. "You are such a good girl. Go that way. Go on. That's where they found you." When she hesitated he pushed her, and she half turned and fell. Small rocks in the sand jammed into the heels of her hands.

Sonnie made it back to her feet, only to have Romano shove her again, knock her down again. "You're almost there," he said, waiting over her. "This is a place of memories for you. Here you will remember it all and then we can help you."

If she attempted to get up, he'd only hit her again. She stayed where she was.

"Up you come," Romano said, his tone easy and pleasant. He grabbed her by the neck of her shirt, hauled her up, and threw her.

Sonnie landed so hard her teeth rammed together. Every bone and muscle hurt. "You're going to kill me," she said. "Do it. Do it now. I don't care anymore."

"Oh, no, sweet one. I love you as a sister, remember? Whatever I do is for your sake. I want to help you. Tell me what you remember." Looming over her, his face lost its artificial calm. "You are where you were found that night. You were unconscious. But you weren't unconscious when you saw that wall grow closer, were you? Tonight you knew again the terror you'd felt then. You were supposed to die. The Fates intended it. They must have. But you didn't because you didn't buckle your belt."

"I undid it."

He straightened and stared down at her, his face a mask of hatred. "Did you?"

She couldn't close her mouth. Her eyes stretched so wide they ached.

"You undid your belt. Well, well, so you do remember something. Why did you undo the belt?"

"I don't know. I can't remember."

He kicked her knee. "Why? I don't believe you can't remember. You're pretending so you can protect yourself."

"No. I don't remember. All I know is my hand went to the belt. Perhaps because I feared for my baby. Don't do this. Let me go."

"But you couldn't try to stop the car? Wouldn't that be the first thing to do before you killed my little niece?"

"Stop." Almost no sound came with the word. "Stop it. You don't know what happened. My darling, my baby—stop it."

"You stop me. How would you do that?" He caught up a handful of rough coral sand and threw it into her face. "Did you lose consciousness before you were thrown, perhaps?"

Sonnie brushed at the sand, scratching her skin as she did so. "I don't know."

"Think hard. Perhaps you were thrown around inside the car and you struck something."

Sonnie's world turned red and black. "Hit me," she said. "Hit me so hard." She fleetingly touched her cheekbone.

"What hit you?"

"I don't know." The pictures came and went. The snatches of sound. The sensations.

"But it was you who decided you wanted to die, wasn't it?"

"It wasn't, Romano." Her sobs disgusted her. They were proof of her terror. "I didn't want to die. I don't. I wanted to look after my baby. Believe me. Please believe me." No one would come this way now. It was too late. The last plane from Miami had landed a long time ago.

"Someone will see the Jag," she said, grasping for hope. "They'll see it and come to see who's here. You aren't allowed to park here."

"No one will come," he said. "And if they do we will be contrite lovers. I will say the right things, and if you value yourself, you will say nothing. And we will leave. Simple. But I do not expect company."

"I can't tell you any more."

"So you say, but I believe I can change your mind. Scared little rabbit that you are."

On her bottom, she scooted away from him.

He laughed again. "You are sliding through sand that cradled your baby, Sonnie."

She couldn't cry anymore.

Two strides brought him over her again, and he grabbed her hair to yank her head from side to side. "You killed my brother's child. Your unbalanced mind took his heir away. But you are going to learn to behave. With the help of experts, I will teach you. Now think again. What else do you remember? Think of the Volvo moving faster and faster.''

Her brain became fuzzy. He tore at her scalp. Now he pulled her head from side to side, then back and forth. ''Faster and faster,'' he said. ''Why would you do that if you didn't have suicide in mind?''

''I have never been suicidal. I had everything to live for.''

''But you'd fallen out of love with Frank, hadn't you? *Hadn't* you?'' With the heel of one hand he slammed her against the hardened sand again. ''You'd decided you were going to tell him that night.''

Her head ached so badly she couldn't lift it. She hadn't the strength to try to fight him.

''I thought and thought about it. Sitting beside your bed night after night, I thought about it. You were going to tell him, but when I arrived without him, you went crazy and rushed to your car. You were beside yourself. The anger you never let anyone see came to the surface. Once in the car the real Sonnie came out, and you decided that if you couldn't have your way, you'd die and take the baby with you. Why? To make sure Frank never got his hands on any of your money. You'd changed your will, hadn't you? Your trust was to be held for your children while Frank got no part of it. You'd set out to hurt him by cutting him off. Were you so unbalanced that you decided to die rather than risk his finding a way to hang on to you and have anything that was yours?''

''It wouldn't work the way you say,'' she told him. ''No, he would inherit.''

''Liar,'' he said. ''And you're going to pay. If it takes me the rest of my life, you're going to be charged with manslaughter for the death of my niece. My God, I cannot bear it. First I must make you well; then I must do what Frank would want. You had best pray that you are beyond rescuing from your insanity.

''Say it now,'' he shouted. ''Say it. Say you deliberately murdered the little girl.''

"I didn't."

He came down on top of her, clamped his hand over her mouth and nose. "You did it. Nod your head or you die right here." Keeping his hand over her face, he dragged her until she felt waves soak her pants and shirt.

"Say it!"

She shook her head.

Romano dragged her deeper. The thundering water broke over her, washed over her face, filled her ears, and seeped up her nose. She coughed and struggled.

Using her hair, he dragged her head free of the water. "Admit it. You did it deliberately. You're unbalanced. You've always been unbalanced."

"N-n-no."

Romano pushed her head under the water and held it there. She struggled but found no power in her arms and legs. Water burned her eyes and her throat. She gagged.

"I tried to save you," she heard Romano say. "But it was too late. You ran from me back there and I couldn't see you at first. When I found you . . . well."

Summoning every last vestige of strength, Sonnie jackknifed her knees into his crotch. Romano howled and released her just long enough for Sonnie to wriggle sideways. But then he was on her again, howling in Italian she didn't understand.

Water splashed about her. It rose in great fins that broke in white foam.

A bellow broke through the frenzied, swelling babble.

Romano fell on top of Sonnie. She choked. The fight went out of her.

He was heavy, but then his weight lifted. She raised her head, spitting out water, gasping for air, and she rolled to her knees. Salt water bubbled from her nose and mouth.

"Son of a bitch," a familiar voice hollered. "You're dead, bastard. You're dead meat."

Locked together in the surf, Romano and Chris fought. Only another second seemed to pass before Romano went, headfirst, into deeper water. Chris followed, yelling as he went. "You're history, killer. I tried to save you, but you ran from me and I couldn't see you at first. When I did . . . well? And all because you're a bundle of grief over the death of your brother. Think that'll hold up in court?''

Sonnie made it to her feet and waded, doubled over, toward the struggling pair. The sound of connecting flesh and bone terrified her.

She reached them and launched herself at Chris's back. With more strength than she ever remembered having, Sonnie landed where she could wrap her arms around Chris's back, and held on. He grappled with her hands, but she held on.

''Don't kill him, Chris. He isn't worth it. Let him go.''

''Like hell.''

Sonnie tightened her hold. She hiked herself higher onto his back, gripped him with her legs, and crossed her wrists over his eyes.

''Let me go, Sonnie. For God's sake.''

She closed her eyes and clung, afraid that she would weaken.

Splashing sounded, and past her legs scrambled Romano. He coughed and cursed and moved faster than any man should be able to move after the assault he'd just suffered.

Chris managed to swing Sonnie around his body and half drag, half carry her to the beach. ''You shouldn't have done that,'' he said through his teeth. ''You're going to have to explain why you did. Dammit, he's getting away.''

''Good,'' Sonnie said. ''I won't have you tried for murder.''

The Jag's engine burst to life, lights came on, and the car screeched backward before Romano swung onto the road and roared away.

Panting, Chris watched, and when the noise began to fade he took Sonnie's hand and rushed her along so fast she scarcely kept her footing. ''Everything's changed,'' he told her when they were beside his Harley. ''When you said you thought people had tried to convince you to die, you probably told the truth. And I think you just managed to save one of those people.''

Twenty-seven

Sonnie remained seated on the sand with her knees pulled up and her arms wrapped around her calves.

"Bastard," Chris said, staring at the place where the Jag had been. "What the hell was happening here? Why?"

"He's berserk." Sonnie's voice broke. "Berserk. I don't know what happened. I want it to stop. D'you hear me? It's got to stop."

Chris bent over her. "Sonnie—"

"Don't *touch* me." She moaned. "I can't take it anymore. I want to be quiet. I want to be alone."

That wasn't an option he could offer. "Don't go to pieces on me now. We've got to move. Everything's going to happen fast now."

"I don't care."

"You don't care? It looked to me like he was trying to drown you. And he'd have gladly killed me. But you don't care?"

"I thought Romano was my friend. Even when Frank was . . ." She rested her forehead on her knees. "What a fool I was. I've got to have time to think. I don't *know* what it all means. Let me think."

Even when Frank was . . . When he was what? She still

didn't trust him enough to tell the whole story. But who was he to talk on that topic? Roy had told her something of the mess in New York. He, Chris, hadn't even given her a clue, and he still wasn't ready to talk about any of it.

"Sonnie, we can't waste time here."

"The hell we can't." She scooted away from him. "You just said Romano tried to drown me. He beat me and tried to drown me, Chris. I almost didn't have any time left to waste. I'm falling apart."

"You're soaked, darlin'," he told Sonnie, squatting beside her. He stroked her hair. When she looked at him he barely managed to stop himself from flinching.

But she wasn't going to hit him. He almost wished she would, if it helped.

"You're wet, too," she said.

"Yeah, you're right. Let's get back and change."

"Get back where?" He felt her grow limp. The fight had gone out of her. "Where can we go?"

He touched her sopping back and winced. "Come on, Sonnie. Please. I've got to see if you're hurt. We can go to Roy and Bo."

"No. I'm too embarrassed. I'm a disaster in many installments. I'm not going there like this."

"The cabin out back, then."

"They'll see the lights and come to check on us. Then Aiden will show up."

His patience slipped. "On your feet." He bobbed up, hooked a hand beneath each of her arms, and pulled her in front of him. "I don't want pneumonia. I don't have time. And you don't want pneumonia. Come on; I've got a blanket in my roll." And, despite what he'd told Billy Keith earlier, he did have his passenger seat on the bike.

"I'm going to be okay," she said. "Mostly I'm shocked. But I'll figure out what . . . I'll figure it out. I have to."

"We have to. You've pulled me too far in to expect me to step out now. You wanted me on your side when I didn't want any part of you. You wouldn't let me turn away, and now I

won't. We're going where we can get dry and decide what comes next.''

Dragging her feet, she went with him and did nothing to help him when he produced a towel to rub her hair, her arms and legs, when he brushed away sand that had stuck to her wet clothes, or when he wrapped her in the blanket he took from his bedroll.

Her apathy unnerved him, but he kept on smiling and making inane comments.

When she was enveloped in the blanket he continued to rub her down. He took first one hand, then the other, and chafed them until the icy clamminess faded.

''Okay,'' he said, drawing her against him and rubbing her back, ''that's the best I can do out here. Now we've got to find a warm, dry haven. A hotel? A motel?''

''I don't like those places.''

''We can't stay here.''

''Ena would take us in. She's so lonely, she'd be glad. We'd be helping her and she'd be helping us.''

Chris didn't relish going to Ena's place. To take in a boarder like Edward, she had to be odd, and odd was something he'd just as soon avoid.

''May I use your phone? You do have one?''

''Sure.'' He produced it from a saddlebag. ''Darn it, we don't know the number.'' The instant he grinned, he knew he'd made a bad move.

Sonnie snatched the phone and said, ''I just happen to remember Ena's number,'' before dialing. Almost at once she said, ''Ena? It's Sonnie. How are you?''

The woman was many bricks short of a wall. Or so Chris had decided from the day they met. She would fuss over Sonnie. She would fuss over *him* if he wasn't careful to maintain a glacial demeanor.

''Yes, yes,'' Sonnie said. She opened her mouth and nodded, clearly waiting for a chance to break in. ''Ena, I'm with Chris and we need a place to stay for the night. I know this is a terrible imposition, but would it be possible for us to come to you? There wouldn't be any call to go to any trouble. Sleeping bags would—oh, you're so kind to me, Ena. I don't know how I'll ever pay you back, but I will try. Yes. Yes. No. We're down by the ocean on South Roosevelt. I know I'm being silly, but I'm not ready to go back to my house, and''—she glanced at Chris—''and Chris doesn't want to disturb his brother by taking me there again tonight. Okay, see you soon.'' Quickly she clicked off the phone.

''That, ma'am, was a lie I heard you tell. I'm more than happy to take you to my brother's place.''

She frowned and said, ''So I lied. I'm not an angel and never was, regardless of what my parents think. You could drop me at Ena's and go back to the Nail yourself.''

No matter what had passed between them, he had no right to be disappointed that she didn't mind being separated from him.

''But I wish you wouldn't do that,'' she said, bowing her head so he couldn't see her face.

He smiled—just a little. ''Well, if it'll make you feel safer, I suppose I can come with you and stay there.''

Still she looked at the ground. ''Don't put yourself out. I'm not helpless. I'll manage just fine on my own.''

Roy frequently warned him to think before he spoke, just in case he later regretted what he'd said.

''Maybe a cab will come along,'' Sonnie said. ''Drat this storm. Everything slows down when they start watching for hurricanes. And they've been watching for them since I got here.''

''A cab won't come tonight. They don't bother to drive out here once the last plane's in.''

''The phone,'' she said. ''I'll call for one.''

She'd handed it back to Chris, who looked at it and managed an exasperated frown. ''The battery's gone,'' he said. ''Darn it.''

The wind blew so hard he had to support her or she couldn't have stood in one place. Blowing sand stung his face. The night raged. A sound like a train whistling in a distant tunnel went on and on and grew louder. ''We've got to get inside somewhere,'' he said, bending over her.

"I'm sorry, Chris. I've become your Waterloo, haven't I?"

Time for the honest approach. "You surely have not. It takes someone a whole lot bigger and meaner than you to upset me, sweetheart. Anyway, I was trying to play hard to get. Wherever you're going, I'm going. On the bike. It won't take long to get to Just Ena's." It didn't matter where they went anymore as long as it was out of this darkness.

He took away the blanket, and Sonnie said, "I'm cold."

The nylon windbreaker he kept handy at all times would help that. "Let's get this on you. The blanket might be a disaster on the bike."

She giggled. "I feel like a little kid being pushed into pajamas when I'm still wet. Thanks, Chris. I think you'd be great with little kids, by the way. You've got good hands. Gentle hands."

For an instant he looked at his hands. "Let's go." He might have what she called gentle hands, but he'd stopped thinking they'd ever hold a child of his own.

Once they were on the highway again, he called Roy and told him Sonnie was safe. He also said they wouldn't be back tonight, and was grateful his brother didn't ask questions.

A sharp jab in his already bruised ribs got all of his attention. "What?" he yelled over his shoulder.

"Liar," Sonnie yelled back. "There's nothing wrong with the battery."

He grinned into the wind and shook his head.

Sonnie rested against his back and held him tightly.

They reached Truman Avenue too quickly for Chris. He took the bike all the way to the house steps. Carrying a flashlight and with a shawl wrapped around her, Ena emerged before he switched off the engine.

"I'm so grateful you've come," she said when Chris and Sonnie had dismounted. "I don't know what you must think of me. I haven't been any help at all, have I? I'm grieving for Edward. Who would have thought you could become attached to someone you hardly know? But that's no excuse. You needed me and I've been selfish. Oh, it's such a wild night. Do get in here."

Chris ushered Sonnie ahead of him. He wasn't prepared for Ena's shriek when she saw Sonnie clearly.

"What's happened? Oh, my, what has happened to you? Oh, you poor dear." Ena wrapped Sonnie in her arms so that she could hardly walk without falling over the woman's feet.

On the short drive from the beach, Chris had decided what he must get done in as little time as possible. He had to talk to Sonnie, carefully, about his visit to the hospital. Then, whether she wanted to or not, he had to know what had preceded the scene he'd walked into on the beach. And he also needed to ask Ena a few questions. She could be the only person with the right missing puzzle pieces—but only if she turned out to be really observant. Or, perhaps, really nosy.

Ena took Sonnie into a sitting room that managed to be overcrowded and tidy at the same time. "I'm going for some water. That face has to be cleaned. How did it happen?"

"Don't," Sonnie said, turning her face away. "I'll do it."

"Thanks anyway," Chris said. "Thank you, Ena, but the best thing for Sonnie will be a hot shower. Those are only scratches. She fell on the sand. These things happen."

"Oh." Ena opened and closed her mouth several times. She wore no makeup, and Chris was surprised by the thought that she looked younger without it. "Well, then, I'll take her to the bathroom. I've got two nice rooms with a bathroom between. You'll both be very comfortable. You need dry things and sleep. I'll see what I can find."

Two rooms. He said, "Thank you, Ena." Of course two rooms. She was old-fashioned and she had no way of knowing that at least Chris would be happier if she had only one spare room. "I keep a change of clothes on my bike. Old habit that pays off sometimes. May I ask you a couple of questions?"

Her lips came together.

"You're the one who might be able to help us. Since you're next door to Sonnie's place."

"She needs to get in that shower."

"Of course she does. This won't take more than a few minutes. Have you seen anyone next door? Anyone or anything in the last twenty-four hours?"

"Sonnie's face is bleeding," Ena said, and she sounded tearful. "What is all this dreadfulness? Did you fall, or were you pushed?"

Sonnie blinked and glanced at him. "I ... fell. I'm a bit clumsy sometimes."

"Ena?" Chris said. "Have you seen anything?"

"I've tried not to," she blurted. "That sounds so childish, but it's true. I've hardly been outside this house for days. I'm frightened. Silly, aren't I? I'm frightened to leave my own house even in daylight. How can everything be carrying on as if nothing's happened when Edward was burned to death like that? Why is it as if nothing's different out there?"

Chris didn't set her right on the subject of Edward's death. "It feels like that whenever someone we know dies."

"Thank you," Ena said. "You're a nice man."

"He is," Sonnie said.

Unsmiling, she stared at him, and he'd have liked nothing better than to kiss her.

"So you haven't seen anything, Ena?" Sonnie said.

"The workers came back. They were there for hours. I haven't seen that side of the house, but I imagine it's almost back to normal now."

Sonnie turned up the corners of her mouth. "That's something, isn't it? We've got to try to get back to normal."

"Anything else?" Chris asked, afraid Ena would clam up again if he didn't press her.

"Just the man who looks like Sonnie's dear husband."

"Romano?" he and Sonnie said in unison.

"My brother-in-law," Sonnie added.

"I expect so. He's very good-looking, just like our Mr. Giacano. Drives a Jaguar."

"That's Romano," Sonnie said.

"He didn't stay long," Ena told them. "Not more than a quarter of an hour, perhaps. That was after the workmen left, but the blond man was still there."

Chris and Sonnie looked at each other again. "What blond man?" Chris said.

"Oh, I don't know, really. Long, curly blond hair and a hat

with a big brim. He went in once the workmen left. He had a
duffel bag. He doesn't stand up straight. Sort of shuffles as if
he's old, only I don't think he is.''

Sonnie's expression was blank, or blank but for the confusion
that filled her dark eyes. "He went into the house?"

"Oh, yes. Used a key, so I assumed you knew him."

Chris shook his head slightly at Sonnie and said, "We do.
Nothing to worry about there. Did he leave when Romano
came?"

"No. Like I said, Romano went inside, too. For about fifteen
minutes. Then he left, but I didn't see the other man again."

Sonnie looked as if she might ask questions best left alone.

"Marcus is the type to take a nap at the drop of a hat."
Chris laughed. "Maybe I should say at the drop of his hat.
Don't you ladies worry about a thing. I'll go over there and
make sure he hasn't slept through an appointment or something.
And I'll make sure Wimpy's got plenty of food and water."

"Funny how that dog stays over there," Ena said. "Must
be because of . . . Dogs sense things, don't they? That's the
last place he saw Edward."

If it was possible, Sonnie turned even paler. "They put in
a pet door for him," she said faintly. "The workmen did."

He didn't want to ask, but he had to. "Ena, do you remember
the lilies you brought to Sonnie?"

Ena frowned and said, "They weren't from me."

"I know, but I wonder if you remember the message you
were asked to give when you delivered them."

"Oh, there wasn't one. I wasn't told to say anything."

"Well," Chris said, "I wasn't sure. Sonnie, why don't you
take your shower and get really warm. I'll check on you when
Ena's got you tucked in."

Sonnie didn't have to say a word for him to know she was
close to begging him not to leave.

He went quickly.

"I wish he wouldn't go out there in this storm," Sonnie
said. "Ena, can I talk to you? You've been so kind to me."

"You can say anything to me. I'm just a woman on her

own who spends her life wishing she had someone to take care of. If I can do something to help you, I'll be a happy woman.''

Sonnie shivered inside the nylon jacket she still wore. ''I'm so muddled up. I don't know what's happening to me or why. But I do know that for some reason things are happening to me. I don't want to talk about them all, but . . . Oh, I don't even know how to explain what I'm feeling. Ena, someone's trying to drive me mad.'' She bit her lip and waited to be told she was imagining things.

''Why would they do that?'' Ena said, sitting beside Sonnie on the orange chintz sofa. ''You've suffered so much. Everyone should want you to be happy. Could you be imagining things?''

She must be careful what she said. She'd become convinced that she hadn't crossed that narrow line between sanity and insanity, but if Romano could find a way to make people believe she had, they'd put her away. Sonnie waggled her head. ''See, even you think I'm probably nuts.''

''No! No, I don't. But with what's gone on—about Edward, I mean—we're all on edge. Think of me staying inside this house because I'm afraid to go out. You aren't nuts; you're just human. And can you believe the police? They haven't even contacted me to say if they know any more than they did.''

''I haven't heard from them either.'' She got up and approached the window. From now on she would keep her own counsel about things she couldn't prove. ''Put out the lights, will you? So we can see outside better.''

Ena did as she was asked, and Sonnie stood near the lace curtains at a window that faced the side of her house. Ena joined her. ''Ooh, Chris is out there. Look.''

''Yes.'' She saw his large, shadowy form walking slowly along the path that surrounded the house. He carried a flashlight and swept its beam from side to side, covering not only the path, but the surrounding areas. ''He's looking for something.''

''What a handsome man,'' Ena said. ''You know, I shouldn't mention this—with you being married, I mean—but I think he really likes you.''

Sonnie was glad Ena couldn't see her blush. ''Most of all, he's an honorable man.''

''He behaves as if he's investigated things before.''

''You're observant,'' Sonnie said. ''He used to be with the NYPD.''

''Why did he leave?''

That was a topic Chris still hadn't chosen to visit with Sonnie. ''He wanted a change. He thought he could use his talents elsewhere, but first he decided to come and spend time with his brother. They're very close.''

''Mmm.'' Ena sounded noncommittal. ''He's going all around the house, isn't he?''

''Looks that way.''

''That man with the long curls was . . . unusual-looking. I think his legs hurt.''

If he'd fallen from the chandelier in her hall, Sonnie was very sure his legs hurt. And she was also very sure that he had been the person stretched out at the foot of the stairs. But what was he doing coming back and going inside? Why wasn't he dead, or at least too injured to stand up at all?

''Are you sure you didn't see . . . Marcus leave again?''

''Oh, yes. He didn't leave. That Romano is very handsome, but he doesn't look as if he's a kind man. Very angry, I'd say.''

''Romano has a great many responsibilities.'' Sonnie had always tried not to hate, but tonight she'd learned to hate Romano. ''With Frank missing, Romano's running the family business alone.'' He'd always run it alone—but he'd kept up the pretense that Frank was an active partner.

Only a short time had passed since Romano had learned of Frank's death, yet he'd talked about marrying her. The thought amazed Sonnie. He'd spoken as if he could do whatever he wanted to do with her. And he'd sounded as if he wanted to gain control of her money. If Frank had shown up when she'd expected him, she would have told him that she'd discovered how he'd taken advantage of her ignorance when they'd made a new will after they married. He'd have learned that with the help of an excellent lawyer, she'd been able to protect her trust fund—the trust fund she wasn't old enough to touch even now.

''Don't you want to talk any more then?'' Ena said.

Sonnie spread her hands and said, "I was miles away. I'm sorry."

"You and your husband are part of that business, too, then? The one with that Romano. What kind of business is it?"

Sonnie made a vague gesture. "We're exporters. Mostly of surplus goods to third-world countries. There's such incredible need out there." She knew almost nothing about the business.

"I say," Ena whispered. "What a wonderful thing to dedicate your lives to. Not that I'd expect anything less of you."

Sonnie wanted to see Chris come through the front door.

"I'm going to take you upstairs," Ena said. "You can get started on your shower while I find a nightie of some sort. I'll put your things through the washer and dryer so they're ready for the morning. And I'll get my first-aid kit out."

Hanging back wouldn't help a thing. Sonnie followed Ena up the stairs and along a crooked corridor to a room at the very end.

"Apart from my bedroom, this is my favorite. If I'd ever been lucky enough to have a little girl, this would be the room I'd want for her."

White eyelet flounces were everywhere: the floor-length bed-skirt of a double sleigh bed, edging pillow shams atop a puffy duvet. Two barrel-shaped chairs were also covered with white eyelet and edged with threaded pink ribbon. The rug was pale pink. The ceiling was a deep rose color, while the walls were the green of a soft spring meadow. An elaborate doll house sat atop a table, and beautifully dressed dolls lined a window seat covered with rose-colored velvet.

"How lovely," Sonnie said around the lump in her throat. "I really like it." Two more dolls sat at a small table set for tea. Any little girl would love it here.

"Thank you," Ena said. "I had a little girl, you know. I don't mention her, but you've got a loving heart. She died when she was very little. My husband was so devastated, he couldn't stay afterward, so he left me. I don't blame him anymore. I haven't seen him since."

"Ena," Sonnie said. She threaded her fingers together and searched for the right words. "We mothers—I mean—you know I lost my baby. She was a little girl, too. And I still miss her even though I never saw her alive. So much pain.''

Ena nodded. "Only those who have been through it can understand. Other people can help us by letting us talk sometimes, but they can't really understand.''

"My mother lost three babies before me," Sonnie said. "Three little girls. She's never said a lot, but she told me in case I needed to know for medical reasons, and I think she could hardly stop herself from crying even years after it happened.''

"You'll have more babies," Ena said, and opened a door from the bedroom into a bathroom. "You're young and you'll be completely healthy again one day. I hope I'll see your children. Come on in here.''

Sonnie did as she was told. Ena took big white towels from a cupboard above the toilet. She turned on a heated towel rack and set the towels there. "Eucalyptus soap," she said, unwrapping a big bar. "I love the way it smells. And there's shampoo and rinse and a clean brush and comb. Toothbrush and toothpaste. I'll come back with a nightgown. Just leave your clothes on the floor. I'll knock and put the nightie inside the door for you. Do you want a hot drink?''

Sonnie wanted to be alone, to stop talking. "No, thank you. I just need sleep.''

"I'm sure. Here's the first-aid kit. Clean those scratches well, mind. You've got bruises, too. You must have fallen very hard.''

"I did." And now she had to have a plan for dealing with Romano. And Billy. It seemed more and more obvious that they were attempting to interfere with her very freedom. Romano's behavior had been unbalanced. More than unbalanced. She shuddered. He was bound to move on her again—to make sure she didn't tell anyone what he'd done to her.

Ena's sharp look wasn't lost on Sonnie, and she smiled. "I'm cold to the bone," she said. "Thanks for everything.''

"I wouldn't have it any other way. Now get into that shower.''

Sonnie waited until the door was closed and turned on the

shower. She shed her clothes with difficulty. Everything wanted to cling to her damp body.

The hot water felt like tiny spikes on her tender skin.

Chris had said he'd talk to her when he got back. What could be taking him so long?

Ena hadn't seen the blond man leave. He could have attacked Chris in the dark. He could have hit him on the head before Chris had a chance to defend himself.

She must hold on and keep hoping for a normal life again. If she gave up, it would mean the end.

Sonnie turned off the shower and clung to the faucets. Steam filled the windowless space. The shower curtain was pink, with raised pink flowers all over it. If she let go of the faucets, she'd fall. Her foot hurt—her right foot, where it had been crushed. Nerves jumped in her left hip.

She'd been so sad for so long. Alone with the baby growing inside her. Pretending to her parents that she was happy and her marriage was fine, that Frank kept in constant touch.

That night she'd left for the airport . . .

Her mind felt clear. She couldn't remember much, but she'd begun, so that could change. Frank couldn't have called the other night, yet his voice had sounded so real in her mind. She must control the urge to talk about what was happening to her, or she'd be handing Romano the excuse he wanted. He wanted an excuse to dominate her.

With Frank dead, whatever he had left in his estate should go to Sonnie, shouldn't it? Romano didn't want her. He wanted a legal right to take whatever she had, and he'd be happy to shut her away in a sanitarium as soon as he could. And Billy wanted that, too. She was with the psychiatrist, but that didn't have to mean she wasn't involved with Romano, planning with Romano.

Mad people were often convinced of conspiracies against them.

The night she'd left for the airport she'd made up her mind about something. Yes, she'd made a decision and intended to tell Frank because she was afraid her sadness was bad for the baby. Bad for Jacqueline.

On the way to the airport she'd rehearsed.

What had she rehearsed? When did memory stop and noth-ingness begin?

She'd rehearsed what she would say to Frank about the sadness. That was it. But he would be angry. He'd told her he was in a hurry and wanted her to do something for him.

Sonnie pulled the shower curtain aside a little. Beside the sink was a folded nightgown. It appeared to be made of white cotton with a high neck edged with lace. Her clothes were gone.

She stepped onto the bath mat and began toweling herself dry. Her skin prickled as if the blood were only now starting to flow back properly.

There was a high wire fence near the area where private planes parked. Even at night, high-powered lights illuminated the current assortment of equipment.

Sonnie had pulled the Volvo in near the fence and waited. There hadn't been enough air in the night to fill her lungs. Fear, fear of Frank's anger had all but suffocated her.

She'd intended to ask him for a divorce.

Twenty-eight

The pair of maroon-and-white-striped pajama bottoms Ena had pressed on him would make great pedal pushers—for someone. Chris waited in the spartan room he'd been given until the house felt silent. Ena had explained that the bathroom had two doors, one from the room Sonnie was using, and one from the hallway.

He rummaged through his saddlebags and found dry shorts. After he'd stripped and put his wet things into the plastic bag Ena had provided, he pulled on the starched cotton pants, slipped his Glock 17 and a flashlight into a supposed toiletry bag, and ventured outside the room. Also according to Ena's instructions, he left the bag of clothes on a metal tray she'd placed on the floor.

When he opened the bathroom door, the atmosphere inside was still steamy and smelled of eucalyptus. A big, damp towel hung from the shower rod. Beads of water clung to the shower walls and puddled together on the bottom of the tub.

He wanted to talk to Sonnie. He *had* to talk to Sonnie. He'd told her he'd check in on her when he got back.

Well, he was back.

Not a sound came from her room.

So much for thinking she'd be too worried about him to sleep.

He stripped and got into the shower. If he thought it would make her safe, he'd take Sonnie away from Key West. But she wouldn't be safe unless he could force those who intended to do her harm to make just the right *wrong* move, *and* keep her alive at the same time.

He took a large, already wet bar of soap in hand and studied it. A whole bunch of guys would get a laugh if they could see him looking at that soap and thinking about it sliding over Sonnie's skin.

Unfortunately, he was all alone in the shower. If rubbing that soap over his own body gave him a hard-on, well, he might as well be grateful, because it wasn't going away anytime soon.

The sight of a hand, a fist, extending past the curtain and into the shower, jarred his spine. The fist knocked on tile.

Chris grinned. He sidestepped closer and kissed Sonnie's wet knuckles.

The hand withdrew at once.

With his back to the beating stream of water, he continued to wash. He unscrewed the shampoo, emptied a puddle into his palm, and rubbed his hair.

And, through the shower curtain, he watched the moving shadow.

At first she remained still.

Then she paced.

Finally he saw her approach the door to her room and he stuck his head out. "Hi, there, Sonnie. Where you goin'?"

The white cotton gown she wore resembled a larger version of something a Victorian child might have worn. It covered her from neck to ankles. But the cotton wasn't heavy-duty, and steam was being kind to Chris. "I asked where you're goin'?" he said, appreciating the shades, and shapes, of her body inside that gauzy number.

Her smile was sheepish. "I got cold feet," she said. "You told me we'd talk when you got back. I heard you showering, so I thought I'd come and talk to you in here. But that's way too intimate, isn't it?"

"Sit on the toilet seat," he told her. "Surely it's intimate. I'm willing to try that on for size if you are."

He stepped back beneath the water to rinse, but kept his attention on her lovely shadow. She didn't hesitate long before accepting his invitation to sit down. She raised her voice to say, "I was so worried about you. That man Ena talked about—"

"There wasn't anyone in the house."

"But who was he? What did he want there? He went inside, Chris."

"I know, I know. I can't answer your questions, but he's not there now. The carpenters are doing a great job. Everything looks almost better than new."

"Yes, good." She didn't sound excited.

"We do have our work cut out for us," he said. "I don't mean there's any reason to panic, but I think we're getting close enough to our problem to make the players real antsy."

His towel was outside the shower.

He was a big boy. "Would you mind handing me a towel?" He hauled back the curtain and felt pretty satisfied with his nonchalance.

Sonnie didn't fare so well. She knew it when she'd taken a second or so too long to pass the towel, and her face turned hot.

"Thanks," he said, toweling his hair rather than covering any part of his body. "The hot water felt great. Did you clean those scratches well enough?" He got out of the shower.

What did you say to a naked man when you were sitting on a toilet seat while he checked the skin on your face? *My, what nice teeth you have?*

"I'm going to go over these one more time," he said.

No, he wasn't, not if he expected her to remain conscious. "You don't need to bother, Chris."

He was already pouring antiseptic solution on a cotton ball. "This is going to sting a bit."

When he moved, the tattoo on his shoulder undulated. "That tattoo is out of character," she said, and got a sideways glance. "Isn't it?"

"Not at all." The manacled woman curled up a little, then stretched out as he put his upper arm at his side. "Nothing like some good, old-fashioned S and M. Love that pain. Love women who love that pain."

As promised, the antiseptic stung. Sonnie drew air through her teeth.

"How do you like being led around on a collar and leash?" Chris said, dampening another cotton ball to continue this particular torture. "Nude, of course."

"Sounds okay." Sometimes she amazed herself. "But I do appreciate a man with fresh ideas. Everyone does the leash thing."

"Do they?" The cotton balls landed in the wastebasket. "You keep on surprising me. Sexy talk is no more natural to you than flirting. And you, ma'am, do not have a flirtatious bone in your body. But you're game, Sonnie. You don't back away from giving as good as you get."

"I think that's supposed to be a compliment." A compliment she wasn't sure she should enjoy.

Chris put a foot on the side of the tub while he dried a leg. The man did have great legs. The hair all over his body was very dark. His buttocks flexed; a deep scar on one side also flexed.

"What happened to you?" she asked. "What caused the wound?"

He slapped a hand over the part in question. "That's my war wound. Nothing really. We had a disagreement over the appropriate way for a man to get his point across to a woman, and guess what? He had a gun, and he had no sense of humor. That was a real nuisance to me for some time. It's tough when you can't sit down.

"I was lucky, though. The guy had lousy aim. See?" Still presenting his back, he moved closer. "Feel how deep it is."

Holding her breath, Sonnie passed her fingertips over his muscular flesh. "Very deep, but it doesn't . . . You feel nice."

"Uh-huh. About the aim. Guess what he was aiming for?" Sonnie stroked the cheek and the back of his thigh.

"Can you guess what he was aiming for?" Chris asked again.

Her fingers between his thighs brought them together like clamps that trapped her hand. Sonnie followed the line of his spine with her eyes. She concentrated on the question. "Oh, that's sick. It's awful. Why would he want to shoot you there?"

"Because a bullet in the heart usually guarantees death."

Sonnie suffered another fierce flush, but she laughed with him, and she wasn't quick enough to stop him from drawing her hand all the way through his legs and holding it over what made him feel so very masculine.

This time the big reaction came from Chris. He made incoherent sounds and moved against her palm.

Sonnie grew tight in places that felt good that way, and she kissed his scar with lips that lingered. "You're a bad man, Chris Talon," she said when she rested her cheek where her mouth had been. "You play with my mind—and my body."

"And you don't like it?" He sounded as if he fought for every breath.

"I shouldn't. And we should be dealing with serious stuff."

"We already are," he said. "What we've started together isn't going away anytime soon. Thank God."

"You know what I mean." She grew hotter and hotter.

"We're going to deal with that—soon." He stopped moving, and straightened—but kept his hand over hers. He was so hard. "How are you doing, Sonnie?"

She wasn't going to play any more games. "Shocked, but okay."

"You've got guts."

The urge to make a crack about her sanity was difficult to swallow.

He released her hand and faced her. "You and I are going to be joined at the hip from now on. Can you handle that idea?"

Her eyes were at the level of his navel. His abdominal muscles were solid ridges. "If you think I have to stay close to you all the time, I'm going to trust your judgment." *Oh, what a penance.*

"You know I can see right through this, don't you?" He

gathered a handful of cotton on either side of her breasts and pulled it tight. "Funny. Such a prudish thing, yet so sexy. I'd like to eat it off you. Or maybe tear it off in bites, hmm?"

She spread her hands on his abdomen and urged him closer. What she felt for him was overwhelming. Looking up into his tensed features, she was almost afraid of that intensity. "How did you find me on that beach, Chris?"

"I drove this island from one side to the other, and from top to bottom. I did it over and over again. I was desperate by the time I just happened to notice Romano's Jag by the side of the road."

She looked away.

"You can't hold anything back anymore," he said. "I can feel the walls closing in on us. What happened to bring you to that point?"

If she was supposed to think clearly, there had to be more distance between them. She got up and sidled past him. "He came to the Nail and said he needed to talk to me. He gave me Frank's medallion and he cried. I felt sorry for him. Don't blame Roy. What was he supposed to say when my brother-in-law said he needed some of my time?"

Chris took her place on the toilet set. He ran his fingers through his hair, sending drops of water onto his shoulders. "But what happened?"

"He drove me all the way to Miami. And he got madder and madder the farther he went. Sometimes he drove slowly; then he'd travel miles and miles at the kind of speed that made me expect to die at any moment."

"F—friggin' bastard."

She started to lower herself to the side of the tub. Chris reached for her hand and pulled her to stand beside him. Then he tipped her to sit on his lap.

"He said wild things. He told me he's going to marry me now and I'm going to do whatever he tells me to do." She didn't want to talk about money angles, or about Billy and Frank's supposed plot against her. "When I wouldn't cooperate, he hit me. Then he started to hound me about the accident, about what I remember. He took me to that wall by the beach and parked. And he kept on hounding me.''

Chris held her by the waist. What she felt beneath her bottom made it almost impossible to concentrate.

''What I don't get is why he attacked you. How could he expect to get anywhere with you if he got violent?''

''Because Frank did it.'' She squeezed her eyes shut and gritted her teeth. She had never before said that aloud.

''I know,'' Chris said, and he stroked her hair back so gently that his touch was a phantom. ''I figured that out a long time ago.''

She felt so ashamed. ''I married too young, and I didn't want to go to my family and admit I'd made a stupid mistake by going against their wishes.''

''I know, I know.''

''I think Romano and Billy want me in a sanitarium. And Romano wants to be my husband so he can control everything that's mine.''

''Don't worry. They'll never pull it off. Not as long as I'm still breathing.''

''Please don't even say that.'' She wrapped her arms around his head and held his face to her breasts. ''I don't know what's going to happen, but I can't even think about you getting hurt.''

Chris lifted her and set her down astride his lap. The gown rode up her thighs and settled around her hips.

''Chris,'' she said, and rested her brow on his shoulder. ''Is this really wrong?''

''No,'' he said simply. ''It's really right. I thought I'd closed this part of my life off. The part that needs to feel what I feel for you. My future was never supposed to include another woman I cared a damn about. Sonnie—oh, hell—what I feel for you is lethal, or it will be if we have to say good-bye.''

Thinking only became more of a feat. The most intimate parts of their bodies pressed together. Sonnie was afraid to move even an inch.

''I went to the hospital in Miami,'' Chris said. ''And I talked a records officer out of some information I think is going to underscore what we're already thinking.''

"That Romano and Billy have been trying to kill me ever since I had the accident?"

His eyes half closed and she guessed he was having at least as much trouble concentrating as she was. "When you line everything up, it's very incriminating. Sonnie—oh, lady, I think we're going to have to postpone this discussion, at least for a while."

She crossed her arms and pulled the nightgown over her head.

Chris's lips parted. His chest expanded. Never taking his eyes from her face, he lifted her and brought her down on his erection. Their bodies joined as if they were halves of the same whole.

He held her there, not moving, just breathing hard and watching her eyes. "Does this hurt your hip?" He smoothed the scars there. "Don't lie; just fess up."

"It's not hurting. Nothing's hurting. I want to tell you something."

Restraint was costing him dearly. The distended veins at his temples said what he didn't say. "Tell away."

"I remembered something about that night. I was angry. I'd found out how Frank took advantage of me because I was too dumb to know what he was up to. He arranged a new will for us. I won't go into it now, but it meant I didn't have anything that was mine anymore.

"I went to the airport to tell him I'd taken care of that."

Chris shifted the tiniest bit and Sonnie squeezed herself tightly about him.

"And I was going to tell him I wanted a divorce."

He was utterly still, utterly focused on her. "You're sure?"

"Yes. I always knew I was angry about something, but I wasn't sure about all of it. Tonight I remembered."

His smile puzzled her. "What's funny?" she asked.

"Not a darned thing. I just happen to think those are the best words I ever heard. That you intended to divorce him."

"Chris, I don't think I can stay like—"

"I surely can't." And he gripped her hips again to shift her, to begin again what they'd known once before.

Abruptly he stopped and reached between her legs. "I'm going too fast," he said.

She pulled his hand away. "No, sir, not too fast at all. This is what I want. Time for play later, maybe."

"I like the way you know your own mind." He held her breasts, kissed each one, and managed to draw smothered gasps from her when he concentrated on her nipples. "Sensitive?" he said, his voice muffled.

Sonnie worked to make him move with her.

He moved.

Burying his face in her neck, he used his strong buttock muscles to drive and retreat. Sonnie hovered on the edge, longing to go over, yet wishing she could hang on, feeling just this, for a very long time.

Holding her bottom, Chris got up. He managed not to come out of her while he went to a wall and supported her there. She crossed her ankles behind his back and gave herself up to the beat inside her body, her breasts, deep in her womb. He kissed her again and again. They reached for each other, wound around each other, and gave and received of each other.

And Chris pushed inside her again and again.

He shuddered, and so did Sonnie. Their cries were muffled against shoulders that would bear teeth marks.

Then there was a stillness that seethed, a silence that roared. And gradually heavy peace settled, and Sonnie slowly lowered her feet to the floor.

She didn't know how long they stood there, clinging.

"Is there room for me in your bed?" Chris asked at last.

Sonnie took him by the hand. He grabbed a handful of tousled clothing from the counter and let her lead him into her bedroom.

Chris saw a bed with pale covers along one wall. Sonnie climbed in first. Chris followed, placing his bag and pants on the floor. He rolled toward her and found her facing him. In the darkness, her teeth showed white in a smile and her eyes glinted.

As long as he was with her, he was convinced she would be safe. Romano would be running scared after their scuffle, but the man was a coward who picked on women, not the kind who would confront someone bigger and stronger.

"What are you thinking?" Sonnie asked.

"That at least for tonight I'd like to just be with you. Maybe I should be too disciplined to take any time off from what I've got to do, but I'm only a man in ... Sonnie, I can't promise a thing yet. I don't know what's ahead for me because I can't see it clearly. But you've stopped being a woman I just feel protective toward."

He paused and Sonnie said, "I love you, Chris," and didn't care if she might be making a fool of herself.

His hand, a hand strong enough to crush things that got in his way, curved over her shoulder with warm tenderness. "You don't have to say a thing," she told him. "I only wanted you to know."

"I'm not supposed to be afraid of things," he said. "I'm surely not supposed to admit it if I am. But I love you, Sonnie, and that does scare me."

She wouldn't ask him to explain why, but she would get as close to him as she could, and hug him as tightly as her arms would hug.

The kind of excited hope she felt was new. He hugged her back and managed to touch her in a dozen little ways guaranteed to arouse her again.

"What would Ena think if she knew we were in here together?" Sonnie said, giggling. "I don't think she'd approve."

"She's well-meaning," Chris said, and his fingers found their way to the slick flesh between her legs. "But I agree with you; she probably wouldn't approve."

He used his thumb, making small, unbearably wonderful circles while two fingers passed inside her.

Sonnie held his penis, fluttered her fingertips over the end until he moaned.

If she kept on touching him that way, Chris didn't think he could even pretend to be happy with going slowly. He did love her. All his promises cut in stone, the ones that said "never," had crumbled.

Damn. She was flicking her tongue back and forth over one of his nipples. She might not be a woman of vast experience, but she certainly classified as a natural.

He speeded his attention to her pleasure and she forgot teasing him. Instead she arched away from him and actually gripped his forearm, urged him on. He felt the ripple of her climax, and realized that, for the first time in his life, he'd found someone who matched him, fit with him, complemented him as if she had been designed for him—and as if he'd been designed for her.

"Whatever happens," he told her, "you and I are right for each other. I'm never going to forget that, and I want you to keep telling yourself it's true."

Drawing short breaths, Sonnie kissed him. "I won't have to try hard," she said when she drew away. "Can we make love again, please?"

He rubbed his nose against hers. "I'll take it under consideration."

"Oh, thank you," she said with laughter in her voice, and rose over him, pushing him to his back.

Chris embraced her—and frowned. He placed a hand behind her neck, and clamped his other arm around her waist. "Keep still," he whispered. "Let me listen."

She went rigid, but didn't say anything.

The room was warm, yet he felt cold. His spine grew tight. He'd feel better if his gun was in his hand and Sonnie wasn't on top of him.

They were being watched.

Hair rose on the back of his neck. "It's okay," he said against her ear. "Just hang on and stay calm. Slide off me, sweetheart, but don't make any sudden moves."

She did as he asked, settling stiffly at his side.

Making as little rustle as possible, he made contact with the toiletry bag and eased out the Glock. This was the ultimate vulnerability, the ultimate bad scene. His gut, and his gut had rarely been wrong, told him they were seen by someone they couldn't see, which meant he couldn't know where an attack would come from.

His eyes were well adjusted to the darkness. He swept as much of the room as he could without lifting his head.

There.

The next breath he took stayed right where it was.

As swiftly as he dared, he swapped the gun for the flashlight. "I'm going to turn on a light," he told Sonnie. "Just stay still."

Click. The noise the flashlight made had the impact of gunshot on his brain, but the beam instantly found what he'd seen.

Directly above the bed, something alive gleamed. Then it was gone and Chris leaped from the bed to pull on his shorts. "Stay where you are," he told Sonnie.

"Forget it," she told him, already on her way to the bathroom. She was back at his side in seconds and pulling her nightgown over her head. "What's going on? Chris, what is it?"

He switched off the flashlight. "If I put the lights on in here, we lose any advantage we might have, and it isn't much as it is. You've got to stay here, Sonnie. You'll handicap me if you don't. And you'll put yourself into more danger than you have to."

"I'm coming with you." She'd scream if he didn't give her a straight answer. "Tell me what's happening."

He held her by the upper arm and went toward the door. "There's someone above this room. There's a hole in the ceiling. I saw an eye watching us."

Twenty-nine

Finding the way to the attic was easy. After all, he'd been there before. Dark stairs tucked into the opposite end of the upper hallway rose to a door, the door that had been Edward's. No light showed around its ill-fitting edges.

"Please stay here," Chris told Sonnie. Only seconds went by before he heard her bare feet climbing behind him.

At the top he threw open the door, then gritted his teeth at the noise it made when it hit an inside wall. Holding Sonnie behind him, he listened.

"There's no one there," Sonnie said aloud, jolting him. "There isn't. Do you smell something? Sweet? Sweet and perfumed. Where do I know that from?"

Chris shook his head, and still he waited. The feeling of a malevolent presence had faded. He switched on his flashlight and swept the area. He hadn't expected to see the room almost completely cleared of Edward's possessions. A sagging couch flanked a table and a chair. On the other side of the table, a single bed—tidily made and covered with a faded patchwork quilt—extended from the wall. A portable vinyl wardrobe shared space with a chest of drawers, and several trunks lined the wall behind the door. The obscene posters had left fade marks.

Chris turned on overhead lightbulbs that hung, unshaded, from wires. Crouched, weapon at the ready, he entered.

"They've gone," Sonnie said, walking in as if he weren't still practicing caution. "But you're right. We'd better not make much noise. Hey, look at this."

He couldn't help smiling at her jaunty obliviousness. "Let's keep it down, sweetheart."

She looked back at him, but pointed to the floor where a braided rug had been left turned back.

"There may be no one around now," he said, "but I'll bet your boots someone just left in a hurry." The dormer was open. Another trunk stood beneath it, and when Chris cautiously looked outside he saw a short flight of rough wooden steps leading down to a second-story balcony at the back of the house.

He closed and locked the window and joined Sonnie, who was on her knees with her face pressed to the floor. She moved aside and pointed.

The hole the carpet should have hidden gave a view of the bed below. Chris pulled the carpet farther back and found more holes that offered a variety of views on Sonnie's borrowed bedroom. "Did you notice any sawdust down there?" Chris asked. "These were drilled very recently."

Sonnie said, "No sawdust. D'you think Ena knew?"

"That someone's been in her attic again? What do you think?"

"Could she be unaware?"

He studied the room. "No. But I guess there could be reasons why she ignores whoever it is. She wasn't expecting your call, so there was nothing planned about this—not long-term. Could be someone overheard her talking to you on the phone, then drilled holes. Or she told someone you were coming and they drilled the holes."

"And cleaned up before we got here? That sounds . . . Wow, it sounds far-fetched."

"You don't know how far-fetched things can get, kiddo. Desperate people can accomplish a lot in a short time. I'm going downstairs to find Ena now."

"No," Sonnie said. "If she really does have another weird boarder, she's weird, too. We'd better just get out of here."

"Unless we feel like following whoever went that way"—he inclined his head toward the dormer—"we stand a good chance of running into Ena anyway. Better we bumble in on her all puzzled and wondering if she knows there's been someone hanging out in her attic, and making holes in the floor to watch people."

"She isn't going to admit it."

"She surely isn't. But the way she reacts—" He shook a hand for silence. The sound of footsteps, soft but sure, came from the hallway below. He wished he could get Sonnie safely out of here.

He listened intently. Sonnie turned an ear toward the door. She looked at him sharply and he nodded—and made a decision that could prove a killer. "Only one thing to do," he said loudly.

"Tell Ena?" Sonnie responded. She must also have picked up that the footsteps had paused at the bottom of the stairs to the attic.

"You don't think we should, do you?" he told her. "She's been through a lot. But she's got to know about this."

The owner of the feet started up the stairs, and Chris didn't know whether to be relieved or suspicious because there was no attempt to muffle the noise.

"Sonnie? Chris?"

He met Sonnie's eyes and they both mouthed, *Ena.*

"Up here," he called out, then said, "It's Ena."

She arrived on the threshold with a blue scarf over her hair, her face shiny with cream, and wearing a white, quilted cotton robe that reached her feet.

"Ena," Sonnie said, going to meet her. "We don't know what to think about this, but—"

"Why are you up here?" Ena asked. She appeared honestly puzzled. "I'm not a narrow-minded woman, but there are things that don't seem right. I mean, if the two of you are . . . well, if you are, it's not my place to judge, but you should have respect for being in someone else's home. Were you afraid I'd

. . . well, afraid I'd hear you? You shouldn't just go looking around for privacy like this. Not in my house.''

Chris hadn't anticipated her reaction. ''Who lives in this room?''

She frowned. ''Lives? That's cruel. No one lives here anymore. It's a spare room now. You ought to get to your beds, or bed, if that's what you want. This is all upsetting enough without you walking around almost naked.'' She indicated Chris in his shorts, but was quick to shift her attention to Sonnie. ''And you. Well. It might be better if you didn't have anything on at all. That pretty nightie looks like a rag and it doesn't cover you decently. I suppose it's my fault, but I didn't know you intended to carry on like this.''

The twitch at the corners of Sonnie's mouth didn't help Chris control his own urge to laugh. ''I think we'd better explain ourselves,'' he said. ''Come and see this, please, Ena. Holes drilled in the floor. If you get down and look, you'll see what got Sonnie scared enough to want me to come up here with her.'' He did smile while he avoided catching Sonnie's eye. He could feel her indignation at his interpretation of what had really happened.

Ena went to the biggest of the holes. She didn't kneel to examine it, but stood staring down, utter disbelief making her eyes round.

Sonnie took a step toward the woman and said, ''Ena?''

''Who would do something like that?'' Ena said without raising her face. ''Vandalism. And how did they get in here, that's what I'd like to know?''

''He was watching Sonnie,'' Chris said.

Sonnie set her chin in a way that gave him pause. ''Chris and I were both being watched,'' she said. ''That looks straight down on the bed where I'm sleeping.''

''Supposed to be sleeping,'' Ena said.

''That's right,'' Sonnie said with the kind of vaguely aggressive chutzpa Chris would never have expected from her. ''I'm pretty edgy. Chris is one of the only human beings I know I can trust. I wanted him with me—in my bed where I can feel him. I still do want him there, and anywhere else I happen to be. I've learned about trust the hard way. If you get the chance, you'd better grab it.''

Ena appeared disconcerted. ''There's a lot of truth in that. But you've got a husband, Sonnie.''

Still basking in her accolades, Chris waited with interest for her response to Ena's latest salvo.

''No,'' Sonnie said. ''According to news my brother-in-law has, I am not married. Frank is dead. And he probably has been since shortly after he disappeared. I'm sad to know that. Really sad. But we weren't going to stay together, Ena.''

Ena's brow knitted. She placed one hand over her mouth and the other over her heart, and stumbled to sit on the bed.

''I'm sorry to shock you,'' Sonnie said, ''but these things happen. People change and they can't always hold a marriage together.''

''I don't believe in that,'' Ena said brokenly. ''I believe that when you say, 'until death do us part,' that's what it means.''

Chris went to the vinyl wardrobe and unzipped the front opening. He wasn't surprised to find it empty.

''Death has parted Frank and me,'' Sonnie said. ''But you don't know what went before, why I had to make a decision to do what I don't believe in and divorce him.''

She doesn't believe in divorce. Neither, Chris thought, did he in many cases, but sometimes those decisions were taken out of your hands. The surge of satisfaction at hearing Sonnie give her opinion on the topic might be way out of line, but he'd chose to enjoy the sensation.

''You're a nice girl,'' Ena said, catching Chris off guard. ''You could have mentioned how my husband and I are divorced, but you didn't.''

''That wasn't something you chose,'' Sonnie said.

Chris checked the trunks and the chest of drawers and scored nothing but a set of keys, a heavy box of businesslike tools, a flashlight, and a short list of women's names, none of which meant anything to him. Careful not to be seen, he pocketed the piece of paper. There was also a card with an address in Miami, but with no name attached to it. All these items were in the same trunk and covered with a gray blanket. Chris made no comment about his find. Since the women were deep into their discussion of what did or did not constitute an acceptable reason for dumping a spouse, and were moving to a place where they commiserated with each other, he was free to concentrate on making certain he didn't miss anything.

"Can you imagine someone getting in here and using this place without my knowing anything about it?"

No, Chris thought.

"I sleep on the ground floor, you know. Edward preferred being able to go up and down to the bathroom in privacy. I suppose I should move upstairs now that he's gone." She sighed and looked at her hands. "I miss him, you know. I'm sure you think he was very strange, but he wasn't really. Just different. But he was so kind to me. He looked after me always."

"I'm here now," Chris said, intending to make no such offer. But what the hell, he'd promised himself years ago that he'd never be the selfish, misogynistic bastard his old man had been. "At least for a while. You can count on me, Ena. Just get a message to me. I'll give you my cell phone number so you can reach me if you need to. Sonnie and I will look after you until you're more sure of yourself, won't we?"

Sonnie's long, speculative stare suggested she thought he might be going overboard, but she recovered quickly enough to smile at Ena.

"The point is that we do have to look into who's been up here. And why. You do agree, Ena?"

The last thing he expected was to see moisture in her eyes. "Can't we just make sure he doesn't have a way to get back in and let it go? I don't want to deal with the police anymore. They aren't nice to me."

Chris thought about that. "I'm not sure. Although we could probably let it go for a day or two while I make some inquiries. But if I can't turn up anything conclusive, the police must be brought in." He was well aware that they should be called at once.

Ena sniffed and made a valiant and visible effort to collect herself. "I understand, but you will try first, won't you?"

"I promise I will. Now, I want you to go to bed and get some rest. I'll make sure everything's locked up tight."

"Thank you, Christopher," Ena said with great formality. "I feel I can trust you, too."

"It's Christian," he told her. "Which is your bedroom?"

"The room behind the parlor. But I want you to get to bed, too." She gave Chris and Sonnie a benevolent smile. "You make such a nice couple. I hope you'll be blessed with happiness. You deserve it. And children. I think you need children."

She turned and trod rapidly from the attic, holding her robe up to display shapely ankles.

Sonnie smiled at him, a smile he wasn't sure he liked. "What?" he said.

"Nothing," she told him. "I never thought to ask if you actually wanted children."

"Why would you?" he said gruffly. "It's not the kind of topic you bring up over lunch."

"But do you?"

How typical of a woman not to miss an opportunity to ask uncomfortable questions. "Maybe. Circumstances have to be right for those things. We can go back to bed now."

"You're joking," Sonnie said. She stood in the middle of the room with her fists on her hips, and the raw light from above turned her prim nightie into a provocative effort resembling a clever use of randomly shaded plastic wrap.

Chris straightened the carpet. "Our nosy friend won't be back tonight."

"But we do have to find out who he is and why he was here."

"Do you believe Ena's story?"

She considered. "I guess so. Do you?"

"I don't know yet." He thought of what he'd found and wondered where the items fit in. "We might as well try to get some sleep, though. There isn't much I can do tonight." In fact there was probably nothing he could do, but he'd discovered some interesting facts this evening, and as soon as the sun was up, he intended to follow up a few leads.

He offered her a hand and she held it. Chris took it to his

lips and kissed the backs of her fingers, all the while grinning at her.

Sonnie turned red.

"Am I missing something?" he said. "You get embarrassed when I kiss your hand."

"What I think about every time you touch me is embarrassing. It's got to be your fault, because I'm not like that."

"Like *that?*" He liked it when she blushed. "Like what? A woman who has sexy thoughts because she enjoys sex?"

She cast her eyes downward.

"Hey, so you enjoy sex. I enjoy it, too, with you. I suggest we go to my room, make sure there aren't any inconvenient peepholes in the ceiling, and see what we can come up with to really embarrass you."

Her face looked as if it might throb with heat. Chris ringed her neck loosely with his hands. He waited until she looked him fully in the face, then kissed her until she fought for breath.

"Come on," he said. "I've got one or two ideas. Y'know, I really like you on top. It's a great view."

She turned away and headed for the stairs.

Grinning, and feeling his body already primed for what it expected, he followed her.

Moving slowly, Sonnie got out of bed. She stretched, very aware of how sore she was, and in how many places. Christian Talon continued to sleep, one arm thrown over his head and the sheets bundled low on his hips. Just looking at him started sensations she had to ignore. The time for business had arrived.

She showered quickly, but when she pushed back the curtain, Chris was seated—naked—on the toilet lid, arms crossed, obviously waiting for her to appear. A towel was draped across his knees. He beckoned her to him and began drying her skin. This required that he feel every inch of her—after rubbing it down—to make sure she wasn't still damp. And Chris missed not one inch, no matter where it was.

"You must spend a lot of time planning ways to torture women," she told him.

"Just one woman," he said, and slid to his knees in front of her. "Have I told you I think you have the most delectable belly? Well, you do." He licked swirls around her navel, poked his tongue inside until the sensation caused her to cling to his shoulders.

"Good, huh? Mmm, and you taste so good." Gripping one of her thighs in each hand, he parted her legs enough to allow him to flip his tongue into the hair at her pubic area and find something that he obviously knew wouldn't easily rebuff him.

"Stop it, Chris," she said, but without conviction. The tension already mounted. She managed to surround his penis and start a little torture of her own.

She climaxed and fell against him, holding handfuls of his hair and pressing his face to her midriff. "Give me a few seconds," she said. "You're a wicked man. But I like it. Your turn next."

"Too late," he said. "It isn't going to be easy, but I'll have to wait."

"No."

"Yes. I need to focus. I won't if I get sidetracked—much as I would love to get sidetracked with you for a long, long time. Sonnie, you do know we're coming to the end of all this, don't you? You do feel that we can't go on for much longer without finding out exactly what's happening to you, and why?"

His words turned her clammy. "I guess. Although it's almost like it's going to go on forever."

He shook his head. "We're too close. They're going to start to make more and more rash moves until they give us some very obvious leads. And we'll be ready. I'd like to get over to your house. I looked around last night, but I'd like to do it again in daylight. I also need to take another look at the yard."

"Why?"

"Probably no reason. I'm just following up what could be a clue."

Ena had left their clean, dry clothes outside their bedroom doors. Chris retrieved them.

"What do we say to her?" Sonnie asked.

''Nothing. Not at once. If she wakes up when we're on our way out, I'll think of something. Otherwise I'm sure she'll follow us next door as soon as she's up and dressed. Leave her to me.''

Sonnie wasn't in the mood to argue. She still felt Chris's hands on her, and the way he felt in her hands. Who knew for sure how wrong she was to be falling in love with him at such a time, but she was and there didn't seem a thing she could do about it.

Chris unbolted the front door and let them out into yet another morning overcast with a heavy cloud layer. Heat assaulted them already, and the wind had dropped, leaving another uneasy calm behind. ''I almost wish the darn hurricane would come and get it over with,'' she told him. ''It's like it keeps on terrorizing us.''

''This is about number five to play peekaboo,'' he said. ''I don't like 'em any more than you do.''

They used the gap in the shrubs favored by Ena and didn't notice Aiden until they'd climbed the veranda steps. He'd stretched out on the porch swing. A couple of pillows from chairs propped his head.

''About time,'' he said without opening his eyes. ''I've been here for hours.''

''Hours?'' Chris said.

''At least half an hour. Did you two have a nice night?''

''That sounds personal,'' Chris said. ''I suppose my flapping-lipped brother said you'd find me somewhere over here.''

''I suppose he did. I've got more on the moped. The one Romano rented the night of Sonnie's accident.''

''Yeah? Let's have it.''

''Coffee first. That means inside. So are you two really compatible?''

Sonnie hoped he was talking about their opinions on politics, or religion, or maybe the state of health care in the country.

''Chris, are you?'' Aiden said.

The look on Chris's face suggested he was also uncertain what Aiden had in mind. ''Sonnie and I agree on a number of things.''

"Good. Sounds great. I always believe in being able to discuss sex with a partner. It gets a lot of the awkwardness out of the way up front. And later on it makes it easier to deal with any disappointed expectations."

"Thanks, Flynn," Chris said, sounding anything but grateful. "I didn't know you were such an expert on relationships."

"I read a lot," Aiden said. "Open this door. I'll make the coffee. We've got a lot to talk about."

"And I've got a lot of things to check out," Chris said. "So do you."

Once inside her house, the men went directly to the kitchen. Sonnie looked toward the upper floor. She climbed slowly, aware of how little true rest she'd gotten the previous night. Starting with the spare room, she checked to see the condition of the place. The workmen had done a good job, and everything seemed back to normal. The spare room was now completely empty and freshly painted. She went from room to room, not stopping for more than a few minutes until she got to Jacqueline's nursery. Such a pretty room. All it needed was a baby to make it complete.

Sonnie thought of the conversation with Chris, but quickly dismissed it. Clearly he wasn't interested in discussing children, not children with whom he had any personal connection. Two narrow windows, each closed off with white wooden shutters, allowed filtered light through the slats. The day was too gray to brighten the room much.

She left again and went into the master bedroom. The draperies were wide open. Frank's rocking chair stood with its back to the French doors, unmoving in the still air. She ought to take it in. The sight of it depressed her.

A faint sound made her spin around, her hand at her throat. Wimpy had curled up on the pillows—between the pillows—and fixed Sonnie with a baleful stare.

"Rough life," Sonnie said. "I suppose one of these days we're going to have to decide who you belong to." Promptly, Wimpy jumped from the bed and sat at her feet. The dog looked up and Sonnie shook her head. When she left the bedroom,

Wimpy followed, and stayed close behind every step of the way.

Chris was speaking as she approached the kitchen. "Romano and Sonnie's sister Billy kept constant vigil. Says so right in the records, and I found a nurse who remembered. She took care of Sonnie part of the time. She told me Romano often sat beside the bed all night, and Billy took over in the morning. The parents came and went but seemed too upset to stay a long time."

"And you think you can make this add up to Romano and Billy wanting Sonnie dead?"

"If she heard voices telling her to die, to go join her baby, who was it most likely to be? A nurse? I don't think so. And there's a write-up on the incident when a catheter was found pulled out. It was Billy who raised the alarm—although a staff member had seen a change on a monitor and was already entering the room. Evidently Billy went into hysterics and had to be sedated. She said she didn't think Sonnie wanted to go on and suggested she'd pulled the catheter out herself. It's noted that since Sonnie hadn't regained consciousness at the time, it was amazing. But no one questioned whether or not there'd been any foul play.

"Then there's yesterday's disaster. Without a lot of luck, Sonnie might be dead by now. Romano gave it a good try."

Sonnie might have turned back if Wimpy hadn't decided to scurry ahead into the kitchen.

"Hey, Sonnie," Aiden called, "come and have coffee. I made it. That means it's the best."

"What do I do now?" she asked when she confronted the two men. "I heard what you were talking about."

"If you'd left the hospital and gone home to a happy, uncomplicated life, we wouldn't be here," Chris said. "I didn't want to take you seriously. You know that. But too much has happened now. We've got to take everything seriously."

"What Romano did to me yesterday was crazy, wasn't it?" she asked, not expecting a response. "If he were himself— even though he now knows Frank is dead—but if he were himself, he'd never do a thing like that. He was trying to shock me.''

"He was trying to see if you'd break," Chris said. "He was doing his best to find out if you could be pushed far enough to remember things that would be dangerous to him. I can only think he and Billy tried to finish you off in the hospital—probably for money reasons—and they're scared you'll suddenly recall everything and turn them in. And don't forget that when I arrived he'd given up and decided to kill you. Or he'd snapped, would be closer to the truth.''

She didn't want to talk about that. "But if they thought Frank was still alive . . . If they expected him to come back, they'd assume he'd be the beneficiary of my estate. It's true that according to Frank's will, Romano was appointed to oversee his estate, and essentially stand in for Frank. Supposedly I couldn't touch anything without Romano's approval. They obviously suspect, but they don't know for sure that I was able to make sure my trust fund was safe from them.''

Chris and Aiden stared at each other.

"What is it?" she asked. "What are you thinking?"

"It's too bad we didn't know that from the outset," Chris said. "Know what I think? I think Romano probably found out his brother was dead months ago—while you were so ill, Sonnie. Since he would be a much richer man with you dead, too, and he's apparently had some business reversals, it makes sense—if he's the kind of man we think he is—for him to want to help you join Frank as soon as possible.''

"But my own sister?"

"We don't have the proof yet," Chris said and she felt how he hated making these suggestions at all.

"Oh, I think we do," Aiden said. "The minute Sonnie showed up here, Romano was right behind her. Then Billy. He must have told her to get down here—and bring her tame shrink with her. Want to bet what they might have had in mind for Dr. Lesley to do?''

"Billy was the one who knew I was coming," Sonnie said, subdued. "She was the only one I told. That means she's the one who sent Romano down here. They came to make sure they could control me.''

''And because there's something here that frightens them— frightens them if you're here,'' Chris said. ''Something to do with what happened here.''

''Romano only pretended to be good to me,'' Sonnie told them. ''He used to apologize for Frank's behavior. All that was an act. Billy's made mistakes, but should I really believe she'd try to hurt me?''

Chris detested the beaten expression on Sonnie's face. ''We don't have any final proof that she did,'' he said. ''And we also don't know if Romano had something to hold over her.''

Aiden poured a mug of coffee and gave it to Sonnie. ''I found a guy at the airfield who remembered a ruckus because Romano rented a moped the night you were hurt. I mentioned this already. But the whole story is that he never took it back to the rental agency. A couple of days later he said the machine was stolen and paid for it in full. The agency told him it was covered by insurance, but he still insisted on paying for it. Does that make any sense to anyone?''

The kind of sense it made to Chris was best kept to himself for now.

''No,'' Aiden said when there was no response. ''But there is a black moped in Ena's garage. It's covered up with a tarp, but it's in perfect running order and the plates are stolen— probably to replace the ones from the rental agency. This is exactly the same model as the blue one Romano left with, and the new paint job isn't professional. There's blue paint underneath.''

''My, haven't we been busy?'' Chris said, but he was grateful for the good legwork.

''Those of us who are experts on such things as paint jobs— although I won't go so far as to put this in the same league as the number that's been done on my pink pony—know about these things.''

Chris slapped a hand to his brow and moaned. ''I may need aspirin. I can't take another discussion of the Barbiemobile this morning.''

"As I was saying. The paint job is amateurish, but it tells us what we want to know. Romano kept that moped and stored it in Ena's garage. The only good news is that Ena doesn't own a car, and from the look of the garage, she never goes in there. So we can assume she didn't know anything about it."

"I'm having difficulty believing one supposedly sane woman can know so little about *anything*," Sonnie said.

Chris got up and pressed her into a chair. He disciplined himself not to do more than hold her arms. Every time he looked at her, let alone touched her, his pulse did double time. He had a bad case, and he'd better start praying she felt something similar toward him.

"I want to know where Romano is," he said, making sure he didn't telegraph how desperate he felt at the thought of not knowing the man's location. "Aiden—"

"Already being done. They're checking for him at roadblocks on the overseas road, and at the airports. Nothing yet."

"I don't see why he'd want to keep the moped," Sonnie said. "He could have bought his own."

"He did buy his own. But he didn't have to deal with a lot of paperwork or with people who would take note of him, and maybe talk. Sonnie, aren't you due at the Nail?"

In other words, they wanted her out of their hair. "Yes," she said, although she didn't know if she was.

"I'll run you over," Chris said. He took a card from his pocket and handed it to Aiden. "See what you can make of this, okay? I'm going to pay a visit and ask some questions. Keep your phone on."

"Will do," Aiden said, studying the card and frowning. He looked up and appeared about to say something more, but changed his mind. "I'll get going now. They're talking about us at least getting clipped by this next storm. That could make it real nasty around here."

"No," Sonnie said. She slopped hot coffee over her fingers and set the mug down. "No, you can't go, Chris."

Both men stared at her.

"I . . ." She mustn't sound possessive. "I don't think it's a good idea for you to be out there on your own."

Aiden smothered a laugh, and looked embarrassed.

Sonnie cleared her throat. "Okay, I might as well be honest. I'm afraid to let you go, Chris. Something might happen to you. And I'm afraid when you're not with me."

The following silence was heavy with awkwardness.

"You've got a right to be scared," Aiden said. "Not that I understand why a lout like Christian Talon would make you feel any safer. But, hey, there's nothing to worry about, is there, Chris?"

"Not a thing." He spoke fast, maybe too fast. "Aiden has some legwork to get through and so do I. Nothing dangerous. Just boring stuff. We'll be in contact all the time. If we sit around staring at each other and doing nothing, we'll never put this thing to rest. The sooner I go, the sooner I'll get back. Okay, sweetheart?"

Arguing wouldn't accomplish a thing. "Okay," she said, although it wasn't. "You get going. Both of you. I feel like a good walk. I need fresh air. I also want to check in with Ena again this morning. I feel so sorry for her."

Both men had gotten up. Sonnie didn't miss the sad way Aiden watched when Chris bent to kiss her. He kissed her for a long time. She turned in the chair and reached her arms around his neck.

"Ena's first; then you go straight to Ray and Bo, okay?" he said.

"Okay." They released each other slowly, and she was sure he was as reluctant as she.

"You two do intend to see each other again, don't you?" Aiden said. "You might want to leave something for later."

"You're jealous," Chris said.

"You're right," Aiden told him. "Let's go."

Chris followed, raising his brows at Sonnie when he passed her. Men, Sonnie decided, could be so obtuse. Aiden was lonely, and neither his pink Mustang nor his special Cadillac were filling up the empty spaces in his life.

When they'd left, stillness filled the house. Wimpy continued to follow Sonnie wherever she went. First she returned to Ena's house and knocked.

After waiting for several minutes, she tried the door and found it unlocked. Perhaps she and Chris had failed to lock it when they left. Sonnie went inside and called "Ena" several times. A search of the whole house produced no sign of its owner. Sonnie checked the gardens but still didn't find her friend.

The bed in the room behind the parlor was made. There was no sign of Ena having used the kitchen that morning.

Sonnie detested the tightening of her skin, and the way her scalp prickled. Ena could come and go as she pleased.

But wouldn't she wait to see Chris and Sonnie that morning?

They hadn't waited to see her. . . .

Where would she go so early in the day?

Sonnie should call Chris.

And tell him what?

Panic wouldn't accomplish a thing. She would go back to her own place and give some thought to organization. A call to her parents was long overdue. What should she tell them about Romano?

On an overcast day, the purple bougainvillea was blindingly brilliant. Nothing moved. Not a suggestion of a breeze did anything to cool off the mounting heat.

She didn't have to go home. There was no reason not to go to the street and keep on walking—except for the need to overcome irrational fear, and to deal with the presence of one small, bug-eyed dog who looked at her as if she were his salvation.

"Okay, Wimp, let's get you fed, you nuisance." She liked having him with her. He asked nothing but that she love him and make him feel safe. Odd how some simple needs crossed so many boundaries.

She went inside and promptly called her parents. Their worry oozed along the lines. They both wanted her to come home at once, and they urged her to listen to Billy's friend, the good doctor, whom they respected. Neither of them mentioned either Romano or Frank, and Sonnie chose to avoid the topic, too. They almost certainly wouldn't believe her if she told them what Romano had done to her.

As soon as she hung up, the phone rang. She picked up again and Aiden's unmistakable voice said, "Sonnie. You heard from Chris?"

"No. Did you try his phone?"

"Idiot's got it turned off."

"I haven't heard," she said, calling on simple discipline to stop herself from defending Chris's intellect. "What's going on?" Chris hadn't turned on his phone, that was all. It didn't mean something had happened to him.

"I got something, that's all," Aiden said. "And I want Chris to check some things out. Do you know a guy called Cory Bledsoe?"

"At the club. He's the athletic director. Or he's supposed to be. Romano's been covering for him. He left for some reason."

"Yeah? But you don't know him personally?"

"I've met him. Nice enough man, if you don't mind the way he hovers."

"Any talk about him?"

Sonnie considered. "Well, he does have a bit of a reputation as a ladies' man. But I don't know any specifics."

"Could be unimportant. I'll get hold of Chris eventually. If you hear from him, please let him know I called."

"Will do," Sonnie said, and hung up once more.

Wimpy had left on a sniffing expedition. Sonnie reminded herself that every inch of this house had been examined, and went to the kitchen to heat a mug of coffee in the microwave.

She scoured the sink until the buzzer went off, then climbed the stairs, mug in hand. A nap sounded better than she ever remembered. Yesterday's ordeal had taken a lot out of her, and she hadn't had much sleep last night.

Mostly she didn't feel like doing anything but waiting for Chris.

With the coffee on her bedside table, she plumped up her pillows and stretched out with her head propped. Better than a nap, just being comfortable and having the time to think about Chris was an irresistible idea.

Yet again the phone rang, and when she picked up Chris said, "Why didn't you go to the Nail?"

She must have summoned him up just by thinking about him. She smiled and said, "I decided to take a nap instead."

There was a short silence before Chris said, "Tired you out, huh?"

"You wish you were here?"

"You've got it. I'd like to be there with you. I'd like to keep informed of where you are, though, Sonnie. Are you staying there, or do you plan to go to the Nail?"

"Not till this evening. Aiden called. He said to tell you that if I heard from you. He tried to contact you but your phone was off."

"It has to be for now," Chris said, but didn't elaborate more.

And Sonnie didn't press him. "Aiden asked questions about Cory Bledsoe but he didn't tell me why."

"Shit," Chris said, "I need to talk to Aiden. Listen, don't leave your house before you hear from me. Got that?"

"Yes."

"Good. Later." He hung up.

Chris was fine.

Sonnie took a mouthful of coffee that was growing cold and rested against the pillows. The palms beyond the balcony had grown tall in the years since she and Frank had bought the house.

Frank was dead. That was a thought that didn't make sense. He'd been so vibrant, so self-assured. Frank smiled at everyone—even Sonnie if there was someone around who might see. How sad. They had seemed blessed, bound to have a golden life together. So soon he'd let the pretense fall away, and she'd found out he liked to have her on his arm—or perhaps to have her name and connections on his arm—but he hadn't even liked her at all. She'd become a nuisance to him.

She wished he were alive and happy. Once they'd divorced he'd have had no difficulty finding a much more suitable woman to share his life.

A *bang, bang, bang* startled her. She sat up and saw at once what was making the noise. Outside on the balcony, Frank's chair rocked madly back and forth, hammering at the frame on the French door.

Sonnie jumped from the bed and went to open the doors. She had to push the chair away in order to go outside.

She gripped the chair to pull it away from the doors, but stopped and looked at it. The last time she'd noticed it, it had stood farther along the balcony—well away from the windows. She couldn't have seen it without coming outside.

And there was no wind now.

She gave it a push.

It rocked, but not much. Frank had chosen the long runners that guaranteed soft motion. He'd had the chair made because he liked to sit out here at night—on his own. There hadn't been a chair for Sonnie, not that she minded. She'd been glad for him to find peace wherever he could.

Even if the chair had been moved while the cleanup from the fire was under way, that wouldn't explain why it started rocking all on its own, and rocking so hard it banged the window.

Sonnie leaned over the balcony railings and scanned the area for signs of an intruder onto the property. She didn't see anyone.

Her heart beat faster. If she mentioned the incident to anyone they'd say it was petty and unimportant. It *was* petty and unimportant, and she wouldn't mention it. She hauled the chair well away and back out of sight of the bedroom and returned inside. She locked the door and sat on the bed again.

At any other time or in any other place, she would be deciding who might take pleasure in childish pranks.

But these weren't pranks.

She crawled under the quilt. The air conditioning was on and the house was cool. It felt good—safe—to be warm. The house was locked up and Chris and Aiden were in touch. She had nothing to fear. And she was regaining enough confidence to feel sure of herself.

Consciousness slipped slowly, comfortably away. Images

crowded her mind, mostly of Chris. Christian. They could go away and forget everything here.

Her warm, safe feeling grew deeper.

One sound penetrated. Just a faint sound somewhere above her head. She turned onto her back but didn't open her eyes. A soft, soft sobbing. A baby sobbing.

Sonnie did open her eyes then. Awake? She didn't know. The noise stopped. Had she ever heard it at all?

Twilight sleep claimed her again and she went with it. She was healing. If she weren't, she wouldn't be able to stay here like this and think logically about what was happening to her.

A baby's distant sobs sounded again. When she opened her eyes, she didn't hear them anymore.

She wasn't coping at all. As long as she was around other people she felt almost normal, but not when she was alone. Maybe she did need treatment. What could it hurt?

"Go. Go. Go." Her mouth dried out. She gathered the quilt to her neck. A man's voice high in the room—stuttering the word. *"She's waiting. Go."*

Sonnie resisted the urge to cover her head. She did settle even lower in the bed. No, she would not give in to this. And she would not blame other people for the condition she was in.

She located the bottle of sleeping pills in the bedside table and went to the bathroom for water. The glass was missing so she returned to take the medication with cold coffee.

She almost dropped the mug. She'd forgotten she was holding it. And she recalled being told the medicine was strong and she'd have to lie down when she'd taken it. Sonnie did so and felt herself begin to float.

Her eyelids were too heavy to open, so she didn't try.

When she parted her lids again, the light from outside had begun to dim. She was still so tired, her limbs so heavy.

A baby cried. A brokenhearted baby sobbed. Neglected and alone.

Sonnie began to cry, too. If her mind had been destroyed, but enough had been left intact to give her periods when she felt she was normal, she would suffer like this as long as she lived. No good to anyone. She should go away where no one knew her, and no one could be worried for her.

The child's noises went away, and Sonnie felt herself going away, too.

A scream tore through the house. Sonnie sat up and covered her ears. "Stop it," she cried. "Chris, I need you."

Another scream somewhere overhead, and an explosive sound. Metal wrenched from metal, and sliding rubber. She smelled burning rubber.

She leaped from bed and her legs wouldn't hold her. She slid to the floor. The noise was all around her. Bigger and bigger. The screaming went on and on.

Sonnie panted, and whispered, "Please stop. Let me go." She was finished now. Taking in a big breath she shouted, "Let me go," and huddled in a ball on the carpet.

The unmistakable roar of igniting flames brought her own screams to join the others. A searing current, a draft of intense heat engulfed her, stole her breath.

She collapsed and waited to die. She wanted to die now.

Sensation faded.

Sonnie opened her eyes and thought, dimly, that a lot of time had passed. Near darkness pressed the windows. She should gather a few things and leave—and not tell anyone where she was going. She owed the people who cared for her that much. If she could find a way to get better, she'd return; otherwise they would never hear from her again.

The baby cried. Her throat sounded hoarse and she hiccuped. An exhausted plea for comfort.

Pain assaulted every joint, but Sonnie used the side of the bed to pull herself upright. This time the crying didn't stop.

How many hours had she slept? Darkness had fallen. If the phone had rung, she hadn't heard it.

She pressed her ears to try to drown out the sound of the baby, but she heard it just the same.

She staggered across the room and opened the door to the hallway. The baby's cries became louder.

Now the noise wasn't disembodied. It came from Jacqueline's room. Sonnie felt weak and sick. She swallowed again and again, willing herself not to vomit.

Too light-headed to walk without holding on to the wall, she turned the handle on the nursery door and pushed it open carefully.

Grayness crowded every corner, but the white flounced bassinet almost shone in its dim surroundings.

The rocking bassinet.

Sonnie stepped, very cautiously, closer.

The desperate crying came from the baby's swaying bed.

Inside the bed, tiny arms and legs flailed.

Thirty

He'd meant it when he told Sonnie he thought they were nearing a resolution. What he hadn't told her was that he wasn't sure he was relieved at the prospect. The two scenarios that scared the hell out of him were that everything would come down and he'd be in the wrong place at the wrong time—or that Sonnie was mentally unbalanced.

Why didn't he just say it like it was? He had no choice but to see this thing through to the end, but he knew the end might cost him his newfound hope for the future: Sonnie.

Chris had left his bike in the club's employee parking lot. He went along a walkway to one of the enclosed pools and let himself in by an age-old but very skilled cop trick. He reached over the gate and released the lock from the inside.

He had called a few minutes earlier and asked for "Billy Keith in twenty-seven," to which the front desk clerk obligingly replied, "Twelve, sir. I'll ring for you." Trusting people could be so helpful. Chris had let the phone ring until the clerk came back on the line and said, "I'm sorry. There's no answer. We don't have a mailbox system, but I can take a message for Ms. Keith and make sure she gets it when she comes back in."

"She's out?"

"Yes."

"You sure of that?"

"Oh, absolutely, sir," the man said. "She's difficult to miss, if you know what I mean."

"I do indeed." So why had they both wasted time ringing the room? "Thanks for trying. I'll call back."

Chris walked along a pathway of crushed white rock as if he knew exactly where he was going. There'd probably never be a better chance than now to take a look at Billy's room. He already knew that Romano wasn't at the club today. Sonnie had checked and been told he'd gone to Stock Island and would be there overnight. That meant a look at his room could come after Billy's.

A woman in a bikini and carrying what resembled a good-size vase filled with a blue, paper parasol–decked drink, pushed through a door from the building. Chris promptly strode in that direction and held the door open for her.

If her mouth hadn't been full, she would doubtless have engaged him in deep conversation. As it was, she stared and sputtered—and Chris escaped into a corridor papered with palm-strewn foil.

Seedy was the word that came to mind. A new do would definitely be in order, not that Chris gave a damn.

He found room twelve so fast, he paused. This was all too easy.

The place hadn't yet graduated to key cards. *Thank God.* Another ten seconds and Chris was inside.

With one hand at the clip-on holster he wore at his waist under a denim jacket, he planned his approach and started with the bathroom. He turned up nothing of interest, except for a stash of masculine toiletries. Dr. Lesley, no doubt. Just as well Detective Talon was ex. He'd definitely lost his touch. True, the doc hadn't been very visible since he'd been here, but that didn't mean he wasn't around. And why wouldn't he and Billy be sharing a room?

Chris moved even faster. He opened one of two closets and went through pockets as rapidly as he could. Dr. Lesley's clothes hung there, and Chris saw no reason not to search them, too. He checked a shelf above, and moved clothes aside to see if anything had been taped to the wall behind. Nothing. And the clothing yielded nothing.

Someone knocked on the door.

Chris prepared to shut himself in the closet.

Another knock. Chris said, ''Yes?'' and quit breathing.

''Housekeeping.''

''Later,'' he said, shaking his head. If you belonged in a room, you didn't usually knock on the door before entering.

With Jim Lesley unaccounted for, every second became even more precious. Chris threw open the second closet. That was when he saw a leather satchel tossed on a shelf in the nearest bedside table. The bed was a vast effort covered with, yep, palm trees on blue. The walls and ceiling were blue. The carpet was blue. The club had definitely gone the watery tropical route. He supposed he could say it sort of fit in with the private pool he could see in a courtyard beyond sliding glass doors.

The satchel looked feminine.

He started on a short dress encrusted with silver sequins. A jacket hung on top had pockets. But for a used tissue, the pockets were empty.

Shit. He'd look in the bag.

Made of the kind of leather that sucked fingers into its tan softness, it closed with one of those snap buckles that was pretty close to ski-boot style. This buckle was gold. Chis slipped it open and looked inside. A small bottle of Coco. A lipstick—Shiseido. A powder compact—Shiseido. Money. Loose money. Chris sank his fingers into several inches of bills and brought up a handful of hundreds, fifties, and the odd grand. The lady was very relaxed about security around here—and she liked to deal in cash.

An inside zippered pouch yielded several pens and two leather-bound notebooks. Chris flipped through one, and at last he found something that really surprised him. Billy Keith kept a record of her dreams. He dropped that little tome back into its ''safe place'' and opened the other book.

Numbers. Telephone numbers. Addresses. Random notes that she wrote almost in code because she didn't bother to complete a thought, and grammar wasn't Billy's forte. She liked to make shapes with words. A shopping list in the shape of a fish blowing bubbles. What she wanted the hairdresser to do for her took on the shape of a hair dryer. Evidently the gentleman also gave interesting massages.

The shape of a gun with a long barrel consisted of nothing but names written so that it was impossible to tell which first names went with which last names.

One name stood out. Ginger-Pearl. Chris scanned for last names that might help him remember where he'd first seen them.

He didn't need to. He eased a couple of fingers into a back pocket in his jeans, drew out the list of names he'd found in Ena's attic, and found Ginger-Pearl with ease. Last name Smith. And the rest of the names used to make Billy's artistic gun were also on the list.

The project had yielded something useful, even if Chris still had to find out exactly what, but he could be walked in on at any moment. Back at the closet, the search went on. And one after the other, pieces of clothing yielded nothing. In the midst of Billy's expensive and flashy wardrobe, he found a black sweatsuit made of some soft microfiber. It looked very un-Billy.

Chris took the jacket off the hanger and checked the size, just to be certain Lesley's clothing hadn't gotten mixed in. Nope, this was Billy's. Probably used as warm-ups before playing tennis, or whatever she did with her time when she wasn't being a nuisance to Sonnie.

In the right front pocket of the jacket, he found a black silk stocking cap and gloves. Glancing down, Chris noted black sports shoes with black socks stuffed inside. Even Detective Talon at his least sharp could figure out how useful this number would be at night if a person didn't want to be seen.

He ought to leave.

In the left jacket pocket Chris hit pay dirt—so to speak. He withdrew his hand and looked at pale grit crammed beneath his fingernails. That led him to examine the gloves more closely. *Oh, baby, you'll never get into Special Forces.* The fingertips and palms of the gloves were soiled gray-white. When he shook out one glove, a powdery substance flew.

Chris stuffed the gloves away, felt around for a small sample of what he'd found to take away, and put it in his own pocket. He smacked his hands together to remove any residue.

Now he wanted to see Sonnie so badly it hurt. He hadn't come up with anything a resourceful person couldn't explain away, but the evidence was good enough for him—it tied Billy Keith in somewhere, and now he'd have to find out where that was.

Aiden had gone to Miami to see what he could find out about the address Chris had discovered at Ena's. Chris was grateful he'd decided to take on the list of names himself. He needed some time alone with a telephone directory. And he needed to persuade Ena to allow him to poke around in her house. He thought he could do that.

A peach-colored teddy and negligee slipped from its hanger to the floor. Chris gathered it up, trying to visualize Sonnie in anything trimmed with ostrich feathers. He failed.

He also felt a familiar old friend: all systems on alert.

The sound he heard at the door this time wasn't a knock— or the voice of a maid.

What he heard at the door was someone fumbling to insert a key. Escape was out of the question. He yanked pillows against the headboard and propped himself against them just as Jim Lesley meandered in, looking at the keys in his hand.

Chris seized the only defense he might pull off. "You," he said. "What the . . . What are you doing letting yourself in here?"

For an instant the man's calm slipped. He looked quickly at Chris. "Talon?"

"Yeah, Talon. I'm waiting for Billy."

Lesley shut the door. "Does she know you're waiting?"

Chris settled back on the pillows. "Couldn't reach her before she left."

"So she doesn't know. How did you get in here?"

Chris gave his best innocent smile. "Just a little skill I

picked up along the way.'' He laughed as if hugely enamored of his joke.

The doctor said, ''Cute, but there are going to be questions.'' He inclined his head. ''She's something, isn't she? Billy? That's what this is all about. You're one more man she's bowled over without even knowing she's done it. Happens all the time. You want something of hers, is that it? Look, you don't have to make excuses to me. Nothing too unusual about that as long as you don't let it get out of hand.''

Now the guy was analyzing him, but at least he showed no sign of having any idea about the real reason Chris was there.

''You should see her in that,'' Lesley said, pointing.

Chris turned to see that he'd managed to drop the teddy and negligee again, and wisps of silk with ostrich feathers attached were visible under the closet door. ''I bet she looks great,'' Chris said. ''Look, this was a bad idea. I don't know what got into me, but I'd better clear out before I make a total fool of myself.''

''Billy won't be back for a while. I'm a believer in grabbing opportunities, Chris. I've been hoping for a chance to talk to you. I'd say this was the perfect chance.''

Chris didn't want a cozy chat with Jim, but he also didn't want to miss anything useful the man might inadvertently say.

The doctor went to the second closet, opened the door, and picked up the fallen lingerie. He carried it to the bed and stood over Chris. ''It's soft,'' he said, holding it to his mouth, then rubbing it against his cheek and neck. ''Here, take this. She doesn't use it, but you can.'' He winked and gave Chris the belt from the robe. ''Just let me know if you want any ideas. Erotic stimulation is one of my areas of special interest. It's been useful in my practice. A happy patient is a docile patient— as long as they keep getting more of what they want. That's my motto.''

Chris squelched the urge to toss the belt aside. Instead he wound it quickly and stuffed it into one of his jacket pockets. ''Thanks, Doc. I haven't had much chance to get to know you, but I can see why Billy feels comfortable with you. She needs a strong, innovative man, doesn't she?''

"I like to think it's something like that. Chris, it's Sonnie I want to talk to you about."

Chris wasn't surprised by the switch in topic.

"I don't think your interest in her is purely professional. And I'm sure Billy's right when she says Sonnie isn't your type—not sexually. You're a man who must need a woman with an appetite to match his own. And the kind of physical stamina to match. Obviously Sonnie can't satisfy you, but I think you care about her as a friend. Am I right?"

Chris would like to smash the charming, sympathetic smile right off the hypocrite's face. "Sonnie's worth caring about. She's very special."

"That's exactly what I expected you to say, and it makes what I want to tell you much easier. How much do you know about schizophrenia?"

"Not a lot outside of it's being when people have delusions."

"A simple explanation, but certainly true to a degree in some cases. The presence of conviction—by the patient—that the patient is being persecuted is almost always demonstrated. I've no doubt you've heard about these poor, beleaguered souls being tormented by the belief that they hear voices—real voices, of course."

Chris supposed that if one charged by the hour, one might learn never to use one word where seven or eight would do. "I have heard that, yes."

"The good news is that there have been significant advances in the treatment of schizophrenia. Often we employ the type of cognitive therapy used for cases of severe clinical depression. And we're scoring successes. Especially where a supportive family is involved.

"Perhaps I can give you a sketch of what may happen. A patient may be convinced that there is a malevolent force set on destroying him or her. The patient hears this force, or can produce signs that it exists. Our cognitive approach is to make the patient spend time alone. Then we start to prove that this, for want of a better term, this force is not waiting somewhere, out there to do mischief, but that it in fact originated within the patient himself. By forcing the patient to confront the truth—in lucid moments, of course—we can make progress.

"Chris, Sonnie hears voices, doesn't she?"

He'd learned to show nothing of what he was thinking. He drew on that skill now.

Jim smiled again. "All right. Loyalty is very admirable. From what I've been told, I know Sonnie hears voices. In fact, as hard as this may be for you to accept, I believe she has a very severe emotional illness that may well be schizophrenia. Complete rest and intensive treatment is her only chance for recovery. But I can't force her to accept my opinion, not that I've given her my opinion, or would do so unless someone with the right authority requested me to do so."

"The right authority?" Chris said.

Jim sighed and inclined his head sadly. "Someone who eventually takes over responsibility for her because she can no longer continue to function adequately in the regular world."

Every word made Chris feel a little angrier. These people already had Sonnie locked away and under constant supervision. And Chris didn't know if there was truly a plot afoot to accomplish this, or if Sonnie really needed help. He would not consider that possibility until he'd done his best to help Sonnie sort her way through whatever was going on.

"What do you say?" Jim asked. "Will you help us to help Sonnie?"

Chris got no chance to answer.

Romano Giacano burst into the room. He pushed Jim Lesley aside hard enough to send the man stumbling over an ottoman. Failing to catch his balance, Lesley fell and slammed into a wall.

"You're a violent man," Chris said, bracing himself for a fight. "I'm glad you're here. We've got some unfinished business."

"We certainly do," Romano said. "You have become a nuisance. You are in my way. That is something I will not tolerate. Jim, get out of here. Wait in my room."

Jim Lesley made much of hauling himself from the floor.

He stumbled again and slid to his knees, holding his head as if he were injured.

"Games are over, Giacano," Chris said, standing and taking a step toward the man. "I suggest you go on your way. When you've cooled off, we'll talk about why you're into victimizing women."

"The only time I intend to spend with you is right now," Romano said.

"When will you learn you are not in charge of the world?" Chris said.

Romano turned away to look at Jim Lesley. When he turned back he held a Smith Airweight in his right hand. Its short barrel gleamed. "You have meddled in my business for the last time."

Thirty-one

The thought of using the telephone frightened Sonnie. She heard that there were instruments that could be used to listen to other people's phone conversations.

Perhaps that was how they were getting information on her, how they knew when she'd be alone. Listening to her phone calls could have given them a lot of details Sonnie didn't want them to have.

They would use the information against her.

What could she do? There was no noise anymore. It had stopped when she went into Jacqueline's room and found the battery-powered doll in the bassinet. Sonnie had bought that doll for Jacqueline, for when she was old enough to enjoy it. They were cruel, these faceless enemies. They wanted her to be forever waiting for them to taunt her.

She tiptoed downstairs, watching to be sure there wasn't anyone stretched out on the floor anywhere. That man was injured. She knew it for sure now. He'd show up again just as soon as he was well enough to crawl from wherever he was hiding.

Gravel crunched beneath tires in the driveway.

Sonnie stood quite still in the hallway and waited.

Ena had talked about a man with the same kind of hair—

long blond curls—going into her house. Into this house. Sonnie peered around. And he had been injured. He bent over and hobbled. He was here with her somewhere.

She must find the courage to return to Ena's and hope she'd be there now. Sonnie was worried about Ena. She'd been under such strain and she was completely alone.

Cautiously Sonnie went and opened the front door to peer out. But she remembered she'd just heard a car arrive and started to close the door again.

Billy stopped her. "Sonnie, it's me, Billy. I tried to call but there was no answer."

Sonnie didn't think she remembered hearing the phone ring. "I'm very busy," she managed to say. "This isn't a good time for a visit, but thank you for coming anyway."

"I've got to talk to you—*now*," Billy said, and pushed the door so hard that Sonnie staggered back. "Oh," Billy cried. "Oh, Sonnie, what is it? What's happened to you? I'm calling Jim right now."

"Don't," Sonnie said. "I must ask you to leave. You have no right to force yourself on me."

Billy held up both hands. "All right. Okay. I won't call anyone. Just let me talk to you. I've had a shock, Baby. And I know you have, too."

Sonnie stared at her. "You do?" This could be another trick.

"Sonnie," Billy wailed suddenly. "Oh, Sonnie, you're my sister and I love you. You're not yourself. Please let me take care of you. Your face. The scratches. My God, what's happened?"

"Nothing." Even though she ached in so many places, she stood straighter. "There's nothing wrong with me. Why would you think there was?"

"You look ill. You've been crying. I can tell you have. And your hair's a mess. Your clothes. And, Sonnie, the doll. Why are you holding a doll as if it were a baby?"

She didn't care what anyone thought about that. "I'm going to find a safe place for her." Sonnie fingered the locket at her neck. She'd hidden Frank's medallion where she didn't have to see it. "It's time for me to take charge and care for myself and whatever matters to me. I'm getting stronger all the time. I don't need any help." But she did wish there was some hope left that Chris wouldn't turn away from her. She'd already put him through too much.

They had made love.

Each time that had been as much or more her idea than his. She shouldn't have let it happen. She shouldn't have fallen in love with him. He couldn't be expected to stay around a woman who was only part of what she'd once been, a woman with so many problems that even she couldn't see a way out.

Billy was looking at her with apprehension in her eyes.

"It's okay," Sonnie said. "I'm not dangerous or anything like that. I'm just absorbed in making decisions. I did speak to Mom and Dad to let them know I'm fine. I don't think they're convinced. When you talk to them, will you try to put their minds at rest?"

Billy hesitated, but then she said, "Yes. Yes, I'll tell them. Not because I think you're in good shape, but because I don't think it will help you if you're worrying about them as well as yourself." She locked the front door. "Is everything else around here locked up?"

"Everything that needs to be." There was something strange about Billy's behavior.

"Can we sit in the parlor? I've always liked that room."

The fastest way to get rid of Billy was to let her have her own way. "If you want to." Sonnie led the way and sat on one of the chintz couches that no longer brought her any pleasure.

"I'm horrified," Billy said, taking a seat at the opposite end of the same couch. "I don't know how else to explain what I feel. Horrified. I love you, Sonnie. We've had our ups and downs. We certainly haven't always agreed—on a lot of things. But I don't think we've ever stopped caring about each other, have we?"

Sonnie looked into her sister's eyes. "No, I don't think so."

Tears welled in those eyes. "Thank you for saying that. I'm muddled up. I don't know what's wrong here, but something is. I don't know. . . . Your safety is so important to me. I'm afraid you're not safe. That can't be. I can't just allow that to be.''

"Hush," Sonnie said, the urge to comfort automatic. "It's all right. Thank you for caring."

Billy sat straighter. "I not only care *about* you—I'm going to care *for* you. Sonnie, I've spoken with Romano."

"Oh." Hugging herself, Sonnie turned on the couch to face the room. "I don't think we should talk about Romano. I never want to see him again."

"I've failed at everything," Billy said abruptly. "I'm a loving woman. I care about people. But I've allowed myself to be sidetracked so many times. And jealousy has almost destroyed me. I could never cope with not being the most sought after, the woman everyone looked at and envied. I've felt all that begin to slip. After all, I'm not as young as I used to be."

It all sounded so sincere. Sonnie didn't believe a word of it, but she'd play along. "You're absolutely gorgeous and you know it. You stop conversation in any room you enter."

"Thanks. But even if it's true, there has to be more in my life than that. I want to turn the clock back. I want you and me to be the way we were when we were kids. We always felt more like sisters than half-sisters.

"Sonnie, Romano confessed what he did to you."

Sonnie put her head in her hands.

"He told me he took you on a long drive and frightened you. He knows you aren't a good passenger. He said he drove slowly, then very fast, and then he took you to that horrible place and—"

"Stop."

"We have to be able to talk about it. He said he wanted to shock your memory back."

"But why like that?" Sonnie asked. "Why would he do something so despicable? I tried to get away."

Billy scooted closer to Sonnie on the couch. "Did he hurt you?"

"Yes." But she didn't want to think about what Romano

had done. "I always thought he was my friend. What an idiot he must think I am."

"I think he's under too much stress. I'm sure his business is failing."

"That doesn't excuse him," Sonnie said quietly. "And the business isn't only his. Frank has a lot of money tied up there, too."

"Frank's dead," Billy said. She patted Sonnie's knee. "What exactly did Romano do to hurt you yesterday? I need to know."

"Why . . . Okay, I'll tell you. He pretended he was going to crash the car into that wall."

"I know."

"When I tried to get away, he chased me onto the beach and knocked me down. That's where I got the scratches. And he hit me. He threw me onto some rocks. Then I think he intended to drown me." Repeating what had happened aloud sounded bizarre. "He went crazy. He'd already said he intended to marry me so he could control me—or anything I happen to own."

Billy reached for Sonnie's hand. "I know what we've got to do. We've got to get away from here, and I don't mean by running to the folks. They don't cope with anything that upsets their comfortable routine."

"I can't leave," Sonnie told her. "Not yet. Maybe soon, but I still have things to accomplish here." She couldn't, wouldn't leave unless she became certain there was no future with Chris.

"How long will it take you to finish up and be ready?" Billy asked.

"I'm not sure."

"Sonnie"—Billy squeezed her hand—"I don't know what the whole story is with Romano. I used to think the way you did—that he was such a good friend. Now he scares me. I think he'd kill to get what he wants. With both you and Frank dead, everything goes to him. And I know too much. You can fill in the blanks. If I didn't think he's desperate enough to convince himself he can get away with it, I might hope he'd come to his senses. We can't take that risk.''

Where was Chris?

Billy got up. She leaned over Sonnie and hugged her. ''We're going to be okay, Baby,'' she said, and kissed Sonnie's cheek. ''Romano took off for Stock Island. He's going to be gone overnight at least. I told him I'd call him in the morning to find out his plans. He thinks I'm working with him and that I'll help him do what he wants to do. Then he plans to get rid of me. I'm sure of it, Baby. We've got to help each other.''

Sonnie looked up into her sister's face. ''I want you to leave Key West now,'' she told her. If Billy was being honest with her, Sonnie had an obligation to tell her to get away from Romano and Key West. ''Billy, *now*. I don't want you to go back to that club, and I don't want you to speak to Romano again.''

Billy's mouth tightened. ''You aren't well enough to make any decisions. Leave that to me. We'll go away together.''

They would go nowhere together. Billy had only one agenda—to get Sonnie away from anyone who might truly be on her side.

Sonnie wanted Billy to leave. Calling her bluff might pull that off. ''Wait with me until Chris comes. If he agrees, we'll go straight to the police.''

''No.'' Billy shook her head, swung her hair from side to side. ''Chris Talon seems like a decent enough guy—in spite of the Harley-Davidson and the tattoos. But we have to make our own decisions. Be ready by ten in the morning. Take as little as you can. In fact, dress as if you were going to work at that bar and bring a purse with any personal papers you've got with you. Nothing else. That way we don't draw any attention.''

''Chris only has one tattoo. I like it.''

Billy gave her a speculative sideways glance. ''Do you now? You don't stop surprising me, little sister. I do believe there's a whole wild side to you. That would be the side you've been hiding all these years.''

''You may be right.'' In fact, Billy *was* right. ''Regardless, I want you to wait for him with me. We need his advice.''

Billy straightened. Her face was rigid with anger. "I don't need advice from him, thanks. In fact, I want you to promise me something. Don't mention I've been here. Will you do that for me?"

"Why? What difference would it make if he knew?"

"I don't know," Billy said. "And neither do you, not for sure. Ten in the morning. Just a purse with your papers in it."

Romano Giacano might have been born with a silver spoon in his mouth, but he'd also been born a rebel. Papa had made an arrangement with the authorities in their small Italian hometown that his eldest son would be driven home, rather than to the police station, when he got into trouble. That arrangement had cost the family plenty, and it had allowed Romano to run with the wildest thugs in the countryside, and to learn how to fight as dirty as it took to win. He was still smarting from his poor showing against Talon the previous evening. He could hardly believe his luck that a rematch was presenting itself so quickly.

The idiot doctor was down and staying down—the smartest move Romano had ever seen him make.

Talon stood relaxed, his arms hanging loosely at his sides and his feet planted far enough apart to telegraph to Romano that he was confronted by a man he'd never be able to take down easily.

But he would take him down.

"This time you're dead, Talon," Romano said, motioning with the gun. "Yesterday you caught me off guard. Today I'm ready for you. Come on. Let's see how good you really are."

Talon didn't move. He said, "The gun wins every time. I don't have to do a thing to help you prove that." And the bastard smiled.

"Romano," Jim Lesley said, rising to his feet. "This is a bad idea. Killing is wrong. It never accomplishes—"

"I do not need lectures from a witch doctor, or whatever you are supposed to be. I suggest you get out of here. The scene will not be pretty by the time I finish."

"No," Lesley said. "No. I implore you to stop this at once."

Romano responded by backhanding the quack across the face. He felt blood spatter the back of his hand and spared the man a disgusted glance. He probably had a broken nose.

Without waiting another moment, and while Talon wasted time saying, "Get a cold cloth on that nose, Doc," Romano shoved the gun into a pocket, let out a roar, and launched himself. He would prove he was physically superior to Sonnie's trained pet. Talon confounded him by rolling a shoulder down, catching Romano beneath the diaphragm, and straightening enough to send him over his back and crashing into a fake potted palm.

The fucking pot broke on his knee, and blood soaked the leg of his pants almost instantly. "You freak," he yelled. "You are nothing. You have had your piece of luck. Now we play the game my way."

Expressionless, Talon had turned to face him again. Still he didn't initiate a move.

"Let's talk about this," Jim Lesley said. "Please. This isn't accomplishing a thing."

Romano was bleeding all over the carpet. So much for trying to fight fair. He fumbled for the gun.

"Looking for this?" Talon held out the Smith Airweight. "You can have it. Later. I'll call for some medical help."

"No," Romano said. He'd misjudged this scene. "Get me a towel, Jim."

"I'm not leaving you two alone until I'm sure you won't try killing each other again."

Romano shrugged and offered up his empty palms. "My opponent has the advantage, and"—he couldn't afford to let his need to punish ruin everything—"and I'm going to ask you to accept my apology, Talon. I've been through a great deal. Damn it to hell. I cannot expect you to care what I feel— or to forgive me for my bad behavior."

Chris had never been vengeful, but with Romano Giacano he might break his record.

"Listen to him," Jim Lesley said. "Give him a chance to explain himself."

"Get him a towel," Chris said. Showing Giacano even the

smallest chink in enemy armor could be a huge mistake. "From what I can see, you're going to need stitches."

"Don't worry about me." This was a whole new Romano. Romano the martyr.

"I don't intend to worry about you. Nice piece. You always armed?"

"You can keep it," Romano said. "I should not have it. My temper is too unpredictable."

Chris wasn't fooled. "I guess that's why you should also never take a woman for a drive, hmm?"

"Go easy," Jim Lesley said, returning from the bathroom with a towel. "He's in a bad place. You can see that." He tossed the towel to Romano.

"Did you know he beats up on women, Doc?"

Romano shook his head repeatedly. "Never again." He tore his pant leg open and pressed the towel over a jagged wound.

"He's trying to get his head straight," Jim said. "At least hear him out."

"I'm listening," Chris said. He didn't intend to give Romano a whole lot of time. "Come on. Come on. Let's hear how you think you can explain yourself."

"I want a chance to apologize. Not just to you, not even mainly to you. It's Sonnie who deserves an explanation, and my promise that the man she saw yesterday wasn't really me. I love her as the dearest of friends. Even if she forgives me, I will not forgive myself."

"You're breaking my heart," Chris said.

Romano kept his eyes downcast and applied more pressure to his knee. "My brother—my baby brother—is dead. It is not supposed to be that he should die before me. I should not have done what I did to Sonnie, but I am suffering, and knowing that she doesn't care that my brother—her husband—has been brutally murdered has been too much."

"Did you know Sonnie planned to divorce Frank?" Chris asked. "She intended to tell him that when he was due to arrive in Key West, but didn't."

"I know this." Romano wiped the back of a hand across his eyes. "She told me that she'd begun making plans. And then I found out that she'd looked into making changes in her will—Frank's will."

"Surely she couldn't do that without her husband."

Giacano's laugh was ugly. "She intended to prove he had no right to her trust. It predated her wedding, and she planned to divorce Frank before she came of age to access the funds."

"How do you know that?" Chris asked.

"Billy mentioned it. She and Sonnie have always shared everything. But I'm not making that an excuse for what I did. She won't listen to me, Talon, but you could talk her into giving me another chance.

"She's not well. We all know that. I haven't helped, but I want to turn that around. She needs treatment before it's too late to reclaim the Sonnie we've known. Voices." He raised his gaze to the ceiling. "Have you heard the voices she talks about?"

Excitement all but overwhelmed Chris. "Can't say I have." How interesting that Romano should talk about those voices and look upward as he did so. "How about you?"

"No," Romano said. "Neither has Billy." He glanced upward again.

"So we're all pulling for Sonnie, is that right?" he said, barely able to stop himself from running out of the room and going for the Harley as fast as he could.

"We most certainly are," Romano said.

"Count on it," Jim Lesley said.

"Great. I'll be in touch after I talk to Sonnie."

He left the room and immediately saw Billy Keith at the end of the corridor. Her back was to him while she talked to someone in the lobby. A room opposite and to the left stood open, with a housekeeping trolley outside. He was out of options.

Chris dodged behind the trolley and entered the room. He heard water running. The bathroom was being cleaned.

Encountering Billy was out of the question now. He positioned himself at the back of the door. The carpet in the corridor muffled footsteps, but he heard them, and through the crack between the door and the jamb he saw Billy arrive at room twelve. It was Jim Lesley who appeared before she could use her key. He looked up and down the corridor and said, "Did you see Talon?"

Billy made her own check of the corridor. "No. He was here?"

"Yes. Romano's injured his knee. Probably needs sutures, but I'll take care of that. Then we need to start moving. Talon knows too much."

Thirty-two

Heading for Old Town and Truman Avenue, Chris made repeated attempts to reach Sonnie by phone.

She didn't pick up.

He knew what he was looking for. For the first time since he'd grudgingly allowed himself to be drawn into Sonnie's intrigue, he felt completely convinced that she wasn't imagining any of the events that had frightened her. Fear might intensify her reactions, but she wouldn't be human if it didn't.

Chris rode over the sidewalk and shot into the driveway of Sonnie's house. He didn't know how long he had before the trio at the club made a move, but the afternoon sun beat down, and he did know that most of this day was past and time was unlikely to be on his side.

He slid to a halt and jumped off the bike.

The front door stood open and Wimpy sat there, blinking against the sun.

"Psst." Someone was behind the dense shrubbery at the base of the veranda steps. "Pretend you don't hear me." Aiden Flynn's voice. "But listen up."

"I can't just stand here."

"Sit on the steps, schmuck. Sonnie's over at Ena's. She doesn't know I'm here. I spoke with Roy and he's worried about you and Sonnie. Says you're taking too long to get things cleaned up.''

As ordered, Chris sat on the steps. Wimpy skittered beside him and hopped on his lap. "This could be the day we've been waiting for. I think this thing's breaking.''

"Me, too,'' Flynn said.

From where he sat, Chris could see Flynn crouched behind the shrubs. "Any particular reason for the theatrics?''

"I think so.'' Flynn must have felt Chris's eyes on him but he made no attempt to turn in his direction. "I barely made it out of sight when the local heat came calling.''

"If you were where you are now, you didn't make it.''

"I wasn't.''

"Okay, so what's up?''

Flynn said, "I dropped here so I could watch for Sonnie to come back—or for someone else to approach Ena's house. I heard what the cops asked Sonnie, though. Someone tried to get out of Miami—international flight—using Edward Miller's papers.''

"Where the hell does that fit in?'' Chris gripped the edge of the step on which he sat. Wimpy promptly planted his forefeet on his chest and studied him closely. The big question was, Who had tried to use Miller's papers? "It's all going down. I knew it. Do we know who the guy is? He didn't make it out, so where is he now?''

"I don't have an ID on him yet, but we'll get it. He's in a Miami hospital and under heavy guard. They arrested him and he collapsed. Then they discovered he'd been beaten—only in places that didn't show when he was dressed—and burned. Poor devil's got infected cigarette burns on his penis and scrotum.''

"God.'' Chris shuddered; then he looked directly at Flynn. "Those fools didn't say that to Sonnie, did they?''

"You bet your boots they did. Shock was what they had in mind. They think she's mixed up in all this. What would you think if you had a stiff show up in a woman's house, then the stiff's papers—missing when the body was found—are used by a guy who talks about Sonnie when he's unconscious?''

Chris wiped his palms on his thighs. By the time the runt

dog finished with him, he could plan on missing a shower. "What d'you mean, talked about her?"

"Just said her name. Damn, it's turned hot. I know I'm not going to get out of this hole before a damn hurricane hits."

"You said you don't know who he is," Chris said. "The police must have said his name to Sonnie."

"She asked. They don't know, either. He wasn't talking about that."

"Who would it be?" Chris took Romano's gun from one pocket and put it into another while he retrieved the list of names.

"I've told you we'll find out. What's with the toy pistol?"

"I confiscated it from Romano Giacano. Actually he gave it to me when he decided to switch tactics from killing me to confessing his wrongdoings and trying to get me to ease his way with Sonnie. How long has she been over there?"

"Maybe fifteen minutes. She went as soon as the cops left."

"Did you get a good look at her?" Chris said. "She look okay?"

"I guess. Listen up and don't interrupt me. I made it to Miami and back in record time. Finding that address was easy. House is owned by a couple. They're away at the moment and there's a house sitter. Unfortunately the couple keep to themselves, so the neighbor I found home couldn't tell me too much. I remembered an old buddy on the force in Tampa. I got really lucky. He was still around and he's running some checks for us. Reckons he'll have names by the end of the day. I told him your E-mail moniker and he'll get to us that way. It'll probably fall flat, but we can hope."

Chris grunted. He'd caught sight of the pink Mustang parked a hundred or so yards up the street. "That car's a liability. See it once and you never forget it."

"I know," Flynn said, almost purring. "Isn't she something? Kinda like your Harley—unforgettable. Fortunately no one connects me to the car or either of us to you. I'm Wally the phantom, remember?"

"If you say so. I'm going to check on Sonnie." He got up and left without looking back. Entering Ena's yard by the gap in the shrubbery fence, he could see that the draperies remained drawn and Sonnie had shut the front door after she was inside.

Chris opened the door and called out "Sonnie" at once. He didn't want to shake her up.

He heard footsteps overhead and started up the stairs. "Sonnie? Ena?"

"I'm here," Sonnie answered. "You came back."

Chris frowned and continued up. "I came back. I said I'd come back. What are you doing?"

She met him at the top of the stairs. "Everything looks exactly the way we left it this morning. Ena was already gone then. She hasn't been back. Not as far as I can see."

"Wait right there," he told her and walked swiftly toward the attic stairs.

He'd returned, Sonnie thought. If she were superstitious she'd be afraid to feel relieved, but she wasn't superstitious.

"Okay," she heard him say. "I want to take a closer look at this." He arrived with a large toolbox and ushered her ahead of him down the stairs.

She followed him into the kitchen with its cluttered cat theme. He put the metal box on Ena's scrubbed, white wood table. He opened it and quickly removed a variety of items. "Tell me what you're doing," she said.

"These are drill bits," he said, opening a small blue metal case. "Several missing." He lifted out a tray to reveal a large compartment below. Another blue case, this one much larger than the first, was empty. "Drill should be in here."

"Maybe it was used to make those holes in the floor—ceiling."

"Uh-huh, but it's not in the attic. Unless whoever went out of the window up there took a drill and bits with him, I'd have expected to find them. I'm going upstairs again."

"Don't, Chris," Sonnie said. "I'm afraid Ena will walk in and get upset that we're poking around here."

"We're looking after her interests as well as ours," Chris said.

She couldn't argue with him. Instead she followed back up

the stairs and along to the room where she'd spent the night—where they'd spent the night.

Chris looked around. He took a bamboo nightstand from beside the bed and climbed on it. Sonnie said, "Be careful. What are you doing?"

He had to bow his head to avoid hitting it on the ceiling. "I thought these were low," he said, and he reached to finger the hole over the bed. "Start looking for a drill."

He confused her, but Sonnie opened drawers and felt around. She went to a freestanding wardrobe and opened it. No clothes hung there. "Everything's so empty here," she said. "I don't know how you live in a place and have so much empty storage."

Chris didn't comment. He went into the bathroom, and returned after a few minutes. Lying on his stomach, he lifted the bedskirt and searched beneath. Sonnie heard a muffled "Shit," but couldn't smile.

"Nothing here," he said as he got to his feet, brushing off his jeans and jean jacket.

Without another word he left and ran downstairs. Sonnie caught up with him in the kitchen, where he was going through the garbage. "What's your best guess about the man they've got in the hospital in Miami?" he said, still rummaging.

"How do you know about that?"

"You don't want me to know?"

"Of course I do, but I haven't had a chance to tell you, so—"

"My buddy Flynn was eavesdropping. Shit," he repeated, pushing the garbage back under the sink and looking around. He opened a drawer in the table. A tidy line of wooden spoons greeted them. "She's got stuff where you can see it, and nothing in places where stuff wouldn't be seen."

"The police said they were bound to find out who the man is. They weren't very nice to me, but I think they suspect me of being in on something awful."

Chris went from drawer to drawer and was shutting the last one when he grew still. He drew out a plastic bag and opened it.

"What?" Sonnie said.

He held it open where she could see inside. "Sawdust? In a kitchen drawer?" She reached inside to touch the fine wood shavings and felt something hard. "A nail in a bag of sawdust?" she said, withdrawing the nail.

"And pieces of painter's tape at the top of the bag," Chris said. "Theory?"

Sonnie shrugged. "I pass."

"Someone made a hole in the bedroom ceiling with that nail—just to mark the spot. They dropped the nail into the bag, then taped the bag to the ceiling with painters' masking tape. Won't pull off the paint. After that he went to the attic, found the tiny hole, and drilled another one on that spot, making it big enough to give a clear view into the room below. Take away the bag with the sawdust, and there you have it. Could be the other holes were made with nothing more sophisticated than the nail—or maybe a bigger nail. The sawdust was added to the rest. But why put this bag in a kitchen drawer, and where's the drill?"

"And who did it?" Sonnie said.

Chris's phone rang. He picked up and said, "Yeah?"

"It's Mustang Man. Just making sure you've got the phone on. I told Roy to go into your shack and keep an eye on incoming E-mail. That okay?"

"Would it matter if I said it wasn't?"

"My friend in Tampa could be getting back to us at any time. Chris, I don't think we should hang around any longer than we have to—with you in that house, that is. I don't feel good about it."

"We'll be over there shortly." Chris switched off. "Just as soon as I'm convinced I can't find the damn drill."

Sonnie kept right behind him. Whenever possible, she helped by searching cupboards or drawers or wardrobes. "This house is too empty," she said. "Just like you said. Everything is where you can see it."

"Yup," Chris said. "But Ena didn't have time to do any packing, did she?"

"I don't think so." She'd be happy just to watch Chris forever. He moved smoothly, performed tasks deftly and without wasteful fumbling. Even set in concentration, his face was more handsome than any other. His mouth tilted up very slightly, but that tilt had nothing to do with smiling right now. And she loved his hands. She knew they could break things, but they could also be so careful.

"Sonnie, what's the matter with you?"

She started. He'd caught her staring at his hands and doing absolutely nothing. "I'm fine," she said. "I was just trying to think of somewhere clever to look for a drill."

He took his time looking away again.

Chris's phone rang again. "Yeah," he said, scowling this time.

He straightened slowly, listening intently. "Could be a coincidence. I'll check that out."

Once more he switched off, and this time he caught Sonnie off guard by whipping her into his arms and holding her tight. "We've got to concentrate. I've got to concentrate. I can't do that without the right inspiration. You're the right inspiration. A minute out for a necessity."

Sonnie looked up at him and he kissed her. He put a lot of thought, a lot of finesse into that kiss. When this woman kissed you, you knew you'd been kissed. And it wasn't ending. Sonnie seemed determined to make contact with every cell that made up his mouth. They both withdrew at the same instant. Sonnie rubbed his chest and smiled at him. On tiptoe again, she nibbled his jaw, blew into his ear.

Take-charge time. Holding her just far enough away to allow the tasting party to go on, it was his turn to grin. "I could have my way with you, darlin'," he said, and homed in to kiss her mouth. "But I'm goin' to be merciful just now." He still held her, but he'd always been a man who multitasked well.

"You've got a gun," Sonnie said, this time trying to put some distance between them. "You could kill someone with that."

The old dilemma: how did a man with a cop history tell a woman that the reason for carrying a gun was to try to calm a situation down, not to kill? Although Chris knew he could pull the trigger if he needed to.

"Chris," Sonnie said. "You're not a cop anymore. Why the gun?"

"Habit," he told her, absolutely honest. "You'll never find a cop, active or otherwise, who doesn't have a gun."

He could tell he'd made no points with his explanation.

"Guns frighten me," Sonnie said.

"That's healthy. They aren't toys. Sonnie, now we have to make every second count. I'm going to call the hospitals in Miami and see if I can track down the man who took Edward's papers. The police could leave you alone and be just as far ahead. But I would put money on the guy with the papers having been in your house—killing Edward so he could get at the papers he needed."

"Surely the cops must be thinking along those lines."

"Some cops may be. I'm going to make some calls. Keep looking for the drill."

Sonnie continued in the kitchen, where she could hear what Chris was up to.

He made three calls before the expression on his face lightened. "Surely I can hold," he said. "Sonnie, I think I've got it. She's checking."

Sonnie nodded and went on to finish with every drawer in the kitchen. Nothing.

"Hey," she said, "best hiding place of all. Right in front of our faces." A drill rested on the back of a framed picture that had been left facedown on the bucket rest of a small ladder.

Chris mouthed *Yes,* then said, "You're sure? He's been beaten, and he's got burns on his body. I'm supposed to relieve the cop who's guarding him now." He covered the mouthpiece and said, "Good job on the drill. I may have found the right hospital. From the way they're behaving, they've got to have a patient under guard. At least they didn't deny it."

He'd put the list of names on the counter and didn't try to stop Sonnie from picking it up. She took the phone book Chris was no longer using and began flipping through pages and, where available, adding numbers beside names.

"Still here," Chris said into the mouthpiece. "That's our man. What's his condition? Yes. I do thank you for your time.

Excuse me? I didn't quite hear that. Oh, I see. You're a gem, nurse. Make sure he's taken good care of until I can get there.

"I'm damned." He hung up and said, "Cory Bledsoe. How about that? The only other person we're going to tell about this is Flynn. Sonnie, things are going to get really dirty. You heard what happened to Bledsoe—can you believe he was trying to use Miller's papers?"

"I can believe anything," she told him. "I'll check again, but I think I've got all the listed numbers."

He took the list back from her and stuck it into a jacket pocket. "Cory Bledsoe had access to Edward Miller's possessions. And he had to have time to search for what he wanted."

"So he's been in this house, too," Sonnie said. "He must have been because all of Edward's things were here. I'm glad we've already found what we were looking for. Edward's room gave me the creeps."

Chris drummed his finger on a counter.

"Hey, Edward's room's empty," Sonnie said.

"You've got that right. And it shouldn't be unless the police told Ena she could clean up in there. I want to get back to your house. And I want this drill." He returned to the kitchen and grabbed the box containing bits. "I might need it."

"Why?" Sonnie asked. "What would you drill?"

"Nothing if I find what I want quickly." He could hope.

The phone rang yet again. "Yeah," Chris said. "F—frig it, Flynn. I don't have time to appease my brother right now. I've got to deal with something over there, and fast."

He listened to Aiden again. "Okay, okay, I'm on my way right now. I'll be setting down a drill and some bits by your shrubbery. Get them inside; then make yourself scarce again. By the way, the guy who tried to use Edward Miller's documents is Cory Bledsoe. He's the athletic director at the club, and . . . Yeah, well, I'm telling you now. Watch your back."

"Why are we going to Roy and Bo's?" Sonnie asked.

"You wouldn't be if I could leave you here." With the drill and box of bits in one arm he walked toward the door. "Come on, damn it. When we get there, you stay at the Nail. Got that? I'll be at my place."

She didn't agree or disagree, but she walked with him to the Harley and admired the nonchalant way he slid the drill and bits into some bushes. The items quickly disappeared. Chris glanced at her and said, "Let's go." In other words, he didn't want her to ask more questions.

They set off for Duval, passing a woman raking palm fronds a few houses from Sonnie's. Chris yelled, "Hold on, I'm going back."

She clung to his jacket while he made a U-turn and came to a stop near the woman. "Hi," he said. "Do you know of any property for sale around here?"

"Depends what you want," she said. "Nothing right here. Maybe farther out, I don't know."

"Thanks anyway," Chris said. "I thought you might have heard about something about to come on the market."

"No," the woman said. "Best you go to the realtors. They know."

"Would they know about rental properties, too?"

Sonnie had no idea what was on his mind.

"Rentals are mostly word-of-mouth around here," the woman said. "Any vacancies, they're filled right away. That's a rental"—she pointed to a house across the street—"and the one next to it."

"Nothing this side, though?"

"No—oh, sure." Her tanned skin gleamed and her gray hair was cut to a short buzz. "That one. Not next to me, but next to that. And there are lots of good boardinghouses."

Chris thanked her and set off again. "Ena's renting," Sonnie shouted. "Been renting a long time, I guess."

"Nothing to be lost by stopping at a realtor's and seeing what we can find out."

"About Ena's house? Why would we do that?"

"To see if she's been in touch with them about leaving."

He stopped at the first realty office they came to. "You want to come?"

"No. You'll be quicker without me."

"Okay." She heard his relief and smiled. He wasn't used to toting a civilian along when he was working.

He ran through a door plastered with ads.

Someone tapped her arm and she spun around.

"Don't scream." The man from the Nail, the one who'd threatened her, stood there. Today he wore a neat, button-down shirt—navy blue with a red stripe around each sleeve.

Sonnie glanced toward the realty office.

"No, no," the man said. "Don't be scared. I just wanted to see you, that's all."

Another psychopath. "Get away," she told him. "Come any closer and I'll scream so loud you'll be buried in people."

He was clean shaven and she noticed his well-pressed pants and brown loafers. And his wedding ring.

"What is it with you?" Sonnie said. "Are you sick? Other than the kind of sick we already know about?"

He shook his head and said, "Please keep your voice down. I just want to ask you a favor. That's what I've been trying to do for days."

Sonnie prayed for Chris to come back.

"Look," the man said, and he pulled a photo from his pocket. "This is my wife. If she knew I got drunk the way I did, I don't know what she'd do to me."

Sonnie gave the photo of a dark-haired woman a cursory glance.

"I'm really sorry I was such an ass—I mean, so rude to you. I'd gone out with a group of the boys. Convention. You know how it is."

She didn't. And she didn't care.

"Margie's arriving this afternoon. For our second honeymoon. Will you promise not to ... Well, if you did see her ..."

"Don't worry," she told him, with an urge to laugh. "But you'd better go away before my friend gets back. He's bigger than me."

"Thank you." The man sighed and wiped sweat from his brow. He backed away. "Oh, thank you." He backed up until he bumped into a police barrier, and turned to hurry away.

Sonnie didn't know whether or not she felt relieved. She'd believed him. So now she'd checked off one vague suspect. Big deal.

When there was time, she'd tell Chris.

Ten minutes passed before he reappeared. He carried a sheaf of pamphlets. When he reached Sonnie he seemed about to say something. Instead he pushed the pamphlets into a saddlebag and mounted the bike.

"Chris," she said, indignant. "Are you going to tell me what they said in there?"

"Ena's place is owned by a woman who moved to Atlanta to live with her daughter. That was last year. I said I'd be interested in renting the property. The agent took out the file on the place. He said he thought the lease on it was coming up in a month or so." Chris turned until he could look at Sonnie. "The house was rented by Ena Fishbine. She used a P.O. box in Miami. Good references. She's paid up for two more months. She moved in a few days before you arrived. Didn't you tell me she talked about seeing you and Frank when you lived here together?"

"Yes. Roy was there. But . . . There was always a woman next door. I saw her. She . . . She kept to herself. I didn't meet her." A woman who parked her car at the foot of the front steps while she carried in her groceries. "A blond woman. Like Ena."

"But not Ena," Chris said.

Sonnie thought back. "I didn't take much notice. Chris, it doesn't make sense that Ena would be mixed up in this, does it?"

He faced forward again. "It may not make sense, but she's involved. That woman is a newcomer to Key West. Why should she lie about that?"

The sun had brought out throngs of tourists and other members of the aimless. They wandered, eating out of bags, looking in windows, overflowing the curbs on narrow Duval Street. And everywhere the music played. A serpentine of tie-dye-clad teens forced Chris to a halt. They danced across the street to the strains of their leader's boom box.

But it took only a couple more minutes to reach the alley at the back of the Nail. "Please go tell Roy I'm out here," Chris said. "I've got to get to the computer."

Sonnie ran to the back door and let herself into the bar. She grabbed Roy's arm, said, "I'm borrowing him, Bo," and dragged Roy outside. "Chris is getting on his computer. Evidently it's very important. I don't know why."

"About one more hour, Sonnie, girl, and I'd have rounded up a posse to hunt the pair of you down."

Sonnie knocked on Chris's door, but walked in without being invited. Roy overtook her and stood behind his brother.

"Who's that?" Roy asked. Sonnie couldn't see the screen.

"Friend of Flynn's in Tampa went looking for names to match an address I found," Chris said. "I don't know who they are. Mitchell and Annette Roberts. Doesn't ring any bells, but their address was in Ena's attic. I'm sure it wouldn't have been if we hadn't showed up last night."

"Here's an attached file from our helper."

Sonnie edged behind the two men to stand on the other side of Chris. "Mitchell and Annette Roberts," she said. "Why would they mean anything to us? Who knows where the furniture in that attic came from? Could have been a garage sale or something."

"You're right," Chris said. "But Annette's got a record. She's done time—more than once. That's why we're about to see a mug shot."

"What did she do?" Sonnie asked.

"Stalker," Chris replied. "Malicious mischief. Harassment. And here she is."

The unflattering shot was of Ena. Dark haired, younger, but still Ena.

Thirty-three

Chris looked sideways at Sonnie. She walked with more difficulty than usual.

"I know it isn't far to your house, but I still think we should take my bike," he said. "Or use Roy's car."

"Walking does me good. I haven't exercised enough lately. And it probably takes about the same length of time anyway."

Even in the short time they'd been at Roy and Bo's, the crowds had swelled. They passed the brilliant white facade of St. Paul's Church and heard organ music. Sonnie pressed Chris's arm and climbed to the forecourt. She peered in through the open doors and saw a man playing a grand piano in the center of the nave. "Come on," she called to Chris, urging him to join her. "Listen. 'Greensleeves.' Visions of cool English brooks and butterflies, gentle sunshine and peace. Think I might be stressed?"

"Have you been to England?"

She shook her head no. "But I'd like to. Frank . . . Frank went there lots of times, of course."

"But he never took you."

Sonnie knew Chris wasn't asking a question. "It's still there, and there's still time."

He smiled. "We're both overdue some hours in quiet places,

Sonnie.'' Sliding an arm around her shoulders, he whispered in her ear, ''We're going to make it happen, darlin'. You and me and the kind of life we both need.''

When she looked at him, her features were sharp, her expression searching. ''What does that mean?''

What does it mean? ''I want you and me to be together. For as long as our forever turns out to be. Does that explain enough?''

She pulled him into the shade. ''Look at me, Chris. You're sorry for me. You'd like to fix me. But maybe I'm not fixable.''

''We both know better than that. You became the center of some kind of plot. I admit it's more complicated than I thought, but it's starting to show all of its faces. I want you because I want you. The whole package. How about you?''

She closed her eyes and rested her brow on his chest. ''After you left this morning, I went to take a nap. I woke up because Frank's old rocking chair was banging against the windows. It wasn't even there before. More voices. More noises. A baby sobbing as if her heart was broken. I went into Jacqueline's room and saw what I thought was a baby moving in the bassinet. It was a battery-operated doll I bought for when Jacqueline got older. Then I fell apart. But it's all explainable. I could have put that doll in the bed. I could have moved the rocking chair.

''Chris, I may be mentally ill. You can't tie yourself to an insane woman.''

He held one of her elbows and jerked her toward him. ''Don't you ever say that again. Will you marry me, Sonnie?''

She began to cry. She couldn't help it.

Chris bent to kiss away the tears. ''Answer me. Will you throw your lot in with a wreck like me?''

''Now whose putting himself down?''

He kissed the side of her neck. ''I'd like to try to have children of our own. I'd take very good care of you. We'd make sure everything went fine.''

''Christian Talon, you're deliberately making me cry. I'd love to marry you. And I'd love us to try to have children. But I'm up to my teeth in uncertainties. We've got to get past those first.''

"All right. Good enough. We have a tentative agreement. Now we're going to move so fast there'll be some people who don't know what slugged 'em."

He hurried, but sensed when he was going too fast. Without ceremony, he hauled Sonnie onto a wall, turned, and wrapped his arms under her legs. "Piggyback time. Hold on tight."

Alternately jogging and executing unlikely dance steps, he got them to Sonnie's place in record time. The pink Mustang had gone, the front door was closed, and there was still no sign of activity next door.

"Just let me do my thing, okay?" he said. "I want you to wait in your bedroom and don't ask any questions until I come to you."

"Okay." She didn't sound enthusiastic.

Chris urged her into her room and shut the door. Immediately he retrieved the drill and bits from the parlor where Flynn had left them and returned upstairs as quietly as he could.

He found a trapdoor into the attic in a spare bedroom closet. The trap had a recessed ring, and by standing on a stool he was able to slide the trap open. An obviously new length of rope with a knot in the end dropped down. A tug on this produced steps that glided noiselessly downward. All very well designed and oiled—and new. The police had been here before him. They'd searched the attic after Edward's murder. But what Chris was hoping to find might not be evident to anyone who wasn't looking for it.

The flashlight he'd brought was powerful. If there were visitors before he'd finished, and his theory was correct, he might have to turn off the heavy-duty flashlight. Then he'd have to rely on a small pocket light.

Once at the top of the steps, he hauled them up, closed the trap, and put on the flashlight. Wide wooden slats had been laid between beams. A man might praise his luck for having his job made so much easier and safer, only in this case, Chris knew the extra care had been taken for others.

The idea of coming up here had started to form when he'd been in the attic next door. That and the way Romano had looked upward when he spoke of what Sonnie insisted she'd heard. This attic wouldn't allow anyone but a child to stand upright. He crawled forward on hands and knees, examining everything around him as he went.

A sharp turn took him into a wider space. Chris got close to the ductwork that ran the length of the area and curved around and out of sight toward whatever was beyond this place. He took the small flashlight from his pocket and moved slowly along, examining the air-conditioning ducts. When he reached the farthest end of the space he'd drawn a blank, but then he saw a large, dark kit bag that closed with a drawstring.

The police wouldn't have missed it.

He pulled it open and lifted some of the contents into the beam of his light. Top hats, wigs, cloaks, glittery things . . . silk scarves. Edward's theatrical gear.

The police hadn't missed it because it hadn't been there immediately after the fire. Someone had brought it later, used it later.

He took out the Glock and checked it, then replaced it in the holster. He preferred to stick his weapon in the waist of his pants, but he was running into too many situations when he needed to be sure the piece couldn't fall.

The sharp turn took him along another narrow corridor, then into one more spacious area. There was another bag there, a grip. This contained cans of food and blankets, and tools— including a drill. So much for hunting down the one next door.

Some hours ago Chris had begun to see that there could be two parallel operations under way against Sonnie. Cory Bledsoe was the player who didn't fit. Calls to several of the women on the list hadn't provided much, except for the fact that they'd all worked at the club and they'd left because of harassment. They didn't want to explain, but he got a marked reaction to the mention of Cory's name. One woman still worked at the club, and she was frightened for her job. She had a small child and no husband and didn't want Mr. Bledsoe to think she'd talked about him. Chris told her she wouldn't have to worry about Mr. Bledsoe anymore because the man was opting to leave the club himself. Then the dam broke and he learned more about the sexual excesses of Cory than he wanted to know.

Why didn't the woman report her boss? No one would believe what she said. It was too weird. He used to make her strip and lie on his bed, and if she moved, he hit her. He would roll up her paycheck and insert it into her vagina, then use it to make her climax. More recently he'd wanted her to masturbate in front of him. Sometimes he'd want sex with her, but he never climaxed. And she had to be careful not to let him get her alone when she was working because if she had a full tray in her hands, he'd pull her skirt up to her waist and she'd have to all but drop the tray to cover herself. She didn't want to say any more, but the golf pro who supposedly left with a married woman had decided he couldn't work for Bledsoe. This happened after the pro was invited for drinks with Cory, only to find himself expected to take part in having sex with a number of women while Cory watched.

Why didn't anyone squeal?

Because Cory said he had something on each of them, and his own record was squeaky clean. Chris had heard all he needed to hear.

What did Cory have to do with Sonnie?

Chris continued to scrutinize the ducts, and then he found what he was looking for. At one point a separate branch left the main line. He figured this must be connected to a vent into a bedroom. He wasn't sure which one. Where the joints had originally come together, there were scratches, and the seams had been forced apart. Inefficient for the cooling system, but possibly useful for other things. He shone the flashlight into the opening and instantly saw that he hadn't been far off in his theory about drills. Pinpoints of light showed against the sloping walls, and when he bent to look at the other side of the ductwork, he saw where a number of holes had been drilled.

Chris made his way back to the second floor and went to Sonnie's room. Wearing a fresh white cotton jumpsuit, and with her hair brushed back and coiled at her nape, she sat on the side of her bed. Beside her was a scattering of powdery valentine heart candies—each one faceup, where she could read what it said.

She looked abashed. "I'm too nervous to just sit here. Frank loved these. He always kept them in his drawer."

"No accounting for taste." He wrinkled his nose at the sweet, perfumed scent of them. "Sonnie, I've found what I expected to find. In the attic. There's nothing wrong with you, sweetheart. I want you to stay where you are. Expect to hear your name." He wafted a hand airily. "Somewhere up there. If you do, shout back to me."

Sonnie crossed her ankles and sat rigidly upright.

Chris made another expedition to the attic. When he reached the first duct that had been tampered with, he put his mouth close to the metal and said, "Sonnie?" He raised his voice and repeated, "Sonnie?"

"Yes," came her answer.

"Does that sound as if it's floating by the ceiling?"

"Yes."

"Well, it is. It's coming through holes in the air-conditioning ductwork. Now walk around upstairs and see if you hear me again."

He crawled all over the attic and found join after join pried open, and more holes drilled in between. He continued to shout, and Sonnie continued to respond. "Okay, let me take a few photos. There's a cape and some wigs I want you to look at. Try to relax till I'm done."

Sonnie smiled so hard her face hurt. She shouldn't be so happy to learn she'd been set up, but she was. They'd done a great job of convincing her she was losing her mind. But, thanks to Chris, they'd failed. She walked downstairs, aware of the toes on her right foot being swollen. Once all this was behind her, she'd concentrate on getting the best of treatment to help her manage her injuries better. And, when it was time, she'd go ahead with the facial plastic surgery.

And maybe she and Chris would have a life together. But she needed to make sure she could also be independent. She ought to have something she could do. Maybe she'd like to study interior design. She'd often been told she had a flair for creating appealing home spaces. Why not make something of that?

Wimpy showed up with leaves sticking out of his fur. She set him on a chair in the parlor and picked them out. Then she spread a throw and settled him on top. He rested back, and she would almost swear he made a swooning noise.

She heard the front door open and started for the foyer. They hadn't locked it? If she yelled, would Chris hear her? She should stay where she was. The wind was picking up yet again and could have blown the door open.

Wimpy whined.

Sonnie retreated to sit beside him and stroke him. She bent over him and whispered, "It's okay. I'm here."

Someone wearing sneakers was taking his or her time to walk across the tiled floor in the foyer. Every few steps, the noise stopped. The person mounted the stairs.

Chris. What if they surprised Chris?

If she did anything impetuous, she could cause him to be harmed. This could be someone who'd wandered off the street looking for shelter—or to steal.

Minutes had never passed so slowly for Sonnie. And as they passed, her terror mounted. She heard footfalls overhead, but they were still soft, light.

Please don't let Chris call out again.

Wimpy made pathetic snuffling noises and croaking half growls that seemed to surprise him more than Sonnie.

If Chris climbed out of the attic he could walk directly into harm's way without expecting anything to happen. Sure, he had a gun, but would there be time to use it if he was totally surprised?

She didn't want to think about him shooting someone.

The intruder was going through every bedroom. So slowly. So slowly before he descended the stairs making a sound as if he took a step, then brought the second foot to meet it. As if he was injured.

Could Cory Bledsoe have escaped and come back? Who

knew what his part was in all this? He'd been injured—tortured, really. Perhaps that happened because someone else wasn't happy with whatever he was supposed to have done about her. Now he might be here to try to prove he could do the job better.

He came toward the parlor.

A sound came from overhead, a ringing. She turned cold, then hot. Chris's cell phone. A faint ringing, but surely the intruder would hear and wonder where it came from.

Sonnie stood up with Wimpy in her arms. Her heart beat hard. "Hush," she told the dog, "don't be frightened." But she knew the message was for herself.

The door swung open, catching on carpet as it always did so that it had to be repeatedly pushed.

"Oh, Sonnie, there you are. I didn't know where I'd look for you next. No one knows I'm here—yet. But they'll catch up."

Wimpy struggled and Sonnie couldn't hold him anymore. He dropped to the floor and stood there, panting.

"Come here and let me look at you, Sonnie." Frank Giacano, so like his brother facially, had always been much thinner, but never as thin as he was now. Now he was little more than skin stretched over bone. His eyes still had the liquid quality Sonnie had fallen in love with, and with his facial bones accentuated he was almost unbearably handsome. "I came to you first, to let you know how important you are to me."

She blinked to clear her vision, and felt light-headed. Everything in the room seemed to tilt away at an angle. She took a step to steady herself, but her legs wouldn't stay braced.

"*Cara mia,*" Frank said. "You have been through so much, and now I have shocked you. Come, let me help you to bed. But first you must introduce me to my child."

She felt him hold her wrists, but could do nothing to resist, or to help herself. "I don't want to go to bed, thank you," she said, aware of the enormity of this exchange.

Frank released her. He laced his emaciated fingers together, and she saw how he trembled. A purplish hue shaded his deepened eye sockets. "Tell me what I should do," he said. "I . . . I don't know what to do."

"Perhaps you should sit down." What should she tell him to do? She didn't want him here—he frightened her, yet she was sorry for him.

Frank sat on the couch, just as she'd suggested. His clothes hung from his shoulders. On his feet he wore canvas sneakers with holes across the toes. His hair, black when she'd last seen him, hung to his shoulders and was liberally streaked with gray.

Sonnie had never expected to feel pity for Frank, but she pitied him now. "What have they done to you?" she asked him. "I'll call a doctor."

"No," he told her, smiling faintly. "A doctor cannot help. There's a lot I'd like to share with you, but not tonight, not so soon. Tonight I only need to be with you."

He had never treated her with either such gentleness or such singular attention. "I will tell you that I was abducted," he said. "They took me from place to place until I no longer knew where I was. At first they said they intended to hold me for ransom. Then they said I would become more valuable as a hostage they could offer in exchange for some of their own people. I never even knew who they were. But you don't need to worry about that. Sonnie, I've had a long, lonely time to think. I missed you so much. In the middle of all that time, all I could concentrate on was you, on needing to be with you and take care of you. I have prayed that you will allow me a new chance. Allow us to start again, Sonnie. Please."

Chris descended the stairs so fast he barely touched them. A jumbled call had come for him, jumbled but with enough detail for him to get the message. He had to get to Roy. One of those damned old wooden racks over the bar at the Nail had come loose. Glasses had cascaded down, and Roy had been in the line of fire. He'd been rushed to the emergency room at the hospital on Stock Island.

"Sonnie, where are you?" he yelled, and skidded to a halt in the doorway to the parlor.

"Chris?" Sonnie said. "It's Frank."

He needed no introduction to recognize the man—even though he'd never seen him. "Back from the dead," he said, too bemused to temper his reactions.

"Sonnie?" Frank Giacano said. "Who is this man?"

"A friend," Sonnie said. "My good friend." She kept her eyes trained on Chris's as if he could magically change what was happening—or make it go away.

"I have to leave," Chris said. "Now. I want you to come with me."

"Trouble?" Sonnie asked.

He would not discuss anything personal in front of a stranger he hated on sight. "Yes. Let's go."

Sonnie stood close enough to her husband for him to grasp her hand. "Don't leave me," he said—begged. "I could come with you, if you must go."

"Frank"—Sonnie looked at him—"wait for me here. I'll come back as soon as I can."

The man stood up and clutched her arm. "Please, no." He fought, unsuccessfully, against tears. "I can't bear to be alone again." Turning his attention to Chris, he said, "Give me some time with my wife, please. I don't know you, but if you are her friend, then allow her to comfort me."

"I can't—" He'd started to say he couldn't leave her with him. "Sonnie? I've got to go."

Fear stretched the skin over her facial bones. He felt how she held back questions about whatever was troubling him. "Go," she said. "I'll be fine. But get back as soon as you can, okay?"

"Okay." Still he couldn't make himself leave. "Sonnie, maybe—"

"Just go." Her eyes were moistly luminous. "Now. Hurry."

"Yes. You're right. I'll call the second I can." He couldn't make himself look at Giacano again. The most important thing to carry with him was that Sonnie didn't want to be with Frank—she stayed because her husband was pathetic and in obvious need of help.

Chris walked out, and when Sonnie finally drew her gaze

from the spot where he'd stood, she looked into Frank's sad face. "Did you find someone else while I was gone?" he said. "How can I blame you? I can't. Loneliness and fear are too much for someone as weak as you. But I am with you now, and I will always be with you." His trembling grip turned to steel on her fingers.

Thirty-four

"What in hell's name is going on around here?" Chris said, walking into the guest house. He glared at Roy. "There's a hurricane brewing out there. For real this time. If it doesn't hit us straight on, we'll still get bounced around good. I get a call from some maniac—don't ask me who—telling me there's been an accident and you've been carved like the Thanksgiving turkey, so I grab a cab and rush to Stock Island, only to find out they don't know a thing about any accident at the Rusty Nail. Then I get back here to find Pep tending the bar on a busy night and you two hanging out in *my* pad. What gives?"

Occasionally shaking rain from the hat he held, Roy stood behind Bo at Chris's computer. He spared Chris a glance, but only that. Bo sat at the keyboard, apparently checking Chris's E-mail.

"Is anyone going to talk to me before I have to leave again?" Chris said.

Flynn came through the open door, said, "Hi, all," and went directly to swing a leg over the Harley's saddle and sit.

"This day started out as a fraud," Flynn said. "Sunshine to fool us. Just listened to the weather. They reckon we're going to get the edge of a hurricane by sometime tonight.

They're not talking about evacuation, but they are suggesting battening things down.''

"Thanks for the weather forecast. I don't lean on your Mustang; get the hell off my Harley,'' Chris said, not caring how juvenile he sounded. "Then go away, all of you. Do something useful, like find something to batten. But first, did something fall on you in the bar, Roy? Did you have to go to the hospital? And did you get someone to call me?''

"I don't know what you're talking about,'' Roy said. "You see any sign of me needing to go to the hospital? We came over because Aiden called in and said we should watch for a message from some friend of his. Haven't seen anything since we got here.''

"Right,'' Chris said. "So I fell for a setup. I'm outa here.'' And his heart did nasty, suffocating things.

Flynn sounded the Harley's horn, sending all hands to ears. Then he grinned and said, "Got your attention.''

Fortunately the urge to land a punch on Aiden's grinning mouth didn't last long enough for Chris to follow through. "Frank Giacano surfaced again. He's at Sonnie's. Looks like he's wrecked, but I don't trust him. I've got to get back there.''

"Holy hell,'' Aiden muttered. "What a shock. You think he's dangerous to her?''

"No,'' Chris said with complete honesty. "I just don't like her being with him. And I want to know who called me— called me away, folks.''

"Well, it wasn't Frank Giacano if he was with Sonnie, was it?'' Bo pointed out. "You'd better cool it, Christian J., or you could end up looking possessive and overbearing and all the things Sonnie didn't like in good ol' Frank.''

"Yeah,'' Aiden said. "And the way it is now, I think she loves you. Now, that doesn't say much for her judgment, it's true, but who ever understood the way a woman's mind works? And I think you love her, schmuck.''

Chris rubbed his skinned knuckles. "I do.''

"Glad we've got that straight,'' Roy said. "What do you know that I don't know?''

"This has been a wild day.'' Chris wiped at rainwater that

ran from his hair. "Everything Sonnie talked about happened. The voices, the whole thing. It would take too long to go into it now." He checked the clip in his gun and pulled his jacket over the weapon again.

Flynn stood up. "Seems tonight's the night. Showdown time. We'd better get on the road. Cory Bledsoe's going to be brought back to Key West under guard. Seems the local boys have kindly volunteered to cooperate by staging a little get-together designed to bring on the songbirds."

"I don't get it," Chris said.

"Neither did I until—did I mention I flew up to Miami?— I didn't get it till I got into the hospital and managed not to get assassinated for being NYPD. All it took was humility on my part. I'd *looove* to work in Miami." He rolled his eyes. "But we need to get Sonnie out of the way. That means out of her house, because that's where the action's expected to take place. Don't worry; we've got time. No need to panic her."

"Quit yakking," Chris said. "Flynn, travel with me. That Mustang is a beauteous thing, but it does get noticed. Roy, I think it might be—"

"You know where I'll be if you need me," Roy said. The voice was light again, but the eyes were old and scared. "Be careful though."

Chris looked away and went for the computer. He leaned over Bo's shoulder. "I'll just make sure nothing else came in." He looked at the list of mail and said, "No. Hey, Flynn, there is something else from your buddy. Subject says it's for you."

Wind hammered the metal building and the walls moved. Chris glanced from Roy to Flynn, but neither of them commented.

Flynn left the bike and opened the post. " 'Annette Roberts's husband was a magician,' " he read aloud. " 'Got a picture of him from a local newspaper archive. Probably won't help, but I've attached it. Later.' "

The downloaded picture opened on the screen. Flynn turned to Chris and Roy and said, "Now, that's a face I know."

"Edward Miller," Chris said, "alias Mitchell Roberts. This has been weird, but it's getting weirder. Edward was Ena's husband. Write back to the guy. Thank him, and we'll get going. One of us had better stick close to Sonnie. Then it's time to see what the club contingent is up to. By the way, I ought to mention that they think they might be happier with me dead, so I'll be keeping my eyes open wide.''

"Shit," Roy said with feeling. "That means the plans go this way. Aiden, you go to the club. I'll be watching Chris's back wherever he chooses to be while he's watching Sonnie."

"Who made you chief?" Chris said.

"I did," Roy told him. "And that's the way it's going to be until I'm not needed."

Sonnie wanted to leave. She wanted to go in search of Chris and never come back. But she couldn't do anything but remain where she was until he contacted her.

Talking to Frank had already exhausted her, and she wanted to escape the haunted stare from his sunken eyes.

"Sit with me in the kitchen," he said. He had paced the room for most of the last hour, stopping from time to time to look at her where she sat on the couch. "I will make us coffee. We have a great deal to talk about. We have a future to plan, *cara*. And I have to find a way to grieve for our child without making you suffer again."

Sonnie made straightening her jumpsuit an excuse for avoiding Frank's outstretched hand. When she'd told him Jacqueline had died, he sobbed and pointed an accusing finger at her before he begged her forgiveness for his selfishness. She didn't want to touch him. She got up and went ahead of him into the kitchen.

"I don't want to freshen your pain, but you said there was a crash and you lost the baby. And you were seriously injured."

She began making the coffee herself. "The Volvo looked as if it had already been to the wrecking yard. I saw pictures."

"You lost control. I got an old newspaper clipping and it detailed your injuries."

"They assume I lost control. I don't remember anything." He bemused her. "If you've seen a clipping, you know the whole story.'' When did he get a clipping, and where? And the clipping would have detailed their baby's death.

"I wanted to hear about it from you,'' Frank said. He stood beside her and lifted her hair away from her scars. "So horrible. I noticed at once, but why dwell on what can't be changed? You will never look the same. And there were so many bruises and lacerations. The broken jaw. The hip. Your toes. It's amazing you didn't die.''

He was the same old Frank, the same man who dwelled on the superficial. "Yes. I have a lot of other scars from lacerations.'' She didn't care how repulsive he found the details. "On my back. And from burns on my hip.''

Frank's mouth turned down. "I am so sorry. It must be very hard for a woman like you to have so much visible damage.''

"No, Frank. I was never the one concerned about physical appearance. Remember? That was you. How did you escape?''

"They got careless for just long enough. A crowd of tourists wandered into an area where they didn't belong. Those men ordered them away, I can tell you. And I wandered away with them. I had been brought to the States, to D.C. for some reason. I had no documents, but I went to someone who could produce enough ID for me to be able to establish that I am who I say I am, and flew down here at once. I'm not kidding myself, though. I'd give it twenty-four hours at the most before the press gets a hint and they descend.''

Rain hit the windows so hard the panes rattled. The sky had turned a deep purple, and wind drew down the palms like loaded slingshots.

Sonnie gave Frank a mug of steaming coffee. "I need to go out, Frank. You'll be fine here. Did you talk to Romano yet?''

The expression on his face shocked her. Something very near hate made hard brackets for his mouth. He quickly produced a smile. "I wanted to see no one but you, Sonnie. You are the one I have wronged. I had months to think about that and to suffer about that.''

"You look tired,'' she told him. "Take a nap while I'm out. Can I get you anything?'' She was desperate to go to Chris.

"I'm not tired. And you know I never nap. Don't leave me." He patted the chair beside his. "I just want to look at you. I'm sure the baby would have looked just like you."

Sonnie closed her eyes. "I should have been able to save her." She began to ache.

"We won't speak of it again unless you want to," Frank said. "But I would like us to start another pregnancy, *cara,* and soon."

Sonnie sat down, but opposite Frank rather than beside him. "You'll have to give me space." She couldn't tell him she wanted no part of him, not now or ever. Just the thought of being intimate with him disgusted her. "I'll have to think things through."

He looked down into his coffee and stirred it slowly with a spoon. "It's the ex-cop, isn't it? Christian Talon. You two have got together and you don't want to give him up. He is different for you, exciting. But tattoos, *cara?*" He smirked. "I understand, but you will get over him. These things happen when a person is lonely and grieving."

"Sonnie? It's me, Billy," Billy called from the foyer.

Sonnie had been too engrossed to hear a car outside, or someone coming into the house.

"Sonnie, where are you?"

"We're in the kitchen," Frank said, grinning, apparently at the prospect of delivering another shock.

"We're to expect the edge of a hurricane. It'll be major winds and a lot of rain, but not the whole thing."

Billy burst in. Wearing black sweats and carrying an oversize black bag—and with her hair drawn back into a single braid—she looked wholesome and appealing.

"Surprise," Frank said, getting up.

Billy dropped her bag. Her mouth opened and remained so.

"It's so good to see you," Frank said, and folded her in an embrace Billy returned with evident pleasure. He put a forefinger on her lips. "Don't start asking questions. Those will have to wait until I get settled in. The press will be a nuisance. Then various government agencies. It'll be busy, but I want to enjoy this time with Sonnie first."

When he released her, Billy said, "Frank. We were told you were dead. Romano was told. We've been beside ourselves. Oh, thank God it wasn't true."

Sonnie's desperation to get away made her head hurt.

"You've got to help me with Sonnie, Frank," Billy said. "I'm sorry to ask at a time like this, but I've got to get her to a place where she can have some peace and some excellent therapy. You can't imagine how hard these months have been on her."

Frank frowned and pushed his mug back and forth on the table. "I'm here now. I can take care of my wife."

"Things have happened," Billy said. "Romano being the biggest problem of all. Your brother thinks you're dead. I'd rather not say this, but he's moving to get his hands on everything that was yours and Sonnie's. He's done terrible things to Sonnie. Those scratches on her face happened when he was trying to force her to remember the accident. And he told her that they were going to marry, and then he'd shut her away."

"The thing is, he's somewhere around, but I don't know where. I think he intends to get to Sonnie and find a way to have her declared incapable of looking after herself. He wants to have her put away—after marrying her."

"He can't marry her," Frank said flatly. "My brother thought I was dead or he would never have behaved so. He was not himself."

"I was supposed to pick you up in the morning, Sonnie," Billy said. "But with Romano out there and angry, I think we should go now. Just grab your bag and come with me."

"I can't." The only place she was going was to Chris.

"Make her come with me, Frank. I'll keep in touch to let you know exactly where we are. I'll find a safe place for us to wait it out. I think Romano will come here—I think he'll be here soon. Can you deal with him?"

Frank shook his head slowly. "You underestimate my brother's love for me. All will be well now that I'm back. But you're right; it will be a good thing to allow us time together, alone. Do as Billy tells you, Sonnie. Get whatever she wants you to get and go with her."

"I'm not sure—"

"I have told you to go," he said, still smiling, but with the old steel in his tone. "Billy will keep in touch, and I'll tell her when it's a good time for you to return."

"All right," Sonnie said to Frank. What was she thinking of? This was the perfect way to get out of here. "I'll go because you do need time alone with Romano."

"Call me," Frank told Billy, and it was on Billy that his warm smile lingered when she left the kitchen with Sonnie.

"Get your things," Billy said. "Your papers."

Why should she need papers? Sonnie thought. Betrayal hurt, and she was increasingly convinced that her own sister wished her harm.

"Everything's already in my bag," Sonnie said, catching up the straw bag she used for shopping. It bulged with accumulated debris she needed to throw out.

Still Billy hesitated. "You've got your birth certificate, driver's license, any legal papers? Your passport? A copy of your will?"

Sonnie sensed a net falling over her. She patted Billy's arm and said, "All present and correct."

Billy said, "Okay, let's go."

Chris crouched behind the shrubbery fence that separated Sonnie's house from the place he'd always think of as being Ena's. He was still playing mental contortions with the Robertses. There seemed to be no connection with Sonnie, or with Key West. And he wished he knew where Ena had gone.

The cell phone gave its single beep and he crouched deeper to reply. "Yeah. Yeah, Flynn. You sure? Can you tell how long ago? I agree with you. I'd lay odds they're on their way here. Billy's not with them, though. She's already here. And Flynn—the black moped from next door is parked at the side of the house. I do believe our Frank may have ridden in on it. I don't have a single fact to substantiate the hunch, but I still think I'm right.

"I'd like to walk in and grab Sonnie. Yeah, I know that

could be a lousy idea. Hold on. Someone's coming out of the house. You start coming this way, Flynn.''

The front door had opened. Sonnie came out, followed by Billy. ''Billy and Sonnie are leaving,'' Chris told Flynn. ''Sonnie's looking around as if she hopes to see something.''

Roy poked him in the back and said, ''She's looking for you. Can't you pull her out of there now?''

''And risk getting her shot by someone who's using her to draw me out? That's only a possibility, but I'm not taking any chances.''

''You're right,'' Flynn said on the phone. ''If Romano and Lesley are on their way to your location, I'll be close behind. If not—''

''Just get here,'' Chris said and tucked the phone back into his breast pocket. ''Wait for Flynn,'' he told Roy. ''I'm going to follow them. I move better on my own.''

Thirty-five

Billy insisted on driving her Porsche, even though Sonnie pointed out that she knew the area better.

"You don't like to drive," Billy told her.

Sonnie didn't press the issue again. Damp from the short walk to the car, they got into the Porsche, and steam on the windows instantly shut out the world. "Would you mind stopping by the Nail?" Sonnie said, doing her best to sound casual.

"Yes, I would mind," Billy said. "What's the matter with you? You heard me promise Frank I'd look after you."

"I don't see why going to the Nail wouldn't be—"

"No," Billy said. "Not now. I'll take you later, if you like—when I know things have settled down."

They left the driveway and headed toward the airport. "Billy," Sonnie said, "it's good of you to want to help out, but you're overreacting. And you're being overbearing. Let's stop and talk about this, please."

Billy gave the car more gas and they shot along South Roosevelt.

Sonnie held on to the door and said, "Where are we going?"

"We're just going. I'm not sure where. I thought we'd look for a nice, quiet place. Maybe we'll let the family know where we are. Maybe we won't. We're going to find that peace we talked about.''

"Okay. How about the beach?''

Billy snickered. "In this weather and at this time of night?''

This would be the worst possible time to tell her sister she didn't want to go anywhere without Chris. She'd be patient, and get in touch with him as quickly as possible.

"Feel that?'' Billy said as the wind buffeted the car. "It doesn't scare me. I feel excited. This is going to be some experience, and it'll change both of our lives.'' She laughed, and the sound was too uncontrolled. Sonnie turned away and rubbed a sweaty space on her window to look out over the beach.

Billy pulled in at the airport and parked near the main doors. "Why are we stopping?'' Sonnie asked.

"Got to pick up a package,'' Billy said. "Sit tight.''

Sonnie waited until she was alone and tried Chris's cell number. He didn't answer.

She was putting the phone away when she felt more than saw someone approach the car. The driver's door opened and the seat slammed forward. Romano climbed into the back, a worried frown marring his striking face. "Don't be angry with Billy,'' he said. "I spoke with her for hours to persuade her to give me this chance to talk to you.''

"No,'' she said. "Please get out of the car.''

The door opened again and Jim Lesley slid in. Billy joined them and pulled away from the curb before Sonnie had time to voice another complaint.

"Hi, Sonnie,'' Jim Lesley said. "I'm hitching a ride with you and Billy.''

"Why are you doing this?'' Sonnie asked Billy. "You said you and I were going to find common ground together.''

"And so we will.'' She paused before leaving the front of the airport and setting off. "Surely you aren't so paranoid that you're afraid of giving rides to two old friends?''

"Please let me out.'' Sonnie unlocked her door.

Billy promptly locked it again. "Don't be a fool. You'll kill yourself.''

Sonnie snapped the lock open again.

"Stop that," Billy said. "Before you make me angry enough to slap you."

Sonnie thought she heard Romano laugh softly.

"Relax, Sonnie," Jim said. "You'll soon feel a whole lot calmer. We're going to concentrate on making you as comfortable as possible."

Clearly Billy was on her way to the overseas highway. "This is a charmed venture," she said. "If the storm had already notched up a bit, we could have gotten unlucky enough to be caught in a swarm of evacuees."

"Obviously these people aren't normal," Romano said. "To me the storm becomes a terrible thing. The sooner we are away, the better."

Sonnie sat very still. She had walked into a trap. Romano and Jim Lesley wouldn't be getting out and going on their way after a "ride." Billy, Romano, and Jim had plans for her. And they weren't plans she'd like.

"You're upset," Jim Lesley said. "Stress is bad for a person who has been suffering as you have for so long. I want you to take some medication. Nothing strong. Just something to calm you."

Something to drug her, Sonny thought. "I prefer not to take medications," she said. "But thank you. I'll ask if I think I want something."

Silence followed and Sonnie watched out the window as they moved rapidly along the overseas highway. Some of the lesser keys, those that could only be reached by boat, repeatedly disappeared behind high waves. When they reached Big Pine Key, the palms bowed almost to the shape of croquet hoops, and garbage rolled as if swept by a giant broom. The car shot to the next stretch that was suspended above the ocean. Sonnie felt as if she were in freefall. Nothing appeared to touch anything else, and the car might well have been riding through foggy air.

Water arced over the roadway, and for moments the surface became real again. Palm fronds littered the way. The occasional coconut bowled along. Billy only drove faster.

"I'm glad people seem to be staying off this road," Jim Lesley said. "Makes it easier."

"You do know I'm sorry about what happened the other evening, don't you, Sonnie?" Romano asked.

"Consider it forgotten," she told him. To antagonize him would be a poor idea. "I'd have expected you to want to be with Frank now." *Mistake, mistake.* She should not open that topic.

"I am shocked," Romano said, but there was anger in his voice. "Jim advised me to wait a little before going to Frank. To give me time to work through my feelings. Of course I am ecstatic that he is back safely, but I am overwhelmed. It is all too much. Jim is kind enough to say he will help me deal with what I feel."

"Billy," Sonnie said, "please could we go slower?"

Instead of slowing down, Billy drove even faster. And she laughed. "This is fun. Lighten up, for God's sake."

"We're being followed," Romano said. "Or I should say, if the motorcycle behind us doesn't pass and go on his way, I think we can assume we're being followed."

"No one even knows what we're doing," Jim Lesley said, but he sounded anxious.

She had confirmation of her fears, Sonnie thought. These people who should be her friends were planning to do her harm.

"Fuck," Billy said. "We're being followed, all right. It's that idiot washed-up cop of Sonnie's."

"Could be a coincidence," Dr. Jim said.

"Damn, I should be driving," Romano said.

Billy laughed. "Just make sure you're strapped in. Just in case things get really good."

They were still over open water, and nothing broke the force of the wind. Sweat made Sonnie's back slick. She held on to the door and the edge of her seat.

"The freakin' fool's coming alongside," Billy said. She looked at the road ahead and saw nothing. There was also nothing behind.

Chris drew level with Billy and motioned for her to roll

down the window. She shook her head and gave the car more gas.

He caught up again and made the same motion.

Billy took the window down a crack. "Get out of my way," she yelled.

"Storm warning has been upgraded," he shouted at her. "Best turn back and get off this highway."

Billy laughed at him, but he was looking at Sonnie, and she couldn't keep tears of longing from her eyes. He set his jaw.

Although Billy rolled the window shut and looked ahead, dismissing Chris, he stayed with the car, riding alongside all the way. His face was stark. His hair streamed. He narrowed his eyes against the wind. Billy held the wheel in a white-knuckled grip and constantly corrected against the battering. Chris seemed to use the car as a partial windbreak. When he parted his lips, his teeth were clenched. He repeatedly ducked his head to find relief from the explosive buffets.

"You've got to get rid of him," Jim said. "You know that."

"I know what I have to do. Romano, keep an eye open behind. Jim, help me watch in front. This will need to be perfectly timed, and we can't have any witnesses. I'll have to concentrate on him, too. He's going to wish he'd opted for hot chocolate in front of the fire."

"Stop it," Sonnie cried. "Leave him alone. He's riding beside us is all."

"Shut up," Billy said. "You were always a whiner." She turned the wheel slightly to the left. Chris veered away, and when he straightened out, Sonnie saw how grim his expression was.

Billy waved as if he'd indicated he was leaving. Chris stayed right where he was. Billy made a more acute turn toward him. Chris evaded her again.

They would kill him if they could.

As if he read her mind, Romano said, "I'd say this was an opportunity sent from God. Play it right and he's one more biker maniac who rode off the highway in a storm. Sharper and faster next time, Billy."

"I don't like this," Dr. Jim said.

Billy jerked the wheel left. Sonnie made a grab and managed to correct their direction very slightly. Billy sent a forearm into her throat and Sonnie went limp. She held her neck and looked directly into Chris's eyes. His anger was mixed with determination. And she could almost hear him telling her to be brave.

Rain had soaked through everything Chris wore. He noticed, but not enough to care. He was grateful he'd followed his instincts and left Roy to wait for Flynn. If they should decide to follow, they would be sure to stay far enough behind.

That bitch Billy had thrown an elbow into Sonnie's throat because she had tried to stop another attempt to force him from the road.

He gestured to Billy to lower the window again. She did so and he knew it was because she was high on the power she felt. "Let Sonnie out and I'll be gone," he called. "I'll back off while you stop; then you can go where you like. I don't care what you do."

The woman's response was to yank the wheel even more sharply than before, and he didn't react quickly enough. His footrest made contact with the side of the Porsche. While he fought not to turn over, he watched a deep gouge open in red paint.

Billy Keith was laughing maniacally. From what he could see, Sonnie was screaming and making futile grabs for the wheel. He saw when Romano Giacano leaned forward and clamped his hands over her face, effectively cutting off her vision and making it impossible for her to pull off another attempt to stop her sister.

But for Sonnie, he'd be making his own moves. Billy slowed suddenly and he overtook.

Instantly he knew his mistake.

The Porsche crossed the center line and made its initial contact at the level of his rear wheel. Chris tried to get out of the way, but the Porsche was too fast. He sustained a vicious clip that ran the length of the Harley—and over his leg.

Pain momentarily dulled him. Wheels slid sideways and he

did what came naturally: slammed down a booted foot to keep the bike from landing on its side.

His knee screamed, and his ankle, but the bike didn't go down. The Porsche made time on him. Billy had to be doing a hundred or more.

The Harley gyrated but settled down, and Chris used a hand to settle his foot on the rest before gunning as hard as he could. He felt himself gain control and went after the Porsche. If he didn't stop them, they might find a way to hide Sonnie so well that no one would see her until she was a hundred and ten. Or they might fabricate a tragic death. But if he did stop them, what would the price be? Who would suffer? If the Porsche went into the ocean . . . It couldn't go into that roiling ocean.

Billy had slowed down again. She must be so pleased with the last maneuver that she intended to go for it again. Chris stayed back, never allowing his front wheel to get closer than a few inches behind the rear of the Porsche.

Sonnie bit Romano's hand. She drove her teeth in and held on, tasting his blood. He cried out like an animal.

"Stop her, Jim," Billy ordered. "Then make sure she can't pull any more stunts."

"Stop all this, Billy," Sonnie said. "Jim, reason with her. Even if she pulls off what she wants, you'll all end up behind bars."

"Why?" Billy said. "Because you'll squeal on us?" She giggled. "You really aren't very worldly, Baby."

"Don't call me that. I hate it. I've always hated it."

"You think I don't know, *Baby?*"

"Brace yourselves," Billy said. "I'm going to try to get a lock on his front wheel. When I shake him loose he'll already look as if the fish have been at him. Then we want him over the edge."

"No," Sonnie pleaded. Once free of her teeth, Romano had gathered her hair into his fist and twisted until she couldn't bear it—but she had to. "Please don't do this. Listen to me,

Billy. We can carry on our way and leave Chris behind. We never have to go back to Key West.''

"Generous of you," Billy said. "But no dice. He's too dangerous to us. Jim, see to the little peacemaker, will you? Wait till I've got the guy's wheel, though."

Sonnie glanced behind her in time to see Jim Lesley filling a hypodermic. She set her teeth and willed herself to foil his efforts.

An earsplitting noise, the sound of tearing metal and rubber, hurt her head—and her heart. They really did intend to kill Chris.

She saw him tip sideways—away from the car this time. Billy screeched with laughter. "See how generous I am. I'm giving our enemy a tow."

Chris was being dragged along the ground.

Rain on the windshield all but obliterated vision. Sonnie gauged what it would take to leap from the car. At least she could use her phone to get help.

Chris knew there was no substitute for leathers; he just didn't like feeling that constrained. This evening he'd gladly have them on and saving his body from some of the damage it was sustaining.

He guessed there was no right way to play this one, but he sure as hell wished Sonnie wasn't in the car. All he could do was hold on. Even a megalomaniac wouldn't have the gall to drive far with a man and his motorcycle trailing from a wheel.

Billy swerved wide to the left, then back again to the right. With each move Chris wore more clothing away. Blood seeped through his jeans leg. The knuckles on both hands bled freely. Twice his face had scraped the ground, but so far he'd sustained no direct hits to the head.

The fear in his belly, and the strain of holding on, mounted with each second. Billy continued to make wide moves designed to send him and his bike into the ocean.

What did they intend to do with Sonnie?

The car slowed suddenly. Then it made sluggish directional

changes. They slowed almost enough for him to get off—but not quite. He made out a lot of movement inside the Porsche but could identify no particular person from this angle.

"You little shit," Romano bellowed at Sonnie. "Look what you've done."

"It was an accident," Sonnie said, not expecting to be believed. "Her arm got in the way of the needle."

"Fuck," Romano said, and put a lock around Sonnie's neck. "Give one to Sonnie. I'll make sure she doesn't screw it up again."

Jim was leaning past Sonnie to steer. "Just hold on, Romano. First things first, unless you want to be the one in the ocean. Sonnie, reach over with a foot and apply the brakes, please."

The central drive shaft made it tough. "Let go of me," she told Romano. "I can't do it with your hands around my neck."

Romano let go, and Sonnie sat on the center console. Jim steered, and she placed her foot on top of Billy's on the pedal. She had to give it all she could to depress the brakes.

Sonnie heard a noise she didn't like coming from the backseat. Glancing over her shoulder, she saw Romano slipping a clip into a silver gun. He leaned behind Jim to look out the window at Chris. "Too bad the poor bastard won't have much time to know how much he hurts. We're stopping, Doc. Send Sonnie to lala land. We can haul Talon over the side, put the two sleeping beauties in the back, and we'll be away."

Jim's bag was on the backseat. He kept one hand on the wheel but managed to take a full hypodermic from the bag and popped off the cap.

Sonnie caught his eye but couldn't bring herself to beg again. They were almost at a stop.

Romano had the gun braced as he timed his shot at Chris.

The hypodermic rose, and Jim looked back and forth between the needle and the road.

They did stop.

Jim drove the needle into Romano's arm, the one that held the gun. Sonnie could imagine the instant ache that would feel like lead to Romano. He looked at his arm with amazement. The gun fell to the seat. He blinked his eyes as if he couldn't see it. Then he slumped, still conscious, but losing it rapidly.

Sonnie leaped from the car and was immediately flattened to its side by the wind and rain. She forced her way around until she was beside Chris. His head rested on the road, and his eyes were closed. There was blood everywhere. Jim joined her and started checking vital signs.

He looked up at her. ''Painful days ahead for your friend,'' he said. ''But he's strong. He'll probably do fine.''

Sonnie knelt beside Chris in several inches of standing water. When she went to touch him, Jim said, ''Better not until we know the extent of his injuries.'' He took out a cell phone and dialed. He started giving information and requesting help, but Sonnie concentrated on Chris. The left leg of his jeans was shredded from hip to ankle, and the flesh beneath was covered with blood. His hands bled, and his face. She wanted desperately to get the weight of the Harley off his left leg.

Glancing up, she narrowed her eyes to see what was moving in their direction, but some distance away yet.

Chris grunted, and when she looked at him again, he'd opened his eyes.

Sirens sounded.

''You've got to come with me,'' Chris said. ''If you leave me, they won't be able to save me. Got that?''

She bent over him and kissed his mouth. ''I think I must have been hurt, too,'' she said. ''I'll just have to get checked over. Aiden's following us.''

''Please say he's not driving his Barbiemobile.''

''How else would I know it was Aiden?''

Thirty-six

Aiden decided he'd been in worse places than a Miami hospital when a case went down.

The local boys had set themselves up with a room—graciously supplied by the nursing staff in the trauma unit—and they kept the door shut at all times. Whatever overtures he'd made on his last visit had obviously been forgotten, or never taken seriously in the first place. He got polite enough nods, but they sure weren't treating him like a buddy.

"How long you reckon we'll be twiddling our thumbs here?" Roy asked. "It's like a party with no cake. And we're still waiting for some of the guests. That's what it feels like to me."

"Frank Giacano's on his way," Aiden said. "All he knows is that Billy and Sonnie got in an accident. They let me make the call and that's what I told him."

"I thought Chris was a goner," Roy said with a quaver in his voice. "Good thing for those goons he's not, or they'd be needing a morgue, not an emergency room and transfers to comfy beds."

"You said it. And I'd help you put 'em there."

They shared an understanding glance.

"I heard a nurse say Billy was conscious and demanding

to be allowed to leave," Aiden said. "She's got a smashed foot, but they've casted it. Evidently she's dressed and just waiting for the word that she can leave. Doesn't know why they insisted on admitting her anyway. Clever move, getting her slapped in here. She doesn't know Romano's a couple of rooms away. They've got a cop in there with him."

Sonnie came along the corridor, past the waiting area where they sat. She carried a Styrofoam cup in each hand. "His lordship says he's starving," she said. "Sent me for rations. Soup and Jell-O."

"He *sent* you for soup and Jell-O?" Roy asked.

"He sent me for a burger and fries," Sonnie said with a wicked glint in her eyes. "This is what he's allowed to have. I guess Billy's yelling that she's being held against her will. Romano's threatening to bring down the country if they don't let him out of here. Jim Lesley's a good guy, by the way. He saved me—and Chris. He may need help to prove he isn't as culpable as the others."

"Yeah," Aiden said. He wasn't too hung up on what happened to Jim Lesley—even if he was sitting in another waiting room looking as if he'd rather be dead, anyway. "Any word on where Bledsoe is?"

Sonnie said, "They were going to take him to Key West, but it's been agreed that he stays here until the cops make up their minds how to handle him. Know an anonymous donor who'd be likely to pay the hospital to keep people in rooms they don't need—for health reasons?"

Aiden said, "Nope, sure don't, but I'm grateful."

"I'd better get these where they're going." Sonnie backed away. "Cold soup and warm Jell-O might bring on something really nasty."

Roy and Aiden laughed. "You make him behave himself," Aiden told her. "But don't forget he's in a tough place. And I don't mean this hospital, or because he's scraped up a bit."

Sonnie forgot the soup and Jell-O and moved in to take one of the turquoise tweed chairs opposite Roy and Aiden. She leaned forward and said, "I think you ought to explain exactly what that means, don't you?"

"Some people have big mouths," Roy said. He tipped his Stetson over his face, crossed his arms, and leaned back in the chair. He stretched out his booted feet, and any casual observer would assume he slept.

"Come on," Sonnie said. "Don't keep me in suspense."

Aiden looked away and said, "It's none of my business."

"Now he remembers," came from the shadow of the Stetson.

"Okay." He was a big boy. He'd jump in with both feet. "Christian J. Talon's one hell of a man. And—although you might think otherwise—he's the best friend I ever had. He's been through hard times. For a long time I wasn't sure he'd ever forgive himself enough to make another life. I'm not saying I believe that when that woman hanged herself in her cell it was Chris's fault. It wasn't. But in his eyes he might as well have strung her up. Then you came along, and *bam*, the old Chris, only even better, started to appear."

For a long time Sonnie didn't say anything. Her hair had dried in tangles. The once white jumpsuit she wore was spattered with mud, the knees black. And over all Chris's blood had dried to rust-colored stains. "He did the same for me," she said—finally.

"Past tense," Aiden said. "Now your husband's back and the picture changes, right? You're a loyal woman, Sonnie. I figure you're torn, too. But your husband says he needs you, so it'll be sayonara, Chris. I like you for what you've done for him. But Sonnie, I'm gonna hate you when you take it all back again."

"Subtle." The Stetson's brim jiggled again. "Is it too late for you to go back to minding your own business?"

Sonnie couldn't take her eyes from Aiden's. While her throat grew so tight she couldn't swallow, she looked into his almost-too-intensely blue eyes and couldn't blame him for taking the part of the man she loved.

She got up. "I can't be disappointed because Frank Giacano isn't dead. Frank's not the man I want, but he is the man I'm married to. Do you think it's easy being me right now?" She left before Aiden could respond and hurried toward Chris's room.

"Sonnie, where are you going?" Seated just inside a room on the left side of the corridor, Billy reached a hand toward her. "Please let me explain."

Sonnie paused but looked away. "No," she told Billy. "Not now."

Awkwardly, Billy stood up. "Romano threatened me. He said he'd kill me if I didn't do what he wanted. You've got to help me."

"I told you, *not now*," Sonnie said, knowing she ought to keep on walking but unable to move. "When are you going to get it that you're done? Finished. You're nothing to me. Less than nothing." She heard her voice rise, and felt the vibration of it inside her head.

"You come here when I tell you," Billy said. "I'm hurt. I need you to help me. You've got to tell them how Romano's always threatened me. You know that's true. He held it over me that he knew things he could tell our folks."

Sonnie looked at the soup and Jell-O in her hands. She couldn't feel the containers.

"You're not yourself," Billy said. "You haven't been for a long time. How could you be after . . . You had a terrible head injury."

Sonnie went slowly into Billy's room. She set down the soup and Jell-O and shut the door.

"Oh, Sonnie," Billy said. "Family sticks together. I knew you wouldn't let me down."

"How? How did you know? Because I'm docile, but not quite right? A few sandwiches short of a picnic? Stuck in blond gear? And you can program me to do and say whatever you want?"

Billy's face twisted. "I'm in pain."

"Yes, so I see." Sonnie looked from her sister's face to her casted foot. "Better get your weight off that." Gently, but firmly, she caught Billy by the arms and pushed, just a little.

"Sonnie!" Billy's eyes opened wide. With a thump she sat

in the chair again. "What are you doing? You could do damage, you crazy bitch."

"Crazy?" The room was too hot. "I'm crazy? Well, sister dear, you haven't seen crazy yet. You ought to know better than to pick on someone with two good arms and two more or less good feet when you aren't doing so well yourself."

"Sonnie—"

"Keep your voice down. Someone might think *you're* crazy and decide *you* need a quiet room somewhere. Somewhere you can be taken really good care of. For your own good."

"Stop it."

"I can't, because I'm crazy. I need to be restrained. I need to be protected from myself. Maybe we can share one of those quiet rooms in Dr. Jim's discreet establishment. Think of it"— she leaned over to grasp the arms of the chair and put her nose within an inch of Billy's—"all those lovely summer days. Side by side beneath the trees in our wheelchairs. Chattering about old times—until we can't remember old times anymore."

"You are nuts," Billy whispered.

Sonnie laughed. "Told you. Glad you believe me."

"I'm going to scream."

"Be my guest. You invited me in here. Yes, why don't you scream? When someone comes I'll tell them you've lost it. I tried to calm you down, but you obviously need psychiatric help."

"Stop it." Billy let out a shuddering sob. She cried, dragging in hoarse little breaths. "All the toes on my right foot are broken. And lots of other little bones. It hurts, Sonnie. Don't be cruel. Get me out of here. Make them believe I didn't do anything wrong."

"Can't do that. Sorry."

"Sonnie! It hurts so much. And I don't even know how it happened."

Your foot got stomped on in the car. "Oh, I'm sure it does hurt. It probably always will. Especially when it rains. Some people think that's an old wives' tale—about injuries aching when the weather's damp. It isn't. It's true. You'll probably develop arthritis in time."

Billy cried louder. She pulled her head as far away from Sonnie as she could. "You're just trying to get your own back. Well, all I've got is an injured foot. At least my face isn't ruined."

"No, it isn't," Sonnie said softly, "but behind your face, inside your head is ruined, isn't it? It's rotten in there. Disgusting."

"Go away."

"Isn't it? Answer me."

"No one's going to believe anything you say after this," Billy said.

"Really?" Sonnie laughed and it felt good. She grabbed a handful of tissues, crammed them into Billy's right hand, and pushed it to her mouth. "Your nose is running. It looks sickening."

"Help," Billy said, but scarcely made a sound. "Help me, someone."

Sonnie straightened. She picked up the cartons of Jell-O and soup and went to the door. "It's too bad they can't cast broken toes. They just have to heal on their own, and you hope they aren't too crooked afterward. Best to stay away from nail polish. It only draws attention you don't want. It's a real nuisance having to buy sensible shoes and give up heels or anything cute. They make some really good orthopedic insoles, though. Just because you have to wear boring shoes, it doesn't mean you can't have some fun with them. Buy cute shoelaces. Silver, maybe. Or the ones that look like neon telephone cords. Those are a great idea, especially when the foot swells. They stretch."

She maneuvered the door open, and left it open.

The feeling of triumph was too short-lived. She longed to lie down and sleep—and forget. She heard Billy crying, but felt nothing.

The amazing Mr. Talon leaned against his pillows and glared. But when he saw Sonnie, his expression changed to one of cheerful stoicism. Despite the cast that enclosed his left leg from hip to toe, dressings that covered sutures in more places than Sonnie had so far counted, a banged-up face, and bandages on his knuckles thick enough to resemble mittens, he contrived to look dashing. A white sheet across his lap shielded the essentials. Everything else was muscular and bare—including his tattoo. The nursing staff was already commenting on that tattoo—and finding excuses to check on "the hunk."

"You okay?" he said. "You look . . . angry?"

"Let it go, please."

He frowned, but said, "Okay. They haven't let Billy go, have they?"

She would like to forget Billy—for good. "No."

"That black outfit she's wearing. Is it sweats?"

"Yes. Please, Chris, don't get worked up. All this can wait for a bit, can't it?"

He shook his head. "Gotta tell someone to check her pockets. Dust and little white rocks in there. They match ones at the club—on the walkways. They were in your foyer. Nothing like them in your gardens. She used them to throw at the chandelier and make it move and clink."

Sonnie realized what he was telling her. "Billy," she said. "Poor, mixed-up Billy."

She did her best not to look at anything but his face. She also did her best not to feel what she felt anyway: a longing to touch as much of him as his injuries allowed, to kiss all those places.

"I don't want you to pity me," he said, "but they did do an open reduction on my knee. I've got pins in there, y'know."

"You're quoting a doctor."

"Yup. Thought it sounded worthy of a lot of sympathy."

One moment she was convinced she must try to at least help Frank get back on track before she left him; the next she couldn't imagine doing anything but staying at Chris's side—forever.

"What is it?" he asked. "What's wrong, Sonnie?"

She evaded the question. "I don't want to hear any complaints about what I've brought you. I was stopped when I came on the floor and told this would be what you'd eat. The soup's cold and the Jell-O's melted. Tough. You don't get any choices and I can't do anything about it.''

"Oh.'' He managed to push his hair back with the fingertips of his right hand. "I guess that's what I'll eat then.''

She put the cups on his bed tray and pulled a chair near the bed. "The police must have given orders for Billy to be detained at the hospital.'' If she ought to feel guilty for what she'd just done to her sister, it wasn't happening. "She's got a badly injured foot, but that's no reason to keep her here. Romano's also here, and Jim. And Cory Bledsoe.

"They've decided they can control things here, and the hospital is going along. The only player they haven't dredged up is Ena. Annette Roberts. But they're hunting for her.

"Do you suppose all this means they think they know what's been going on?''

"That would be my guess,'' Chris said. "They know about the attic at your place now. Would you close the door, please?''

Sonnie felt uncertain, but she did as he asked.

"I'm not hungry anymore,'' he said, and rolled the tray as far away as he could.

"You saved me, Chris.''

"So you've already told me. I'd do it again. Anytime.''

"The cost was too high. You're suffering too much.''

"I'll be hopping around on crutches in no time.''

"I just got a pretty direct warning.'' This seemed like a way for her to broach a subject that couldn't be ignored. "I was told I'd lose friends if I did anything to hurt you.''

"Would you kiss me?'' Chris said. "I think I really need you to kiss me now.''

She closed her eyes and tried to be very calm. He knew what they needed to talk about. Avoidance wouldn't change reality.

"Sonnie, don't do this to me. Come to me. Let me feel you.''

He'd come close to being killed for her because he loved her. And she wasn't sure she wouldn't die if he stopped loving her. Barely able to see through a haze of tears, she went to him and, very gingerly, kissed him. But if she'd had any plans to withdraw, she could forget them. Dressings or no dressings, he held the back of her head and kissed her. The man was a wizard with his mouth. If they gave out awards for killer kisses, Chris Talon would win first place, hands down.

He slid his fingertips down her arms until he could hold her hands. His eyes were pure green now. "I'm not giving up on you. Not ever. I don't care if you decide you've got to be Frank Giacano's support group—that you've got to stand by him. That's the kind of thing I expect from you. But I will be there, darlin'. I will be a shout away at all times."

"I can't live without you." She couldn't close her mouth when she finished. The words had tumbled out—a small but powerful torrent beyond her control. "I can't," she whispered.

Chris brought first one, then her other hand to his lips. "I'm not going to live without you," he said. "But I'm not blasé enough to believe we can have what we've already had again until you make peace with it. Does Frank want to work it out?"

"He said he did. He said he wanted to start another pregnancy as soon as possible."

Chris felt instantly enraged. He breathed in through his mouth.

"But he hasn't changed, Chris. And the things he said— how would he know about you? He does, in detail. And when I told him the baby had died, he cried as if it was a new shock; then he said he'd read all about it in a newspaper clipping."

Chris pressed his lips together.

Sonnie said, "He's the same as he always was. And he sent me on that drive with Billy. He ordered me to go with her. I think he knew something about what was going to happen."

"What do you think their plan was?"

"To put me in a sanitarium and keep me drugged. My parents would have been brought in, and of course they'd have agreed that Frank needed access to my trust to cover my expenses. Frank and Romano separately planned to use me for their own gain. Romano had no idea what Frank was up to, but I think they're both in big trouble and they'd do anything to dig their way out. And my sister is as involved as they are." She could no longer pretend otherwise.

Chris thought she was close to the truth about Frank and Romano. He wouldn't push her on the subject of Billy, but he was glad they both realized she was as guilty as hell. "Detective Whittle is in charge here. He's a good man, straight. He told me they're suspicious about how Frank was able to slip his captors after almost nine months and just walk away. Frank says he was in Europe with these goons, but there's no record of his coming back into the States. And he's got an answer for anything they throw at him, every little detail. They also think he arranged for an anonymous tip to break in media-land because the press and TV started to arrive in Key West late this afternoon. Truman Avenue looks like the who's who of 'Inquiring minds want to know.' We don't believe that happened accidentally."

Her sad and tired face caused him to wish he'd kept the last bit to himself. She had to know what kind of publicity hound she'd married.

The ferocity with which she slapped her hands over her ears caught him off guard. And it scared the hell out of him. He didn't say a word, but figured he'd wait until she was ready to share whatever had upset her.

"My foot," she said, and her face contorted. She sat on the chair, pulled her right ankle across her left knee, and held her sandaled foot as if it were freshly wounded. "In the Volvo. Just like with Billy. Someone stamped on my foot to keep it on the pedal—to make me give the car more gas. And when Romano drove me at that wall the other night, he said something about doing that—that I should do it to him, I think.

"It wasn't an accident I hit that wall. I couldn't have done anything to stop it. He stamped on my foot and turned the wheel. He turned the car toward the wall."

Any color she'd had fled her face.

"Take it easy," he told her. "Just let it come."

"That's why I went to Key West again, isn't it? Because I knew I had to find out what really happened to me. I don't panic easily, Chris. Nothing I was told made any sense, but who would listen to a woman who couldn't remember the truth?"

"Who was *he*, Sonnie?" Chris asked as quietly as he could.

"I don't . . . Well, I don't know. They said I was alone in the car." She glanced downward. "We were alone, Jacqueline and I."

"But someone slammed your foot on the accelerator. Unless he wanted to die, he'd have to jump clear, wouldn't he? And to do that he'd have to be fit, really fit. His timing would have to be either perfect or instinctive."

"We were alone," she said, and shook her head. "No, we weren't. Pain, so much pain in my foot—and my ankle. I undid my belt. Then I hit the side of my head here''—she touched her right temple, then her jaw—"and here. And I couldn't stay then."

"You mean you lost consciousness?"

"Maybe. I must have."

He mustn't push too hard. "You're doing just fine. Great. You don't have to worry about it now. I don't suppose you recall what you hit your head on."

When she bowed her face and looked up at him, her deep blue eyes held sorrow, confusion.

He said, "Forget I asked. We've still got some rocky times to get through tonight. The hospital isn't going to put up with being used as an interrogation center for long. They'll want all of us out of here."

"Not you," she said, still far away. "They'll make you stay."

This wasn't a good time for argument, so he grunted.

"I didn't hit anything," she said. "He hit me. He shouted at me, and hit me until it was all black."

Keeping his hands relaxed on the sheet took a whole lot of willpower. "Unconsciousness feels like that. I surely know how it feels. What did he shout?"

"I don't remember."

"No." Damn, so close but so far away. "And you still can't think who he was?"

Her expression cleared. "No, I can't. But I got a feeling just then. And I've already started to bring it back, haven't I?"

"You surely have. Now quit worrying about it. You've got

as long as it takes.'' *And will you take it with me, Sonnie? Will you decide in favor of me? Please, will you stay with me for the rest of our lives? I'm trying to be so reasonable here, but I don't know how I'll be if you leave me.*

She surprised him by standing up. ''I don't regret being with you—*with* you.'' Faint brushes of red stained her cheeks. ''I wanted you from the moment I met you. You're steady and strong, and although I knew you couldn't be interested in me, I wanted your strength and certainty for myself. You never pushed yourself on me.''

Hardly trusting himself to exhibit any of that legendary strength, he said, ''I didn't have to fall for you. I couldn't seem to help myself, though. And I'd do it all over again, and again. Only I don't have to, because I'll never stop loving you.''

Moving close enough to trace the damn tattoo he'd acquired to help complete his biker image, she inclined her head and smiled faintly. ''I've got to work on learning to like myself. Find out if I *do* like myself. I like you, Chris. There is nothing about you that doesn't turn me on.'' The smile became broad. ''Look what you've done to me. I never used to say things like that. Now I hope I don't ever have to go back to being prissy.''

His own grin faded fast. ''What are we going to do? You have to call it.''

Being careful to avoid wounds, she smoothed his hair away from his face, watching her own fingers as she did so. ''We're going to believe we'll be together again. If that's what you want.''

The word *believe* grated, but he said, ''It's what I want. When?'' He had to hear her tell him it wouldn't be long.

''I don't know. Not long. But there are things I have to do.''

The door opened without a prior knock and Detective Whittle came in. He held Cory Bledsoe by the elbow. ''Excuse me,'' the detective said, ''but we won't take long with this. Would you mind waiting outside, miss?''

''She'll be fine here,'' Chris said. ''She needs to stay.''

Whittle, a blond man with sharp gray eyes, raised his brows but nodded. Sonnie felt his authority. He wore it low-key but comfortably. In charge, Whittle.

"We've been talking to Mr. Bledsoe about how he came to be in possession of a dead man's passport and papers. We've been talking a lot, but he can't seem to come up with an answer. What I'd like from you, Mr. Talon, is your permission to mention the information you shared with me about Mr. Bledsoe."

Bledsoe showed none of the congenial assurance Sonnie expected from him. "You were in my house," she said, never intending to say anything. "You tried to frighten me by pretending to be dead in the foyer. And you went back there again. Ena saw you."

"I don't know any Ena," Bledsoe said, not looking at her. "I've never been in your house."

"You must have worn a wig."

"Sonnie," Chris said gently, and shook his head.

Detective Whittle flexed his shoulders. "Sure you know Ena. Annette Roberts, really. You were looking for a way to get out of the country, so you paid Annette for her dead husband's papers."

Bledsoe raised his face. He wore the expression of a horse confronted with flames. "I didn't."

"Okay if I say something?" Chris asked, and the detective gave a short nod. "You didn't pay Annette for her husband's papers?"

"No."

"What did you pay her for?"

"Nothing. I need to sit down."

"Was it Romano you were paying? Paying off by terrorizing Sonnie? He and Billy wanted to drive her mad—or make it seem as if she might be mad."

"No."

"I found a list of women's names in Annette Roberts's attic. Didn't mean a thing till I found the same names written in a notebook that belongs to Billy Keith."

Cory's eyes flickered rapidly between Chris and Detective Whittle. Sonnie could smell his fear.

"Your ex–tennis pro left because you wanted him to perform sex acts in front of you, didn't he?" Chris said.

''Who told you that?'' Cory panted and bared his teeth. ''You don't have any proof.''

''Remember Ginger-Pearl? She moved on. But you had plenty of other victims. You shouldn't have been in such a hurry to get Romano to work for the club. What did you do to make him go digging for dirt on you?''

''Nothing.''

Chris laughed and said, ''That's not what he says. He says the whole plan was yours. All of it.''

''It's a damn lie,'' Cory said. His face contorted. ''I can't stand it.''

Whittle eased the man onto the chair Sonnie had vacated. ''Sit a minute. We'll go and see what Romano says when the two of you are face-to-face.''

Ashen, Cory closed his eyes and shook his head no. ''I don't ever want to look at that bastard again. He did this to me. With help from her.''

''Her?'' Chris said mildly.

''Billy Keith. She isn't human. She lit her own cigarette so she could help him. All I did was tell him I knew he was getting it on with her and that''—he glanced at Sonnie—''that if he didn't share the goods with me, I'd see if someone would pay to know about the two of them. They seemed okay with it. But when I'd finished—''

''Finished?'' Whittle asked.

Cory swallowed. ''She egged me on. She wanted me. But afterward they said it wouldn't be a good time for me to start spreading rumors. I said I wouldn't, but they worked me over anyway. Then they took me to the attic at Sonnie's house. They said if I did what they wanted, they'd let me go and no one would ever find out about—about the stuff at the club. You know the rest. I made a mistake and got away without the passport. I'd found it in the attic. I had to go back for it. Can I lie down?''

Whittle pulled Cory to his feet and walked him slowly from the room.

''They're going to arrest Billy, aren't they?'' Sonnie said. She also needed to lie down. ''And Romano.''

"After what they did on that road, they were already headed in that direction. But I think we can now be certain who tried to make everyone—including you—question your sanity. Cruel SOBs. I told Whittle what I found in that attic. And at Ena's. He's smart enough to ask KWPD to deal with that end. They'll secure everything."

"My sister hates me," Sonnie said. Bitterness didn't make good company. "I wonder why—the deep reason?"

"Because she's jealous of anyone or anything wonderful."

"Chris, I'd like to turn some sort of key and switch it all off. Send it away but leave you and me together."

"The key will turn in time, sweetheart."

Whittle stuck his head into the room again. "Nurse says it's time for your beauty sleep," he told Chris. "Your husband's here now, Mrs. Giacano. He'd like to talk to you."

"No way," Chris said. He made a move and dropped back on his pillows. "She's not to be alone with that man. You understand, Whittle?"

"I understand what you just said, Mr. Talon."

"Then leave her here."

"We need you," Detective Whittle said to Sonnie. "You can refuse to come, but we'd appreciate it if you did."

"Don't—"

"I have to," Sonnie said. "There's nothing to worry about. I'll be kept safe." She knew she would, but she also knew Chris was suffering both mentally and physically, and all because she'd forced him to notice her. She went to the door with the detective. "See you."

"When?" she heard Chris mutter, but she left without answering him.

Thirty-seven

He hadn't gone through so much only to lose to someone else in the end. Frank ignored the plainclothes policeman who sat just inside the door twiddling his thumbs—literally.

"This place is disgusting," he said. "I want my wife; then I want to get us both out of here."

"Uh-huh."

"Where is she?" He knew the answer, and the cop knew he did. "In that man's room. I'm not even sure she's safe with him." He was damn sure she wasn't.

"She's safe." The guy reversed the direction of his thumbs. "Boss's going to bring her. You heard him say he would."

Sonnie walked in ahead of Whittle.

"You might have been killed," Frank said, and strode to pull her against him. "They planned to have you committed so they could get their hands on your money. Well, it isn't going to happen. These guys will lock them up and throw away the key."

Sonnie pushed him away. "You told me to go with Billy," she said. "You insisted, and you insisted I did what she told me to do."

He spread his hands. "I just got back from hell, *cara*. How was I to know what was going on?"

Someone tapped the door, and Whittle stepped out. The preoccupied cop got fresh interest in his job. He stood up, braced his feet apart, and put his hands behind his back.

"Let's go," Frank said. "They have no right to keep us here. Let's just leave."

Sonnie wanted Frank to leave—alone. She wished she need never see or speak to him again.

He said, "Sonnie?" in the voice he used when he really wanted something. "That man's no good for you. A man who came from nothing and still cannot go anywhere? What good is he? He has no job. He's what they call a bum. And his brother is homosexual."

Whittle came in again, this time with a policeman Sonnie hadn't seen before. Between them, struggling and kicking, was Ena.

They deposited her on a chair and pushed her back down when she tried to get up. "You don't have any right to touch me," she told the police. "I haven't done anything." She noticed Sonnie and actually gave a weak smile.

"If you haven't done anything, you'll be okay, won't you, Annette?" Whittle said. "But you do have priors, and we did tell you why we were bringing you in. And you did say you didn't mind coming to the hospital to identify someone."

"A stiff," she said, and pushed at Whittle. "I thought it was a stiff. She's Sonnie Giacano. Now can I go?"

"Sonnie's not the one we were wondering about."

Sonnie realized Frank was obscured from Ena by one of the policemen. It was Frank they'd brought her to see.

Frank wasn't saying anything. He wasn't moving.

"Do you know this gentleman?" Whittle asked Ena, indicating Frank.

She turned on the chair and her facial contortion weakened Sonnie's already tired legs. "You," Ena said. "I saw the latest news, Frankie."

He turned his back on her.

It took all three policemen to stop Ena from leaping at that back. "You lied to me, you bastard. You said you'd never actually go near her again. You said the other three would do all the dirty work. All I had to do was make sure you knew what was going on. Calling Chris about Roy was going to be the last of it. Then it was going to be you and me. But you told them about me. You told them where I live so they could come and get me. If you hadn't, at least I'd be safe.''

"Shut up, Annette," Frank said.

"I'm not shutting up until it suits me. Hey, you"—she poked Whittle again—"listen up. His brother and her sister pulled off all the tricks. But he was behind it. He knew what they did because Billy told him. The two of them used Romano. And Frank lied to me. He told me we'd be together if I helped. So I did. I gave up sleep to help. Making sure they only did stuff to her when she was alone. Delivering things. Putting a doll in a crib when I should already have been on the run. Made me late, that did. *And* I had to deal with her turning up with the guy she's been sleeping with.''

Frank turned around.

"That's right. I figured you deserved to know the truth, so I watched them with my own eyes.''

Through a hole in the ceiling, Sonnie thought.

Vaguely, she heard Whittle reading Ena her rights. She fought, but handcuffs put an end to that. Her parting words to Frank were, "I'd have stopped you from using Mitch like that if I'd known you'd leave me on my own. He didn't even know why he was there. But I asked him to be there, so he went. I shouldn't have done that to Mitch. I shouldn't have.''

Ena was taken into the corridor, and Sonnie went out, too. She couldn't stay with Frank.

The spectacle that confronted her was Chris in a wheelchair being pushed by a very pretty nurse. A hospital gown, open in the front rather than the back, was secured in place by a sheet tucked around him.

Ena glared at him as she was taken past.

"Good to see you, Ena," Chris said. "Make sure they look after you.''

The only reaction was a snort from one of the cops.

Sonnie swung away and took several steps back into the

room where Frank stood. A policeman rested a restraining hand on his shoulder.

"You," Sonnie said. "How did you know all about Chris? How long ago did you really escape from those people?"

Chris's casted foot drew level with Sonnie. The nurse said, "Five minutes, Mr. Talon. That's all you said you needed. I have to take you back."

Sonnie said, "Thanks for bringing him, nurse. I'll take him back."

The nurse didn't seem sure, but she did as Sonnie suggested.

Whittle joined them almost silently and made sure the door was closed.

Being helpless was foreign to Chris. "What's with Ena?" he said.

"She's just a little bit angry with Mr. Giacano," Whittle said.

"I'll tell you later," Sonnie told Chris. "She believed Frank was going to reward her for watching me and telling him what was happening. She expected him to move in with her."

Ena. That explained a lot, Chris thought.

"It is not a sin to change your mind about a woman," Frank said. "Annette is very sick. She imagines things. She has a history of imagining famous men are in love with her. But what happened was Billy's idea. She planned everything. She hates my dear wife. They told me about her foot, *cara.* You must not blame yourself. It would be difficult to avoid when she was unconscious."

"I'm divorcing you, Frank," Sonnie said. Her eyes closed tightly and she started to slip downward.

Chris made a grab. He succeeded in landing her on top of him, and in causing more pain than he could handle. He bent over her and held on.

One of the policemen lifted Sonnie and set her on a chair. "I told you before," she said to Frank. "You were angry. You said you wouldn't let me go. But I told you I'd divorce you anyway."

"You aren't yourself," Giacano said. He was too close to Sonnie. "You are imagining things again."

"I never imagined anything." Unsteadily, she rose and faced her husband.

"And you were never abducted, Giacano," Chris said through his teeth. "And when you found out Sonnie was returning to Key West, you got crazy-fan Annette Roberts to take the house next door where she could keep you informed. You knew about me because Annette saw me, and you did some homework on me."

"You're guessing."

"Right before her accident, you were in the car with Sonnie. When she told you she wanted a divorce, you did what you have a history of doing so well: you hit her. You knocked her out, then got too scared to do anything but react. You know all about breaking someone's foot. That's what you did to Sonnie. You stamped on her foot—on the gas—and crushed every little bone. Then you jumped. And if you didn't at least scrape yourself up, you're quite a man.

"Your brother was there. He'd followed you in his Jag. And he told you what to do. Get on a plane and get the hell out of Dodge. That's what he told you. And he made up a big fat lie about terrorists. Poor Frank was abducted by terrorists. You were to come back when the time seemed right and sop up the pity and the adoration—and the bucks for your story, and the endorsements you'd pull in.

"But you thought you could do better, so you stuck around, in hiding, having an affair with Billy, laughing at your brother while you plotted against Sonnie."

"You don't have any proof," Giacano said.

"The police have a number of people who will sing without any encouragement. They'll sing to try to save themselves. Then there's the man who was there when you rented the moped. After you walked back to the airport."

"He couldn't have known I wasn't Romano. . . ." Frank's lips remained parted.

Sonnie went for him. With her fists, she beat any part of him he couldn't cover fast enough. "You killed my baby," she said. "You murdered her." She landed a punch on the bridge of his nose, and blood trickled.

"Watch him, Whittle," Chris shouted.

Sonnie's last punch got one of Frank's eyes. He captured her wrists, swung her around to face the room, and trapped her against him with one arm. With the other hand he produced a knife from beneath his sleeve.

"Shit," Chris said. "Didn't anyone frisk him?" It didn't matter that he knew the answer. "Let her go, Giacano," he said. "Let her go and you'll make a point or two."

Frank laughed. "There aren't enough points to get me out of here if I don't have her with me. You want her to stay alive?" The knife came to rest against her neck. "You let me walk us out of here. One move to stop me and she dies."

Chris believed him. His mouth dried and he looked at Whittle. "Let him go."

Whittle said, "Okay, Giacano, you win." And Chris could almost feel the way the man's hand itched to go for his gun.

"Against the wall," Giacano said. "Both of you cops. Get your hands up and don't move an eyebrow."

The two men followed instructions.

Frank edged backward a slow step at a time, never taking his eyes off the police.

Without warning, Sonnie went limp. Giacano hadn't expected resistance from her. He failed to grab her before she fell to the floor.

He raised the knife. "Nothing's changed," he said. "You stay right where you are, and we'll leave very peacefully. Come any nearer and this knife is in her back."

"I don't believe you'd do that to Sonnie," Chris said.

"Try me." Frank Giacano's attention wavered for one instant.

A hollow-point bullet from the Glock opened like a flower in the man's heart.

Epilogue

"You can drown, or you can swim. Decision's yours, Sonnie."

It wasn't that simple.

Nothing ever had been that simple, never would be.

"Roy means you can choose to go down under the weight of hating yourself for what was never your fault," Bo said. "Or you can look up. If you look up, and open yourself up, you'll feel the clean wind blow over you and into you, and it'll fill you with hope. You aren't supposed to be perfect. Nothing to work on in this world if you're perfect. Takes us our lifetimes to do the best we can. It's the trying that counts. The trying turns the ugliest caterpillars into butterflies. You must have been a real pretty caterpillar, and that's why you're the most beautiful butterfly I ever saw. Beautiful and good."

"That's right," Roy said. "Only I never knew you were a philosopher, Bo, or so eloquent."

They sat, one on either side of her, on Smathers Beach. The sun shone; the sea was a perfect, calm blue; the wind was as clean as the wind Bo spoke of. Roy and Bo had come to her house and insisted she talk to them, really talk to them. She'd agreed, as long as they brought her here.

"It's a perfect day," Bo said. "A day for beautiful butterflies like you, Sonnie."

"Beautiful day," she agreed. Her gaze lingered not on the sea or the cloudless sky that met it without a seam, but on scattered rocks some feet away.

"Why did you want to come here?" Roy asked. "Wasn't this—"

"Yes," she said, still looking at the rocks. "That's why. How do you figure out the order of things? Endings and beginnings? It's all a circle, isn't it?"

She felt the two men catch each other's eyes, and she smiled. "No nonverbal allowed, guys."

"Okay," Roy said. "Bo, I can't keep this up."

" 'Course not," Bo told him. "You're a softie. Sonnie, you haven't talked to Chris since . . . Well, it's been days, and you haven't."

"No. There hasn't been an opportunity. He needed to be left alone to heal."

"What does that mean?" Bo said.

"He's never tried to get in touch with me again. I don't blame him."

Roy leaned to see her face. "I'm not getting what you mean by that, but you haven't tried to get in touch with him, have you?"

"That wouldn't be right. I've messed up his life—and I've gone against things I believe in." But she wanted to see him at least once before she tried to do what she'd promised herself she'd do; really make something of herself.

"I can't stand it," Roy said. "I can't. You're both good people. And you're both f—friggin' *stupid.*"

"Roy," Bo said. "Go easy."

Roy stood up. "Do you want to talk to Chris? Don't hem and haw. And if you cry, I'm going to cry. You won't like that. Just gimme a simple answer."

"Yes, of course I do."

"I . . . Oh. Okay, then. Just as well, because if you knew what we went through to get him to agree, you'd feel sorry for us."

"Roy, your mouth will be the end—"

"It's okay," Sonnie told Bo. "If I could sit here on my own awhile, I'd be very grateful. Then, if you'll take me home again, you can tell Chris I'd like to at least talk to him."

"He's on his way here," Roy said, his face crumpled with worry. "They discharged him from the hospital late yesterday and he flew down here. He's at our place. I called him while you were doing whatever you do before you go out."

"Chris is coming here?" She turned around, but all she saw was the nondescript gray pickup that belonged to Roy and Bo. "If he's smart, he'll change his mind. He's not ready for the beach."

"But you're going to talk to him?" Roy said.

Sonnie followed the flight of a single gull. "Of course I am." Even if the thought of facing him stole feeling and left her numb.

Minutes passed in silence. It was Sunday, and few vehicles came and went along South Roosevelt. Despite the sun, the morning wasn't yet very warm, and they were the only people on the beach.

Bo made patterns in the sand with his fingers. When he grew still, Sonnie raised her head to listen, and she heard the engine of Aiden Flynn's Mustang. She'd quickly learned its distinctive sound.

Brushing sand from her full blue skirt, Sonnie got up and faced the road. Aiden pulled in to park behind the pickup. Chris was with him.

Sonnie started up the beach. "He can't come down here," she said. "The wheelchair won't want to move on the sand."

Roy caught her arm. When she paused, he kissed her cheek and said, "My brother's got great taste." He and Bo hurried toward the road, but rather than stop to help Chris, they got into the pickup.

What would she say to him? Did he want her to say anything? Whether he did or not, she wanted him to know everything she was thinking and everything she knew now. And she wanted to thank him—and to say how sorry she was for what she'd brought his way.

Chris was a long time getting out of the car. She saw him gradually draw up to his full height, but Aiden didn't produce the expected wheelchair. Chris settled crutches under his arms and negotiated his way around the hood of the car.

Aiden jumped into the pickup and Roy drove away.

"What—" They wouldn't hear her, so why ask what they thought they were doing? Anyway, it was obvious. They were trying to throw her together with Chris for as long as possible. And they'd decided that forcing her to drive him home in Aiden's car wouldn't hurt.

Chris must need help. He shouldn't be on his feet like that. It hadn't been quite two weeks. He could so easily fall and do more damage.

This was one effort that was almost beyond Chris. He might be a strong man, but at this moment he was also an idiot, an idiot for love. Wasn't that a line in a song? If it wasn't, it should be.

She had stopped coming toward him.

The doctors had warned him that if he should mess up the good work they'd done, he'd suffer—oh, he would surely suffer.

Damn. The least she could do was walk beside him and give him an illusion of safety. "Sonnie," he yelled, "get over here." *Oh, great.*

Instantly she ran. Blue skirt flying around her calves, hair streaming behind her, she ran. And if he didn't look closely, he wouldn't notice she limped. Despite his insecurity on the crutches, he smiled. He was so proud of her.

Proud? As if he had any right to take credit for one thing about this woman.

"You aren't supposed to be on your feet," she said, drawing close. "I know what they told you after surgery. Wheelchair for several weeks at least, with only brief periods on the crutches—for necessities."

He didn't want to be cute, but he said, "This is a necessity."

Frowning, Sonnie stood in front of him. She raised her arms, then let them drop again. First she approached his right side, then his left. "Oh, this is awful," she said. "Men can be so stupid."

"So can women."

"I meant them." She pointed in the direction Roy and Bo's pickup had gone. "Leaving you like this. I'd better help you back to that car and drive you home now."

"Don't do that," he said. "Not that you could make me do anything I didn't want to do."

She didn't tell him he sounded petulant. "Aren't you feeling weak?"

"Yes," he said. "I'd like to go over there and sit down." He pointed beyond the scattering of rocks, beyond the wall, to a place where the running of a thousand tides had carved a solid sandbank.

"It's too far and you can't use crutches on sand," she said, but he was already concentrating hard, swinging himself forward to the tennis shoe he wore on his one usable foot, moving the crutches, waiting until the points stopped sinking, and swinging again. He wore cutoff jeans. Dressings swathed his so-called good leg, and he still had heavy bandages on his hands.

"Whatever I say, you're going to do this." She caught up with him. "I don't know how to help you."

"Stick with me. That'll help. I've got to smell fresh air."

She jogged along sideways, and he wasn't about to lie to himself. He liked feeling her worry about him. Beggars grabbed at whatever they could get.

His shoulders strained, and his back. He breathed hard. "Dammit, I hate feeling weak," he muttered.

"You aren't," Sonnie said. "It takes time. Things come back a bit at a time, and you're going to get completely strong and well again."

He paused to look at her, and to allow his breathing to slow down. "I know," he said. "Patience has never been one of my virtues."

"We could just talk here," she suggested.

"No way." He swung forward again. "Over there or bust. This is good for me."

She wasn't sure he was right, but she admired him.

Admired? What a pathetic word.

It took time, but he made it, turned himself to face the sea, and managed to sit without jarring anything loose. When he stopped puffing, he shook his head and said, "God, this feels great. We've got a lot to say, Sonnie. At least, I hope we do. Let's get started." If he sounded short-tempered, he couldn't do a thing about it. He'd had to work his way up to being ready for this. Now he was ready. Right now.

"Are you chilly?" she asked. "Do you have a coat in the car?"

"I'm scared. How's that for honesty? I'm scared about what we're going to say to each other. How about you?"

"Scared," she said. So serious. Such a very serious, dear face. "We've gone past trying to play with what we say to each other. I know I owe it to you to be absolutely honest—about everything."

He patted the sand beside him. "This may take time. Sit down."

"I do better on my feet. I think it's symbolic."

"If you say so."

"Do you want to go first?"

Oh, no, Chris thought, he surely did not want to go first. "Ladies first," he said.

"Okay." She planted her feet apart and put her hands behind her back. "Because of me, you killed a man."

"Frank Giacano would have killed you. What I did was necessary."

"Because of *me*, you did it," she said. "Because I hounded you until you got involved with my problems. You didn't want to."

"Put it out of your mind."

Sonnie shook her head. She would never forget how Frank had fallen, bleeding, on top of her.

"I know," Chris said. He set his crutches aside. "I'm sorry. That was callous. Of course you won't be able to put it out of your mind. At least not easily. I won't either. I'm not glad I took the man's life, but I'm glad he's dead. Don't ask me to regret feeling that way."

"There's too much, isn't there?" Sonnie said. "Too much baggage. It would be too hard to go forward together."

Chris felt exactly what he'd expected to feel: mad as hell, and sad as hell. "You've had such a number done on you, lady. You may have come a long way, but you could still fit your ego on a pin. Tell me something. Do you think you're worth loving?"

How did you answer a question like that? Sonnie wondered. "Do you?"

"I think I could have been. If I'd had a backbone. If I hadn't allowed myself to be carried away by a man who was too sophisticated for me. Then I'd never have been in that car with him. He'd never have lost his temper so badly he pulled off a crash that caused me to miscarry."

"Finished beating yourself up?"

"I think I forgot everything because I couldn't face the truth. It was my fault."

"And was it your fault your sister was having an affair with your husband? And she was ready to be his ears and eyes while he hid out with Ena, or whatever her name is? And was it your fault your brother-in-law—who was also sleeping with your sister—helped Frank get away? And what about the way Frank made sure Romano thought he was dead? Then he almost killed you because he was so determined to make you do what he wanted you to do. Was that your fault, too?" He couldn't go on.

"Not my fault," Sonnie said. She looked into his face and said, "No, not my fault."

"None of it was your fault. You won't get over everything in a day, but you will get over it. You can do it."

She put her hands to her mouth and nodded. "Yes, I can do it." But not if she didn't have him.

"Will you, Sonnie?"

If you'll help me.

"Sonnie?"

"I'm going to try."

"Are you still . . . I'm not sure how to say this. I wish you wouldn't feel bad about sleeping with me. We could go around in circles about technicalities. You thought Frank was dead. Frank wasn't dead. You should have waited longer. You might never have found out."

"I could have had the willpower to resist."

"Yeah. But if we'd been relying on my willpower it would have happened a lot sooner."

"You did nothing to force me."

"Oh, right." He looked away from her. "If I hadn't put us in the way of the opportunity—on a number of occasions— the question wouldn't have come up. Don't argue with me on this."

"You can be a bit overbearing, can't you?"

He thought about it. "Yeah, yeah, I can."

"Maybe you should work on that."

"Maybe I will if I've got a reason to."

"If we walk away from each other today—for the last time—I will never forget you, Christian Talon." She regarded him directly. No lies, no pretense; she would just tell him the way it was. "I'm not afraid of being alone. I've been alone before. I was married and alone. But I won't really be alone again because I will have you with me—inside my head and heart. I fell in love with you, and I'm in love with you now. But I won't try to tie you to me. Not with a single word. Thank you for everything you've done for me. Believe me when I tell you I will always weep in my heart for causing you pain. And, Chris, know that if you need me, I'll come to you. Wherever you are, I'll come and be whatever you need me to be. You do need more of a woman than I am, and I'm not putting myself down, just being realistic. I'm a canary to your eagle."

"Come here, Sonnie Giacano," he said, pointing to the spot beside his casted knee. "You're honest. I'll do my best to match you. What's all that stuff about Mars and Venus? I heard this joke about this couple who were driving. He's real quiet and she's wondering if she's done something wrong. He's trying to remember when he got his last oil change." He laughed. Sonnie didn't. "Well, anyway, I guess it's all about different ways of communicating. But I'm really going to try because I've got to.''

"Got to?'' she said.

"My life depends on it.''

Sonnie stood on the spot he'd indicated, her hands still behind her back. She would be quiet and listen. She wouldn't tell him that without him her life might keep on ticking along, but she didn't even want to think about how she'd feel.

"I'm not as good with words as you are,'' he said. "I'm going to tell you something about myself. Not the thing in New York. I've got to keep on working my way out of that, and you already know about it.

"Roy and I grew up poor. Real poor. But we wouldn't have had to be that poor if our daddy hadn't been what he was. He was no good. He was mean. He beat our mama—until he got arrested and thrown in jail.

"But there was one thing that happened, the thing I'll never forget. Roy and I will never forget. We were already pretty grown-up, but after that it was as if we'd never been kids at all.''

Sonnie's surroundings faded for her. She saw only the dark-haired man whose face was too pale, his eyes too distant. He looked back at her and shook his head slightly. She was to let him speak until he was through and what he intended to tell her would cause him pain.

"It was dark,'' he said, remembering too vividly. "Roy and I sneaked out to the screened porch at the back of the house. We had to tread carefully because Daddy never got around to replacing planks that rotted out. I was about eight. My teeth kept chattering. It was raining so hard it drummed on the pieces of tin Daddy had used to patch leaks in the roof. Drips still got in. Outside we could see the beam from a lamp swaying. It kind of swung this way and that across the earth. Not earth, mud. Mama was carrying that lamp in her left hand. She cradled the bundle in her right arm and held it tight against her.''

The sea blurred. Chris saw it as if through rain-drenched glass. Something that happened such a long time ago shouldn't still hurt so much.

"Mama set the lamp on the stump Daddy used when he split wood; then she started scrabbling at that sopping ground with the fingers of her one free hand. She kept her cheek on top of the bundle and rocked.

"I asked Roy what she was doing.

" 'I heard Daddy say it was just as well about the baby. . . . He reckoned God knows we ain't got enough as it is. Daddy said there ain't money for no funerals neither. Then he told Mama he'd fix her good if she didn't get rid of it before he came back.' " Chris tried to moisten his dry mouth.

"That's what Roy said to me. We were so scared, I almost wet my pants, but Roy and I went through the rain to Mama and we knelt in the mud with her."

Mama's face had showed shiny white. He'd known she was crying even if the rain did wash the tears away.

"She didn't say anything, but she waved us away. We wouldn't go. Between us we made a grave for a tiny girl child born dead that afternoon—three days after Daddy beat Mama so badly her eyes swelled up. When she was trying to get away from him and begging him to stop, she lost her balance and slipped down the stairs.

"Someone blew the whistle on us. They told the law about Mama being very pregnant, then the baby being gone. Daddy got arrested and did time. When he got out . . . Mama took the bastard back. He wasn't around long. He beat Mama again, but she still begged him not to go. Afterward she made Roy and me promise not to try to do anything to her beloved husband." He set his mouth and glanced away.

Sonnie grabbed for his hand and he wound their fingers together.

"Hush," he told her. "It was a long time ago. Roy and I take care of our mama. We don't know if the old man is dead or alive. We don't care."

"Chris." She was breathing through parted lips, and tears stood on her bottom lids.

"I didn't want to tell you all this—I've never told anyone before—but I owe you. I owe you the story of why I think I turned out the way I did. The way I am now. Because of that night and facing up to how harsh things can get without allowing it to make you stop believing there's anything good in the world.

"My father humiliated my mother. She couldn't hold her head up anywhere because folks knew. But she wouldn't leave him. She wouldn't turn the bastard in.

"Long story short. He's gone and Mama's got a nice little place where she's happy. Roy's made a happy life for himself. I went into the law because I wanted to make a difference. I'm not going to do a number on you and say I was a fool to think I could. I *did*. But I made a bad mistake and I'm still not over it."

"You will be," Sonnie said. If she could, she'd cut the terrible memories out of him and leave him as if they had never happened. She touched his cheek and said, "I'm so glad I met you."

And that was all the humility he was going to take from her for one day. "That's enough," he said, and meant to sound as sharp as he did. "Give me both of your hands and hold on, sweetheart. Or run away now."

She put her other hand in his, too. And she smiled, actually smiled. "I know you're tough," she said, attempting to be solemn once more.

"Okay, laugh away. This is good because we can shave some time off this process. Sonnie, do you remember you said you'd marry me?"

She felt still inside. "Yes. We were outside St. Paul's. But we both knew a lot stood between us and . . . and marriage."

"What's standing between us now?"

"Your bad temper and my insecurity," she said promptly, and felt proud of her forthrightness again.

Chris studied her face from every angle possible when he couldn't move much. "Just looking at you makes me happy. If you're with me all the time, or I know you'll be there when I get home, I'm sure I'll never be bad tempered again."

"Oh, sure. I'll still be insecure."

"Come on. You're not trying. You've come so far. And

with a man like me to show off as your husband, the sky's the limit, kid. You'll be the most confident woman around.''

"That's if I can fight my way through your admirers.''

He watched her mouth, the way it moved as she spoke. "Sonnie.'' He slid his fingers into her hair. "I love your mouth. When you talk, I can't keep my eyes off it. Or when you don't talk. Or any other time. When—when we used to kiss, I walked around feeling your lips on mine. In fact, I still feel them. And I love your eyes and your nose, and your hair, and your neck—''

"Thank you,'' she said. It would be so easy to slide into the place he was clearly offering her, but she wouldn't do it unless she was certain she should. "I think I know what needs to happen.''

Her tone knocked a hole in the progress he thought he'd been making. "Okay. I'm listening.''

"Do you think we should have some time to get to really know each other?''

"Hah. Hell, no, and I'm not sorry for cussing. We *know* each other, my love. Sure, we've got a lot of things to learn yet. But the way to do that is to be married and committed.''

"Yes, well, I'm absolutely not going to risk having you go into anything without full disclosure.''

Chris frowned. "Full disclosure? Is this some sort of legal arrangement we're looking at? I don't need your money. Believe it or not, I have a little money, and when I get back to work, we'll be fine.''

"Back to work? As in, to the police?''

"Yeah. They've got a vacancy here in Key West, and I guess it's mine if I want it. I'd like to stay close to Roy. Of course, if you'd rather move north, we'll move north.''

"No. No, not at all. But I don't think I want us to live in my—''

"Me neither. We'll get a new place. Maybe build, or renovate.''

He was rushing ahead again. "When I said full disclosure, I wasn't talking about money,'' Sonnie said. "I was talking about making sure I don't hold anything back from you.''

Chris couldn't stop himself from grinning. "We're going to do it, aren't we?"

"You're pushing your advantage—or what you think is your advantage." But there was still quite a big hurdle to jump.

"You want to marry in church? St. Paul's, maybe? The old crowd from the Nail would love it."

"I don't know yet," she said.

"You mean you don't know if you'll marry me yet?"

"I mean, I don't know if you'll marry me, Chris. This might not be the best time."

He swallowed. He would be calm and reasonable. "Why, goddamn it?"

She flinched.

"I'm sorry, but I'm stretched a bit thin. Why, Sonnie?"

"Well, it may be nothing. Chris, this is going to sound like something from a soap opera. I may be pregnant. Very early, of course. But I got one of those tests and it—"

"Huh?" His flesh felt hot, but goose bumps shot out all over his skin. He looked at her closely. "Pregnant? Are those tests accurate?"

"They say they're very accurate. But that would mean we— I got pregnant just, well, immediately."

"Hold up. *We* did, not you. Let me see your eyes."

"My eyes." She opened them wide.

"They say a pregnant woman's eyes look different. And they're right! Whoa. Hey, no messing around, Sonnie. We've got to get a move on. I'll ask the minister to come over and talk to us when we get back."

"Chris," Sonnie said, trying for patience and calm while her tummy jumped with excitement. "It may not be true. I was thinking you'd rather wait until I'm sure. I wouldn't want you to marry me just because I'm pregnant."

"She's driving me nuts," he shouted to the sky. "Pregnant or not pregnant, I want you to marry me. If you're pregnant, it's a bonus. If you're not, we'll just have to do something about that. And I do know what to do."

She bowed her head. "I wasn't sure you were that keen on having children."

"Shows what you know. I love kids. Oh, if you aren't pregnant, it'll be fine; we'll just have to concentrate on getting it done."

"Very romantic."

He ignored her. "I'm pushing you too hard." But he had her. He felt in his gut and other important indicators that she was his. "If you'd walk back to the car with me, I'd appreciate it. I just need to regain my confidence about walking with these things." He got up awkwardly, worked the crutches into place, and set off. Once again Sonnie ran sideways beside him.

She held the Mustang door open for him, helped get him settled, and put the crutches in the back. "You okay? Comfortable?"

He wasn't, but he said, "Sure."

Sonnie went around and climbed behind the wheel.

Chris cleared his throat. "Pregnant, hmm?"

"Could be."

"What d'you think the odds are?"

She felt lighthearted. He really wanted a child. "I think they're good. I called a doctor here and he said I should come in to see him in a week, but the over-the-counter tests are very accurate."

"That does it," Chris said. Wincing, he turned sideways, or as sideways as he could manage. He took hold of Sonnie's hands. "Please say you'll marry me. Roy and Bo will vouch that I'm trustworthy. Flynn will probably make jokes, but he'll put in a word for me, too."

Who would put in a word for her? He'd just have to take her at face value.

"So," Chris said.

"That'll be fine."

That'll be fine? "Uh, was that a yes?"

"Yes," she said, and giggled. Then she laughed. "I feel giddy, you silly man. If I let you, you'll have a shrieking female on your hands. Yes, yes, yes. Is that better?"

"Yeah, much better."

"Will you marry me, Christian Talon?"

"Yeah. Maybe we can get it done by tonight."

"By tonight? No way. We've got arrangements to make, and there are formalities."

"Tomorrow, then."

"As soon as possible," Sonnie told him, reaching to kiss his jaw.

He turned his head and captured her mouth with his, and anything sedate was history. He kissed her until she wrapped her arms around his neck, buried her face, and said, "I need air."

"You've got it. Home. Now. We've got stuff to do."

Sonnie turned toward the dash, but she covered her face with her hands and laughed again. She was doing a lot of laughing, and it felt good.

"What's so funny?" Chris said. "Let me in on the joke." Aiden would call him a lucky schmuck. And he'd be right. "Sonnie. Quit teasing me. What's so darn funny?"

"I—I can't drive a stick shift."

He looked at the shift. "You're kidding."

"Oh, no, I'm not. I can't drive this car. You sure can't drive it. And even if I knew how, Aiden's taken the keys with him."

Please turn the page
for an exciting preview
of Stella Cameron's
GLASS HOUSES
an August 2000 hardcover release
from Kensington Publishing Corp.

One

The next sucker who told Aiden Flynn, detective NYPD, to get a life was dead meat.

Lightning crazed the night sky over Hell's Kitchen and kept a man praying for thunder . . . and rain, rain, rain. Why didn't it rain, dammit? And why had he agreed to baby-sit Ryan Hill's orchids? And why didn't he just quit now that Detective Hill had gone AWOL after his upstate vacation with dear ol' Dad? Oh, sure, Dad was too sick to be left alone. Probably needed help in and out of the indoor pool at the mountain spread Ryan liked to brag about.

Ah, hell, the suffocating air, or lack of it, was mangling his nerves. Truth was, curiosity kept him coming upstairs from his own apartment to tend plants belonging to a guy he didn't like. Curiosity and competition. His own orchids would do as well as these if he had the equivalent of a greenhouse, rather than a couple of lousy, make-do cabinets he'd rigged himself.

Living on the top floor of the building, where an old but sturdy wall of windows wrapped over several feet of sun-sucking roof space, Ryan D. Hill's (never mention that the *D* stood for *Douglas*) oncidiums bloomed, one plant after another. Currently, umber and cream blossoms cascaded from small forests of spikes on two specimens. After their initial showing, Aiden's oncidiums hadn't produced one bloom ever.

His cell phone beeped discreetly. What did it say about a man when he was grateful his phone rang? He flipped the instrument open, jabbed at it with his thumb, and said, "Yeah?"

"Vanni here."

"*Finally.* That heap of electronic junk you put together for me is on the fritz again."

"So?" For a boy from a good Italian family in Brooklyn, Vanni Zanetto tended to be short on the words.

"I've got things to do tonight—"

"Places to go?" Vanni said dead flat. "People to see? Sure, I know. Enjoy. How's my dog?"

"Boss is just fine. And he's my dog. Don't change the subject. That damned computer turns Greek on me. No kidding. Not a moment's warning, and everything just translates into Greek. Looks like Greek to me anyway. I'm spending my time getting out and getting in again."

"Lucky guy. Congratulations. Is she a good looker?" Vanni could be too quick to live.

"Save that," Aiden said. "But make sure your mama doesn't find out what a dirty mind you've got. Just get over here and work your magic, buddy."

A sigh wafted, long and theatrical, across the distance between them. "Mama was askin' about you, Aiden. She's got another nice girl she wants you to meet."

"Have you met her?"

"No, but—"

"Sure. I should trust your mama again. I haven't forgotten Milly the garlic lover."

"So what's wrong with liking a little garlic?"

"Vanni, the woman had to be using the stuff as body lotion. She might even have been substituting garlic rubs for showers. How the hell would I know?" He felt guilty for knocking Milly. "Hey, she's a nice girl, just not my type of nice girl, okay?"

"But this new one—"

"Will you come fix my computer, partner? It'll take me all night to do it myself."

"You'd never manage it yourself," Vanni said.

"I'll let that pass. I gotta get online if I'm going to get any sleep. You know how cranky I am if I don't get any sleep before I go on duty—and you're the one who'll have to listen to me."

"Hey, Aiden, old buddy, why don't you hop in your pink panther and get over here? We could drop in at Sully's and—"

"Pink pony." By accident or design, Vanni couldn't seem to get right Aiden's favorite wheels, his mint condition '67 pink Mustang—or any car in his beloved collection. "I'm not going anywhere but online. Thanks, anyway."

"*Damn it*, Aiden." Vanni's temper wasn't hard to rouse. "When are you goin' to quit foolin' around with people you know you'll never meet and get out in the world?"

"I'm out there every day. It doesn't have much to recommend it."

"Listen. I'll say this slow and quiet," Vanni told him. "Just see how slow and quiet I can be. That's because I care about you. I worry because you're living some sort of surreal existence with a bunch of virtual pals. You do it because you feel safe with 'em. They'll never ring your bell in the middle of the night and ask if you want company or expect you to make some sort of move on 'em."

"Vanni—"

"Let me finish. You're lonely, but you're scared shitless of commitment."

Aiden felt his temper begin a burn. "You just stepped way over the line. And where's the woman you've committed yourself to, huh?"

Vanni delivered another world-class sigh. "We're gonna talk. Later. And there's nothing wrong with Italian girls. I'll get there when I can—but only 'cause I want to visit Boss." He broke the connection.

"Nice Italian girls," Aiden muttered. It wasn't that he hadn't met wonderful Italian women, but he was allergic to being fixed up by or with anyone.

Ryan D's grow lights were all functioning perfectly, his fans oscillating nicely. Too bad.

On a fancy desk with the curved lines of Scandinavian furniture, and made of teak and sleek stainless steel, sat Ryan's computer monitor with its impressive twenty-one-inch screen. Beneath the desk on a conveniently wheeled trolley was his computer tower. Aiden couldn't recall how many gigabytes the miraculous hard drive boasted, nor how much memory Detective Hill repeatedly mentioned. If Aiden didn't know better, he'd wonder about his own memory, but he knew himself too well, and the less than generous habit he had of forgetting what was either unimportant or annoying.

There was Ryan's machine—undoubtedly in perfect operating condition and faster than anything Aiden got to use, while one floor down the ''bargain'' beast Vanni had assembled groaned and refused to heel.

Aiden approached the big screen in its luminous blue case. Who had ever even seen a luminous blue case on a computer monitor? The keyboard was one of those two-part jobs—one for the left hand and one for the right hand—also blue. Large enough for most people to curl a whole hand around, the mouse occupied its own miniature Oriental carpet.

Which led to another question: With all of his money, why did Ryan D. need to bother his fetid little brain, and his delicate sensibilities, with the business of being a homicide detective? Maybe rather than having to look after his now sick father, Ryan had finally twigged to how unsuited he was to life among the unsavory. Maybe he would never come back at all.

A guy could hope.

Aiden sat in Ryan's soft gray leather chair and morosely regarded the dark screen. From time to time an orange light flashed below and he heard a perfect life form churning softly within the machine.

He tried his own hand on the mouse. He'd probably have to use it with the last two digits of his fingers. He tested his theory and jerked his hand away instantly. Too late. A faint snapping, and a list appeared—Ryan's incoming mail. After two weeks that list was likely to be long enough to make an orderly mind cringe.

Vanni would take his own sweet time getting here. Why not check E-mail from this machine? Ryan wouldn't mind—and since he'd never know, it didn't matter anyway.

"Nope, Aiden. You can wait." He got up and scanned the bank of wall switches that controlled Ryan's orchid setup.

The list on the computer screen rolled up. Another post came in, and another.

It couldn't hurt to take a look at his own mail from here.

Lightning cracked again and he glanced at rooftops briefly illuminated. Thunder followed almost at once—low thunder that rumbled on and on like the sound of boulders gathering speed down a mountainside.

"And here comes the rain," he muttered and breathed long and deep. "Oh, yeah." First the big showy drops that needed space to spatter, but blessedly soon a torrent that clattered on Ryan's coveted overhead glass.

Rain made Aiden's soul open up. He could breathe again.

OliviaFitz@bargain.uk was the first entry he actually read on Ryan's list.

Who'd have thought it? Aiden grinned. The crown prince of the Seventeenth Precinct was a closet bargain shopper. Maybe the Ferragamo dress shoes he wore to work were knock-offs.

There was OliviaFitz again. And again. At first he read the names of the people writing to Ryan idly. Soon enough he leaned forward to examine the times on Ms. Olivia's posts. They had arrived from half an hour to an hour apart. Why would someone need to write a series of messages rather than one long one?

None of his damn business.

A siren soared outside and Aiden smiled. The sound of his city at night. New York being New York. He liked everything about the place.

Thunder roared again, shaking the old building.

Ryan's miraculous machine and its view panel didn't even flicker.

The top post on the E-mail list was highlighted. Aiden tapped the mouse and watched OliviaFitz's message unfold on the screen.

One of the blessings about being a cop was that it took a lot to make you feel guilty. Hey, maybe there was something here that Ryan needed to know about—now.

Rain fell even harder. The lights over Ryan's orchids spread an eerie blue glow that cast reflections of the plants on the windows. Beyond the orchids, Aiden could see himself at a distance, and the door behind him. He shifted uneasily, then felt stupid.

Ryan Hill wasn't buying phony Ferragamos online.

Good to hear from you again, Sam. You're so logical and I do appreciate your advice.

Sam?

I will think about accepting the kill fee for the London Style *layout, but it's awfully strange for the magazine to change its mind. Even if I didn't need the money for this commission, I could really use the credit. Cheerio, Olivia.*

Nothing Ryan needed to know there. She must have the wrong address for her Sam. But what, he wondered, was a kill fee? He might consider it a foreign term for a hit contract, but the context didn't fit.

Maybe it would be kind to take a look at another post from her and see if he ought to let her know Sam wasn't reading what she wrote. Evidently she was a Brit. Wouldn't hurt to do his bit for international relations.

It still amazes me to think about the way we stumbled on each other. Imagine you writing to me by mistake, just trying to remember an address and getting me. Life

*is so odd. How can we only have met a few weeks ago?
It feels as if we've known each other forever.*

And Vanni thought his partner was lonely? The way Olivia
wrote to her Sam made Aiden pity her. He might even feel sad
if he could remember how.

*Having a dog yourself, you'll understand how I felt
about Wilbur. He was just in too much pain to go on. I
stayed with him at the end. We'd been pals for eleven
years, since I was fifteen. Felt like forever. Even though
it's more than two years later, there's still a hole where
he used to be. Forgive me for going on about it. You've
been so understanding. This is strange, but I can feel
how kind you are.*

*Your Boswell sounds a dear. How perfectly awful that
those bad men hit his mouth with a baseball bat. I'm
sure it was very expensive to have some of his teeth
capped with metal, but you're the kind of person who
wouldn't spare any expense to help an animal.*

Aiden's eyes glazed. Well, hell. That was it. Ryan Hill was
Sam, had to be since he'd evidently claimed ownership of
Aiden's Boswell—Boss to people he didn't hate. Very few
called the dog Boss. *Bad men? Baseball bat?* Wait till Vanni
got a load of this. Ryan Hill, alias Sam, and a dog hater, trying
to impress some Brit female with his generosity to animals.
And lying about Aiden's Boss, an ornery retired canine corps
dog who had earned his titanium mashers by keeping his teeth
embedded in a rapist's arm while the crazy bastard slammed
away at the animal's mouth with the butt of an empty gun.
And Olivia could feel how kind Ryan was?

*Anyway, thank you for writing back so quickly. How
do you stand the climate in New York? I melt when the
temperature gets close to 80. I must admit that you make
Hell's Kitchen sound intriguing.*

Dear Ryan was definitely Dear Sam. So the stud who boasted that he had a woman for every night of the week and some to spare still went looking for extra jollies among those people Vanni called "virtual pals." Who'd have thought it?

Are you sure you have an extra room I could use? Oh, what am I saying? I know I won't come, but it is awfully sweet of you to offer. Toodles, Olivia.

The message had been sent about two hours ago.

He ought to check his mail and get out of here.

Slowly, he clicked on Olivia's next post and felt an unfamiliar rush of remorse. He was snooping out of idle curiosity—and boredom.

Sam: Thank you for saying you do mean it about the room. As I already wrote, I really appreciate the offer.

Aiden fell back in the chair and stared. Obviously Ryan had read and responded to the first post Aiden had read. Ryan was communicating with Olivia from wherever he was right now. He was picking up his E-mail at a remote location and answering Olivia from that location.

If he brought her here it would be obvious he'd lied about the dog. Which meant he didn't intend to bring her here. Why would he lie about something like that?

It was just a game. People played these games all the time. As Olivia said, she would never come to the States.

Ryan might hate Boss, but the feeling was more than mutual. So what? This was fiction—mostly fiction.

Okay. I'm just going to tell you the truth. I'm frightened, Sam, and you're the only one likely to give me sensible advice. While I was out today someone must have searched the house. I know what you'll be thinking: Why am I just writing about it now? They searched my darkroom—nowhere else—and I only just went down there. It's in the basement. I probably wouldn't have known they'd been here at all if I wasn't so compulsive about keeping my work organized.

This is weird, but I think I know what they may have been searching for: the photos for Penny Biggles's London Style *layout. I don't know what made me take the prints and negs with me when I went out—I just did. Maybe it was what you told me that made me more cautious. I rang up* London Style *a little while ago. They don't know anything about the kill fee that man called to offer me. I photographed this London house for Penny— fabulous place—and some of the shots will be used to illustrate an article being written about her work—at least, I hope they will. Penny was the designer. Whoever was in here didn't take anything as far as I can tell. They must have wanted these.*

London Style *told me they still expect to use the piece. So the call about someone coming here to see me and bringing money—the kill fee—but wanting to have the pictures in case they could place them was a hoax, right? Which means my photographs are valuable to someone. The authorities are the best ones to deal with this now. My friend Mark Donnely is an inspector at Scotland Yard. He's bound to have a good idea.*

Aiden let the screen go black and stood up. He'd taken the prying too far.

Stella Cameron

"A premier author of romantic suspense."